T   E

SIMON TEMPRELL was born in Chesterfield, Derby-shire, and raised in nearby Clowne. He attended the Plymouth Art and Design College before moving to London in 1982. After working as a window dresser at Harrods, he started his own interior design business in 1986, moving to Brussels in 1990 and Washington DC in 1992.

Continuing his design business, he lives in Virginia, and began writing as a hobby in 1994. *The Rich Man's Table* is his first published novel, and others are ready to follow.

SIMON TEMPRELL

THE
RICH MAN'S
TABLE

PAN BOOKS

First published 2000 by Pan Books
an imprint of Macmillan Publishers Ltd
25 Eccleston Place, London SW1W 9NF
Basingstoke and Oxford
Associated companies throughout the world
www.macmillan.co.uk

ISBN 0 330 37637 3

135798642

A CIP catalogue record for this book is available from
the British Library

Phototypeset by Intype London Ltd
Printed and bound in Great Britain
by Mackays of Chatham plc, Chatham, Kent

For Christian
Pom Pom De Pom

ACKNOWLEDGEMENTS

I would like to mention the following people, without whom this book would not have been written.

My friend and mentor Sam Schwartz who made me believe that I could tell a story worth listening to.

My brother Gary who told me I would not fail because I never do.

My agent Anne Dewe who took a chance because she saw something in my work that many others were afraid to tackle.

My editor Peter Lavery who went out on a limb and made my dream come true.

And last, but by no means least, I would like to thank my parents who never fail to stand by me even when they think I'm bonkers.

Without all of you I could not have accomplished any of this.

Thank you.

And desiring to be fed with the crumbs
which fell from the rich man's table

Luke 16 v 21

PART ONE

CHAPTER ONE

There are topiary trees outside Craven's Hotel.

No fairy lights or flags or polished brass.

Just the name *Craven's* etched on a modest chrome square at each side of the revolving doors.

Craven's is well known by people who are in the know.

It was created by Felicity Craven.

We don't see much of her on the telly these days, not since she ran that detective agency with Adam Faith and Twiggy.

She used to be on at nine o'clock on Friday nights.

Her show looks very dated these days, with all those white leather sofas and bell-bottoms. But she's holding up remarkably well. In fact, one might even say that she looks better today than she did in the seventies.

Here she is, Felicity Craven, holding one of her little board meetings in the second-floor conference room of her hotel . . .

'Quite frankly I will not tolerate this kind of infantile behaviour any longer!' snaps pristine Felicity Craven in her black tube of jersey wool. She is holding up a grubby photocopy of a rather impressive-looking penis. 'I don't know who's doing this, but it's getting beyond a joke.'

Nobody sniggers. Nobody giggles. When Felicity Craven speaks, everyone else in the room is paid to remain silent.

'If this happens again, I will be forced to keep the Xerox room under strict lock and key. We are supposed to be running an *adult* operation here, not some kindergarten playground. I thought you were all professionals, but perhaps I am wrong.' And Felicity lifts up a delicate wrist to arrange her hair. Her bracelets are made of ebony: they slither and clatter down her arm like stylish teething rings.

She has the beginnings of a headache. She has been up since five-thirty, and tonight there is another late-night reception. Felicity works hard. She practically never stops, for even when she's relaxing, she seems to be doing something that anyone else would consider hard labour. She is tireless, and she is relentless in her pursuit of perfection. Hell to live with, hell to work with, but one hell of a business manager.

The door to the conference room is upholstered in rich chocolate-brown velvet with brass studs and a handle shaped like a golden antler. It opens without much of a sound, and a neatly dressed girl steps in.

'There's a call for you, Miss Craven. It's confidential. Would you like to take it in my office?' The announcer at the door is Prudence Wilton, one of the PR girls, who just got back from a three-month nervous breakdown.

'What does *confidential* mean, Prudence? *Who* is calling?'

'It's a policeman, Miss Craven. I really do think that it would be better if you took it in my office.' Prudence backs out into the corridor as though she has just addressed the Queen. Well, in a way she has.

'Oh, what a bother!' sighs the much beleaguered Felicity, with her chunky shoes from Hobbs and her seductive perfume of tuberose and orchid. 'Kathy, give out these details of the tenth anniversary celebrations to everyone here, and I will see what this is all about.'

Although Felicity Craven is the figurehead and creator of Craven's Hotel, it is her younger brother, Sebastian, who owns the deeds to the property. Their father left everything to Sebastian because he figured Felicity was already set up nicely with her billionaire husband. Their father had not realized just how tight Felicity's husband David was with his hard-earned billions. As much as he adored his daughter, Humphrey Craven III was old-fashioned enough to believe that everything should go to his son and heir. He left his wife Sabrina the house in Hampstead, and enough money to keep her for the rest of her life in the style to which she was accustomed.

Sebastian has very little to do with the day-to-day running of Craven's. He pops in now and then to see if there's anything he can do, but Felicity is too self-sufficient, too *perfect* in everything she does, to allow Sebastian any kind of responsibility.

He is good-looking.

Tall and blond.

Felicity uses her brother as a suitable escort whenever she has an important business meeting, but, apart from that, he is superfluous to her needs. Unlike his turbo-powered sister, Sebastian has absolutely no desire to slog away at an eighteen-hour day if he can get away with doing nothing. He is generous and kind, and because of this he has an awful lot of friends. Felicity calls them his 'sycophants', and she is scathing about her brother's wasted potential.

Today we find Sebastian hovering in a dark little corridor behind the kitchens. This is where the store cupboards are. This is where he has arranged to meet Wayne Briggs, the under-porter.

'I reckon it's going to cost you a bit more this time, sir,' says Wayne, appearing from the shadows like a ghost, cocking a roguish eyebrow.

'You've got a bloody nerve! I thought we had a deal?'

'Deal was you get your end away whenever you feel randy, and I get the going rate. Well, the going rate just went up to a hundred and fifty nicker.'

'Daylight robbery! What happened to common decency? It was only fifty quid the first time.'

'The cost of common decency just went up, sir, and there's nothing decent about a gentleman taking advantage of a minor in the storage cupboard of his own hotel. I expect it could be construed as sexual harassment as well, seeing as how I work here. I could get you on both counts with the help of a good solicitor.'

'What do you mean, "minor"? You're eighteen. I checked your employment files.'

'I lied. Knew I wouldn't get the job if they thought I was just a school-leaver. I'll be seventeen in August. That makes me a minor, in my book.'

Sebastian feels winded. It is the kind of sickening situation he has been expecting for most of his adult life. Like a house built over a fault line, Sebastian lives every day just waiting for the first blip on the seismograph: and here it is. A minute, inky-black line that portends disaster.

A scandal.

A media scoop with all the flashlights and tabloid rhetoric that will hound him out of society.

His family will be mortified.

'You little shit! After all I've done for you, I can't believe you're being so short-sighted.'

'I reckon you're the one with the vision problem, Mr Craven. Now hand over the readies or I'll blow the whistle.'

'If you want to make some money, why don't you bugger off back from where you came? You're fired!'

Wayne laughs. He moves up close to Sebastian, his breath warm and sweet, and he runs his tongue across his lips.

'I wouldn't do that if I were you. Just give me the money and I'll say no more.'

Sebastian reaches for his wallet.

Wayne pockets the money wordlessly. He puts one hand over Sebastian's crotch, kisses him on the cheek and slips out of the corridor, leaving Sebastian to drown in his own fearful speculations.

Prudence Wilton has a small office, but like everything in Felicity's hotel it is beautifully decorated. The walls are pale French-grey shantung. The window is draped so heavily with interlined curtains and swags that Prudence has to keep the lights on even during the sunniest of days. Today, though, it isn't sunny. It's raining: interminable London rain that seems deliberately colourless.

'This is Felicity Craven.'

There seems to be a lot of static on the line.

'Hello? This is Felicity Craven speaking.' She perches herself impatiently on the edge of Prudence's desk, half a mind on the crooked picture over by the filing cabinet, a Chinese watercolour in a silver-leaf frame. It cost £350, and it is *crooked*.

'Miss Craven, this is Paul Buccanan. I'm sorry, this seems to be rather a bad line.'

'Paul, what is all this about? Prudence told me you were a policeman. Is everything all right over there?' Felicity glares at Prudence, who is hovering by the doorway pretending not to listen.

'I wanted to get to you before the media start hounding you. I'm afraid I have some frightfully bad news.'

Now Felicity is paying attention. When her husband's personal assistant calls all the way from Kuwait to tell her some bad news, it must certainly be something worse than a cancelled flight or a drop in the oil prices.

'What is it, Paul? Is it David?'

A double-decker glides silently past the window in the gloaming of the wet February afternoon. The top deck is brightly illuminated, and garish with colour.

'There was an explosion at the plant. Just a small explosion, but David and three of our men were badly injured. Felicity, I'm afraid that David was killed . . .' Paul is swallowed by static, but the crucial words have come through.

David is dead.

David Samuel Glendale, oil tycoon, property magnate and father to Felicity's children, has been killed in an explosion. How can this be? Surely things like this never happen to Felicity Craven, in her charmed circle of light?

The telephone line is dead. There is nothing more to be told. Felicity replaces the receiver and walks slowly over to the filing cabinet to straighten the Chinese watercolour.

'You know how I cannot abide imperfection,' she whispers absently, as she shifts the frame a few millimetres to the left.

In the mirror opposite, she catches sight of a woman she barely knows.

Eyes like ebony. Skin like peaches and cream. If it

wasn't for her mother's Scandinavian blood, she could almost be a perfect English Rose.

'Are you all right, Miss Craven?' questions little Prudence Wilton, her cardigan scrunched up in her fist.

'Perfectly,' replies Felicity in a defensive tone that could have snipped the heads off a hardy annual. She has never been one to show her feelings in public.

'Please tell everyone that the meeting is postponed and that I will be in my office. I need to make a few calls, and I do not wish to be disturbed.' Felicity glances at Prudence and sees her grey little face all puckered up with tears. 'Now come on, Prudence, that's the last thing I need to see right now.'

'Oh, Miss Craven, he was such a lovely . . .'

But Felicity has already gone. She has turned the corner in a wake of tuberose and orchid. She is walking with purpose in her clunky shoes and her black jersey-wool dress. The lift doors open as though by royal command, and in the lift there is an elderly gentleman leaning precariously on a Zimmer frame. He reminds Felicity of her greenhouse tomatoes, bent and crooked inside their protective wire frames.

'How are you enjoying your stay with us, Mr Rheinhold? Everything to your satisfaction, I trust?'

'Oh yes, thank you, Miss Craven. One so looks forward to a comfortable room when one is up in London. One finds it all rather bewildering these days, what with the drug addicts and the whores.'

Felicity hasn't the slightest clue what the old man

is talking about, but she offers him her best complimentary smile and waits for him to shuffle out of the
lift into the black marble lobby.

Garard the concierge rushes across to grab her
attention. Apparently there are two men from *The
Times* to see her. Will she grant them a few minutes?
Right at that moment, Felicity sees several reporters
congregating by the revolving glass doors.

'Tell them all I have absolutely no comment at this
moment, Garard. It is imperative that I have some
private time to myself.' And she waves her bangles
and her diamonds as she disappears through the mirrored door into her inner sanctum. It is all she can do
to keep herself upright. She wants to collapse like a
house of cards. She wants to crawl on her hands and
knees. She longs to be in her bedroom with the Thai
silk and the view across the lake.

Her assistant, Marissa, is waiting for her with
tragedy smudged across her face like charcoal.

'Not now, Marissa,' is all she can say as she passes
by and enters her office. She closes the door behind
her. It is a hefty door made of a wonderful burr walnut,
inlaid with black diamonds of ebonized oak. The room
is silently purring. It is the very *essence* of Felicity.

This is where she belongs. This is where, finally,
she can allow her emotions to take over as she throws
herself across the velvet sofa.

David is dead.

She keeps repeating it over and over in her head,

like a demented mantra. The truth refuses to materialize.

'Oh, my God!' She says the words out loud, as though to test them on the air. Her voice sounds small, and it soaks into the soft furnishings like spilled milk.

'David is dead.' And this time her words are stronger, slicing through the faux painted atmosphere.

Felicity thinks of the children. It was only two days ago that she waved David off outside the house, with Sascha hugging his waist and Josh shouting from the bedroom window.

The implications are enormous.

Surprisingly she finds tears in her eyes. They are the silent, poetic tears of a screen actress, but they are tears nonetheless, and it is years since Felicity allowed herself the luxury.

They call her cold.

They call her insensitive.

Whatever happens now, she must be alert. For the wolves will be at the door as soon as the first newspaper announces David's tragic demise.

Wipe away your tears, Felicity. You need to be strong, you need to be resilient.

Slowly, from beneath the fragile layer of shock and disbelief, a small diamond of providence emerges from the coal-black depths of her confusion.

It catches her breath.

It halts her tears.

And somewhere way up high, like light through a chink in the rock, Felicity recognizes her freedom.

The freedom to be herself at last.

'David is dead,' she repeats to herself.

There is something almost musical about those words.

CHAPTER TWO

From the sublime to the ridiculous.

Isn't that what people say when they go from one end of the social scale to the other?

Well, Felicity and Sebastian Craven have no real understanding of what goes on outside their own enclosed kingdom of wealth and self-importance, so why should they be interested in the plight of those less fortunate than themselves?

Let us travel a few miles up the motorway, forty miles or so away from Craven's Hotel, where there are fields and hedgerows and low-flying aircraft coming in and out of Luton airport.

The house has a name as well as a number.

Wychwood.

It was one of the things that attracted Claire Brown to it in the estate agent's blurb. It's something she has always wanted – a house with a name, like Four Chimneys in *The Railway Children*. She has tried running the name around in her mind a few times, seeing if it might not be too pretentious for her to refer to the house by its name when inviting friends over for dinner.

'Do come over to *Wychwood* for cocktails on Saturday evening.'

Or: 'Let's spend the weekend at *Wychwood*. We can take a picnic down to the lake.'

Of course there is no lake at The Acorns. It's a Barratt housing estate that was built in the mid-eighties, and Claire Brown is mortgaged up to the hilt with her one-bedroomed, red-brick house that is sandwiched between two others, artfully arranged so as not to appear terraced.

Staggered housing.

That is the same as terraced, but it gives the illusion of something less *northern*. If you are a regular viewer of *Coronation Street*, then you will be familiar with the set-up.

Claire Brown lives a life of illusion. How else could she drag herself through the tedium of it all? Every day would be the same, nine to five.

Bus, train, then tube.

Tube, train, then bus.

A girlie magazine in the morning and a copy of the *Evening Standard* on the way home. Sometimes, as a treat, she might buy a bag of Revels to eat on the bus.

During the light mornings of summer, Claire is all Dorothy Perkins in pale floral prints.

In the dark evenings of winter she is bundled in quilted cotton from BHS and footwear from Freeman Hardy & Willis.

Claire works for Glendale Estates & Associates.

The company owned by the recently deceased David Glendale, Felicity Craven's late husband.

Claire is office assistant to a man named Robin Bleesdale, who runs the promotions department for the company. Office assistant is a modern name for a secretary. There are five office assistants in Claire's typing pool, and they sit there all day with their headphones and their keyboards, and they eat Pot Noodle and tuna-salad sandwiches in the canteen between twelve and one. There is absolutely no possibility of glamour. Unless, of course, one gets hopelessly drunk at the staff Christmas party and ends up in a five-star hotel bedroom with the managing director.

How could Claire have done such a sluttish thing?

Down-to-earth Claire, with her Ikea furniture and her Marks & Spencer duvet: she must have had one too many champagne cocktails. And maybe the alcohol didn't mix very well with the pills she is taking for her sciatica. It says on the bottle Do Not Use with Alcohol: it also warns against driving or operating machinery, but Claire can't just sit at home with the curtains drawn watching *Neighbours*, simply because she's on prescription drugs.

So, when she hears the terrible news that David Glendale has been killed in an explosion in the Middle East, naturally she is upset. So upset, in fact, that she has to excuse herself from the typing pool and jam her face into a wad of toilet paper to stifle her sobs, in the steel-grey cubicle of the Ladies'. She gets mascara on her new top. Her eyes swell up like bee stings and she can feel one of her migraines coming on.

'Are you all right in there, Claire?' shouts Margaret, the typist with the smoker's cough and the perm that looks like kapok.

'I'm fine, thanks. Just a bit of a headache.'

'Can I get you some paracetamol?'

'No thanks. I'll be out in a minute.'

That poor, poor man. He had everything going for him: a huge international business, a famous, fabulous wife, two adorable children and a body that still makes Claire's knickers damp with excitement.

And she has seen that body. Every inch of it.

For it was David Glendale who took Claire Brown's maidenhead on 21 December in a deluxe suite of the Dorchester Hotel, with Robin Bleesdale having it off with Lynda Watson from Accounting in the adjoining room.

I suppose you might call it a late-night business meeting. A private conference.

It was certainly an early Christmas bonus for Claire and Lynda, who had never seen inside the directors' offices, let alone a suite at the Dorchester. It was a privilege they would have been foolish to refuse.

Like saying no to a free bag of assorted Continental chocolates from Thornton's.

Chapter Three

Felicity Craven is at the church on the eve of her husband's funeral. She faces a dilemma.

The silk is the wrong shade.

Can she trust no one these days? She had specifically asked them to swag the coffin in *anthracite* shot through with darkest *amethyst*, and what does she get? Black and sodding purple! That's the last time she orders anything from those incompetent bastards up in Bradford.

If there is one thing that Felicity knows about, it is colour. After all, it is her business as creative director of Craven's. In one bedroom alone she used thirteen different shades of grey, from slate to ash. In another she confidently juxtaposed magenta and tangerine on an eighteenth-century canopy bed. She is known for her sumptuous use of colour and her penchant for black. She once owned a little boutique on the King's Road in the late seventies called Black Magic, where she specialized in selling home accessories and fabrics in every shade of black imaginable. It failed miserably as a business, but she got a lot of media coverage from it at a time when her personal star was fading.

That was just before she met David.

David Samuel Glendale.

He was already a rich man, even in those days. They were introduced at an extravagant ball given in honour of Bubbles Rothermere. They sat at the same table. It was horrible food and the wine was corked. David and Felicity left before dessert was served, and they did a Joan Collins number going up in the lift to his apartment.

Torn Zandra Rhodes taffeta.

Spunk on her Janet Reger knickers.

She had been married before, you see, so she had very little to be moralistic about. Her first husband had lasted about three months, and then he was carted away to a drug rehab centre where he fell in love with a heroin addict and never came back. He's quite famous now, in a minor TV celebrity kind of way.

Felicity was twenty-nine when she married David. The wedding was up in Scotland where his family live. It was all bagpipes and men in kilts. Felicity had her dress designed by the up-and-coming Emanuels, way before Princess Di made them famous for their puffy, frilly confections. When she looks at the pictures now, she wants to puke. She looked like one of those cheap toilet-roll covers with a plastic doll's head stuck on the top. She had a Wendy Craig hairstyle and *lip-gloss*. Christ!

'Where do you want these, Miss Craven?' asks one of the decorators.

Felicity inspects the arum lilies as one might check a cauliflower for slugs. 'Put them over there next to the draperies, but pull out all this ghastly gypsophila. Whoever told them to do such a thing? It looks like something from an Esso station.'

'Yes, Miss Craven.'

Felicity sits at the edge of one highly polished pew. The service is tomorrow morning and nobody can believe that she has taken on the arrangements for the funeral herself. They think she is being brave and heroic – one last perfect gesture for her beloved husband.

And to an extent they are right. For Felicity mourns David's death, even though she welcomes the undeniable advantages of becoming his widow.

Felicity knows that this event will be on every news broadcast, in every newspaper and probably photographed for *The Tatler* and *Town & Country*. She knows that her so-called best friends will be looking out for just one thing for which to criticize her. Eagle eyes will be pinned to every floral tribute, every flounce of silk, every pinch-pleat in her hastily commissioned dress from Bruce Oldfield. She can't afford to offer them ammunition against her. This is probably her finest hour. She will not slip up.

The coffin must remain closed. There is to be no viewing, because there is no body to view – just a few blown-up pieces of him. A hand with his wedding ring. Part of his scalp with his famously gorgeous hair still attached. And, funnily enough, most of his tight little backside with the incongruous tattoo of the Playboy logo – a joke from a previous relationship with a bunny girl in New York. Felicity had always hated that tattoo, and it's almost as though David is having one last laugh at her expense by leaving her his arse, one final gesture of his opinion on their marriage.

David knew that the love between them had perished. He knew that Felicity thought more of her children, her house and her hotel than she did of him.

By the time he died, their marriage was as wrung out as a dishcloth.

Felicity doubts that she ever really loved David in the conventional sense. But they had been friends in the early days. Felicity had her hotel and David had his business. They became so highly polished, so unapproachable with power and wealth, that Felicity often wondered who on earth she was married to. She didn't even know what brand of deodorant he used – imagine how embarrassing that would have been if they had ever been forced to take part in *Mr & Mrs*! (Highly unlikely, but an amusing thought.)

Their sex life was always good. He was an expert in bed: unselfish, and considerate to her womanly needs. But it wasn't often that they got the chance to do it once the excitement of the wedding was over. She became pregnant with Sascha almost immediately, and just eighteen months later she was carrying Josh. Heavily pregnant in a South Molton Street maternity smock.

'Your car is here, Miss Craven.'

Felicity checks her watch. Right on time! At least *somebody* can get it right. She straightens the hem of her jacket and gives final instructions to the decorators. It is dark outside, and a little windy. She hopes that it will die down before tomorrow, otherwise it might mess up her plans for the floral canopy down the driveway.

There is a full moon riding the clouds. The sky is almost purple, like a bruise. Her chauffeur is called James – naturally – and he is standing by the open door of her car with moonlight glinting on the reflective peak of his perfectly maintained cap. He has the Craven's logo embroidered on his breast pocket, and a respectful expression embroidered on his face.

'Good evening, Miss Craven.'

'Good evening, James.' Felicity bends to climb into the back of the limo.

It is warm inside, and softly illuminated by a pair of chrome and opaque-glass sconces. There is a cocktail cabinet, a telephone and a small TV screen. Classical music plays, purring along with the unobtrusive sound of the idling engine.

'Hello, darling,' smiles Felicity.

'Good God, you look like Eva Perón!'

'It's my grieving widow, darling. I thought the chignon was rather a poignant touch,' smiles Felicity, patting her hair.

'Sometimes, Fliss, I forget that you were once an actress.' And the man in the cashmere jacket reaches across to touch Felicity's cheek with the back of his wonderfully warm hand.

CHAPTER FOUR

The family house is in Hampstead, in one of those celebrity-studded streets where every other building boasts a pale blue ceramic plaque declaring the past residency of somebody illustrious like Gerald du Maurier or Hattie Jacques. Trees create a shadowed tunnel of dancing light along the road, where gas lamps punctuate the cobbled pavement at regular intervals. It could be a set for a BBC play.

Sebastian drives up to the imposing gates and punches in the code number. Nothing happens. He punches in the number a second time, leaning as far as he can out of the car window to reach the buttons. He is careful not to catch his expensively tailored sleeve on the framework of the door. Still nothing happens, and so, with a heavy sigh of impatience, he presses the intercom button. No doubt Mummy has been buggering around with the security system again.

He can hear the dogs barking inside the house.

'Hello?' It's Mummy's voice, scratchy and tremulous. 'What do you want?' she demands. The dogs continue to bark frantically in the background.

'It's me, Mummy. Let me in!'

'Felicity?' questions the voice.

'Do I sound like Felicity, Mummy? It's *Sebastian*. Now please open the gates, will you.'

'Are you here about the clock?'

More wild barking.

'What are you talking about? It's me – Sebastian. Your one and only son.'

'He's not here,' says the crackling voice.

'What?'

'Sebastian – he isn't here. You'll have to come back another day. Get down, Snap!' she screams.

'Get Mrs Leigh! Tell her there's somebody at the gates who wants to come in.' Sebastian is jamming his face up to the entryphone.

'We don't want anything. Go away!' and the intercom clicks off.

'Christ!' shouts Sebastian, hitting the keypad like someone jammed in a lift.

Mrs Leigh, the housekeeper, finally comes to the intercom and Sebastian is granted entry. He swerves up the gravel driveway and screeches to a sudden halt outside the house.

The house is a glorious hotchpotch of barley-twist chimneys and mullioned windows. Rambling roses, dead at this time of year, and verdant ivy crawl liberally over the façade, padding out the hard edges and giving the house an upholstered appearance, like a huge, fat tea cosy. He can hear the dogs throwing themselves against the inside of the studded oak door.

Sebastian climbs out of his car, grabs his briefcase and approaches the front porch, home to the boot-scraper and the walking sticks. As he pushes open the door, he releases three miniature poodles, all of them wearing party hats and ruffled collars. They leap around him like demented children, and he stumbles into the entrance hall with the dogs attempting to trip him at every step. They race past him, shrieking and barking and jumping on the marble tiles.

'These dogs are bloody barmy,' says Sebastian, but there is no one there to hear him.

The hall is a marvellous open area, rather gloomy but magnificently atmospheric. The dark oak staircase rises to a central landing area, and then divides itself into a symmetrical pair of staircases branching off in opposite directions and opening out into a pair of balconies draped with heavy old kilims and tapestries. The marble floors are worn and yellowed with age, undulating like a chequered blanket. There is a large octagonal table in the centre, veneered and sagging upon an octagonal rug of indeterminate colour. A gloriously untidy arrangement of winter roses and berries spills drunkenly over the sides of a crystal urn, scattering petals across the polished wood and on to the floor.

A pair of painted doors shudders open and light floods through from the room beyond. The dogs skid over into the slab of lamplight, falling over themselves and knocking their party hats askew.

'Ah, Mummy!' says Sebastian affectionately. 'What is all this nonsense about a clock? And why wouldn't you let me in?'

Sabrina Craven steps forward apprehensively, peering into the gloom of the hall with her slender hand raised to shield her eyes.

'Is that you, Sebastian darling?' she asks uncertainly.

'Yes, it's me. Who else did you think it could be? I did tell you yesterday that I'd be popping over.'

Sebastian switches on the chandelier and the hall is doused in a bleak, white light. Sabrina Craven looks startled and she steps back, almost falling over one of the poodles as it chases around her feet.

She is wearing a pair of white thigh-length boots with zips, and a white leather miniskirt with a wide belt made of silver chain mail. Her billowing blouse is coffee-coloured chiffon with a kind of Pierrot collar and cuffs, through which Sebastian can clearly see the outline of her black bra. Her hair is styled in what used to be called an 'urchin' cut, and she is wearing false eyelashes. It's her Emma Peel look.

'Don't I get a kiss, then?' Sebastian asks, approaching his mother. Sabrina reaches out to grab him. She is wearing a ring on every finger, and on her thumbs, some of which appear to be nothing more than huge chunks of coloured plastic. One of the rings is a plastic chrysanthemum. Her fingernails are painted white.

'Who are you?' she asks, clasping Sebastian weakly and staring into his face with her wild, spidery eyes.

'Oh, for crying out loud, Mummy!' snaps Sebastian wearily. 'I'm going into the study. Why don't you put

Snap, Crackle and Pop into the kitchen and ask Mrs Leigh to bring us some tea and biscuits?'

'Have you seen Greville?' asks Sabrina, twisting a plastic clip-on earring until it falls off in her hand.

'Daddy's dead, Mummy. You know that! He's been dead for seven years. You put flowers on his grave just the other day when Felicity took you over to the cemetery. I'm going into the study now. Obviously there's no point in trying to communicate with you this evening.'

Sebastian strides through the double doors, through the chintzy sitting room and into the oak-panelled study with the empty fireplace and tartan carpet. He can still hear his mother talking to herself in the hallway, apparently unaware that she has been deserted.

He closes the study door and picks up the house telephone to speak to Mrs Leigh.

'I'm in the study, Mrs Leigh. Mother is really quite alarmingly bad this evening. Has she been like it all day?'

'I'm afraid so, Mr Sebastian. I called the doctor earlier, but he just told me to up her dose. There's not much he can do, really. I caught her out by the gates in her nightie this morning. She reckoned she was waiting for a letter from Mr Craven. She thinks he's still alive.'

'Could you bring me some tea please, Mrs Leigh? And some of your flapjack, if you've got any handy.'

'Of course, Mr Sebastian.'

Sebastian sits in the velvet-covered wing chair by the fireplace. When he crosses his legs, one can see that his worsted socks are monogrammed.

He must speak to Felicity about Mummy again. Obviously his sister has too much on her plate at the moment with the funeral and everything, but they really should come to a decision about the nursing home in Dorset. It seems that Sabrina's bad days are far outweighing the good, and she now needs constant professional attention.

Suddenly a blast of music ricochets through the house from somewhere upstairs.

'Bugger!' cries Sebastian. 'She's found the bloody records again!' And he dashes out of the library, with Petula Clark bellowing ahead of him.

In the bedroom that used to be the nursery Sabrina is go-go dancing on a footstool, gyrating her hips in time with the music and tossing her head back and forth in a most alarming manner. She is a Carnaby Street relic, an old woman in a time warp that never even belonged to her in the first place. Mrs Leigh has switched off the record player, but the music obviously continues inside Sabrina's head.

'Come on now, Mrs Craven. Let's get you off to bed, shall we?' And the faithful servant leads her mistress towards the master bedroom, offering Sebastian a look over her shoulder as they leave the room.

On the nursery shelves there are still memories of Enid Blyton, and Robertson's plaster golliwogs, arranged in a semicircle, play their chipped musical instruments. There are bars on the windows and ABCs around the frieze on the walls. And in the cupboard at the side of the fireplace Sebastian knows that he will find the Oxo tin filled with dominoes and marbles, and the wooden blocks with the farmyard scenes. It strikes him as terribly sad to remember Mummy as she was in those days. Mummy in her wonderfully glamorous ballgowns, on her way to a dance. Mummy with her scent and her talcum, coming in on a path of light from the landing to kiss them goodnight.

Feeling nostalgic and just a little old, Sebastian returns to the library with a heavy heart. Who would ever have predicted that life would turn out like this? Felicity is a stranger these days, so caught up in her self-made world that she barely has time for her family and friends. Mummy is clearly one step away from the loony-bin, Daddy is dead and Sebastian is a tormented homosexual who daren't even admit to himself that this isn't just a phase he's going through.

'When are you going to get married?' they ask.

He endures the dinner parties with the convenient seating arrangements: always a spare seat beside old Sebastian, ready to be filled with someone else's idea of a suitable partner. He has tried to conform. He has dated and dined, kissed and cuddled, but he has never allowed things to go any further. The ladies think he is a gentleman. The press have labelled him 'a confirmed bachelor'.

Sebastian wonders what would happen if he just screwed the lot of them and told the truth about himself. Bugger the blackmailing little Wayne Briggses of this world!

The cost of common decency just went up, sir.

The mere thought of such a perilous action sends him rattling through the liquor on the tray in the drawing room. Some things do not bear thinking about.

CHAPTER FIVE

Wayne Briggs.

He writes his name over and over again, as though attempting to reaffirm to himself who he really is.

He writes with a biro on the inside of a cornflakes box. Untidy, uneducated handwriting that is barely joined up, and the lines slant dangerously close to the edge as though his name is slipping, tumbling downward towards oblivion.

On the rare occasion that he has to write something presentable, he uses Basildon Bond with the lines already printed.

'You've got a mental blockage, son,' announced Mr Greenspan at Loughton Comprehensive. So Wayne would sit at the back of the class with a pocketful of Refreshers and a copy of *Melody Maker*. They didn't even bother to check if he'd done his homework. He was ignored. And he was glad. Because Wayne Briggs knew he wasn't stupid.

Theydon Bois. That's where they lived.

Sounds so fucking posh, but it's nothing but a dump.

Oh yes, there are big houses there, with double garages and crunchy driveways, but the Briggses didn't live in one of those. They had a rented flat above a sweet shop. Mr Briggs had asbestosis and had to sit by the electric fire all day, while Mrs Briggs sold sherbet lemons and Winter Mixture to the snotty-nosed kids from the private school up the road.

Most afternoons Wayne skived off school and sat in the playground, going higher and higher on the kiddy swings until the framework rocked and creaked.

Until he thought he might actually go right over the top bar and into space.

He liked to imagine that there was some sort of time portal just above that top bar, and that if he could only get up there he would vanish through the invisible gate into another time zone, like on *The X-Files*. He would like to go back to the time when they had highwaymen and guillotines – and stupid women with bulging tits, screaming as they had their jewels ripped from their bodies. Wayne would have liked that.

At weekends he used to catch the bus out to Epping Forest. It was quiet there, and in the autumn it was a secret place. He felt like Robin Hood. Quite often, usually late in the afternoon or early evening before it got too dark, Wayne would spy on shagging couples who thought they were alone in the bracken. Bare bums blotchy and thrusting. Used condoms under the damp leaves. Didn't these people know about the snakes that lived in the undergrowth? Weren't they scared that an adder might suddenly pop up and bite them on the arse?

About a week after his sixteenth birthday, Wayne walked away from Loughton Comprehensive a free agent. Shit, it was such a weird feeling! Like getting out of prison must feel. On his first day of freedom, he took the Central line into London and played in the arcades on Leicester Square until he ran out of money.

Leicester Square is just a short distance from Piccadilly. Wayne had heard stories about that place. Stories of old perverts who paid big money for pretty young boys such as himself. Anyway, he couldn't get back home without some cash, so he decided to give it a try. It was surprisingly easy. Ten quid for about three minutes in an alley behind Boots. Somebody disturbed them and the man scarpered before he even shot his load.

You see, Wayne Briggs lied to Sebastian Craven when he said that he was under age. Wayne is almost nineteen now. A very young-looking, old-acting nineteen. He has seen more of life in the last three years than most of us would want to see in a lifetime. Two years on the Dilly with his own pimp, and a motley bunch of mates who taught him the ethics of the street. In its own way it was a good time. The winters were hard, but the money was pretty good, and he got his own place. A bedsit in Soho where his window looked down on a courtyard gay bar that was all lit up in the summer, with blokes on the fire escape holding beer bottles, and the thump of dance music.

Then one night he tricked with Sebastian Craven. It was an all-nighter. One hundred nicker for a night of sex in a very posh flat belonging to a friend of the punter's. King-size bed, gold taps in the bathroom – that kind of thing. And breakfast the next morning. Couldn't be bad.

That was the turning point. Sebastian offered him a job in his hotel. A decent wage, a safe occupation and easy access for a quick shag in the cleaning cupboard whenever Sebastian got the urge. The perfect job.

Wayne Briggs writes his name.

Over and over on the inside of a cornflakes packet.

He knows he's not stupid.

Less than a year at Craven's and he's already been promoted.

Chapter Six

It isn't really spying.

Claire is in her bathroom being sick, so I don't think she really cares if we have a little look around her house. It isn't as though we're total strangers.

Let's start in her kitchen. It seems like a sensible place to begin, and it's right off the front-door entry-way with the doormat and the coat hooks. It's a kitchen-diner, and has a breakfast bar just big enough for two people to sit opposite each other. Claire likes to keep the vertical blinds closed, so that none of the neighbours can look in and see her eating alone every evening.

Sometimes it's beans on toast.

Sometimes it might be a microwave meal from Sainsbury's. She isn't fussy.

Claire uses her central-heating boiler as a notice-board. Colourful novelty magnets hold postcards and electricity bills in place, and there's a clever little notepad with a magnetic strip on the back and a holder for a pen. SHOPPING LIST, it says on the top of each page in pink block capitals. She has already written *Toothpaste* and *Weetabix* in her neat, secretary's writing.

There is a washing machine and drier, a cooker and

a fridge-freezer. Not much work surface, but a decent amount of storage space in the overhead cupboards from Magnet & Southern. Everything is spotlessly clean. Even her water is clean. She filters it into a little plastic jug before she makes her tea in the morning.

The living room is next.

It is surprisingly bare. Beige walls and beige carpet, and there are vertical blinds on all the windows – including the patio doors that open out on to her little garden. There is only just enough room for the sofa and one chair. She has a fake fireplace with an electric fire that glows in the dark, pretending to be real flames. Above the mantelpiece there is just one picture – a framed poster from Athena of a woman in a long frock swooning on to a chaise longue.

You know the kind of thing.

At the top of the stairs Claire is wondering if she ought to cancel her blind date. She feels awful, and the last thing she wants to do is spend the evening with some boring stranger in a pub she has never even been to before. The thing is, she doesn't have his phone number and this was arranged two weeks ago.

Before David Glendale died.

Before she missed her second period.

She steels herself and goes through into the little room that contains her wardrobes. It's supposed to be a second bedroom, but it isn't big enough for anything larger than a cot, so she uses it as her dressing room. She put the wardrobes together herself, and they lean against each other like conspirators, creaking ominously whenever she opens the doors. She had been unable to follow the instructions, and so she had improvised with superglue and staples. There was an alarming pile of nails and screws left over at the end, but they have held up so far.

She chooses the skirt and blouse from River Island, but then she remembers that the last time she wore it had been to the Christmas party. She gets out her Principles dress instead, and digs through the boxes at the bottom of the wardrobe to find a suitable pair of shoes. It's no fun getting dressed up for something you're not interested in doing. She'll just stay for one quick drink, and then she'll make an excuse about an early start tomorrow. He'll probably have the same agenda in mind. Claire wonders if he's taking care choosing what *he* wears – do men do that kind of thing? His name is Duncan and he's a civil servant – whatever that might be! Claire thinks it's something to do with the Council or the government. Something in a cubicle with a computer and a swivel chair.

She has to rush: the number twenty-nine leaves the corner of her estate at seven-fifteen sharp, and if she misses it there won't be another until half past. They've arranged to meet at eight in the Jolly Roger. It's a pub she passes on her way to work every day, but she has never been inside. Sometimes, in the summer, she sees women and children sitting on the wall outside with bags of crisps and straws in pop bottles. But not tonight – it's February and it's drizzling.

Claire is early, of course. She has to go into the pub

on her own and she feels highly conspicuous. She keeps her head down and her hands in her pockets. She bumps into a slot machine and bangs her forehead. How embarrassing! People are looking at her and wondering why she's here. She sits at the first available table and puts on an act of searching through her handbag for something important. She makes tutting noises as though she really can't find whatever it is she's looking for. The jukebox is playing 'Sugar Baby Love', and there is a strong whiff of minced beef.

It's only ten to eight. The barman is casting suspicious looks her way as he polishes his glasses. She takes off her coat and folds it carefully on the seat beside her. What if Duncan never shows up? She could be sitting here for hours like a lemon, and all the time he might be at home watching *Brookside* while she sits there waiting for him to arrive. She decides to give him till half past, and then she's off home.

'You must be Claire.'

She jumps so violently that the little round table leaps up in the air and the ashtray skids on to the carpet. She barely sees the man who has just addressed her; she's too busy scurrying under the upholstered bench on her hands and knees.

'I am sorry. Did I startle you?' asks the man with the trench coat and the Michael Caine glasses. He is so tall that Claire has to crane her neck to see the top of his head.

'Duncan Fraser.' He extends his hand. It is chilled

from the drizzle outside, and there are coarse black hairs on the back of every finger.

'I'm sorry, I'm not normally so nervous. It's just that I've never been in here before, and I really wasn't sure if you were going to show up.'

'I think I'd better start by getting you a drink. What'll it be?'

'Erm, I'll have a gin and orange.'

'Fair enough,' says Duncan with a friendly smile. Claire watches him as he approaches the barman. He seems very confident. Not at all what she had expected. She had certainly not imagined that he would be so tall. He must be well over six foot. Claire is only five feet two inches in her bare feet.

Duncan returns with their drinks and takes off his coat. He's a corduroys-and-jumper kind of man.

'Well, I am glad that we've finally met, Claire,' he says, wiping the froth off his top lip as he takes a first swig of his beer. 'You can never be sure how these things are going to turn out. I expect it's even more nerve-racking for a woman.'

'I've never done this before, actually. I just saw your ad and you sounded very nice, so I thought I'd give it a whirl. I have to admit that I very nearly didn't come tonight. I've been feeling a bit under the weather.'

'Oh, I'm sorry to hear that. I'd hate to think I'd dragged you out on such a horrid evening if you weren't feeling up to it. We could have made it another night, you know.'

'I didn't have your number,' says Claire, jiggling the ice cube in her glass.

'We don't have to stay here late. Perhaps we could get together for dinner one evening, when you're feeling better?'

He's a bit of a fast mover, thinks Claire, hiding her rising blood pressure under a layer of indifferent platitudes.

They have a second drink. The pub is getting busier, and Claire is beginning to enjoy herself. For a moment she forgets about her dilemma, and then it falls back in her lap like a breeze-block. It's like suddenly remembering a dentist's appointment.

'Are you all right, Claire?' asks Duncan. 'You look a bit uncertain. I do hope I'm not keeping you here when you would rather be at home.'

'Oh, I'm sorry, Duncan. It honestly isn't you. My mind was wandering. I'm glad I came. This is much more cheerful than an early night at home with a packet of gypsy creams and a library book.' Claire is flushed. In this light she looks almost angelic.

'I'm glad I came, too. I have to admit, I was more than a little doubtful about all this. After I placed the ad in the paper I had strong reservations. There's quite a stigma attached to classified advertising, and an awful lot of trust involved.'

'You could have been an axe murderer,' smiles Claire.

'You could have been Glenn Close,' says Duncan.

Claire remembers that film. The scene at the

kitchen sink with Michael Douglas giving her one up against the stainless steel. Claire flushes an even deeper shade of pink.

'Can I offer you a lift home, Claire?' asks Duncan when the barman is shouting last orders. There are quite a few empty glasses on their table, but Duncan sensibly switched to alcohol-free after his second half-pint. Claire can feel the gin glazing her eyes. It makes her reckless and slightly dizzy.

'That's very kind of you. I don't live very far.' And together they leave the Jolly Roger as though they have known each other all their lives.

Duncan has one of those cars with wooden panels on the side. *It looks like a little Tudor house on wheels*, thinks Claire stupidly. She stumbles on the edge of the pavement, but Duncan is there to catch her elbow.

'Oops!' they both say together.

Inside, the car smells of pipe tobacco and damp carpet. There is no seat belt on Claire's side, and Duncan apologizes. They laugh about the girls outside the chip shop with their dyed green hair and the shoes that make them look handicapped.

'We shouldn't laugh,' says Claire. 'I can still hear *my* mum going on about my platform shoes and fluorescent-green bomber jacket.'

'You don't look old enough to remember any of that,' says Duncan.

'I'm thirty-four.' *How unladylike, and on a first date!*

'I'm a bit older than you,' says Duncan. 'I missed that whole seventies period myself. I was a bit of a recluse, I think – kept myself to myself. I preferred reading and listening to my dad's old jazz records to going out with kids my own age. I've always been a bit of a fuddy-duddy.'

'I don't think you're a fuddy-duddy,' says Claire, resting an impetuous hand gently on the sleeve of Duncan's gear-changing arm. He looks too big for the car. His head is slanted forward to avoid hitting the roof.

'Is this you, then?' he asks as they pull up at the entrance to The Acorns.

'Yes. You can drop me off here. I live just inside.' Better not let him see her house just yet. She isn't *that* drunk.

'So how about that dinner, then?' he asks, smiling in the half-light of the dashboard.

'I think I would like that very much.'

'Does the weekend work for you?'

'That's fine.'

'How about if I pick you up here at half past seven on Saturday night? You've got my phone number now, so you can call me if you need to cancel.'

'Lovely. I'll see you then.'

And Claire gets out of the half-timbered car, and waves goodbye as Duncan makes a U-turn and trundles off towards the main road.

Tomorrow I must go to the doctor's.

There's no point in going out to dinner if she's already got a bun in the oven.

CHAPTER SEVEN

'You know when you said that I could pass for a thirty-year-old – did you mean it, darling?'

Felicity is in bed with Ross, her lover of six years.

He's the man in the cashmere jacket. The man in the back of the limo.

He is the husband of Felicity's friend Cybil, and the ex-business partner of Felicity's dead husband David.

They have just made love for the second time since the last of the funeral party left, and now it is after eleven. There's a fireplace in the bedroom, and the pair of them are draped across the bed like a Renaissance painting, in the wavering light of the spitting hickory logs.

'Oh, Fliss, you're not going to start obsessing about your age again, are you, darling? How many times do I have to tell you? You are absolutely amazing,' strokes Ross.

'For my age . . .'

'For *any* age. There must be thousands of fat, spotty teenagers who would give up their first-born to have a body like yours. Just look at these tits . . .' He cups one of her firm breasts in the palm of his hand, jiggling it slightly as though testing for ripeness. ' . . . Now, unless you've been telling porky-pies about silicone implants, I'd say this pair have stood the test of time in a most outstanding fashion. Hell, I'm getting a hard-on just touching them!'

'Oh, Ross, you are so reassuring. I don't know what my life would be like without you. All those wasted years, darling – I was a virtual *toadstool*. I thank God, or whatever else is watching over me, for sending you to me.' Felicity kisses Ross's shoulder lightly and then reaches over him to get another Fauchon rum truffle from the bedside table.

'You know, I see more of you than I do of Cybil, these days. She seems to have accepted the fact, over the years, that she and I are merely living together out of habit and security. I'm pretty sure she's been bonking some fourteen-year-old from the local grammar school. He's always hanging around our house doing odd jobs in his gym shorts.'

'Well, if she isn't, she certainly should be, darling. After all, you can't blame her for wanting a bit of romance.'

'I don't think it's romance she's looking for. Her whole life is romance. No, what Cybil wants is just a bit of the other, and somebody who's prepared to be subservient to her every sexual whim. A grammar-school boy fits the bill perfectly.'

'Who'd have believed it, eh? David is off our hands without us even having to try. It's almost as though it were predestined.'

'The gods are on our side, darling. Anyway, you

deserve a little happiness after all those years with him. Well, now we're free, and we can tell the world to sod off, and do whatever we please. First thing would be a nice long cruise around the Caribbean.'

'What about Cybil? What will you tell her? Surely you're not thinking of leaving her, are you? I don't think that would be a very good idea at this stage.'

'Oh, of course not, Fliss! That would be disastrous, and there really is no need to upset the apple cart. Now that your mean bastard of a husband is out of the way, you and I can finally have some fun. You know, I always suspected he knew about the two of us. Ever since that episode in St Tropez with the anise and the bikini top.'

Felicity is examining another truffle, and enjoying the powdery feel of the cocoa on her fingertips.

'Darling, of course David knew about us. Hell, most of London knows about us – it's hardly a secret. Anyway, David was too busy with his precious business deals to worry about my little affairs.'

'You had the ultimate marriage of convenience. Wealth and prestige for you, and glamour and panache for David. You were the perfect couple.'

'Hardly, darling! David was miserly and stubborn, and if it weren't for the children we would have split up years ago.'

'You are a rare creature, Felicity Craven. I could gobble you up!' grins Ross with his broadest smile. He flings his arms around her and bites her neck playfully.

'I think it all went marvellously well, don't you, darling?'

'What?'

'The funeral and everything.'

'Marvellous, my angel! You were the absolute picture of grief. That riding-hat thing with the black chiffon was a touch of genius. You looked every inch an Evelyn Waugh heroine. I overheard somebody in the church whispering that you were probably setting a new trend.'

'How wonderful! I might just drop a couple of eight by tens over to *Vogue* next week. Bruce's little black number went down like a house on fire! Isn't he just the *sweetest* man? It isn't very often one meets a fashion designer these days who isn't foreign or a screaming queen.'

'Aren't most of your friends screaming queens?' replies Ross, stroking Felicity's arm in repetitive circles. 'Screaming queens, or bitter, fortysomething women with vendettas against their ex-husbands?'

'One has to humour everyone in my business, darling. I couldn't give a toss about them, if the truth be told,' says Felicity, twisting a hank of Ross's silky hair between her fingers.

'And I thought you were a liberal, darling! You're just as bigoted as the rest of us when it comes down to it.'

'One puts on a charitable face for the press. Quite frankly I can't stomach the thought of two chaps having it off. Still, at least they've got style, I suppose, so who cares what they get up to in the privacy of their own bedrooms.'

'Is there any more of that champers left, love?'

'Darling, in this house there is *always* more champers. The only question is: Dom or Veuve?'

And they laugh, because everything is going their way.

Paragons of excess.

Drinking their fine champagne by firelight in a fifteen-bedroom, Palladian-style house with a Victorian orangery, and gardens designed by Capability Brown.

CHAPTER EIGHT

Sebastian is sitting on the edge of his bed staring at the telephone as though he expects it to ring. He is hesitant, especially after the recent episode with Wayne Briggs. He wonders if this is how it feels to be an alcoholic: staring at a phone receiver like it's a bottle of Scotch.

Why should he feel so ashamed?

Perhaps because he has just been labelled London's fifteenth most eligible bachelor. How everyone would snigger if they knew.

Finally he picks up the receiver and dials the number he has torn from the back of a newspaper. He hears the digital response and then a ringing tone. A man answers.

'Hello, Boyzone.'

'Rick, this is Sebastian Craven.'

'Sebastian! We haven't heard from you in yonks. Where the hell have you been? I read somewhere that you were getting engaged. We had a laugh here in the office, I can tell you!' Rick has a voice that could shatter glass.

'Oh, you know how it is,' replies Sebastian. 'Those ridiculous tabloids and their mindless speculations.

One only has to take a gal to the pictures these days and one is practically married. Actually I called because I'm totally fed up and feeling just the tiniest bit lonely this evening.'

'Well, we can soon remedy that for you,' says Rick enthusiastically.

Sebastian can hear him rustling through some papers, and then he says: 'If you'd called just half an hour ago I could have sent Zach over, but he's out for the evening now. Stone is free after one, but I seem to remember that you and he didn't quite hit it off the last time.'

'Is that the redhead with the foreign accent?' asks Sebastian, screwing up his eyes, trying to remember.

'That's right. He's very popular but not, perhaps, *your* usual type, darling. I think I've got just the thing! A fairly new lad called Günter. Very spirited, and proving to be a great success since he joined us last month. Aryan blond, blue eyes, very special,' drawls Rick conspiratorially.

'The usual arrangements?' asks Sebastian.

'Five for the night, mate.'

'That's a bit steep!' exclaims Sebastian in a wounded tone.

'Overheads, mate. Everything's going up these days. And he is very special . . .' cajoles Rick.

'Five, then. I'll meet him in my apartment lobby at twelve-thirty,' says Sebastian. He puts down the receiver.

It is already half past eleven.

Sebastian doesn't mess around with the Piccadilly rent boys these days. Not since he met Wayne. It's too dangerous, and he just can't risk the chances of being caught. He had thought that having Wayne work at the hotel would be the perfect solution, but now it looks as though he's got himself into a bit of a mess. Wayne is proving to be more of a handful than he'd imagined.

Little slag!

He throws on some jeans and an oilskin jacket, and grabs his wallet. There's a very convenient cashpoint machine on the corner, so he doesn't have to get too wet running out into the rain to get some money. He has to draw from two different accounts in order to get the required amount – the system refuses to allow more than three hundred pounds in one twenty-four-hour period from either account. Then he pops into the all-night off-licence to get a couple of bottles of champagne, and dashes home to put them in the freezer. He just has time for a quick shower and a tidy-up in the bedroom before his date arrives.

Rick has very strict policies regarding his boys: payment up front, house calls only, and nothing kinky unless you are prepared to pay for it. Sebastian knows the ritual. He can see most of the lobby area through the spyhole in his door, so he checks two or three times before he catches sight of the escort sitting patiently on one of the upholstered armchairs, flipping idly through a very old magazine he has picked up from the coffee table. Sebastian can't tell from his fish-eye view if the boy is attractive or not, but he is definitely very blond. He opens the door and steps out into the lobby.

He isn't as boyishly innocent as Rick's usual chaps – rather short when he stands up, and dressed in a somewhat unbecoming pair of white jeans. He looks nervous, and this endears him to Sebastian, who is always rather nervous himself on these occasions. He smiles encouragingly and the boy smiles back.

'I wasn't sure if I should wait out here,' the boy says. 'You never know, with these places, if you're allowed to just come in and sit down.' He has no trace of a German accent: in fact he sounds a bit *common*. And he certainly isn't a day younger than twenty-five.

'It's Günter, right?' asks Sebastian.

The boy looks a little confused, and then he smiles again and says, 'Oh, yes!' in the way one might nod and smile in the face of an incomprehensible foreigner.

'You'd better come in,' says Sebastian, standing aside and offering him the open door.

'Oh, I don't think so. I'm here on business,' says Günter, his expression changing suddenly. A little hostility, perhaps?

Suddenly the penny drops and Sebastian says, 'Ah!' with a how-stupid-of-me smile. 'This is for you,' he says, producing the fat envelope from his pocket and holding it towards him.

Günter crosses the lobby and reaches for the envelope, but Sebastian pulls it away, teasingly.

'Look, I don't know what your game is, mate,

but . . .' says the boy, just before Sebastian takes his arm and pulls him into his apartment, closing the door and pressing him up against it with one arm around his waist.

Why does all this have to be so sordid?

'Look, the money's all there. Please don't mess me around. I'm nervous enough as it is,' says Sebastian, waving the envelope in Günter's face. 'I've got some champagne in the fridge . . . I thought we could just sit and talk for a while. We've got all night.'

He leans forward in an attempt to kiss the boy, but is immediately pushed roughly away.

'What the fuck do you think you're playing at?' screams the boy, and he brings his knee up right in Sebastian's groin with alarming ferocity. Sebastian doubles over in star-spangled pain, scattering twenty-pound notes across the floor, moaning spasmodically. The stupid boy has gone out into the lobby, where he is screaming blue murder, drawing attention from an incredibly striking blond boy in cut-off denims and Timberland boots, who is standing just inside the lobby entrance. The shouting and swearing scares away the other blond and doors begin opening.

Sebastian hears one of his neighbours say, 'Somebody call the police!' and he knows then that he is doomed.

CHAPTER NINE

'Oh, not again!' exclaims Claire, in her winter coat.

She looks down at the unmentionable mound on her doorstep and tries to decide whether she should just leave it and dash off to meet Duncan, or quickly clear it away just in case he pops back for a coffee after dinner. She is a tidy girl and she doesn't want the cat poo getting on her new shoes, so she grabs a sheet of yesterday's *Evening Standard* from the breakfast bar and scoops up the feline faeces, her mouth twisted into a distasteful little knot. She can feel it, all squidgy inside the paper – thank goodness it isn't still warm, or she might have gagged!

She doesn't notice the grainy photograph of Sebastian on the piece of newspaper she's holding. She doesn't even know who Sebastian Craven is, so why should she recognize him?

SOCIETY PLAYBOY IN RENT-BOY RUMPUS!

Claire is too busy stuffing the offensive bundle into her dustbin. Now she's reaching for the Dettol under the sink. She's going to be late if she doesn't watch it, and it won't look good to be late for a second date – if she dares even to call it that. She still hasn't made it to the doctor's; every morning she thinks, *One more day,*

I'll wait just one more day. But she knows she's fooling herself.

On the corner of the estate, Duncan is waiting for her in his funny little car. It looks as though he might have washed it as a mark of respect. The orange street lights make everything brown and grey; the colours of February. Claire can see him peering out over the steering wheel, with his head bobbed down like a contortionist in a magic box. His glasses glint through the windscreen.

'Hello, Duncan. I'm sorry I'm a bit late, but next door's cat pooed on my doorstep, and I had to clean it up before I could come out.' Claire believes in honesty.

'Oh dear, that doesn't sound very savoury,' laughs Duncan from the driver's seat.

'I don't mind really, it's a dear little thing, but I just wish it would find somewhere else to do its business. I always thought cats were supposed to be clean animals.'

'Maybe you just got one of the neighbourhood rebels,' jokes Duncan in a puff of tobacco smoke and leather.

'You smell nice,' comments Claire as she slams the passenger door shut. 'Is that aftershave you're wearing?'

Duncan ponders for a moment, staring into space as though recounting his recent ablutions in systematic detail. 'Not aftershave. It must be Imperial Leather or Right Guard – one or the other.'

'It smells nice. Kind of . . . comfy.'

'Sorry about the smoke. I only light my pipe when I'm on my own. I hope you don't mind. My friends always comment on it whenever they get in the car.'

'My dad used to smoke a pipe. I've always liked the smell, actually. Far nicer than cigarettes, or those blasted cigars that all the young lads are waving about these days.'

'Did you notice anything?' asks Duncan, a slight undertone of excitement shivering beneath the surface of his question.

Claire looks at him, then at the dashboard. What on earth does he mean?

'Erm . . . not really, Duncan.'

'The seat belt. I've had them install a seat belt on the passenger side. Now you don't have to worry so much about going flying whenever I take a corner a bit too fast.'

'Is this for me?' asks Claire, pulling the belt forward and backward as though it's a pair of braces. She looks at Duncan with bright anticipation.

'Just for you, Claire. It never really mattered to me before.'

Claire snaps herself into her seat with a comforting click, hiding her pleasure under the seat belt as though her life might fall down without it.

He takes her to St Albans. It's Saturday night and the streets are full of weekend people. The pavements are still wet from a recent shower and the light from Laura

Ashley spills out on to the road like petrol in the puddles. Girls in high heels and thin coats huddle together and dash over to the pub. Boys in baggy jeans and woollen caps take lethargic strides towards the chippy, where the sharp tang of salt and vinegar bites the wind. It's like being on holiday, thinks Claire. She doesn't come to St Albans very often, even though she only lives a few miles away. It isn't very convenient by bus, and the train is too expensive.

'Here, take my arm,' offers Duncan, keeping his hand in his coat pocket but offering her his elbow. She links her arm through his and they walk through the cobbled streets of the town centre like they've been doing it for years. Claire wants somebody to see her. Somebody from the office, perhaps. Somebody who might go back to the typing pool on Monday morning and say: 'You'll never guess who I saw on Saturday night – arm-in-arm with a hulking great man in the middle of St Albans.'

The wind makes her eyes run. She shields her face in Duncan's voluminous oilskin. It has the smell of him that she already recognizes, and for some ridiculous reason she suddenly wants to cry.

'Are you all right, Claire?' he asks, looking down at her from his great height.

'I'm fine, thank you. It's just the wind getting in my eyes.'

'Quick, before it turns red!' he laughs, tugging her over the pedestrian crossing so that her feet seem to fly away behind her. When they reach the other side they're a little breathless, and they pause in the shelter of a covered doorway.

'Blimey!' laughs Claire, flicking her hair out of her eyes. Funny how something as simple as crossing the road can be so exciting when you're not on your own. 'Where are you taking me?' she asks.

'To the Tie Rack.'

'Tie Rack? For *dinner*?' she asks, with understandable scepticism.

'The *Thai* Rack – it's a play on words. I hope you like Thai food, Claire.'

'I've never had it,' she admits.

'Then you're in for a treat. Come on, we're nearly there.'

'It's all delicious,' enthuses Duncan as Claire looks at the menu.

'It's all double Dutch to me. You'll have to steer me in the right direction, otherwise I'm going to make a pig's ear of it.'

'Do you like spicy food?'

'You mean like curry?'

'Well, sort of.'

'I don't like it if it makes my eyes run. I had a vegetable thing from Marks & Spencer's once that had curry in it, and I had to throw it away.' Claire fiddles with the chopsticks, hoping desperately that they are going to bring her a knife and fork.

'Well, let's play safe and order things that aren't

going to be too much of a shock to your system. Would you like some wine?'

'Lovely.'

She is admiring the beautiful colours of the silk tunic that their waitress is wearing. The colours of a parrot. And such small feet! Everyone is talking, but quietly, and some people at another table are being served tiny liqueur glasses that have been set on fire.

'Look at that!' she whispers.

'It's ouzo – a kind of aniseed syrup – with a coffee bean in the top. We used to call them Witches' Hats, because the flame makes a cone above the glass. We could have one later.'

'How do you drink it?' asks Claire. 'Doesn't it burn your mouth?'

Duncan laughs at her naivety. 'You blow it out first,' he says.

It is the most fantastic dinner she has ever had. There are miniature kebab things on skewers which they dip into something like peanut butter, and a cucumber salad with something perfumed sprinkled over it. There are huge chunks of succulent chicken cooked in a little pottery casserole dish with a lid, which has onions and spices and something like floppy lettuce shredded up in it. Claire is so full she can hardly sit up straight.

'We've eaten every last bit,' regards Duncan, finishing his wine.

'It was lovely! I'm stuffed.'

'Are you going to have this last drop?' Duncan holds up the bottle.

'Ohh, I couldn't. I'm already tipsy.'

'Well I can't drink it, I'm driving. It would be a shame to waste it.'

'Go on, then, you've twisted my arm.' Claire holds out her glass. She's looking at Duncan's fingers on the bottle. They are thick and solid and his nails are square and clean. She likes the rectangular patches of black hair just above his knuckles and on the back of his hand, spreading up beneath his shirt-cuff. Something about his shirt-cuff gets her all fidgety and she can't look him in the eye.

'Can I ask you what happened to your wife?' asks Claire, noticing the wedding band still on his finger. She knows from the classified ad that his wife is dead.

'Yes. She tumbled down some stone steps when we were on holiday in the Cotswolds three years ago. It knocked her out and she went into a coma. They had her on life support but she never recovered. In the end we had to give up and switch off the machine.'

'Oh, Duncan, that must have been horrible for you. How can they expect anyone to make such a momentous decision for someone they love?' Claire is suddenly sober and crushed with concern.

'It wasn't easy, but it was either that or an endless limbo. She was dead already; it was just the machine that was doing the breathing.' Duncan shrugs and smiles. His eyes behind his glasses are inscrutable, but Claire thinks she knows how he's feeling.

'How long had you been married?'

'Seven years. We met in Edinburgh, actually, at the Festival.'

Claire has never been to Edinburgh and she doesn't know what the Festival is, but it sounds romantic and she nods in silent sympathy.

'You're the first woman I've been out with since it happened. I hope that doesn't frighten you, Claire.'

She hides behind a massive swig of Blue Nun.

'I was worried that I might start making comparisons between someone new and Chrissy – my wife – but you're so different from her that somehow I don't make a connection between the two of you. There's something refreshingly simple about you.'

'That's me – simple!' giggles Claire, embarrassed and uncomfortable.

'No, I don't mean *simple* in that way. You're just . . . unpretentious, I suppose. You seem to see everything through new eyes. You make me feel as though I'm seeing it for the first time too. Does that make sense?' Duncan is leaning forward, with question marks in his earnest spectacles.

'I haven't done much in my life, Duncan. I am thirty-four years old and I have never had a real relationship beyond a few occasional dates. I've never been on an aeroplane, and I've never been further north than Doncaster. I've been in the same job for nine years and I've never been promoted, even though the other girls around me are getting moved up all the time. Dependable, they call me. They think I'm like a bloody washing machine with a limitless warranty – good old Claire! Come rain or shine, she'll always be in at ten to nine to plug in the coffee pot and wipe out the mugs.' Claire surprises herself with the words that vomit out of her mouth.

'I'm sorry if I've offended you,' says Duncan.

'It's not you, it's me. Nothing ever *happens*. It always seems to happen to somebody else.'

'Perhaps something is going to start happening very soon. How can you know, if you don't wake up every morning and wonder, will it be today? If you give up wondering, surely you give up on the intrinsic quality of life?'

'The *intrinsic* quality of my life at the moment, Duncan, is somewhere between birth and death. I feel like I'm just hanging here, like a shirt at the dry-cleaner's, waiting to be moved on up the conveyor belt. Just a plain, ordinary, white cotton shirt. My mother used to call me Lizzie Dripping. "Always moping around," she'd say. "Always looking like a wet weekend." And she'd try to get me out on the street to play with the neighbours' kids. I suppose I was anti-social even then.'

'Are your parents still alive?' asks Duncan.

'Nope. They died in a car accident in ninety-one. Five miles outside Chester – on their way home from a traction-engine rally. Dead before the ambulance arrived.'

'I'm sorry.'

'Oh, I'm over it now. I just feel, since then, that

there should be somebody to talk to. I don't really like being on my own all the time. Well, I've got the girls at the office, and they're a good laugh, but it's hard at night when I go home. Sometimes I feel as though I act too desperate – you know, grab at any opportunity, however silly or small it might be. At Christmas I . . .' Claire falters at this point, realizing that she is allowing her tongue to run away with her. 'I think I've had enough of this wine; it's going straight to my head.' She laughs nervously.

'I don't understand how you've escaped the clutches of some other chap before now,' says Duncan, accepting the bill from the waitress with the tiny feet.

'How can I get "clutched" if I'm permanently locked away?'

'Well, we'll have to do something about opening up a few doors for you, won't we?'

'Oh, let me give you something towards that!' exclaims Claire as he hands over his credit card.

'This was my treat. I'll let you buy dinner for me next time.'

There's something about that 'next time' that makes Claire feel buoyant, and as they leave the restaurant together, she takes Duncan's arm without even being asked.

Chapter Ten

'This cannot be true!' screams Felicity Craven, tossing the legal papers at her solicitor and turning her back on him to glare out of the window overlooking Cavendish Square.

'Felicity, David changed these papers in 1996 and they are all authorized and signed by the relevant witnesses. You can appeal, of course, but they look pretty watertight to me. It's going to be a struggle convincing the courts that you're entitled to anything more than what he has provided in this will.'

Felicity can barely breathe, she is so angry. How *dare* he? How *dare* her bastard of a husband virtually cut her out of everything she was legally entitled to? What did she ever do to antagonize him into such a cruel and vindictive action against her? She pulls on the beads of her necklace. She stares at the shoppers scurrying in and out of John Lewis; the line of people waiting to use the cashpoint machine. Will she be reduced to *that*? Shopping at John Lewis and getting her cash from a hole in the wall? Oh, God, it doesn't bear thinking about!

She turns to face her solicitor again. He is sitting at his desk with his hands folded on the leather blotter.

He looks as though he has no suggestions to appease her, and she wants to smack him across the face for being so bloody negative. At a hundred and seventy pounds an hour, she expects more than just, 'I'm sorry, there's very little we can do.'

'How am I supposed to survive on two million? I can't even buy a decent house for that! He never told me that Blythwood belonged to the corporation. Does this mean we're going to be thrown out on our arses?'

'Blythwood was mortgaged through Glendale Estates and is therefore legally an asset of the corporation. The directors must make the decision on the house, but surely there'll be no problems from that department?'

'You've got to be joking! They hate my bloody guts! Not one of them has a civil tongue in their head, and they're all as dense as manure. They're going to love pulling the rug out from under me; they've been waiting for a moment like this for years, ever since Daddy bought the hotel and stole their biggest client in the process.'

'But you have no financial claim over Craven's. Sebastian owns the property. At least you're getting your annual salary – and that is a not inconsiderable amount of money compared to the average person on the street.'

'But I am *not* the average person on the street!' yells Felicity, almost stamping her foot in frustration. 'I am Felicity Craven and this is the most awful embarrassment of my entire life! David has left with me a legacy of social ridicule. I am going to be the laughing stock of London. I can almost hear the table talk already.'

'At least he hasn't forgotten the children,' reminds the solicitor.

'Hah! What a generous soul he was! Trust funds that don't come into effect until they're both twenty-one. Sascha is only thirteen and Josh is barely out of short trousers. Who's going to support them for the interim period, I'd like to know? Who's going to fork out for public school now?'

'I believe David has made provision for the children's school fees until they are old enough to claim their personal inheritance. Yes, here it is – section 17A.'

'Oh, I'm not interested, Philip!' snaps Felicity, raking elegant fingers through expensively conditioned hair. 'Who is this *woman* in Texas he's left everything to? Surely we can go after her for fraud, or something?'

'I believe she was his mistress, Felicity. Apparently they had been friends for several years. The fact that she has two of his children—'

'Oh, shut up. I don't need to hear it all again. The bastard! The absolute fucking bastard!' Felicity clenches her fists and returns to the window. The trees are bare. The sky is the colour of concrete, and just as soulless. She is very late for her lunch with Ross. He will be sitting in the champagne bar of The Ivy, probably on his third drink, and wearing something expensive his wife bought him for Christmas. For once the thought of Ross does not excite her.

She has bigger fish to fry.

CHAPTER ELEVEN

Sebastian cannot decide between the game pie and the toad-in-the-hole. Hubert, the waiter, stands patiently with his pad in one hand (a silver chain connecting this to his belt strap) and his ballpoint poised expectantly above it. Hubert has been working at The Forum longer than Sebastian has been dining there. Sebastian's father first brought him to the club on the occasion of his sixth birthday. He can still remember the grown-up smell of cigars and leather, and the discreet mumble of male voices blending with the maroon-flocked walls and the tobacco-brown oil paintings, each with its own individual brass light. Nothing changes at The Forum. It is one of the rules of the club:

No women (except on Ladies' Day, although that is about to be changed despite much fuss from the older members).

No drunkenness (unless it is utterly dignified and unobtrusive).

No radical changes that might disorientate the members (unless absolutely necessary – like the plumbing in the library bathrooms).

'I think I'll go for the game pie, Hubert, and can I

have another whisky when you've got a minute?' asks Sebastian, returning the menu with a sidewards glance towards the sweet trolley, half a mind on the sherry trifle.

'Very good, sir. And will you be taking wine with your luncheon? We've just replenished our stock of the Burgundy you favour.' Hubert maintains a stoic expression of disinterest whenever he speaks to the club members, rather like a bored ticket collector or a member of the royal family.

'Mmm. Jolly good idea, Hubert. Bring me a bottle of that, and some Ashbourne water.'

'By the way, sir, I do hope you don't mind, but we were all most alarmed by that nasty business in the papers. We do hope that you have sorted out those Fleet Street blackguards.'

'Thank you, Hubert.' Sebastian is appalled that they've been talking about him in the servants' quarters, but he must appear neutral at all costs. It's one thing that his fellow club members are whispering about him behind their wing chairs; it is altogether another for the waiters to be throwing his scandal around in the kitchens like a piece of wet fish.

Hubert disappears, and Sebastian surveys the dining room with indifference. It is all so familiar to him that he could be sitting in his own home. He knows every detail, every nuance of the room, from the number of shades on the chandeliers (eight), to the repetitive order of Latin mottoes printed around the cornice in faded gold leaf. When he was ten years old he had written down every golden word, and translated them from his Latin vocabulary. The most incongruous of these mottoes is, to his mind: *Tempora mutantur, et nos mutamur in illis*. Which translates as: *Times change, and we change with them*. Sebastian has always thought that the motto of The Forum should be: *Times change, but we remain the same*.

Sebastian was twenty-six years old in 1990 when his father, Humphrey Craven III, died of prostate cancer. His mother Sabrina went to Monaco for six months after the funeral and came back with a new husband – Hector Meltonbury, an old family friend with gout and a reputation for being a bit of a gambler. The wedding had taken place in secret, with Sebastian's mother wearing an unsuitable dress and attended by two anonymous bridesmaids. It had caused quite a tabloid scandal of its own at the time. Sebastian and Felicity were presented with an album of photographs and a new stepfather. There had been a reception at The Forum in lieu of a wedding banquet, and Sebastian had spent the entire occasion avoiding his mother, who swept around the room in a Bill Blass evening gown with her hair piled up in a ridiculous heap of pin-curls.

Hector died of a heart attack the following summer, leaving Sabrina penniless except for the small inheritance from Sebastian's father. It was about that time that she began to show signs of mental fatigue.

The game pie arrives with the bottle of Burgundy. Sebastian is in a desultory frame of mind as he eats his lunch. Fragmented thoughts drop carelessly through his head like scraps of torn paper. He is concerned about his mother's state of health. He had found her this morning, naked except for a black g-string and tasselled go-go bra, climbing over the garage roof in search of an injured bird she had seen hobbling past her bedroom window. 'It was a dove, darling, a beautiful white dove with a broken wing,' she cried, as Sebastian dragged her back through her window.

Sebastian has watched his mother deteriorate over recent years. Loneliness and a loss of purpose in her life has left her retrospective, clinging to the glamorous world she moved in during her younger days as a society hostess. A kind of pathetic shadow of her former self, she hangs on to her fading former identity and refuses to acknowledge the fact that she is old enough to be collecting a pension. She has no sense of dignity, and because of this she has become a reclusive woman, trapped in her self-made world like a time-warp oddity from the pages of a 1977 knitting pattern. Like a clock that has stopped, Sabrina Craven-Meltonbury has ceased to move on from the final halcyon days of her notoriety. Firmly embedded in the late seventies, glued in an aspic of her own making, she refuses to recognize the passage of time.

As for his sister, Felicity has been horrid since the rent-boy scandal hit the newspapers. It is as though she blames Sebastian personally for making *her* life more difficult.

'If you must be a pervert, can you not do it in

private?' she had yelled. 'Must the entire family be subjected to yet more scandal and ridicule just because you had the disgusting desire to sleep with a young boy? How can you even contemplate such sickening behaviour? Have you never thought of going to see a doctor? There are treatments, you know, for people like you – electric-shock therapy and drugs from America. What were you thinking of?'

Sabrina had sat between them in the family drawing room, seemingly unaware of the argument, until at one point she had spoken up in a most lucid and remarkable manner.

'There's nothing wrong with being homosexual, Felicity. I have had many homosexual friends over the years and they have all been jolly nice. And what about dear Randolph? You have always adored him.'

'Randolph is a *decorator*, Mummy! They're practically *obliged* to be queer! Anyway, that's different. He had the decency to marry Daisy Compton-Bracknell, so nobody really cares what he gets up to in the privacy of his own bedroom.'

'I don't see how that makes any difference, darling,' continued Sabrina. 'He's still an old queen, and everyone knows that Daisy Compton-Bracknell is a dyke!'

Sebastian had laughed at that point, partly due to the fact that he was at his wits' end with the awful publicity and the sudden downfall of his social credibility. It was all rather crushing to one's ego.

Felicity now refuses to speak to Sebastian, and she

told the press that she was 'ashamed and disgusted' by her brother's behaviour. Several gay organizations have labelled her a bigot since she decried homosexuality as a 'grave and disruptive sin' on CNN.

'I'd rather you didn't come into the hotel,' she had told Sebastian. 'It will lower the tone of the place and I don't want my customers thinking that I advocate your sexual preferences. There are *children* to think of.'

'Oh, sod off, Felicity! Anybody would think that butter wouldn't melt in your mouth to hear you talk. What about you and Ross Peters? I'm sure *Hello!* magazine would love to do a cover story about that.'

'At least he's the opposite sex, brother dear! Why don't you emigrate to Greece, or America? You'll probably be right at home on that Kestrel Street in San Francisco. Isn't that where all the poofs hang out?'

'Castro, actually. If you're going to make acerbic remarks about minority groups then at least attempt to back up your ridiculous arguments with some factual information regarding your claims. You know you have really amazed me, Felicity. I never knew you were so sanctimonious. Why are you so afraid of my being gay?'

Felicity had looked at him with that withering look of hers and said, simply, 'Because it is an imperfection. And you know how much I despise imperfection.'

Sebastian finds himself doubting her convenient form of logic. He knows what an obsessive-compulsive kind of person his sister is. He has seen her, in full evening dress, on her hands and knees on the kitchen tiles, trying to move the refrigerator because it was half an inch further over to the left than it should have been. He has seen her actually crying because a dinner party has been 'ruined' by an inappropriate flower arrangement, or by a touch too much salt in the oyster bisque. But Felicity cannot saddle her extreme prejudices on her pernickety idiosyncrasies. She has no reason and no authority to make sweeping statements about homosexuals, or blacks, or any other persecuted minority, just because she would prefer her world to be 'perfect'. Unlike flowers, people cannot be arranged. And, unlike fabric, people cannot be returned to the mill to change their colour. Some things just *are*.

Sebastian is beginning to sound just a touch militant. This is something he has never thought about before, and it startles him with a sharp, indignant sting. For such a long time now he has been ashamed of his sexuality, hiding it beneath his coat like a stolen apple. Clandestine couplings in shameful, secret places, and making sure that none of his little 'friends' ever got closer than a handshake when it was all over. It is a dirty affair. It is a phase he will never outgrow. Now he has no reason to keep his life under wraps, and he finds it to be a liberating experience. He already has Mummy's approbation, and he feels sure that most of his friends will stand behind him once the heat is off.

Strangely enough, he doesn't have any gay friends – none that he knows of, anyway. He doesn't really mix in fashionable circles, and the social scene around

Chelsea and Mayfair really isn't synonymous with sexual liberalism. Sebastian would feel out of place in Soho or Earl's Court, and only twice has he been to gay bars in London, and both times he was so nervous he couldn't even bring himself to buy a drink.

Sebastian's thoughts are interrupted by a polite cough. It is Hubert with his coffee.

'Thank you, Hubert.'

There is a rather precious-looking young man at the table by the French windows. He has been glancing at Sebastian for some time now, and their eye contact has become something of a challenge. Sebastian recognizes him as a regular patron of the club, but he has no idea who he is, which is unusual in such a social microcosm as The Forum. The man is affecting a nonchalance that Sebastian suspects is merely self-consciousness. He is slightly over-polished, like a piece of reproduction furniture. His clothes, though impeccably classic in design, are bordering on satirical rather than sartorial elegance. It is as though he is smiling at his own private joke – a discreet prod in the eye of the establishment.

When Sebastian catches the man's eye again they exchange a kind of non-verbal recognition, almost too subtle to explain. It isn't even a nod or a gesture; it is more like an invisible strand of consciousness which snakes between the tables and chairs and joins them together.

The man has already signed his bill, and he offers Sebastian one last glance before he leaves the restaurant. Sebastian hastily finishes his coffee and indicates to Hubert that he would like to leave. Unfortunately Hubert is not the most dynamic of waiters, and it takes him a full three minutes to circumnavigate the room with his silver platter and pen. Sebastian virtually snatches the pen from his hand and scrawls his name flamboyantly on the ticket, before he races out into the main lobby of the building.

The man is nowhere to be seen. Sebastian checks discreetly in the Gents', but, apart from old Gerald and his tip box, the toilets are empty. Sebastian has heard the popular expression 'I'm gutted' quite often, but he has never really understood what it means until this moment. He stands in the hallway between the library and the lobby, feeling thwarted and despondent.

It is going to be a tedious afternoon.

Chapter Twelve

It is confirmed: Claire is pregnant. She has been hoping that it might be stress or an early menopause that has stopped her from bleeding, but the doctor has proffered his assured prognosis and the baby is due on 22 August. He actually gave Claire the date: the very day that will become her child's birthday for the rest of its life. How can she consider an abortion when her baby already has a birthday coming up?

Actually, Claire has never really liked the idea of abortion. It unsettles her to think about the whole moral issue of embryonic murder, and she has read a lot of magazine articles about it. There aren't many things that make Claire uncomfortable, but abortion is definitely one of them.

Along with the death penalty.

And the smoking beagles.

Now she is faced with a bit of a dilemma, and the first thing she does is sit down for a good cry on the bench by the kiddies' playground. Not a very subtle choice of location, but it just happens to be handy on her way home from the clinic.

'Are you all right, love?' asks a kindly woman with a pushchair and sick on her shoulder.

Claire sobs. She can't form any words, so she just waves her tissue around in the air and claws at her mouth.

'I know how you feel, love. Every day I feel like sitting down here and bawling my eyes out. What with the rent and the boyfriend and the bleeding DSS, I sometimes wonder if it's worth getting out from under the duvet of a morning.'

Claire inhales a shuddering gasp of air and blows her nose.

'I'm sorry,' she says.

'That's all right, love. It's good to get it off your chest. What's up, then? Is it a fella? It usually is, you know. Most of my troubles are rooted round some bastard or other.'

'I've just found out that I'm going to have a baby,' heaves Claire through another mouthful of stifled sobs.

'And the fella who knocked you up has done a runner, is that it?'

Claire nods, for the sake of convenience.

'Honestly, men! They're all the same. Sometimes I think them lesbians have got the right idea, although I'm not sure I'd want some woman ferreting around in my nightie.'

What is this woman talking about?

'I've got to go,' says Claire.

'Well, take care then. It'll all sort itself out, love, these things always do. Just when you think things are as bad as they can get, they usually get worse!' And the woman laughs and lights up a cigarette.

A cold breeze rattles the branches of a sycamore tree and clouds hang low on the horizon. 'Brisk' would be a good word to use. February is a moody month, thinks Claire as she sits on the flip-up seat in the bus shelter waiting for the number twenty-nine to appear. It feels funny having a weekday afternoon off work. It's like playing truant, and any minute now some busybody old woman is going to come up to her and say, 'Aren't you supposed to be in school, young lady?'

Now that Claire knows about the baby, she thinks she can feel it moving around in her stomach. It's floating in a sac of fluid, and she wonders what would happen if she jumped up and down. Would it get dizzy? She's heard about women who jump up and down after sex to stop themselves getting pregnant, and she wonders now if it actually works. Like gin in the bathtub, or bent knitting needles? The advert in the glass panel beside her shows a picture of a woman with a basket of laundry. She is pegging out her clothes in the middle of an Alpine meadow. Claire looks at the smiling woman and wishes that she was her, hanging out her washing in an Alpine meadow and smiling because her clothes are going to smell so fresh. It just doesn't seem fair that anyone should be allowed to ponder the delights of one fabric conditioner above another, when Claire has to think about killing her baby. But there are worse things to think about.

Like being locked in a cell on Death Row.

Like watching your children murdered by terrorists.

Like going blind, or deaf, or losing your legs in a mining accident.

The bus comes round the corner, cheerfully green in the bleak winter light. Claire has her monthly pass and there is room on the long side seat at the front, next to the luggage rack. They don't have conductors these days – just a driver with a ticket machine. Nothing's the same as it used to be. Lots of people don't even have their milk delivered these days. They buy cartons of skimmed and semi-skimmed from Sainsbury's, along with their baguettes and their individual servings of *tiramisù*. Claire wishes it was still the old days. She misses the dough rising on the hearth and the three-quarter bed with the plump satin eiderdown.

When she gets home, the house looks unfamiliar to her in the late-afternoon shadows. She switches on the electric coals to make the living room look more cheerful, and makes herself a cup of tea. Funny how a cup of tea can make things feel normal. It's almost as though she could just stay here with her mug of Tetley's, staring into the fireplace, and nothing bad would happen. The baby would never happen. She might go to bed and wake up in the morning and it will all have been a dream. Claire wonders why she knows definitely that this isn't a dream. How come she never looks around herself and thinks, *Am I dreaming?* People who think that must be fooling themselves, because you could never mistake real life for a dream. It's like people who say, 'Why did it happen to me?' Who do they think it's going to happen to?

The next-door neighbour?

The sister-in-law of the woman in the chip shop?

Claire must have been sitting there for much longer than she imagined because it's almost dark and the phone is ringing. It's Duncan, sounding cheerful.

'I thought it might be nice if we drove up to Leicester in the afternoon, and then we can stop at that pub I told you about on the way back. They do a lovely meat and potato pudding, and there's a carvery at weekends.'

'I'm not sure I'm up to it this weekend, Duncan. I'm feeling a bit under the weather,' says Claire, forcing herself to sound normal.

'Oh dear, I hope you're not coming down with that stomach bug that's been going round. We've got three people off with it in my office.'

Oh, dear Duncan, what would you say if you knew the truth?

'Can we give it a miss this weekend, Duncan? Perhaps we could do something next week, instead.'

'I could come round and cook you one of my famous invalid meals. I'm pretty good with eggs and baked beans,' suggests Duncan, sounding slightly desperate.

'That would be lovely, Duncan, but I really do think that I'd rather be on my own this weekend. I just feel wrung out.'

'You should get some iron tablets,' suggests Duncan.

'I'm sorry, Duncan. I hope you don't mind too much.'

'Oh, don't be silly! I can get some work done at home. I've been meaning to fix the garden fence since last autumn, so now I'll have the time to do it.'

'Thanks, Duncan. I'll call you when I feel better, OK?'

'All right, then. Take care.'

'I will. Bye.'

Now he must think she doesn't like him. Now he must be sitting by the phone, wondering what he did wrong. Oh, this is all such a horrible mess. Claire blames herself so bitterly that it comes up in her throat and stings her tonsils like sick. What was she thinking of when she allowed David Glendale to drag her off to the Dorchester? Why did she give up her virginity so easily, having protected it for such a long time? She knows the answer to that – she was scared. Scared that she might never lose it; that she might dry up into an old spinster and never know what it felt like to have a man's lust up inside her. She reads *Cosmopolitan*. She watches Channel 4. Claire needed proof that passion existed, that it wasn't just something made up like the stories they used to tell in the toilets at school.

Now she knows what it feels like. Now she knows what everybody's going on about.

'Oh, my dear girl, you didn't tell me that this was your first time.'

David Glendale had looked down at the bloody sheets, and she had recoiled in guilt and horror.

'I didn't think it was important,' she had answered, feeling small and wounded in the big, big bed.

'I wouldn't have done it if I had known. How old are you?' he had asked, obviously thinking how pathetic she was to have left it so late in life.

'I'm thirty-four,' she had replied, trying to avoid his eyes.

'Did I hurt you?'

Claire shook her head.

'Oh, you poor thing, I'm most terribly sorry. If I had known I would never . . . Oh, God, you are on the pill, aren't you, Claire?'

Claire had panicked.

'Don't be so silly. Of course I am.'

'Thank goodness for that. The last thing you need is to get pregnant after your very first time.' And he had kissed her forehead as though he was her father.

'The room's paid for. You can stay here for the rest of the night if you'd like, but I've got to get going.'

He was pulling on his trousers.

But he was so handsome that Claire couldn't bear the thought of him leaving. She felt so far below him, she couldn't speak. And when he was gone she sat there, in that big, big bed, and cried because it was Christmas and outside it had started to snow.

Claire's doorbell is so loud it makes her jump. It is not the melodic, welcoming sound that heralds the arrival of the man from Littlewoods pools or the florist with a bouquet of roses; rather it is the harsh, jangling sound that portends a doorstep confrontation with a pair of policemen or the bailiffs.

She considers not answering it. But her living-room blinds are open and her fire is on.

It's Dee from over the road. She has her arms folded against the cold and she's wearing a tie-dye T-shirt that appears to have shrunk in the wash. Her belly button is pierced with a silver ring.

'Oh, I'm sorry to disturb you, Claire, but I was wondering if I could use your phone. I recently switched to Mercury and I've had nothing but trouble with it.' Dee has a smoker's voice, ripe with nicotine and lung-clotting tar.

'Sure. Come on in.' Claire stands to one side and closes the door.

'It's brass-monkey weather again. I can't wait for this winter to be over. Still, it's lovely and warm in here.' Dee knows where the phone is. She has a piece of paper with the number she has to call, and Claire leaves her to it while she turns on a couple of lamps in the living room.

When Dee has finished tearing a strip off the operator at Mercury, she comes into the living room and stands in the doorway.

'They make me sick. One day they tell you one thing, and the next they tell you another. I wish I'd just stuck with BT, but I wanted to get cable and it seemed daft not to do both at the same time. Are you still with BT yourself?'

Claire nods. 'Yes. It was enough trouble getting those blokes to come in and mess around with my video when they brought out Channel 5. I had to take three mornings off work just to wait for them to come.'

'Is everything all right, Claire? You look a bit pasty.'

'Oh, I think I might be coming down with something,' says Claire, picking at imaginary lint on her skirt.

'Have you been crying?' asks Dee, coming further into the room. 'You have, haven't you?'

'Oh, it's nothing, Dee. I'm just feeling a bit down, that's all.'

'Anything you want to talk about?'

'Not really. I've got myself into a bit of a pickle and I don't really know how to get myself out. You know how it is.'

Dee perches on the arm of the sofa. 'Tell me about it! I seem to hop from one personal disaster to another. I think it must be genetic. My parents have lived their entire lives in a kind of melodramatic hell,' she laughs lamely.

'I'm pregnant.'

There is a moment of suspended silence.

'Oh,' is all that Dee seems capable of saying.

'And my new boyfriend doesn't know about it. It isn't his, you see.'

'Blimey, Claire, you're a bit of a dark horse! I always had you down as the quiet type.'

'Well, still waters run deep,' says Claire.

'What are you going to do?'

'I honestly don't know. I'm dead against abortion, but to have this baby would ruin my already ruined life.'

'Why are you against abortion?' asks Dee.

'I can't get my mind around the fact that basically it's murder.'

'I've had two.'

'You've had two abortions?'

'Yep! And I don't regret either of them. It's a decision that affects the rest of your life, and I honestly believe that my life would have been a *complete* disaster if I'd been persuaded to give birth to those babies. The doctors tried, you know, to convince me to have them, but I'm a single woman with a decent career, and there wasn't any support from the fathers concerned.'

'But didn't you feel guilty?' asks Claire.

'Not really. I was a bit emotional, but I put that down to the hormones. You see, Claire, those little unformed babies were totally reliant on me for life, and at two months they were barely more than the size of my thumbnail. They couldn't *survive* without me. I wanted to stop the process before it went too far.'

'I might never have another chance,' says Claire. 'I'm getting to that age when it's either now or never.'

'And you think that's a good enough reason to have a baby? Why is it that women get this fixation in their head that they've got to produce a child – like it's

85

some kind of unwritten law? All this crap about women getting broody, and needing to have a baby in order to balance out their hormones. It's all hype. Life is not all about reproduction, Claire. Life is about making choices and trying really hard to enjoy the short amount of time you've got on this crappy little planet. So you bring another unwanted child into the world and you do your very best as a single mother. Did you really achieve anything? Did you do something clever and original that puts you on some kind of pedestal as a model citizen? Having a baby is like shelling peas, Claire! Anybody can do it, and it takes no intelligence and no outstanding effort. Making a success of your own life, taking control and pushing yourself out there against all the odds, now that's what I call bravery and independence.'

Claire doesn't know how to argue her point. 'But if everyone thought like that, Dee, there would be no more human race. If your mother had thought like that, there would be no *you*.'

'So what!' cries Dee. 'If there was no me then I wouldn't be around to know about it. It's like saying if your parents were never killed in that car accident they would be happier today. How can you know that? They're dead. They no longer exist in this life, and therefore they have no claim to any kind of human emotions. It's those uptight conservative types who hold up photos of their children and say that little Dawn would not be here if her mother had chosen an abortion. *It's a child, not a choice*. Well, I believe that it *is* a choice. Every woman has the choice to do with her own body as she will. Nobody can make her do anything she doesn't want to, and you've got to think about yourself for once, Claire. This is about *you*, not the baby.'

'I know you believe what you say, Dee, but I still believe that it's God's decision to give or take life, not ours. I was stupid, I got pregnant, and now I must follow through with the consequences. It doesn't have to ruin my life. I can still go on working; lots of single mothers do, you know – there's even a crèche at our office. I think I've always known that I wanted a baby, but I was beginning to think it would never happen. Well, now it has, and I think I'm glad. At last something's happening to me, and I'm going to make the best of it.'

Claire feels as though she has suddenly come to a definite decision. She says the words and they become true. She thinks the thoughts and they start to make sense.

'Well, it's your life,' says Dee, unconvinced and sceptical. 'But if you ever need a baby-sitter, I'm just over the road.'

'Thanks, Dee,' says Claire.

And the two women hug awkwardly, because it is something they have never done before.

CHAPTER THIRTEEN

It has been a long shift. Seven till three and then six till ten-thirty. Wayne Briggs is shagged out. The tips were good, though. He got a twenty from Bianca Jagger, another twenty from that politician bloke with the toupee, and seventy-five from the American nympho in the Safari Suite.

A good day, all in all.

But he's knackered.

Wayne stops at the chip shop on the way home. They leave him supper under the hotplate at the hotel, but he just couldn't face leftover veal cutlets tonight. He eats his chips out of the soggy, vinegar-drenched newspaper as he walks to his bedsit. He doesn't live in Soho any more. Sebastian urged him to move away from the whores and the temptation of a quick trick. Now Wayne lives in Knightsbridge, of all fucking places. Who'd have thought it, eh? Wayne Briggs, mentally constipated and least likely to succeed at Loughton Comprehensive, living in Knightsbridge. Within walking distance of Harrods, and rubbing shoulders with the likes of Prince Charles and Kevin from *Coronation Street*.

It's only a bedsit, mind. A basement room with its own private entrance and a bit of a yard at the front, below street level so that it's constantly littered with Knightsbridge rubbish. A better class of rubbish than one might find in less refined neighbourhoods: no crisp bags and Coke cans here, it's mainly sandwich boxes from Prêt à Manger and cappuccino cups. Weeds grow in the cracks of the cement, and in the summer there are daisies and little blue flowers that look like violets. Not that Wayne Briggs gives a flying fuck about violets.

The bedsit is fully furnished. It's L-shaped, and the single bed is tucked away around the corner, under the slant of the staircase above. Wayne has a motorbike poster on the wall over the bed. His duvet cover is printed with red and black chevrons. It comes from a collection called Men Only, and it has matching pillowcases and sheets. Very sexy.

He gets terrible reception on his portable telly because he doesn't have an outside aerial. A mate got him the video player, which conveniently fell off the back of a lorry, as these things frequently do.

Funny, that.

Wayne finishes his chips and chucks the newspaper in the bin under the sink. He turns on Capital Radio, gets a beer out of the miniature fridge and reaches for his writing pad.

Basildon Bond.

Blue.

He surveys his list carefully. This is his Bible, his mantra. For Wayne Briggs is most definitely not stupid, even though he can't spell to save his life.

1 Get more money from Mr Craven.
2 Find out some dirt on Miss Craven.
3 Long-term plan: need better job with more money.
4 Don't take no bargains. Wages better than cash.
5 Get a flat and a car.
6 Need connections in another country. USA? Canada?

And then, just like every night before he goes to bed with a copy of *Auto Trader* and a joint, Wayne Briggs checks his supply drawer to ease his mind. To reaffirm that he is prepared for all eventualities.

The drawer is concealed behind a pile of old newspapers under his bed. It's the bottom half of an old bedside cabinet that he has customized especially for the purpose. He pulls away the newspapers and drags the drawer towards him. These are his treasures, his jewels, each item purloined through his network of nefarious friends and acquaintances.

There are two handguns. Boxes of ammunition. Several lethal-looking knives. Marijuana, coke and a few tabs of acid. And two thousand quid in fifties.

Yes, Wayne Briggs is well prepared for all eventualities. Who needs GCSEs and bleeding A levels? Common sense is all it takes these days to forge a career for yourself.

He's on his way up.

CHAPTER FOURTEEN

Felicity's linen cupboard smells of lavender. Lavender that has been plaited into little bundles in Provence and wrapped in silk ribbon to slip between her two-hundred-and-fifty-thread-count Egyptian-cotton sheets.

Claire Brown doesn't have a linen cupboard. She piles her towels and sheets up in the airing cupboard in the bathroom, along with the toilet rolls and tampons.

But Felicity knows nothing of Claire Brown. And even if she did, she would probably say something demeaning and rather rude about Claire's cheap little house. Felicity has no tolerance of those less fortunate than herself. She abhors supermarkets and multi-storey car parks. She refuses to go anywhere near places like Brent Cross shopping centre, and she always stays at home on bank holidays to avoid the snarled traffic and the ice-cream vendors outside the gates of stately homes.

Felicity reaches for a bath towel. She is standing at the top of the back staircase, the small one originally used by the servants. It has carpet now, and finely polished oak banisters. The children are home for the weekend and she can hear them arguing already downstairs in the conservatory. It's raining again and almost dark, although it's only four-fifteen. She hasn't told a soul about David's bastardly will. She's hoping a plan might pop into her head at any moment, and she'll be saved.

'Mummy, will you tell Josh what tantric sex is? He keeps going on about it since he saw that documentary on BBC2, but he doesn't know what he's blathering about!'

'I'm not sure you should even be discussing such things, Sascha. Don't you have anything better to do than argue about things you've picked up on the TV?' Felicity asks her daughter as she descends the stairs.

'Just tell him that there *is* such a thing,' argues Sascha, hands on hips, head thrown back.

'Sascha says that you can have an orgasm without ejaculating,' says Josh, rocking himself furiously in the wicker chair. 'But how can that be possible?'

'Josh!' exclaims Felicity angrily. 'I don't want to hear you saying such things around the house. It's unseemly.'

'But Sting does it!' snaps back Sascha, quick as lightning.

'I don't care what Sting does in his private time. Let's just drop the subject, shall we?'

'I told you . . .' says Sascha to her younger brother.

'You didn't tell me anything, bum-breath!' says Josh.

'Stop it, you two. It's only Friday evening and

already you're getting on my nerves. Sascha, go and tell Mrs Linden that Ross will be joining us for dinner this evening.'

'Why is *he* coming?' asks Josh. 'I thought this was supposed to be a family weekend?'

'Well, he almost *is* family, isn't he, darling? Anyway, I thought you liked him. You certainly weren't complaining when he took you to the London Dungeon.'

'That was only because you made him,' sulks Josh, picking at a scab on his left knee. 'Well, he needn't think he's going to take Daddy's place.'

'Oh, Josh, shut up!' says Sascha. 'You know I don't want to talk about Daddy.' And she rushes off, swatting sudden tears from her eyes.

Felicity, in her emotionless state of bitterness, has forgotten that her children's father died less than two weeks ago. She smiles at Josh and ruffles his hair.

'Mummy!' he complains, patting it back down again.

'Ross isn't trying to take Daddy's place. He's just a very good friend, and anyway he's married to Auntie Cybil. I just felt it would be nice to have a little company this evening.'

'Is he staying the night?'

'I suppose so.'

'And where is he sleeping?'

Felicity feels a faint blush of irritation creeping above the collar of her blouse, but she remains composed when she replies: 'The green room, I expect.'

Josh appears to be satisfied with the answer and reaches for his Game Boy.

Mother has been dismissed.

They eat dinner in the kitchen. It's cosier than the formal dining room, and the children prefer it. But this is no ordinary kitchen, oh, no. This kitchen is L-shaped and it has what Felicity calls a breakfast nook where she has created a kind of circular alcove with fitted benches strewn with cushions. Windows look out across the herb gardens, but tonight the glass is black and streaked with rain. Reflections like circus mirrors loom tall and distorted.

'Oh, do close your mouth when you are eating, Josh,' admonishes Sascha across the stripped-pine table.

'Oh, do close your bum when you fart!' replies Josh through a mouthful of chocolate crème brûlée.

Ross glances at Felicity with a smirk on his face. Felicity raises her eyes to the ceiling, tired of constantly reprimanding her son, and pours coffee.

'I want Coke,' says Josh.

'Well, you know where it is, darling.'

Headlights arch into the private driveway at the back of the house, shattering the windows into millions of tiny crystal beads.

'Who can that be at this time of the evening?'

Ross squints out through the window. 'It looks like a Jag.'

'Uncle Seb!' squeals Sascha, jumping up from her

95

chair and racing upstairs. Josh, with his Coke, follows her.

'Oh, God, what's *he* doing here?' sighs Felicity.

'Perhaps he's come to apologize,' suggests Ross.

'What for? For being queer and making the family a laughing stock? I very much doubt it.'

There are voices in the hallway. Josh reappears first, followed by Sascha and then Sebastian. He is wearing an enormous trench coat which he removes and drapes over the banister.

'Hello, hello!' he says. 'This looks cosy. I see it hasn't taken you long to get your feet under the table, Ross. Where's Cybil? Saving Great Ormond Street again, is she?'

'Hello, Sebastian,' says Ross warily.

'You should have rung,' says Felicity. 'We weren't expecting you.'

'No, I can imagine. Is there any of that coffee going spare?' Sebastian takes a seat at the table and smiles at his sister with saccharine sweetness.

'Help yourself,' she answers indifferently.

'Uncle Seb, are you going to stay the night?' asks Josh, pushing his way on to the bench beside his uncle.

'I don't think so, Josh. Your mother hasn't had time to get a room ready for me.'

'You could sleep in my room. I can use a sleeping bag on the floor.'

'Thanks, Josh, but I really do have to be back in London tonight.'

'So this is just a flying visit, is it?' asks Felicity.

'Listen, kids, why don't you two go on upstairs and watch the telly or something. I want to talk over some business with your mother.'

'Aww,' moans Josh.

'I'm not a kid any more, Uncle Seb. I'm thirteen, you know,' says Sascha.

'I'm sorry, Sash. I keep forgetting. Well, in that case, you won't mind retiring to the drawing room with a glass of sherry, will you?'

'Oh, Uncle Seb, you are so uncool! People don't drink sherry any more, silly!'

'Well, how about champagne then? Don't all young debutantes like champers?'

'Come on, Josh. Obviously our uncle thinks this is 1920.' And they trail off upstairs, leaving the three adults at the kitchen table.

'You've got a nerve turning up like this,' hisses Felicity as soon as the children are out of earshot.

'Can't I even visit my niece and nephew now? I know you don't approve of my lifestyle, sister dear, but I really don't think there's any need to quarantine your children. The last I heard, homosexuality wasn't contagious.' Sebastian speaks with controlled sarcasm.

'You didn't come here to see the children,' says Felicity, resisting the temptation to slap her brother across his cheek. 'You came here to gloat and mock. You've always been one for melodrama, and now you think you've found the perfect excuse to show off! It's just like that blasted flower parade all over again.'

Ross looks at Felicity for an explanation. 'Flower parade?'

'Oh, here we go!' goads Sebastian, turning sideways in his seat to cross his legs. 'It's story time, children!'

'Well, it wasn't so much a flower parade as an outrageous farce that made us the bloody laughing stock of the neighbourhood. Even at thirteen he was willing to do anything to get into the spotlight.'

'Come on then, Felicity, you might as well spit it out for poor old Ross here. He thinks you're delirious!'

'I should have known even then that there was something a bit queer about you. You never played football or cricket or joined in with the fishing trips. You were always too busy dressing up that stupid bear of yours and helping Mummy in the garden. You and Samantha Donoghue and that boy from the greengrocer's. I cannot imagine where the idea for a flower parade came from, but undoubtedly it was one of yours. I can remember that Saturday afternoon as clearly as if it happened yesterday – the day of the church fête, with all those local reporters and the crowning of the Harvest Queen . . .'

'I always fancied myself as the Harvest Queen!' quips Sebastian, grinning.

'I don't think it's very funny, actually. You seem to be taking this latest scandal just as flippantly as you did that ridiculous parade of yours. I thought you would never be capable of embarrassing me as much as you did back then, but I'm beginning to see that you're impervious to personal humiliation. I can see the three of you now, trailing through the vicar's garden on your bikes, all decked out with crêpe paper and ribbons, margarine tubs strapped to your heads with pipe-cleaners and daisies sprouting out of the top. You looked like gypsies! I can remember everybody laughing because you were wearing Mummy's satin hot pants and my velvet cape. And then to see it on the front page of the *Ham & High* the following week – I could have died.'

'We were kids, for Christ's sake! It was a bit of inventive fun that should have been applauded, not ridiculed. There aren't many thirteen-year-olds who could have thought up such an imaginative game. So, it was a bit poofy and I embarrassed you in front of your spotty boyfriend, but I hardly think the episode warrants such derision. I would have thought being rushed to casualty with Derek Johnson's dick locked up your fanny was a far more interesting anecdote. How old were you – eighteen? Tut-tut, Felicity, how selective your memory can be.' Sebastian offers his sister a sympathetic frown.

'Oh, he's just being vindictive now,' says Felicity to Ross. 'He can't win the argument, so he's resorting to mud-slinging in an attempt to camouflage his own ludicrous behaviour. This really is terribly puerile.'

'Felicity, you have spent your entire life dragging me down. You always acted as though you were some kind of superior being, even when you were with Mummy and Father, and you were the most precocious little girl I've ever known. That damned four-poster bed of yours and the ballet lessons with Madam Whatshername. You were the only girl at the gymkhana in full *National Velvet* regalia, and the only person who recited Keats when you went up to collect your rosette. Do you know that I used to lie in my bed at night and think that I wouldn't even cry if you died?'

'Oh, charming! What a horrible thing to say. How is it that you're the one who gets his name plastered all across the papers for getting caught with a rent boy, and yet here you are lambasting me as though *I've* done something wrong? I don't need any of this right now, Sebastian. It may have slipped your mind, but my husband died just two weeks ago and I've got much more important issues at hand. You've dug your own sordid grave, so I suggest that you leave me alone and go and lie in it. I think this evening has proved that you care nothing for me, and so it's probably just as well if we steer clear of one another in future.'

'That suits me just fine. But don't think that this is over, Felicity. It may have slipped *your* narrow little mind, but I'm the one who owns the deeds to Craven's. I would watch your back if I were you – one never knows who's going to be wielding the knife.'

And with that, Sebastian grabs his trench coat and

leaves Felicity and Ross alone at the kitchen table, with the rain beating against the windows.

'Arrogant bastard!' snarls Felicity, screwing up her napkin as if it were her brother's neck.

'Did you really get lover's lock when you were eighteen?' asks Ross.

'If you can't think of anything intelligent to say, why don't you just keep your mouth shut!' snaps Felicity, as she presses her forehead into the palm of her elegant hand.

CHAPTER FIFTEEN

Sebastian feels far from triumphant. In the headlights of his car the rain appears to be glass rods, pelting his roof like pebbles, obscuring his vision and steaming up the windows in the pitch-dark of the night.

It isn't very nice to threaten one's sister.

Even if she is a self-righteous, bigoted bitch.

The woods around Blythwood House close in around the car as Sebastian follows the curving driveway. Occasionally he illuminates the eerie, petrified shadow of a stone statue among the yew trees, and he imagines that he is being watched; scrutinized by secret eyes in the rain.

Felicity has always been a difficult sister to love. When somebody is described as 'driven', they are usually perceived as emotionally paralysed, dispassionate, cold-blooded. Felicity has been accused of all these things during her lifetime, and yet Sebastian continues to hope that somewhere beneath the haute couture veneer there are hidden qualities that have never been given the chance to be seen. The only time Sebastian ever saw his sister cry was at their father's funeral. And even then she didn't cry for the loss of a father; she cried because the funeral had disrupted her plans to visit the Milan fashion shows, a personal invitation to Gianni Versace's home and three days being entertained by the editor of Paris *Vogue*.

When Sebastian inherited Craven's, Felicity had become incensed with fury. She had always believed that the hotel was her creation and was therefore automatically hers when their father died. The reading of the will had been a difficult time. Lots of shouting and curses and blame were unfairly fired around the room like a round of ammunition. If words were bullets, Sebastian would have been killed that day. Slain by his own sister, his only sibling.

Sibling Rivalry – it could be the title of a psychology textbook.

Unlike his sister, Sebastian is not a driven person. He prefers to sit in the back seat of his life, giving orders through the glass partition, drinking champagne and watching the world pass by through tinted windows. He has never wanted the driver's seat. It's too much like hard work: all that navigating, indicating and watching in the rear-view mirror to try to anticipate what might be coming. In the back of the car there's room to spread oneself out. Room to luxuriate in the knowledge that fate is wearing the driver's cap, and all Sebastian has to do is sit back and enjoy the ride.

Sebastian has no intention of disrupting his sister's involvement in Craven's. He makes a tidy profit from her endeavours with the hotel without so much as lifting a finger. Once a year he sits in on the board meeting and the financial summary, but he's what you might call a silent partner. Felicity often jokes that he is more like a silent sponge, soaking up her hard-earned money while she lives on a salary – albeit a very generous one. Unfortunately her miserly husband, billionaire David Glendale, refused to offer her the money to buy Sebastian out, or for her to open a new hotel of her own. David knew how to keep a tight rein on his wife. He didn't love her but she was a damned good investment and she was worth a fortune in public relations. Felicity Craven is something of an icon in certain circles. French and Saunders make jokes about her. Interior designers sometimes refer to a certain shade of darkest charcoal as 'Craven black', and in 1995 she was honoured with the title Britain's Best Dressed Woman – pushing Princess Diana into a close second.

Sebastian is surprised by Felicity's refusal to accept his sexuality. For one who mixes constantly with the glitterati of European society, it seems strange that she is so vociferously against minority groups. In fashionable circles it would seem apparent that at least fifty per cent of the so-called 'confirmed bachelors' in her profession are as bent as a nine-bob note. Of course she patronizes the charity balls for AIDS awareness, smiling in the glare of the flashbulbs as she hands over a generous cheque to somebody from the Terrence Higgins Trust. And she applauds the daring new collections by Jean Paul Gaultier as she sits between Elton John and RuPaul on the edge of a Paris catwalk.

Sebastian suspects that it isn't so much his sexual proclivities that disturb Felicity; it's the fact that he was scandalized across the front page of several newspapers so soon after the rumours of her husband's long-term infidelity. It would be very un-hip to admit that one is homophobic in this day and age, but Sebastian knows that Felicity would prefer him to be a sterilized, sanitized version of his creed, rather than a filthy pervert crawling through the underworld of rent boys and illicit sex.

She wants the French-cuffed Jermyn Street dignity of Sir Ian McKellen, not the sequinned Soho affectations of Julian Clary.

He passes between the imposing stone pillars of the Blythwood estate and turns into the narrow road that leads towards the village. The windscreen wipers arch and return with depressing regularity, and Sebastian has to lean forward in order to see more clearly through the glass. He doesn't see the figure standing in the road until he almost rams into it. He stamps hard on the brakes and the car skids slightly in the wet. The anti-lock feature jerks into action and he comes to an abrupt stop just a few feet away from the woman, who is caught in the glare of his headlights. She has an umbrella, and a coat down to her ankles.

Sebastian winds down his window and rain spits in his face.

'Are you all right?' he shouts into the wind. He feels his voice being lifted and carried away, frail and ineffectual.

The woman approaches the car. She has long red hair, thick and very curly.

'Thank you for stopping, darling!' she says, peering from beneath her oversized golfing umbrella. 'My car broke down and the chances of another coming along here at this time of night are practically zero. Now, I know that as a single woman I am supposed to assume that you're a rapist or a mass murderer, but it's nine-thirty on a Friday night, it's coming down in buckets and I've been standing here for forty minutes waiting for a Good Samaritan. Do you think you could give me a lift into the village? I live about five miles away.'

'You'd better get in,' says Sebastian, flipping the switch on the central locking.

The red-haired lady gets into the car, flapping her umbrella and arranging her skirts as she slams the door and sighs heavily.

'I must have scared you to death standing there like an apparition of doom in the middle of the road.'

'I nearly knocked you down. I couldn't see very well through the rain.'

'You *are* an angel. I've only had the car a week, and it just conked out on me with absolutely no warning.'

Sebastian notices her earrings. They are pendulous clusters of buttons and gold coins, and they tug on her ear lobes.

'I made them myself,' she announces, noticing Sebastian's inquisitive stare. She cups one of the earrings in the palm of her hand. 'Brill, aren't they? The buttons are all antique and the coins are Turkish. I sell them at Camden Lock at the weekends.'

'They're very unusual,' admits Sebastian.

'Unusual meaning weird, right?'

'Well . . .'

'It's OK, darling. I've heard worse things said about my jewellery. *Unusual* and *different* are probably the adjectives most often used. I sold a pair to Cher, you know. She has a mail-order catalogue in the States, and I might be supplying her on a regular basis.'

'Do you live in the village?'

'Just on the other side, actually. In one of the old tithe cottages on Broadbent Lane.'

'Are you one of the fortunate tenants paying a peppercorn rent?'

'That's me, darling – two pounds a week for the rest of my life. Three bedrooms and an outside toilet that still works!'

'I've always admired those cottages. They used to belong to the Blythwood estate, you know, many years ago.'

'That was when there was still an earl living up there at the big house. Apparently he was a bit of a tartar. He had three wives and divorced them all. From the photos I've seen, he was a bit of a dish in his younger days.'

Sebastian puts the car in motion and they cruise along the country road, viewing each other by the putrid green light of the dashboard.

'My sister lives at Blythwood House now.'

'Your sister is Felicity Craven?' asks the woman with undisguised admiration.

Sebastian nods.

'Then you must be Sebastian Craven. How marvellous! I'm getting a lift from one of Britain's most eligible bachelors. You're almost royalty around here, you know.'

'And just like royalty, we have absolutely no right to privacy. The fact that you know instantly who I am would suggest that you have a pretty clear picture of my curriculum vitae, as spelled out by the popular press, would it not?'

'I read the papers, if that's what you mean.'

'And what do the papers tell you?'

'That you've recently had a spot of bad luck. I have a lot of gay friends and I know what goes on. It was just an unfortunate slip-up that any ordinary person would have got away with. Sadly, you are not just an ordinary person, and so there were consequences. The press love to hold up celebrities and prove to us how fallible they can be. I think it's probably jealousy, darling. They just want to *be* you.'

'It isn't much fun. I've recently been wishing I could have been somebody else. Just an ordinary person living an ordinary life . . . you know,' sighs Sebastian.

'Don't kid yourself, darling. I've reinvented myself several times over the years, and it doesn't change the person you are inside. Do you honestly think you could cope with being an ordinary person – as you put it – with mortgage payments, electricity bills and the National Health Service making you wait nine months to have a verruca removed? I can tell you, it's no sodding picnic being on the breadline. Some people were born to take the golden motorway of life, and some of us were left behind on the loose chippings.'

Sebastian likes this woman's voice. He wonders if she is a smoker, for she has a smoker's rasp. She is obviously intelligent and he finds himself charmed by her candour. Her perfume is musky and it drapes itself across the back of her seat like a piece of heavy cloth. It's a good smell.

'You need to turn left here,' she says as they pass through the deserted village.

'How long have you lived here?' asks Sebastian.

'Oh, thirteen years, give or take. I moved here with a friend – she was in a band and she wanted to move out of London. We were lucky to get the cottage. Her father knew a friend of a friend – you know the kind of thing, minor corruption in the housing association.'

'Is your friend still in a band?'

'She emigrated to Oz in eighty-nine. But you can still buy their records – *Threnody*. Have you heard of them?'

'I'm not much of a rock person, I'm afraid.'

'It's the second one, here,' and she indicates the second in a line of six picturesque cottages, blurred and watery through the rain. 'Would you like to come in? I've got some fantastic coffee from Hawaii – real, undiluted Kona.'

'That's very kind, but I really do need to get back to London.'

'Oh, come on, just for a few minutes. My friends will be green with envy if I tell them I had Sebastian Craven round for coffee. It'll do marvels for my street cred.'

Sebastian looks at his watch. 'Well, just for ten minutes then. I really do have to get back.'

'Ace!' laughs the woman, shaking her hair and smiling broadly. She extends her hand. 'Poppy Bentos. As in Fray Bentos – no lumps of fat or gristle guaranteed!'

'Pleased to meet you, Poppy.'

She has a surprisingly strong handshake. It rattles with silver bracelets.

'Come on, then. We'll have to run if we want to avoid this downpour.'

And they leap out of the car and race up the pathway to crouch under the crooked porch, which is tangled with winter branches. In summer these branches must bloom with roses. There is a sign above the door, a ceramic plaque:

THE MOON IN CANCER

'That's an unusual name for a house,' says Sebastian.

'It was the position of the constellations on the day we moved in. My friend was a bit of an astrologer.'

Poppy opens the heavy oak door and flicks a switch. They step inside the cottage and it embraces them with warmth and light. There is a scent of apples and floor polish, of damp and old books.

'Be it ever so humble . . .' says Poppy, unbuttoning her voluminous coat to reveal a rich expanse of purple crushed velvet and bottle-green silk. Her hair tumbles in all directions. Sebastian suspects that it must be coloured, for he has never seen hair so luminously auburn. In full light he can see that she is not pretty. Her nose is too big, her jaw too angular and her skin is slightly pock-marked beneath her heavy foundation. She is what one might describe as impressive, but never beautiful.

'Come through into the kitchen while I make the coffee.'

The kitchen is tiny, with just enough room for two people.

'Not exactly Smallbone, darling, but I like to think of it as bohemian squalor,' says Poppy as she surveys the sagging cabinets and the curling linoleum. 'I haven't done a thing to it since we moved in, and it would cost a bundle to rip it all out.'

'Who did this?' asks Sebastian, pointing to a miniature mural painted between the work surfaces and the wall cupboards.

'It was a joint effort. My friend started it and I finished it after she left. All these people are friends and acquaintances – we used to add another figure every time we met someone new. This is me, and this is Tricia.' She points out a couple of six-inch-high figures leaning against a tree.

'What a super idea.'

'Now you sound like Prince Charles surveying a lightbulb factory in Belgrade.'

'I'm sorry. I didn't mean to . . .'

'Oh, *I'm* sorry. I can come across a bit blunt at times. I'll make the coffee and we'll have a civilized chat. Listen to that rain.'

They both listen. The cottage is besieged on all sides.

'Go and sit down in the living room through there, and I'll bring the coffee when it's ready. Do you like custard creams? I have a passion for them, I'm afraid. I wake up in the middle of the night with an absolute craving, so now I keep a tin right by the bed. If I didn't know better I'd think I was pregnant.'

Sebastian decides not to investigate that statement, and goes through into the living room.

There are the remains of an open fire; cinders glowing softly in the grate. A clock ticks loudly from the mantel, cushions gather on the sagging sofa, armchairs draped with antique shawls recline comfortably in the corners like old ladies settled down for the night. It is a small room with a very low, uneven ceiling. The walls are thick and the windows are deeply recessed. Sebastian can feel a draught from around the bulging panes. He takes a seat in one of the armchairs and finds himself sinking much lower than expected, so that he is almost sitting on the floor amid a mound of cushions.

Poppy appears at the door. 'Oh, I'm sorry! That

chair needs new springs. I quite like it that way, but it's not very practical for the old and infirm. I left my grandmother here one afternoon while I went shopping and she was stuck there for three hours, unable to get up. When I got home all I could see of her was her little feet and one little arm waving frantically from under the cushions.'

'I like this room,' says Sebastian. 'It reflects your personality, I think.'

'Old and tatty, you mean?'

'No, more comfortable and relaxing.'

'I suppose you live in one of those Docklands penthouses, or a converted warehouse?'

'Actually it's much more boring than that – I have a flat in Kensington. Not very exciting, I'm afraid.'

'And I had you down as one of those playboy types. Your sister certainly lives the high life, if the tabloids are anything to go by. She's incredibly glamorous.'

'Yes, she is. She's always been glamorous; she seems to have been born with it.'

'I've stayed at her hotel, you know. I remember the bathroom most of all – that huge, deep marble bath with all those gorgeous smelly things for me to put into it. I had the room that was tarted up to look like Versailles. Everything was upholstered, including the walls. It was amazing.'

'She certainly has a talent,' says Sebastian, remembering that he's with a perfect stranger.

'The coffee's ready. Can you smell it? There's nothing more perfect than the smell of dark, black coffee and the rustle of newspapers on a Sunday morning. The next best thing is meeting someone new, or the sound of rain on a Friday night.'

'You have a knack for conjuring up very evocative images. I've never thought about the actual *smell* of coffee before.'

'I have a joy for life. There is usually beauty in everything if you look hard enough. Well, I say *everything*, but I have yet to find something nice to say about wasps. Bees I can appreciate, but wasps are just a damned nuisance and they sting you indiscriminately. Oh, and I'm not very fond of microwave chips or so-called superglue!' Poppy disappears into the kitchen, leaving Sebastian to smile at her words of wisdom. When she returns she has a tray with the coffee things and a plate of custard creams.

Sebastian stays for much longer than the ten minutes he had originally allocated himself; in fact it is almost midnight when he finally makes a move to leave.

'Do you *have* to go, darling?' asks Poppy. 'I could talk all night, you know, and there's plenty more coffee.'

'If I drink any more of that stuff it'll be Christmas before I get any sleep,' jokes Sebastian, easing himself awkwardly out of the crippled armchair.

'This has been fantastic,' says Poppy, tossing her splendid hair out of her face.

'I have to admit that you've cheered me up considerably. I was feeling rather fed up before I met you.'

'Does this mean we might be friends?'

'Only if you promise me that you're not a tabloid reporter, or some kind of undercover journalist looking for an unauthorized biography.'

'Cross my heart and hope to die.' She opens the door to let Sebastian out. The mantel clock strikes twelve. 'White rabbits,' she says.

'What?'

'It's the first day of March.'

'Looks like it's planning to come in like a lion.'

'That means we've got plenty to look forward to. I think spring is already waiting to burst forth. I saw some primroses this morning, and there are catkins at the end of my garden.'

'Goodnight, Poppy. Thanks for the coffee.'

'Goodnight. Thanks for rescuing me.'

And Sebastian runs to his car, fumbling with his keys in the darkness. When he looks back at the cottage, Poppy is gone. But there on the passenger seat is an antique button. An incongruous symbol of something newly undone.

'White rabbits,' he says.

And he starts up the car and roars off into the night.

CHAPTER SIXTEEN

On Sunday 9 March, Claire Brown sees Duncan's legs for the first time.

And she is suitably impressed!

As the players jostle into the scrum, Duncan's bum is pointing straight at her and his meaty thighs strain against the synthetic fabric of his rugby shorts.

Hamstrings taut.

Buttocks braced.

Then he disappears into a wild tangle of arms and legs as the players vie for the ball. The playing field is churned up and muddy, and Claire finds herself involuntarily shuddering at the thought of so much cold, wet dirt splattering her body. She's glad that she isn't a man, having to do manly things. One of the nice things about being a woman is that there is no obligation to prove the worth of her sex. She doesn't have to roll around on a muddy playing field, or mess around with oily car parts in an unheated garage. There's no necessity to brag about the size of her genitals or to use foul language when addressing a colleague through a partition wall in the Ladies'. Men are constantly being challenged by their peers to be more masculine, more aggressive, more powerful, while women are at liberty just to be themselves.

She knows that she is old-fashioned in her views. Claire was brought up by very traditional parents, who followed the age-old rituals of married life. Father was the breadwinner, getting up at five-thirty every morning with the rattle of the milk float, and coming home at five-thirty with engine grease under his nails. Mother had the dinner on the table by five-thirty-five every evening. She washed the dishes at five-fifty. Father never offered to help. The kitchen sink was no place for a man.

Claire likes a man who knows his place. She enjoys being the weaker sex, oh, yes! – she can hear the feminists screaming at her with outraged indignation, but why shouldn't she be allowed to choose her own role in life? She wants to feel protected and loved, she wants to be soft and pliant in the strong grip of her chosen partner. Let *him* clean out the drainpipes and mow the lawn: Claire wants to be in the kitchen baking pies and ironing his shirts. And at weekends they might go for a drive in the country, with him behind the wheel and her pointing out pretty things along the way.

The referee blows his whistle. The afternoon sky is a solid slab of startling blue, not a cloud in sight. But it's chilly and Claire is wearing her scarf and gloves. When the wind blows she thinks about the revolving clothes dryer her mother had in the back garden, filled with freshly washed sheets on a Monday, flapping and sailing in the wind.

Kite weather, her father used to call it.

Duncan is loping over towards her, forced to squint without his glasses. He has mud caked to his legs and tiny splatters across his face. Through his shirt Claire can see the swell of his chest. He is a big man, and Claire shrinks at the knowledge of what she must tell him today.

'Did you see that?' asks Duncan, wiping his nose with the back of his hand. 'He purposely pushed me into the fence to get at the ball.'

'It's such a rough game. I'm terrified you're going to get hurt.'

'Is there any tea left in that thermos?'

Claire checks to see. 'There's about half a cup.' She empties the flask out into its plastic lid.

'If you're cold, you can go and sit up in the club-house and watch through the window,' suggests Duncan kindly.

'I'm fine. I like watching you. It really is a beautiful day.'

'The first real day of spring, I think,' and he looks up at the sky.

The referee blows his whistle.

'You go inside if you get cold,' Duncan says as he returns to the battlefield, tucking his shirt in where it has worked loose from the elasticated waist of his shorts.

Claire is afraid to tell him about the baby. He's

going to drop her like a hot potato and she'll be alone again, with her decision growing daily inside her stomach. Dee has been to see her every day since she found out. She pretends to come over for other things, but Claire knows that Dee is checking up on her to make sure she's OK. They went out for a pizza on Thursday and laughed so much that Claire was afraid she might have the baby there and then, under the table at Pizza Hut.

'It wouldn't be much of a baby at this stage,' laughed Dee.

'I wouldn't need a pram, I could keep it in my pocket,' said Claire.

'Oh, don't!' said Dee. 'We shouldn't be joking about such things.'

But they had laughed anyway.

Claire called the Psychic Hotline to see if she could get any spiritual advice on how to tell Duncan. She got the number from Sharon at work, who swore that her psychic had forewarned her about her boyfriend's infidelity and a possible trip to an exotic island. Three weeks later Sharon's boyfriend left her for someone else, and Sharon won a weekend on the Isle of Wight through a McDonald's scratch-and-win competition.

Claire's personal psychic was called Karma, and she had a West Country accent. She sensed that Claire was troubled and that she was about to 'embark on an arduous journey'.

'I'm not going anywhere,' Claire had answered.

Karma had quickly assured her that she was talking

about a 'metaphysical journey' – a rite of passage. 'I'm seeing a man in your life, my dear; somebody very important, somebody in a suit. Does the letter S mean anything to you, dear?'

'No.'

'How about the letter D?'

'Yes! Duncan, that's my boyfriend.'

'There you are, my bird, that's the crux of the matter. Duncan is your problem. Am I right?'

'I suppose so. I need to talk to him but I'm not sure how he's going to react.'

'Honesty is always the best policy, my dear. Lies and deceit only lead to heartache and destruction. Karma knows these things, Karma has been through it herself many times. Is it another man, my dear?'

'Not really.'

'Well, I do see good things for you. This is a good time for you to open your soul, but you must act quickly or you'll lose the moment.'

Claire was ready to put the phone down when something Karma said made her clutch harder on the receiver.

'Have you been to see a doctor recently, my dear? I see a man in a white coat and he's giving you some very troubling news. It looks serious – you're not ill, are you, dear?'

'I'm pregnant,' says Claire.

'And is it Duncan's baby?'

'No.'

'Ah, I see. Now it all falls into place. Usually a baby

is a happy occasion; I couldn't quite work out why the doctor looked so serious. You must tell Duncan and accept the outcome, be it good or bad. You must enjoy your life, dear: take every day as if it is a gift.'

And at £1.25 a minute, Claire has taken Karma's advice to heart. She is breathing in, she is listening to her heart. There's a tiny life inside her and she is suddenly bursting with happiness. With Duncan she stands a fifty-fifty chance. If she loses him she must concentrate her attention on the baby. If he sticks around, she has made a promise to go to church next Sunday and light twenty candles – the big ones, at fifty pence each.

When Duncan has showered and dressed, he joins Claire in the clubhouse cafeteria. She's drinking cocoa from a thick-rimmed mug. He looks scrubbed and red, and his hair is wet. Claire can smell the cheap soap and shampoo, and it makes her look at him with such a fierce maternal instinct that she wants to tell him she loves him. What a foolish, silly thing to do! Claire quickly admonishes herself for being ridiculous, and she finishes off her cocoa with a slurp.

'Are you ready?' he asks, rattling his car keys.

'As ready as I'll ever be,' she says, gathering up her tote bag.

They drive to a Beefeater Inn for an early dinner. Steak and chips for Duncan, scampi in a basket for Claire. She refuses a glass of wine on the grounds that it gives her a headache if she drinks too early in the day. She feels conspicuous as she stumbles over her hastily invented excuse, but Duncan seems to be unaware of her falsehood.

When the food arrives, Claire can barely raise her fork to her mouth, and she is certain she will not be able to eat one bite of food without first telling Duncan about the baby. She places her fork into the basket of scampi and plays with her napkin for a while. Duncan is slicing into his sirloin with determination.

'Duncan, there's something I have to tell you. I've been worried sick about it all day and now I've just got to blurt it all out, otherwise I won't be able to enjoy my dinner.' Claire feels as though she needs to dash to the Ladies', but she clenches her thighs and stares at the garish photograph of the apple crumble on the front of the dessert menu propped between the salt and pepper pots.

'Blimey, this sounds serious!' smiles Duncan, chewing on his steak, but drops his cutlery to give Claire his full attention. 'You'd better get it off your chest.'

'I know I've only known you for a few weeks, and I really haven't got a clue where we're going with this relationship, but I like to think that it's going well . . .'

'Of course it's going well. Haven't I told you enough how wonderful it is spending time with you?' Duncan looks concerned, and he reaches across the table to squeeze Claire's hand.

'Well, it might not go too well after I've told you what I've got to say.'

'Oh, God, this is beginning to sound like one of those stomach-clenching moments. Don't tell me there's somebody else, Claire. I honestly couldn't bear it if I thought you'd been lying to me.'

'No, Duncan, there isn't anyone else. But before I met you I had a brief fling with somebody from the office – he was married.'

'*Was* married. Is he not still married?' asks Duncan.

'He was killed last month in an accident.'

Duncan does not disguise the relief on his face when he hears this news. 'I'm sorry. If he still means something to you I can understand that. After all, it took me years to get over Chrissy's death.'

'He meant nothing to me. It was a one-night stand at a time when I really needed some attention. I was nothing to him, just a stupid secretary with loose morals.' Claire feels tears pricking the backs of her eyes.

'Don't say that, Claire. Don't ever say such things about yourself. You're a wonderful person.' Duncan is leaning towards her with concern and kindness. It is this kindness that causes a tear to wriggle its way down Claire's cheek.

'Oh, Duncan, I like you so much, but you have to know that because of that one stupid night, and because of my own lack of responsibility, I got pregnant.'

Duncan nods, but he doesn't appear to react to Claire's announcement.

'I'm almost three months pregnant with his child

and I've decided to keep it.' Claire dabs at her eyes with the napkin, checking the white cotton for mascara.

'You poor thing,' says Duncan, capturing her hand again across the table.

'Mind the mustard!' says Claire, as his cuff dips into the Coleman's.

'You've been keeping all this to yourself for all these weeks? Why didn't you tell me sooner?'

'It's hardly the thing to use as an opener on a blind date, is it? Hello, my name's Claire, and I'm pregnant with a stranger's baby.'

'Of course, this changes things,' says Duncan.

'Well, of course it does,' Claire replies.

'But it really doesn't affect the way I feel about you, Claire. The baby is just another aspect of you that I didn't know existed. Like your sense of humour and your gentleness.'

'You mean you're not going to dump me?' asks Claire cautiously.

'Oh, you silly little monkey, what kind of monster do you think I am? It took me three years to pluck up the courage to write that ad in the classifieds. I'm not going to put myself back at square one for something so silly. You have to believe me, Claire, this doesn't change a thing. And I'm not going to dump you, as you so elegantly put it!'

Claire feels heat surging up from her chest into her face. It burns in her cheeks and whistles in her ears. She has just won the lottery.

'Oh, Duncan,' she says.

And then she bursts into tears, wetting her scampi and bringing their waitress to the table to see if tartare sauce might assuage her misery.

CHAPTER SEVENTEEN

'On 20 April we celebrate ten years of Craven's. Ten celebrity-studded years of superlative service, with an international reputation second to none.' Felicity waves a dismissive hand at the proposals that are scattered across her desk. 'This looks like a bargain weekend at Trust House Forte. We don't pay you forty thousand a year to come up with crap like this. I may as well have done it myself.'

Felicity is seething. She has eaten one too many oysters at lunch and now she's feeling slightly queasy. She isn't one to belch, but she keeps tasting the fishy aftermath of her midday indulgence and she has to cover her mouth discreetly. It's three o'clock and she's tired.

Tired of pointless negotiations with David's lawyers.

Tired of worrying about Sebastian's threat to take over the hotel.

Tired of reading about her personal downfall in the tabloid press.

Even Ross has cancelled their dinner date, and failed to remember their sixth anniversary. No flowers, no call, just a feeble apology when she finally tracked him down at Bibendum, with the rattle of expensive food being served in the background.

TEXAN MISTRESS INHERITS GLENDALE BILLIONS.

Felicity is bowed under the weight of humiliation. Things haven't been this bad since the end of her acting career. Now they show *Ground Zero* on an obscure little cable channel, and she gets fan mail from menopausal women who remember her from the early seventies. The royalties from the reruns aren't even enough to keep her in Fauchon truffles.

If Felicity Craven was a lesser person, she might be weeping from the hopeless frustration of her situation. But tears do not come easily to Felicity, and even as an actress she had been forced to portray the glycerine insincerity of the ingénue.

Felicity knows how easy it is for people to label her superficial and shallow. It's a convenient pigeon-hole favoured by the sermonizing types who appear on those fervent political debates on Sunday-morning TV. Just because a person is more concerned about the length of a hemline than the length of a term in government doesn't necessarily constitute intellectual torpor. Felicity once overheard hotel staff laughing about her in one of the service corridors.

'How do you make Felicity Craven scream twice?'

'I don't know.'

'Screw her senseless and then wipe your dick on her curtains!'

And that's how it has always been. Felicity Craven,

the woman of stone, concerned about nothing but herself and her despotic desire for celebrity and power. But that would suggest that Felicity cared passionately about nothing but her own self-absorbed world, and that would be untrue. Although she might not be a great humanitarian, Felicity *is* a mother, and she cares deeply about her children. In her time she has loved and she has lost, she has given and she has taken, albeit in a quiet fashion and without the gushing sentimentality that some people take as evidence of compassion. Josh calls it her 'spiky love', because she finds it difficult to express emotion without wrapping it in a self-conscious armour of brusqueness. She cannot express her love in so many words, and so she has to find some other way of telling her children how much she loves them.

'There's a call for you, Miss Craven,' announces Felicity's assistant on the intercom.

'I'm in a meeting,' she snaps, glaring at the PR manager and indicating that he should gather up his things and go.

'It's an international call; apparently it's important. A Mrs Schloss from Houston?'

Felicity's heart skips a beat. 'Put her on,' she says, shooing her PR manager away with impatient fingers.

Click.

'Felicity Craven.'

'Miss Craven, this is Angelica Schloss in Houston, Texas. I realize that I am the last person you wish to talk to right now, but I just felt that I had to make contact, for my own sanity at least.'

The woman has a horrible Southern drawl, and Felicity immediately conjures up the image of an overdressed, middle-aged American with shoulder pads and puffed-up hair.

'Why should I care about *your* sanity, Mrs Slosh?'

'It's Schloss.'

'Schloss, slosh, plish, plosh . . . whatever! Call yourself whatever you want. What *do* you want? Are you after another million or two? Well, I've got news for you, Mrs Schloss. You've had every last penny, and I hope it brings you eternal happiness.'

'I detect bitterness in your tone, Miss Craven.'

'How astute of you!'

'I didn't call to argue. I called to see if there was anything I could do to help. I read in the newspaper that you are about to lose your home, and maybe even your business, and I just felt downright awful about it.'

'Well, bless your heart! Excuse me if I sound a trifle hostile, but you *are* the woman who stole my husband, my inheritance and my life. Was it planned? Did you really love David, or did you just see him as a quick way to make some money?'

'I did love him, yes,' says Angelica Schloss, lowering her tone, 'and I honestly believe that he loved me. He certainly loved Tori and Zane.'

Tori and Zane? Sounds like a fucking circus act!

'And what about *my* children? Did he ever tell you how much he loved *them*, Mrs Schloss?'

'Of course he did. Why do you think he never left you? He was a gentleman, the genuine article. We had seven very happy years together.'

'Lucky old you!' sneers Felicity, breaking the eraser off the end of her Pentel retractable pencil.

'I would like to return some of the inheritance to you. That's why I called. I don't need all the money David left us. I wouldn't know what to do with it. We have a lovely home and enough money to keep us comfortably for a lifetime. I couldn't live with myself if I thought you were having to struggle alone in England. I am not a greedy woman, Miss Craven, although I cannot expect you to think kindly of me at this stage.'

Felicity pauses. She doesn't know how to react. Her hesitation alters the silence like a stopped clock.

'I was thinking of five million. I could have it wired to your account on Monday,' says Angelica Schloss.

'Your generosity astounds me, Mrs Schloss. David was worth twenty times that amount. I would have thought ten million was closer to the mark, if you really wanted to be charitable.'

'David always said that you were a mean-spirited woman. This is not a business negotiation, Miss Craven. This is a gift, and I must watch out for my own interests too. I would be happy to extend my offer to, say, seven million, but that is my final offer, take it or leave it. You would be a fool to refuse such a handsome proposal.'

'The fool accepts,' says Felicity, disguising her

triumph. 'Let me give you the name of my solicitor. I would like this to be arranged legally and without condition.'

'Of course. You will not hear from me again, Miss Craven.'

'Oh, I do have one request . . .' says Felicity. 'I want no one to know about our agreement, apart from the lawyers. No newspaper stories, no magazine articles or breakfast TV announcements. I will not have anyone viewing me as a charity case, do you understand?'

'I sure do. I hope you find happiness, honey.'

'Darling, just remember who you are addressing. I am virtually *royalty* in England, and I do not need to be patronized by some Texas whorehouse hick with more money than sense.'

'My, my, what a feisty little mare! David should have left you years ago. My only consolation in all of this is that he was in *my* bed and not yours. Now I suggest that you take my money and keep that foul mouth of yours buttoned. You are one nasty piece of work!'

'And you, my dear, are one self-satisfied cunt! You can keep your crumbs of conscience – I don't need them. Money isn't everything to those of us who were born with it. I can cope quite admirably without accepting handouts from some ill-bred, uncultured American redneck who, by chance, has come into some money. Enjoy your ill-gotten riches, Mrs *Slush*. You can buy an awful lot of cattle with a billion dollars!'

Click.

Felicity is beginning to get a headache.

'I think this calls for a minor celebration, darling!' laughs Felicity, knocking back another Kir royale in the lounge bar of Craven's. She has changed into her Comme des Garçons two-piece and her hair is up in a loose Ivana Trump. She is feeling bitter and twisted.

Like a piece of lemon rind.

'To your heroic sense of decorum!' says Ross, pouring more champagne and offering her his most cynical smile.

'I'm sorry, darling, I know you were counting on me for that cruise around the Caribbean, but I just couldn't take money from that ghastly woman.'

'You know I would have paid for the trip,' says Ross.

People around them are casting surreptitious glances. They make a glamorous couple.

'Who would be so *stupid* as to offer seven million pounds? If the roles had been reversed I wouldn't have given *her* so much as a second thought. She's probably *religious* or something! Can't sleep at night with the weight of it all? Well, she should have thought about that when she started screwing my husband.'

'You could have bought Blythwood outright, and still have had enough left to buy Sebastian out of this place,' says Ross, sounding resentful.

'Darling, Blythwood is worth about twenty-five million on the current market. It was designed by Robert Adam, you know. After the anniversary I'm going to dump Craven's. Let Sebastian cope with his own investments. I don't want to be beholden to anyone ever again. I'm going to buy my own place – a new improved Craven's hotel that puts this homage to the eighties to shame. I'm going to take the kids on holiday at Easter, and I'm going to come back a new woman.'

'When did you come to all these drastic conclusions?' asks Ross. 'Aren't you a bit scared at the thought of starting from scratch?'

'Darling, to coin a rather working-class expression, I am shitting bricks!'

And Felicity empties her glass in one, luxurious gulp.

'What about Disneyland?' enthuses Josh, ruffling the pages of the travel brochure he's holding.

'Oh, darling, that is so *plebeian*. You can go there another time. I want this to be a special holiday, just for the three of us,' says Felicity, ruffling his hair.

'Princess Diana took William and Harry there,' Josh argues, knowing exactly how to pull his mother's strings.

'Well, she was a princess and she was making a statement,' says Felicity.

'This hotel has five swimming pools and a nightclub,' says Sascha, pointing to a five-star monstrosity in Majorca.

'Darling, that's for *charter* people, not for people like us!'

'Belinda Carlton-Hunt went to Majorca with her stepmother. They drank wine out of a watering can,' whines Sascha.

'Exactly!' says Felicity. 'What about Venice?'

'Yuck!' says Josh.

'No beach,' says Sascha. 'And it'll be cold at this time of year.'

'Montserrat would have been lovely, but there's not much of it left these days since that damned volcano ruined everything. I suppose there's always St Croix.'

'Boring.'

'Egypt?'

'Smelly.'

'OK, wise guys, where *do* you want to go – apart from Disneyland and Majorca?' asks Felicity, losing her patience.

'Let's stick a pin in the atlas,' suggests Sascha.

'I'm not going to any Third World country,' insists Felicity.

'The best of three tries. We'll all have a go and then we'll choose the best of the three.'

'All right, but I refuse to go somewhere ridiculous like Iceland or Jersey.'

Sascha opens the atlas, and Josh bends back the pin on his cycling proficiency badge. Josh goes first.

'The Adriatic Sea. You'll have to try again,' says Sascha.

This time he lands smack in the middle of Bosnia.

'My turn!' says Sascha, grabbing the badge from her brother's hand.

Sascha lands close to Buenos Aires.

'Isn't that where Madonna lives?' asks Josh.

'Shut up, Josh! OK, it's Mummy's turn,' interrupts Sascha.

Felicity closes her eyes and stabs the pin into the atlas. It lands right in the dead centre of Kuwait.

'Oh, Mummy!' shrieks Sascha. 'You did that on purpose. How *could* you?' and she races out of the room, her face contorted with disbelief and rage.

'Darling . . .' starts Felicity, but her daughter is out of earshot.

'Looks like it's Bosnia or Buenos Aires, then,' states Josh, unaffected by the outburst.

'Oh, Josh, stop being so silly! Your sister is still very upset over your father.'

'It's probably her hormones,' says Josh. 'Girls her age can move things just with their minds if they want to.'

'Where do you get all this nonsense from?' asks Felicity crossly.

'It's not nonsense, it's *true*. It was on the sci-fi channel.'

'Well, why don't you move *yourself* with just your mind, and go and clear up that mess you left in the conservatory?'

'But what about our holiday?' asks Josh.

'There isn't going to be any holiday if you don't do as you're told. Now scoot!'

Josh gets up from the carpet, scowling, and in a final defiant gesture he kicks the corner of the outstretched atlas with his shoe. Felicity sighs and sits back on her haunches. Sometimes it seems that she just can't get anything right.

The knot of tension in the back of her neck is screwing itself tighter, burning into her muscle like a narrow pole of fire. Her temples are throbbing, her shoulder blades are clenched in a painful spasm. Felicity allows herself to roll over on to the antique Tabriz carpet, pressing the side of her face into the unforgiving texture of the weave.

In a minute she will get some Anadin.

In a minute.

In a minute . . .

CHAPTER EIGHTEEN

His name is Thierry de Leu de Cecil.

A bit of a mouthful but rather poetic, thinks Sebastian, writing it down in order to get the upper- and lower-case letters in the right order. He copies it from the simple white business card with the gold crest.

Belgian aristocracy fallen from grace over several generations. That is how Thierry describes his family name. That is how Thierry de Leu de Cecil introduces himself to Sebastian that afternoon at The Forum.

'I hope you will not be offended if I introduce myself before I leave,' he says as Sebastian lifts a spoonful of spotted dick to his mouth.

'I have seen you here on many occasions and you are, of course, rather famous. Allow me to introduce myself . . .'

And that is how Sebastian first comes to speak to the elegant young man he had spotted a few weeks earlier.

They have coffee together in the library. There are daffodils and parrot tulips in a crystal bowl from Moyses Stevens. There are newspapers strewn on an oversized footstool. There are flecks of gold in Thierry de Leu de Cecil's hazel eyes.

'I have an inexcusable confession to make,' says Thierry. His British accent is impeccable, and yet he carries the unmistakable textbook turn of phrase that indicates foreign nationality. 'Since I read about your unfortunate exposure in the newspapers I have been watching you very closely. It was a revelation to me that you are homosexual. Please . . . do not be offended. I am not passing judgement. I too am a member of the fraternity.'

Sebastian is certain that his pulse picks up several beats when he hears this, but he attempts to remain composed and aloof. He cannot take his eyes off Thierry's prominent Adam's apple, which is so sharply defined that it appears in danger of getting trapped inside the collar of his Jermyn Street shirt.

'I would have preferred a less controversial coming-out parade,' Sebastian says.

Thierry smiles. 'I can see that it was very humiliating for you and for your family. Were they aware of the situation before it came out in the press?'

'Sadly, no. My sister has practically disowned me; she blames me for bringing the family down to the gutter. My mother has been an angel, but I'm not sure if she really understands the implications. She is suffering from a mild form of Alzheimer's and isn't always coherent.'

'I'm sorry to hear that,' says Thierry, dutifully averting his beautiful eyes. 'And your father?'

'My father died several years ago. We are a very small family.'

'I wish I could say the same thing. I come from a gargantuan mess of great-aunts, uncles and second cousins, all of whom claim familial rights over my immediate family. Both my mother and my father are still in good health, I have both grandmothers and one great-grandmother, and they all live in one huge house close to Liège.'

'Do you still live with your family?' asks Sebastian.

'Good God, no! It would drive me batty!'

Sebastian smiles at the use of the colloquialism.

'I have an apartment in Brussels. It belongs to the family, but my parents have no need for it since they took a back seat with the family business. My two brothers run the show now, and they are both married with families of their own.'

'What is your family business?'

'Property mostly. We buy and sell – speculate on the market, that kind of thing. It is difficult to define just exactly how my family have made their money, but they have been very successful. My father was a brilliant businessman in his time.'

'Do you work for the business too?' asks Sebastian, pouring more coffee, wondering if Thierry's straw-blond hair is as soft as it looks.

'In a circumjacent way. We have a small office here in London, and I oversee my own independent branch of the business – a small operation that deals with commercial properties in the UK. Commercial leases, retail rentals, that kind of thing.'

'So you spend a lot of time in England?'

'I am here through the week. I go home at weekends.'

'Can I ask you a very personal question?' Sebastian proffers.

'Of course.'

'Are you in any kind of relationship at the moment?'

'No. I lost my lover, Alfred, to AIDS in 1996.'

It is Sebastian's turn to say how sorry he is.

'Thank you. We were together for almost nine years. I myself was fortunate not to contract the disease. It was a *coup de chance*, a . . . how do you say? A fluke. So many other people were not so lucky.'

Sebastian looks at this beautiful man and finds himself slopping coffee down the leg of his trousers.

'Oh, bugger!' he exclaims.

Thierry hands him a napkin. 'I would offer to wipe it off myself, but this is a public place and I think perhaps you have had enough scandal for one year.'

'What are you doing for the rest of the afternoon?' asks Sebastian, hardly able to focus on the coffee-stained pinstripes.

'I was hoping that perhaps you might be able to advise me. My agenda is empty.'

And, oh, how Sebastian would like to fill Thierry's agenda!

'Let's go,' he says.

The two men stride out into the March sunshine beneath the invisible cloak of their anticipation.

*

Condensation beads the champagne glass and drips into the bathwater. Steam clouds the humid air and obscures the mirror with a smoky haze. It is not an opulent bathroom. There is no marble; there are no gold-plated taps. It is white tile and Sanitan porcelain. It is Wright's Coal Tar, and Badedas turning the water green. The only note of extravagance is the champagne and the mimosa-scented candles from Czech & Speake.

'I feel as though I am underground,' whispers Sebastian reverently. His voice is absorbed by the steam, 'Like being in the Blue John mines in Derbyshire.'

'Blue John?' questions Thierry. 'What is this?'

'It's a kind of semi-precious stone peculiar to a small place called Castleton. I don't think it's very popular these days, but the old mines are jolly interesting.'

'My favourite stone is lapis lazuli,' says Thierry, running his finger down the side of his cold glass. 'It is the kind of stone that can only be used in very small amounts, otherwise it appears vulgar. Like most precious things, lapis lazuli should be treated as an exquisite detail and never an overindulgence.'

'If I heard that from anyone else I would think it terribly pompous,' smiles Sebastian, his hair slicked back with water and his face glowing pink in the candlelight.

'But I *am* pompous, Sebastian; that is something you should know about me. I am arrogant and pompous, and very opinionated on just about every subject. I am never invited to dinner parties because I do not know what the word diplomacy means. My family despair of me.'

'But you are very beautiful,' says Sebastian, pushing his toe up between Thierry's legs, beneath the dissipating foam.

'Ah, but like foie gras I should be appreciated in very small amounts, otherwise one might become sick of such rich food.'

'You are full of it, aren't you?' says Sebastian playfully. 'It's as though everything you say has been rehearsed, like clever quotations from a book. Even when you're naked you sound as though you're addressing a literary association. Where did you learn such marvellous English?'

'At Oxford, of course.'

'Shame. I was at Cambridge. You're probably a bit younger than me, though.'

'Thirty-five.'

'Three years younger. You could pass for thirty.'

'Flattery is as lukewarm to me as this bathwater. Shall we go back to the bedroom?' And Thierry stands up in the bath, so that small islands of foam course down his body, pausing to rest in his pubic hair.

Sebastian levers himself up and they stand face to face, inches apart, staring intensely before they exchange a damp kiss.

'You taste good,' says Sebastian.

'I am a vintage year,' replies Thierry, as he reaches down to grip Sebastian's slippery buttocks.

They climb out of the bath and Thierry hands

Sebastian a large white towel. When he opens the bathroom door, a cool draught of dry air sweeps in and replaces the steam that tumbles out into the corridor. It makes Sebastian's skin tingle. Goose pimples rush to the surface and his nipples harden.

'It's dark outside,' he says.

'We've been in there for over an hour. My fingers are like *des pruneaux*,' says Thierry, holding up his wrinkled hands.

'It's a bit chilly in here.'

'We can light a fire in the bedroom. I am fortunate to have the only fireplace in the whole building. I think the bedroom was originally meant to be the living room, but I switched it all around. We have the logs delivered. I store them in the butler's pantry, as I do not have a butler.'

'We?' asks Sebastian, suddenly alert.

'Oh, my parents sometimes use the apartment at weekends when I'm in Brussels.'

'And the bed?' asks Sebastian, falling back into the rumpled covers.

'It belonged to my grandmother's family. Apparently my father was conceived in it and my grandfather died in it.'

'Presumably on different days,' laughs Sebastian.

Thierry wraps his towel around his waist and brings logs to the fireplace.

The flat is above a toy museum in Bayswater. The ceilings are not particularly high, because they are up on the fourth floor and these were probably servants' quarters at one time. There is a pair of stunted sash windows that look down over a walled garden with a Victorian carousel and a miniature train track. When they arrived at the flat that afternoon, the sound of children and pipe-organ music had accompanied their moans of pleasure as they tore and struggled at buttons and zips.

'It smells of cigarette smoke in here,' says Sebastian. 'Are you a smoker?'

Thierry crouches by the fireplace.

'No, but my parents both smoke. I don't smell it myself.'

'You soon got that going.'

'I am an expert at lighting fires,' says Thierry. Flames engulf the pile of logs and the chimney gutters with the sudden updraught. The room burns bright with elongated shadows, and Sebastian props himself up against the pillows with his hands behind his head.

'I shall make some tea and we can have some of my mother's almond biscuits. Stay right there and keep the bed warm for me.'

Sebastian takes in a deep breath and closes his eyes for a moment. It has all happened so quickly. Just five hours after meeting this man, he feels as though he has been here all his life. It is incredible. He can't remember ever feeling this happy. Delirious, almost.

There is no such thing as love at first sight, but infatuation strikes like an arrow. Sebastian knows all about infatuation. He has fallen victim to its poison dart many times in the past, and each time he has been left wounded and humiliated, in a pool of his own heartache. He boasts that he is hardened to the sting of seduction, and yet he recognizes the unmistakable grasp of its steely fingers. He could walk away now, this instant, and suffer only the most temporary remorse. But Sebastian, like so many others, prefers to hang around in the hope that maybe this time the grit of infatuation will turn itself magically into a pearl.

Matthew Robbins.

The name returns to Sebastian with all the clarity of a fatal accident. In 1976 Matthew Robbins was the most idolized boy in the school. He was head boy, athlete and *deity*.

It was an all-boys school, of course. The kind with boarders and dorms and ivy-covered walls. School-masters swooped in and out of the quadrangles in raven-black cloaks, and four hundred years of history etched the flagstone floors of the Old School. Sebastian was thirteen. Barely past puberty and still not quite sure how semen and urine could come from the same source. Behind the boiler room they used to huddle together during autumn dinner breaks, and discuss the bizarre changes they were experiencing with their adolescent bodies. Pubic hair was a phenomenon in those days, and flies would be whipped open, with backs turned, to display proudly the onset of manhood. Some of the boys were men by the time they were twelve. Jeremy Truscoe was the first boy in their form to ejaculate publicly. Thomas

Wendover was the first to do it twice in one minute. For a while it was their main form of entertainment.

Nobody would openly admit to having a crush on Matthew Robbins, but it was commonplace to boast about having shared a seat with him on the bus or having delivered a message to him from another prefect during break. 'Robbins is coming,' they would whisper as he sauntered out of the library or the assembly hall, usually with his clutch of faithful followers trailing eagerly in his shadow. Sometimes, as he passed, he might offer the boys of the Lower Third a casual comment.

'Straighten your tie, Phillips.'

'Stop gawking, Raleigh. If the wind changes, your face might stay like that.'

And they would fall silent in his wake, holding their breath and wondering if he might turn round. But he never did. People like Matthew Robbins only looked ahead.

A simple twist of fate brought them together that first day of the Michaelmas term. Sebastian was back a day earlier than most of the other boys, owing to his parents having to rush off to Europe for something or other. The school was eerily silent. The dorm was deserted, parquet floors like glass and smelling of polish. It was hot: stagnant, in fact, because the windows were all closed up, and there were dead blue-bottles on the sills.

Matthew Robbins was sitting on the wall up by

the air-raid shelters. He had grown sideburns over the summer vac and he was very tanned.

'You look like you've lost sixpence and found a penny,' shouted Robbins as Sebastian trailed along the edge of the irrigation ditch.

'Hello, Robbins! Did you have a good holiday?' shouted Sebastian, squinting into the sun so that he could barely make out Robbins in its glare.

'Come and tell me what you've been up to, Craven. I'm bloody bored to death. Nobody else is coming up until tomorrow. My parents have buggered off to Switzerland with my sister. She's going to some fancy finishing school.'

And that was how they started talking. They strolled down along the cross-country route and back up to the school from the village. It was almost four o'clock when they reached the science labs and drank water from the swan-necked taps in the chemistry room.

With cold water still dripping from his lips Robbins launched himself unexpectedly on Sebastian, seeking out his face with grappling fingers and heaving him against the wall. His mouth was all-encompassing, swamping Sebastian's face with hungry kisses.

'You are too pretty for your own good, Craven,' he had gasped as he unbuckled his trousers and released his rigid cock from his pants.

Sebastian bolted.

He raced across the cricket pitch and up through the kitchen gardens. All the time he was running he could see Robbins's cock, proudly incongruous against the rough serge of his school trousers.

Run, run, run, with sweat and tears stinging his eyes. Sweat from the heat. Tears from the euphoric confusion jangling like church bells in his head.

And all night, alone in the empty dorm, the smallest sliver of a new moon promised Sebastian a Michaelmas term he was never going to forget. Matthew Robbins wanted him. Matthew Robbins thought he was pretty. Matthew Robbins had offered him salvation in the form of his everlasting love.

The boys returned. Coach-loads and car-loads of boys and their noise. Sebastian hunted all day for Robbins, hanging around outside the chemistry room in the hope that he might return to the scene of the crime. But Robbins was nowhere to be found. By seven that evening Sebastian was beside himself with desperation. He went to the house room of the Upper Sixth and knocked on the door. Fat, spotty Judd answered.

'Robbins, there's somebody here to see you,' Judd shouted over his shoulder.

Robbins came to the door. 'Yes, Craven?' he said, his face as inscrutable as a judge's.

'I came to see if you were all right,' said Sebastian, his voice as small as his courage.

'What are you talking about, lad? Of course I'm all right. Now sod off and leave me alone. I'm busy.' And he slammed the door in Sebastian's face.

Bang!

Matthew Robbins never so much as looked at Sebastian again after that day. It was a pain that troubled Sebastian for years to come. The pain of rejection.

Unrequited infatuation.

How can he lie here in Thierry's four-poster bed and allow himself to think of what might be? He should leave right now, before it's too late. To stay the night would be to face the cold light of day – that grainy dawn that defuses the passion of the night before. The chink in the curtain, the car in the street, the morning after the night before.

'I hope you like Darjeeling. It is all I have,' says Thierry, entering the bedroom with a silver tray pressed to his stomach.

'Splendid,' smiles Sebastian.

'I thought we could have dinner in bed. I have *crevettes* and lobster in the fridge, and there is plenty more champagne. What time do you have to get up in the morning?'

Thierry rests the tray on the edge of the bed, removes his towel and slides beneath the sheets to press himself against Sebastian's side.

'Whenever I wake up,' replies Sebastian.

'Who said anything about going to sleep?' laughs Thierry.

'Who was it that said Belgians don't know how to have a good time?'

'Probably the French.'

'Miaow!'

CHAPTER NINETEEN

On his nineteenth birthday Wayne Briggs goes to the pictures in Leicester Square: a matinée performance because it's cheaper than going after six, and because he's got nothing better to do. It's his day off.

He's feeling a bit miserable today, and he knows it has something to do with his birthday. He called his mum this morning and she rattled on about crap for half an hour, not even bothering to ask him why he had called. She didn't remember that it was his birthday; she was more interested in some stupid affair that's going on over the street. Late-night fights in the garden and police cars at four a.m. Better than the telly, she said.

Wayne has seen a change in Mr Craven lately. He doesn't call him to the cleaning cupboard any more, and he gives Wayne sour looks whenever they bump into each other in the hotel. Wayne couldn't care less as long as he's getting his wages, but he rather misses the sex. It was pretty good. As for Miss Craven, well, Wayne is just biding his time before he pounces on that stuck-up bitch. She told him off yesterday for hanging around in the service corridor. Fuck her! She'll soon see who's in control.

He sees a science-fiction film about life on a distant planet sometime in the future, when Earth has been blown up and the survivors live in underground caves with electricity and manufactured oxygen. There's a mysterious plague and a mutant breed of creatures that inhabit sulphurous caverns. A load of crap, but it wastes an hour or two, and Wayne sits in the back row with a box of raisin Poppets and some beer he smuggled in under his jacket.

The late-afternoon light makes him blink when he comes out into the crowd of tourists looking up at the stupid clock above the Swiss Centre. Jingle-jangle, five o'clock. He doesn't fancy going home just yet, especially on his birthday. Not that it means that much to him, but he feels it's important to do something special. He wonders if any of the lads might be working the Circus. He could pop over there and have a laugh for an hour or two – maybe even have a few beers in Shaftesbury Avenue.

He pauses in the doorway of HMV to fasten his jacket. There's a bloke watching him over by the railings. He's not bad-looking: jeans, trainers and a ski jacket with stripes on the shoulders. Wayne hangs around for a couple of minutes, staring the bloke out, sussing the situation.

He's coming over.

He's fucking gorgeous!

'All right?' says the bloke, smiling.

'All right, mate,' says Wayne, keeping his hands in his pockets and shuffling his feet.

'Are you working?' asks the bloke.

'Depends,' says Wayne. 'What you looking for exactly?'

'Blow job.'

Wayne sees the wedding ring. Usual story.

'Twenty-five,' says Wayne, looking up and down Leicester Square, puffing his cheeks.

'How about twenty?' asks the bloke.

'Have you got somewhere to go?'

'How about the flicks? The porno place down Rupert Street?'

'OK. Have you got the cash?'

The bloke produces twenty quid and Wayne thinks he would have done this one for free. A birthday present, so to speak.

'Come on, then,' he says, and they make off in the direction of Rupert Street.

They have barely turned the corner before two other blokes grab hold of Wayne by his arms and announce themselves as police officers.

'You've been nicked, son!' they say with bright-eyed relish.

It's never happened before.

Wayne has fallen for a bleeding 'pretty policeman'.

Chapter Twenty

Dee's house, though larger than Claire's, is still very cramped. Probably because it's so full of *things*. It's as though Dee has gone through her life without ever throwing anything away. Her style has never developed. She's a poly student at heart.

'How do you water all of these?' asks Claire, inspecting the tangle of spider plants and geraniums on the deep window ledge.

'I don't,' replies Dee, coming in from the kitchen with two glasses of Paul Masson white. 'I water those I can reach, and the others seem to survive by osmosis. Some of them look as though they could do with a little friendly euthanasia.'

Duncan accepts his glass and attempts to get comfortable in the narrow bamboo rocking chair. He has thrown the cushions on the floor, but there still doesn't appear to be sufficient room for his wide frame. Claire offers him a sympathetic smile.

'Are you sure you don't want just half a glass, Claire?' asks Dee.

'No thanks. I'm fine with the Tango.'

'How long have you lived here, Dee?' asks Duncan.

'I moved in the same week as Claire. Our houses

were both finished at the same time. There was snow piled up to the window sills and my radiators weren't working properly. I spent my first night sleeping in the kitchen with the oven on at 425!'

Claire can see Dee's nipples poking through her *Save the Whales* T-shirt. She wonders if Duncan is looking at them. Dee has small breasts, unlike Claire, and she's showing her belly button above the low-slung waistline of her jeans. Claire still can't look at the piercing without an involuntary shudder, but Dee insists it doesn't hurt.

They're listening to Joan Armatrading. It's an LP, warped and scratched with time, and the stylus needs replacing. There's an awful lot of garlic in the air, thick and sickening like a Frenchman's breath. Claire doesn't like garlic, but she won't tell Dee. Dee puts garlic into everything, even if the recipe doesn't call for it.

'Your friend's a bit late,' says Claire, glancing at the clock. It's one of those pre-digital clock radios with numbers that flip down on little white flaps.

'She's always late. Usually I tell her to be here half an hour earlier than I want her, and she still gets here late. I plan accordingly, and never cook anything that can't survive in the oven for several days without spoiling.'

'You look washed out, love,' says Duncan, leaning forward precariously in his unstable chair.

'I haven't been sleeping very well recently. I keep

falling asleep during the day. I nearly nodded off in the office yesterday.'

'It's all downhill from here, Claire,' says Dee. 'Next you'll be getting swollen ankles and backache and you won't be able to climb the stairs without the aid of a winch and two strong fellas with a rope!'

'It's a funny kind of tiredness,' says Claire. 'It's not like being tired in the normal way. It's more like this weight that comes over me, and I just feel that if I don't close my eyes I'll pass out.'

'Are you taking iron pills? You're probably deficient.'

'I'm taking every vitamin under the sun. I spent eighteen quid in Holland & Barrett last week.'

'When's your next doctor's appointment?'

'Tuesday. He's just moved to that new clinic up by Sainsbury's. He's ever so nice – young. Much nicer than old Dr Hodges.'

'Thank God *he* retired when he did. He was an insurance claim just waiting to happen. Apparently he told Miriam Stafford that she had a malignant tumour in her bladder when all it was was some kind of benign cyst. She was off her head with worry for three weeks before they sent her to a specialist. If I could afford it, I'd join BUPA in a flash. The NHS went down the drain years ago.'

The doorbell interrupts Dee's grievances.

'At last!' she says, leaving Claire and Duncan alone for a few seconds as she goes to answer the door.

'This thing is about as comfortable as a straitjacket,' whispers Duncan, wriggling in his rocking chair.

'Shhh, she'll hear you,' giggles Claire.

'And what's with that poster?' he asks, nodding towards a Benetton advertisement pinned to the wall above the fish tank.

'She told me it's worth a lot of money – apparently it was banned or something.'

'I'm not surprised; it's sick!'

Claire's face lights up expectantly as Dee returns with her friend in tow.

'Claire, Duncan, this is my friend Poppy Bentos.'

'As in Fray Bentos – no lumps of fat or gristle guaranteed!' smiles Poppy, extending her hand towards Claire.

'No relation, I presume?' asks Duncan, shaking Poppy's hand.

'I *wish*! I wouldn't be flogging home-made jewellery down at Camden market every weekend if I had a steak-and-kidney pie empire behind me.'

'Poppy makes wonderful jewellery. She's just got a contract to supply Cher with stuff for her mail-order catalogue in America,' says Dee, proudly presenting her friend's attributes.

'These are mine,' says Poppy, tossing back her Titian curls to show them her earrings.

Claire doesn't know what to say. They look like nuts and bolts.

'Extraordinary!' exclaims Duncan, raising his eyebrows.

'I've heard worse,' laughs Poppy, removing her coat to reveal an outfit that reminds Claire of Annie Oakley – a kind of suede fringed jacket with a matching ankle-length skirt. It's something Claire would never dream of wearing, but somehow it seems right on Poppy, who appears larger than life in the cramped little living room.

'I'm gagging for a glass of plonk, darling!' she says, kissing Dee on the cheek and squeezing her arm. Claire feels a bit uncomfortable in the company of extroverts.

'So, Claire – Dee tells me you're going to sprog. How many months are you?'

'Erm, almost three,' stutters Claire from her ungainly position on the Newcastle Brown Ale bean-bag.

'And *you* must be the proud father!' smiles Poppy, directing her faux pas straight at Duncan with all the force of a punch in the face.

There is an implosion of silence. Joan Armatrading has stopped singing, and Duncan is staring at Claire as though she's holding his life-raft. Claire's face is burning and Poppy immediately recognizes her clumsy mistake.

'Oops! I can see I've put my foot in it, as usual. Please, you don't have to answer that question – it was very presumptuous of me. I'm not known for my subtlety. I once asked a woman when her baby was due and she wasn't even pregnant!'

'Here, get some of this down you,' says Dee,

returning with a glass of wine. 'Dinner is ready when you are . . .'

They eat dinner in Dee's dining room. There are patio doors without curtains, and the four of them are reflected in the sullen glass beneath the glare of an overhead light. Dee is vegetarian, so everything is meatless and organic, and they eat it off brown Denby ware.

'This stuff is practically indestructible,' says Dee, dropping her empty dinner plate on the table with an ominous clatter. 'I bought it in 1977 and I've still got the whole set.'

'What was on the pea pods?' asks Claire, trying to make the food that is left on her plate appear less insulting.

'Oh, you mean the mangetout? That was semolina gravy.'

'Hang on a minute, I'm going to have to open the top button of my skirt,' says Poppy, leaning back in her chair.

'I'm stodged!' sighs Claire, patting her stomach.

'That was delicious, Dee. Thank you,' says Duncan. He has barely touched the so-called Red Dragon Pie, which appears to be mainly beans and tomatoes with a surplus of garlic.

'Anybody for coffee?'

'I'll make it, darling,' offers Poppy. 'You go and sit down in the other room and have a rest. You deserve a bit of a breather.'

The food seems stuck in Claire's chest like a wad of

insulating foam. She feels exhausted, and she wants to go home. Home to familiar surroundings: clean sheets and fruit-flavoured Tums. Duncan looks bored stiff, but he keeps smiling and pretending to be interested in what Dee has to say about vivisection and the castration of convicted rapists. Dee has had too much to drink and she's slurring her words. Her cheeks are flushed, which makes her look quite pretty – not so tomboyish. There is a red wine stain on her T-shirt, like a birthmark in the shape of an island. Claire isn't sure which island – she was never any good at geography – but it could be Australia.

Or a hedgehog?

Dee lights up another cigarette and Claire worries about breathing it in. Dee has been smoking all night, and the house is foggy with it. Nobody has thought about Claire, although she has noticed Duncan wafting away the smoke when he thought nobody else was looking. She tries to take in shallow breaths, but that only makes her feel light-headed. When the coffee comes, she'll gulp it down and make a hasty exit. It's already eleven-thirty, well past her bedtime. She's wearing her new knickers, sprinkled with Lily of the Valley talc from Marks, in anticipation of her first night with Duncan, but now she doesn't feel up to it. Sex is the last thing on her mind, and she's glad she never revealed her intentions to Duncan at the onset of the evening. Perhaps she can swing it on Saturday night, after the pictures?

'What is Poppy doing with that coffee?' slurs Dee,

stubbing out her cigarette in one of the spider plants. She staggers out of the living room.

Claire make an apologetic face at Duncan and he gives her one of his kindly, big-bear expressions that makes her feel grateful for everything she has. She feels a rush of affection so powerful it almost brings tears to her eyes.

'You really do look done in. Do you want to give the coffee a miss and go home?' he asks.

'I feel exhausted, and I've got terrible indigestion,' admits Claire, thumping her breastbone.

'I'll go and tell them. I'm sure they'll understand. After all, it's a week night and we've all got to get up in the morning.' Duncan squeezes Claire's shoulder as he passes her. She feels better already. She likes him making decisions for her, and for a moment she reconsiders her earlier thoughts about asking him to spend the night. She knows it sounds rude, but she's been thinking about Duncan's thighs ever since that rugby game. *Burt Reynolds thighs – in the days before his hairpiece.* Claire has a tatty old *Cosmopolitan* in the bottom of her underwear drawer. It's an issue from the seventies which was lining a box of mismatched wool bought at a jumble sale. Burt Reynolds is spread out across a fur rug, with one massive thigh raised just high enough to cover his tackle. Funnily enough, that same issue has an article about Felicity Craven: a lurid piece about how to dress like a slut to keep your man interested.

'Claire!' hisses Duncan, returning from the kitchen

in a fluster. He is wearing the farcical look of a schoolboy who has just put itching powder down the back of his mother's dress. 'You'll never guess what I just saw . . .'

'What?' whispers Claire, catching Duncan's infectious mood of hilarity.

'Poppy and Dee are *snogging* in the kitchen!'

'No!'

'Yes, they're bent over the breakfast bar, and they're all over each other.'

'Did they see you?'

'No, they were too occupied.'

'Blimey! I had no idea.'

Duncan stifles a burst of laughter. Claire puts her finger to her lips and cranes her neck nervously towards the kitchen. Someone is coming with a clatter of coffee cups.

'Here we are, then,' says Poppy, setting the tray down on a stack of old *Spare Rib* magazines.

Claire can't look at Duncan. She can't look at Poppy. She mumbles her 'pardon' and seeks refuge in the toilet. Suddenly it all makes sense: the feminist issues, the cropped haircut, the kd lang albums and the propensity for Doc Marten's and unshaved armpits. Dee is a lesbian, and Claire had absolutely no inkling. Well, why should she? She's never met one before, at least not that she's known. It strikes her as rather interesting – rather *racy*, for want of a better word. All this time Claire has been wanting her life to be more interesting, and now, in the space of a few weeks, she's pregnant, she has a boyfriend and her neighbour turns out to be a lesbian.

What next? she wonders.

She flushes the toilet and runs the cold tap to make them think that she was having a wee.

CHAPTER TWENTY-ONE

Felicity picks up the hideous white tapered candles and smashes them against the corner of her desk. Chunks of candle explode across her office and she is left holding the drooping wicks and a handful of crumbling wax.

Never trust a man in a leather tie.

'Marissa, get in here at once!' screams Felicity.

Marissa, her personal assistant, comes running to the door with half a doughnut in her hand and sugar on her chin. She looks startled and guilty, like someone used to taking the blame for everything.

'When I ask for natural-white candles I expect natural-white candles, not something that looks as though it came wrapped in cellophane from a fucking card shop!' Felicity brandishes what is left of the candles she has smashed. 'What kind of florist *is* this man? I *knew* we should have asked Kenneth Turner to do the job.'

'He wasn't available,' stammers Marissa, wiping her chin with the back of her hand. 'He's doing a party for Fergie in America – Weight Watchers or something.'

'Well, we are definitely not using a florist who doesn't know the difference between natural white and something that belongs in the middle of a plastic flower arrangement. And why did he send us *tapers*, for Christ's sake? Who uses tapers these days? You know I always specify columns. *Church* candles, I said. Surely he knows what a church candle is? And I wanted at least eighty per cent stearin so that they won't drip. These things wouldn't burn long enough to see a Pronuptia bride get through to the hokey-cokey!'

Felicity feels a band of pressure across the bridge of her nose. It is tightening and swelling, as though a tourniquet were being twisted inside her head.

'I'll call him immediately, Miss Craven.'

'Tell him he's lost the contract. Phone Marcus and Phyleda and tell them to get over here a.s.a.p. Fax them the brief for the flowers and ask them to bring samples – today!'

'Yes, Miss Craven.'

'Oh, and Marissa . . .'

'Yes, Miss Craven?'

'What is that foul perfume you're wearing?'

'It's L'Etoile.'

'Well it smells more like a Glade plug-in!'

'Sorry, Miss Craven. I'll remember that.' And Marissa returns to her office with a steeper than usual gradient to her shoulders.

Felicity dumps the candle stubs unceremoniously into her chrome waste bin with supercilious contempt.

Chink, chink go her bangles.

Thump, thump goes the pulse in her temples.

She has to close her eyes and turn up the ionizer for

a few minutes. The odour of Marissa's cheap perfume lingers in the air, and it offends Felicity's delicate senses.

Felicity, who blends her own pot-pourri with essential oils imported from France.

Felicity, who places perfumed candles in every guest room, each one made to her own specifications by a small factory in Holland.

Why does nobody seem to care about these things? How can anyone be happy with second-best? It just doesn't make sense to her.

Like people who live in caravans.

And people who play the lottery.

God forbid they should win. Imagine some ill-equipped person being handed ten million pounds. It's in the newspapers all the time these days – some pathetic chip-shop assistant winning a small fortune and spending it all on satellite TV and holidays in Tenerife. There should be some kind of rating system for lottery winners, something that regulates the pay-out according to the lifestyle of the winner. It just isn't right giving huge amounts of money to the poor; they just don't know what to do with it. Some of them don't even have bank accounts! They cash their giros at the post office and spend all their allowance on Friday night, so that the rest of the week they have to live off baked beans and Mother's Pride.

Felicity has taken more Anadin than the recommended daily dose, and yet her headache seems to be getting progressively worse. It's weighing down her vision, making it difficult to keep her head up. She has so much to do today, and it's only ten-thirty. If she is to make this tenth anniversary celebration her swansong at Craven's, she needs it to be the most wonderful event London has ever seen. The invitations are being accepted daily, and the guest list is impressive, even for Felicity. Everyone from Richard Branson and Elton John, to Herb Ritts and Madonna. The cuisine will be Pacific Rim, with chefs flown in from California and Japan. Slices of raw fish and paper-thin beef sizzling on slabs of heated slate – that kind of thing.

If Felicity is to succeed on her own, she needs this event to attract worldwide media attention. She must call up favours from every contact she has. She must lunch and dine with people she despises. She must talk to *The Tatler* and *Elle* and *The World of Interiors*.

She must sell herself.

The recent article about David's 'secret family' in Texas has been particularly devastating and she needs some positive press. The last thing Felicity needs is pity. She just isn't cut out to be pitiful.

'Miss Craven, the press packs are here.' It is Marissa at the open door, holding a cardboard box. Felicity holds out a weary hand but says nothing.

She removes the lid. Inside are five examples of the press pack that she herself designed for the anniversary dinner.

Each pack consists of a black lacquer container shaped like an oversized cigarette box. A slender silver-grey tassel hangs at the front, with the Craven's emblem embossed into a copper medallion. Inside each box is an invitation printed on grey recycled cardboard, folded origami-style and tied with silk thread and an onyx bead. There is a potted history of Craven's and a short résumé of Felicity's personal history, with black and white photographs and a pair of crystal and gold-leaf chopsticks created exclusively for Felicity by Daum.

'Marissa?'

'Yes, Miss Craven?'

'The thread on these invitations – didn't I specify copper?'

'I think you did, Miss Craven.'

'Well this is *gold*. Get them to send me samples. We'll have to change this before they're sent out.'

'Yes, Miss Craven.'

'Oh, and Marissa?'

'Yes?'

'Call Ross and cancel our lunch date. I'll have a smoked-salmon croissant and some Perrier in my office at one. Close the door, please, and do not disturb me until lunchtime. Hold all calls.'

'Mr Peters has already cancelled, Miss Craven.'

'Why didn't you tell me?' snaps Felicity.

This is the third time he has cancelled in the last week.

'He called just a few minutes ago. He said to apologize, and that he'll phone you when he gets back from Edinburgh.'

'Edinburgh? What the hell is he doing in Edinburgh?'

'He didn't say.'

'Oh, sod him! He's proving to be just about as reliable as everyone else around here.'

Felicity seeks refuge in her velvet sofa.

She doesn't even think about the mess she will make of her linen jacket – and it's a one-off Dolce & Gabbana that cannot be dry-cleaned because of the ridiculously delicate silk lining.

She *must* be feeling pretty bad.

Chapter Twenty-two

How many people can say that they've had beluga caviar smeared around their genitals?

Admittedly it's an acquired taste.

Like olives. And anchovies.

Sebastian did not find the experience particularly sensuous. In fact, the idea of something so gelatinous, black and pungent in such an intimate area of hygienic concern made him eager to dash off to the bathroom in search of soap and water. Thierry apparently has a voracious appetite for food served on anything but a plate.

Dégustation du corps céleste. A sampling of the heavenly body.

'The idea of anything fishy slapped around *my* nooks and crannies is just too close to the old joke about the blind man saying, "Evening, girls!" as he passes the fish market,' says Poppy over a cup of decaffeinated herbal tea.

Sebastian laughs. 'I can see the whipped-cream thing, and the Kim Basinger thing with the honey and chocolate sauce, but Thierry seems to have a much more discerning palate when it comes to sex food.'

'He's Belgian – what do you expect?' laughs Poppy.

'Just thank your lucky stars he isn't German – you could find yourself with sauerkraut around your wiener!'

'It's really strange, Poppy. The sex. I've never come so many times in one night before, and yet Thierry hasn't come once since we met. Sometimes he doesn't even get hard. Oddly enough it doesn't seem to faze him, and he's incredibly good at manipulating me. I can't get enough of him. Do you think I'm going through a belated adolescence?'

'I do hope so, darling. If you missed out on it in your teens, you certainly deserve to experience it before you pop your clogs.'

They're sitting in Poppy's living room. It's late afternoon and the windows are open. There are daffodils in a jam jar, and birdsong floats in from the naked branches of a pear tree.

'What about you?' asks Sebastian. 'You never talk about anyone special in your life. Surely there must be some gentleman lurking in the romantic shadows of your bedroom?'

Poppy avoids Sebastian's eyes. Why does she look so cornered? She plays with her hair and sips her tea before she answers his question.

'Darling, when you've been around the block as many times as I have, you learn to accept the fact that nothing comes easy. There *is* someone in my life, and has been for quite some time now, but it's something I prefer to keep to myself. I'm not trying to be coy or mysterious; it's just a matter of privacy for the other person. Let's just say that I'm getting my garden watered on a regular basis, and leave it at that.' Poppy smiles and plumps her cushion with nervous fingers.

Of course, now Sebastian is intrigued. It's probably a married man, a man with a family and a reputation to uphold, but he doesn't know Poppy well enough yet to invade her privacy any further. She seems to enjoy talking about Sebastian more than she does about herself.

'So tell me about that sister of yours. Has the dragon lady stopped breathing fire and brimstone? I saw her profile in yesterday's *Independent* – very impressive. Does she really keep live peacocks in the grounds of Blythwood?'

'She's gearing herself up for this anniversary gala at the hotel. I haven't seen her since our bust-up, but whenever I go into the hotel there's a frenetic buzz in the air, as though she's just passed through leaving her scent behind her. It's a reign of terror in that place – I sometimes wonder why the staff put up with it. I found her personal assistant sobbing over a mound of table napkins that Felicity had decried as being less than a hundred per cent linen. I sometimes think my sister doesn't have enough happiness in her life, so she has to focus her attention on minute details. She is obsessed to the point of it being an illness.'

'What about that married man of hers – Russ?' asks Poppy, settling into the conversation as though it's a comfortable chair.

'Ross. He's vanished into thin air since he realized

that Felicity was disinherited from David's fortune. I can't say I'm surprised; he always struck me as the gold-digging sort. That article in *Fortune* magazine was a bit of a shocker. None of us knew anything about the Texan and her kids. Although I sometimes despise my sister, I couldn't help feeling sorry for her when I read that. Losing Blythwood is going to hurt her more than anything – she adores that house.'

'Surely her late husband's partners will let her keep it?'

'Quite the opposite. They'll derive great pleasure in taking it away from her. Over the years Felicity has been an absolute cow to most of those men, and I can't blame them for hating her. She's broken up marriages, exposed fraudulent wheeler-dealings and instigated several hostile takeover bids from rival companies with whom she had a personal interest. As far as the directors of Glendale Estates are concerned, she's poison. I've heard David refer to her as the anathema of his life – a sure indication that their marriage was less than wine and roses.'

'Actually, I met someone who works for Glendale Estates last week at a dinner party,' says Poppy. 'Just a minion – a secretary. Rather a mousy type, but pleasant enough. I think she was a bit intimidated by me. I put my foot in it when I assumed that her boyfriend was the father of her child. She's three months pregnant and I just *assumed* . . . you know.'

'So he isn't the father of her child?'

'Apparently not. There was an awkward silence, a

lot of blushing and then I blundered on pretending it hadn't happened. She didn't seem the type who would sleep around, but I suppose she must be something of a dark horse. She's the neighbour of a friend of mine.' Poppy brushes cake crumbs from her skirt. 'So what happens to your sister now?'

'I wish I knew,' sighs Sebastian, pouring himself some tea. 'She has to be out of Blythwood by the end of the year. Presumably she'll have to find more modest accommodation, and she'll continue to work at Craven's as usual. It isn't as though she's going to be penniless. The kids are provided for, so she only has herself to support. It might mean one less visit to the spa in France, one less yard of silk for her bedroom curtains, but Felicity will no doubt continue to lead the life of a duchess.'

'Are you sure it's OK for me to come to the anniversary dinner? I won't be offended if there just isn't room.'

'Don't be silly, of course it's all right. It's *my* hotel, remember? As promised, I've got you sitting between Thierry and Cher. If this doesn't get you a second mail-order contract, nothing will.'

'Oh, I'm so excited!' squeals Poppy, clapping her hands together like a child.

'Actually, I'm feeling rather proud of myself at the moment. I sacked a porter today. It's my very first dismissal and I feel pretty good about it.'

'You sacked somebody? I thought it was virtually

impossible to sack anyone in this day and age, unless they've attempted murder or raped a member of staff.'

'He was prostituting himself with the hotel guests, actually.'

'Christ! How did you approach him? Wasn't it terribly embarrassing?'

'Well, I wimped out actually. I left a note in his locker telling him to clear out, then I took the rest of the day off.'

'How very brave of you, darling! You really *are* management material, aren't you?' laughs Poppy.

They dine at Le Pont de la Tour. It is Thierry's birthday and they are joined by a trendy young woman called Solange. Sebastian has never met her before. She is an old friend of Thierry's from Brussels and she, like Thierry, wears her foreignness with discretion. Solange has on a strange velvet hat that is squashed and slightly comical. She is very attractive in a rather eccentric fashion, and she makes Sebastian feel conservative by comparison. Occasionally she speaks in French when addressing Thierry, but she also speaks immaculate English, and so Sebastian doesn't have to exercise his rather rusty schoolboy French.

'Nonsense! You speak very good French,' teases Thierry, touching Sebastian's hand possessively.

'I'm OK as long as I remain firmly in the present tense,' admits Sebastian. 'I can be *here*, but I can never come from anywhere or go anywhere – I'm stuck without a past or a future.'

'I don't suppose you have any Flemish?' asks Solange. Her lipstick is almost purple.

'None at all,' says Sebastian, 'although I know a few words in Dutch – aren't they very similar?'

'Not really,' she says, with a touch of arrogance. Her eyes are piercing.

'This must be ours,' announces Thierry as their waiter brings them oysters and a bucket of mussels.

Sebastian doesn't spot Wayne Briggs sitting at another table with a flamboyant gentleman who is plying his young companion with champagne and flattery. It is only when Wayne is halfway across the restaurant that Sebastian becomes aware of his presence.

'Mr Craven,' says Wayne, 'good evening. I haven't seen you for ages. You never call these days.'

'Good evening, Wayne. How are you?' Sebastian's expression is rigid. He has no idea how this encounter is going to develop. 'These are my friends Thierry de Leu de Cecil and his friend from Belgium, Solange. This is Wayne Briggs, one of our under-porters at the hotel.'

'*Ex*-under-porter,' corrects Wayne. 'Mr Craven gave me the push yesterday. Apparently I wasn't pulling my weight. Isn't that right, Mr Craven? Well, I wasn't pulling *something* or other – I can't remember the exact words he used.'

'I don't think this is really the right time or place to be going into this, Wayne.'

'Which one of you is getting fucked by this creep?'

Several heads turn at surrounding tables. Solange raises her hand to her neck, and Thierry whispers *Mon dieu* under his breath.

'You listen to me, you little guttersnipe,' growls Sebastian. 'Go back to your table and leave us alone. I will not tolerate this kind of behaviour.'

'Am I embarrassing you, Mr Craven? Oh, do excuse my rudeness. It's just that I thought we had an arrangement.'

'What are you blathering on about?'

'Do I have to spell it out for you?'

'Is everything all right, sir?' asks their waiter, hovering nervously.

'Everything is fine, thank you,' says Sebastian, offering a conciliatory smile. 'Will you excuse me for a few moments?' He pushes his chair back, grabs Wayne's elbow and marches him through the restaurant. He pushes him behind a frosted-glass partition wall.

'What the hell do you think you're playing at?' Sebastian spits through clenched teeth.

'Just trying to capture your attention. You haven't been returning my calls.'

'There didn't seem much point. You can't blackmail me now. Everyone knows what I am: it was on the front page of every newspaper.'

'But don't you think they'd like to know how you were screwing your junior staff? Innocent boys who are under age and too scared to say no to their powerful boss?'

'You little shit!' Sebastian pins Wayne to the glass wall by the collar of his jacket. 'What do you want?'

'A couple of hundred would do nicely for starters,' sneers Wayne, head thrown back, eyes defiant.

'And then what? Blood money for the rest of my life?'

'I'm sure we could come to some agreement. A lump sum perhaps, and reinstatement at the hotel?'

'You've got a nerve. What if I just deny it all – let you go to the police and spin your little fairy story? Who do you think they'll believe?'

'Well there's the physical evidence for starters. They could shine a torch up my arse and see that it's hardly virgin territory.'

'That could have been anyone.'

'Then there's the rather distinctive mole just above your cock. How do you think a meagre under-porter could know about that if he hadn't had his face pushed up against it as he struggled for mercy?'

'Shit!' exclaims Sebastian, feeling sick and conspicuous as waiters pass by them to reach the kitchen. He lets go of Wayne's jacket and runs his hand through his hair. What is he going to do now?

'I'll tell you what, Mr Craven. I'll let you go back to your Belgian friends, and I'll call you tomorrow when you've had time to think about what I've said. It's not as though I'm asking for money for nothing, you know. I'm perfectly happy to offer you the usual services for the right fee. Actually, I rather miss our little meetings. You aren't half bad when it comes to the old rumpy-pumpy!' And Wayne has the audacity to kiss Sebastian full on the lips before he slips around the glass wall and returns to his companion.

'Mr Craven?' says the maître d'. 'There is a telephone call for you.'

'Thank you,' says Sebastian, straightening his tie and following the man to the bar. He imagines it could be Wayne Briggs calling him from a nearby phone box just to taunt him further.

'Uncle Seb? It's Sascha.'

'Sascha darling, what's the matter? How did you know I was here?'

'I called that man who sits in the lobby of your building. He looked up the number for me.'

'What's going on?'

'It's Mummy, she's in hospital. She told me not to call you, but I'm here on my own – we didn't get Josh out of school – and there isn't anyone else to call.'

'What happened? Is she OK?'

'It's her head, she's been having really bad pains and then she fell down the stairs this afternoon. Nobody will tell me anything, and I'm scared.'

'Which hospital are you at?'

'St Thomas's.'

'I'll be over as soon as I can. Just wait for me there, OK?'

Sascha begins to cry. 'What if she dies like Daddy? What will we do then?'

'Now don't talk like that, darling. She's not going to die. Just sit tight and I'll be there right away.'

Sebastian puts the phone down and checks his watch. It's going to take him at least an hour to get to the hospital from east London. For some odd reason the only image that comes to mind is that of Felicity climbing up a ladder in her wedding dress to tear down the floral arrangement above the porch of the church.

'Carnations are for council houses!' she had screamed, scattering flowers and leaves across the churchyard, her veil billowing sideways in a sudden gust of wind.

CHAPTER TWENTY-THREE

The doctor is young. His white coat and stethoscope cannot belie the fact that he is wearing jeans and heavy black shoes. His desk is piled high with untidy stacks of books and papers, among which there are relics of everyday life.

Coffee mugs and biscuit crumbs.

The doctors office is a tiny, claustrophobic room with a dirty window looking out on to another equally dirty window. Daylight is valiantly dim. It is morning, and somewhere beyond the hospital walls there is sunshine. But not here.

'The diagnosis is not very good, I'm afraid.' The doctor plays with the folder spread out across his desk. He flicks through the pages, playing for time. Although the door is closed, the sound of laughter echoes down the corridor.

'It's leukaemia.' He looks up as he says the lethal word. It is a word that stands alone and deadly, like a gun at point-blank range. It is like a poster on the walls of the tube station, ascending on the moving staircase among the West End theatre productions and the adverts for Hennes and Miss Selfridge: *Leukaemia*

Kills. With a toll-free number for the Royal Cancer Society.

'Do you know what that is?' asks the young doctor with the fashionably long sideburns.

Claire nods.

She only came in for a routine check-up. To listen to the heartbeat of her unborn child.

'Your blood work shows a malignant proliferation of white blood cells in your bone marrow, which explains your recent anaemia. Your particular form of the disease is called acute lymphoblastic leukaemia; or ALL for short. With intensive therapy you have a good chance of remission, and we seem to have caught this pretty early on in the game.'

Leukaemia Kills.

My hair is going to fall out and I am going to die. It will be a slow, lingering death and I will gradually waste away to nothing in a hospital bed, with tubes in my arm and people whispering.

'What will happen to my baby?' Claire's voice sounds surprisingly normal. She had imagined it might come out of her throat like a death rattle, rasping and broken.

'You are less than three months pregnant,' says the doctor. 'I am afraid that the form of chemotherapy used to treat ALL is very aggressive, and your baby stands a high chance of miscarriage or deformity. In cases such as this, and with your still being in the first trimester, we normally recommend termination of the foetus.'

'How long do I have to live if I don't have the chemotherapy?'

'I wouldn't recommend that. With the chemotherapy we could extend remission for at least two years. Without it, you may only have as little as six months.'

'So there would be no possibility of ever having another baby?'

'There would be nothing to stop you from getting pregnant again, but even if you are in remission, the strain of carrying a pregnancy through to full term can jeopardize not only your own life but the survival of the baby as well.'

'So this is my last chance,' says Claire, looking directly at the doctor.

'If you're prepared to die for the sake of the baby, then yes, it is your last chance. But there's no guarantee that you'll live long enough to see this pregnancy through without treatment. Miracles do happen; I've seen it myself. People go into remission and live for twenty years without ever having another symptom of the disease. You can't rule out all possibilities, and you must always believe that there is that chance. Leukaemia is a frightening disease, but we can fight it. You really need a few days to consider the consequences of this, but I would like to get you back in as soon as possible to prevent things from developing any further. I can also arrange a counsellor, who will help you come to the right decision.'

'I don't need any social workers telling me what to do.'

'That's not what I'm suggesting. Do you have someone you can talk to at home?'

But Claire has no one.

She catches the number twenty-nine outside the hospital. At this time of day it is filled with headscarves and Tesco bags. She gets a window seat, and an elderly lady squeezes in beside her. She has a walking stick and a string bag filled with fruit and veg.

'Oh, I'm sorry, love!' she says as she prods Claire with a bony elbow. Her face is heavily powdered, and the powder rests in the creases of her cheeks like flour on unkneaded pastry. She has gimlet eyes. Currant eyes, black and sticky in the pastry of her face.

'I'm all sixes and sevens today. I had my Toby put down yesterday and I think I'm still feeling the effects. He had a dicky bladder. Kept weeing on the hearthrug, and in the end I had to make him wear a nappy, but he never took to it. Dogs don't like being all trussed up like that. Got to be cruel to be kind sometimes, haven't you, love?'

Claire offers the woman a tired smile and nods.

'Still, I don't have to worry about going down to our Flo's now. It used to be a right old palaver having to get back on the last bus from Reading so as I could let Toby out to do his business of a night. He was twelve, you know: that's eighty-four in dog years. The vet said he'd had a good life, and she could see I'd looked after him. Got him in 1986, on the Sunday after Prince

Andrew married that Fergie woman – look at them now, eh? It's the Queen I feel sorry for – and Diana's boys, of course. It can't have been easy after their mum died like that. Are you feeling all right, love?'

Claire attempts to brush away the tears which have suddenly blurred her vision. She doesn't have a hanky, not even a Kleenex screwed up in the bottom of her coat pocket. She uses her sleeve and smiles miserably at her neighbour.

'I'm fine. I get awful allergies at this time of year.'

'Oh, I know all about that, love. My little grand-daughter gets hay fever something rotten when the rape comes out. It *looks* lovely – all yellow, like – but it plays havoc with her little eyes. She had to have a ruddy great injection in her bottom last summer. The nurse said she hadn't seen a needle like that since she'd treated horses for diphtheria. Poor little mite.'

Claire stares out of the bus window, and the woman starts talking to someone on the other side of the aisle.

The bus pauses at a traffic light and there is one of those obscure cigarette adverts spread out over a huge billboard. If you didn't live in England, you'd wonder what the hell it was all about: just a piece of purple silk with a razor blade resting in the sensuous folds. Only the government health warning underneath offers a hint to the uninitiated. Claire wonders how much it costs to produce those adverts. She wonders how many people sit around a desk and come up with the next stupid idea. How can there be death in the world when there are people spending thousands of pounds designing adverts like that? It doesn't make sense.

Outside the off-licence there is a woman with a pram. She's talking to another woman with a root perm and her left leg in irons. She wears one of those clumsy-looking platform boots to make her legs the same length. The kind that Claire and Duncan had laughed about so casually outside the chip shop a few weeks ago. Now it doesn't seem so funny.

Claire has a funny thought. She stares at the Walls Ice Cream sign swinging outside the newsagent's. It's yellow and made of metal, and she knows it from her childhood.

Two strawberry Mivvies and a ninety-nine, please.

How can she die when there are Walls Ice Cream signs still swinging in the breeze? How can she die when there are so many episodes of *EastEnders* still to come? And Christmas trees? And Mars bars? And Friday nights? Will the world just come to an end when she dies, or will it carry on going without her, like it always has? Of course she knows the answer, she isn't thick, but it suddenly strikes her as terribly sad. There are things that she'll take with her that nobody else will ever know. Not important things, but little things like soft-boiled eggs and soldiers on a tray in front of *Watch with Mother*. Like the miners' strike and the power cuts, when the corner shop was lit only by candles. Like Catherine wheels and baked potatoes on Bonfire Night, and those boxes of matches that burned green and red when you struck them.

Now she knows why she has to have her baby.

She has to leave something behind. Something that isn't just a fridge-freezer or a Slumberdown Ortho-paedic. Her baby can start where she leaves off. She knows it's going to be a girl, not because the doctors have told her, but because she *feels* it. It will be a girl and it will have everything that Claire never had. She turns to the woman with the powdered face.

'I'm going to have a baby,' she says.

'Are you, love? Well, that's lovely. When's it due?'

'August.'

'You must be over the moon.'

'I am.'

'Have you thought about names yet, or is it a bit too early for that? My daughter called her two Emma and Rose. What do you want to go calling them such funny old-fashioned names for, I said? I wanted her to call one of them Cilla – I've always thought that was a cheerful name – but she just laughed and thought I was making a joke.'

'It's going to be a girl. And I'm going to call her Claire.'

'Oh, lovely! *Claire de lune*. I used to know a Claire when I was at school. Claire Edwards. She came from one of those poor families that smell. At the Christmas party one year the teachers took her and gave her a bath, put her in a pretty little dress and brought her out into the assembly hall smelling of Yardley's talc. We were only about seven or eight at the time and everybody wanted to hold her hand when we did the

Bluebell Windows. She was like a different person in that little dress. Looking back, it was probably a bit cruel of them to do that because the next day she was just smelly old Claire again, and we were all scared of getting the lurgy if she came anywhere near. Children can be very cruel.'

'This is my stop,' says Claire.

'Mind how you go, my love. Eat plenty of oranges and buy yourself a support bra. It's never too early!'

And Claire steps off the bus into the mid-morning sunshine.

She has a lot to do.

And from now on, every day is precious.

CHAPTER TWENTY-FOUR

'Darling, I thought I was having an aneurysm. I just blacked out at the top of the stairs and I came to at the bottom. Fortunately the stair carpet is well padded, otherwise I might have done myself a real injury. One more reason to thank the Lord that I'm rich enough to afford a hundred per cent virgin wool.' Felicity is talking to a friend on the phone. She's wearing dark glasses and has a small plaster on the bridge of her nose.

'No, I've never suffered with my sinuses before. The doctor said it was probably due to the recent change in temperature. I can't say it was particularly pleasant, having them root around up my nostrils like that; I thought they were going to come out of the top of my head at one point. I had about twenty metres of cotton wool stuffed up there until last Friday. I've still got a bit of a black eye, but as long as it's gone before next Tuesday I'll be fine. Poor Sascha had me six feet under. She's been terribly sweet ever since. Keeps bringing me cups of tea and asking if there's anything I need. All Josh wanted to know was how painful it was having a needle pushed up my nose!'

It is the fifteenth of April, Thursday afternoon. Five

days before the tenth anniversary of Craven's. Although Felicity is extremely busy with preparations for the event, her desk is clear. On it sits a small glass bowl of Fire and Ice roses, flown in from some foreign greenhouse, each rose perfectly formed but sadly lacking in perfume; a Tiffany framed photograph of Sascha and Josh, taken by a professional photographer in the grounds of Blythwood; and three Leonidas white chocolate pralines in a tiny presentation box with the Craven's logo embossed on the lid. Felicity has been indulging herself again.

So what's new?

'I must dash, darling. I'm up to my ears with meetings and arrangements. Call me at home tonight and I'll tell you all about that insufferable man from the marquee company – he's been making my life a misery. Ciao, darling!' Felicity replaces her phone and spins around in her chair to look through the window on to the garden. She has paid every resident in the square five hundred quid, and given them an invitation to the dinner, just to get the garden to herself for six days. It is a plain little patch of grass with a couple of trees and black iron railings to keep away the riff-raff. The residents seldom use it: it's too much of a bother to go out there with a key for the gate, just to sit on a weathered old bench in full view of the neighbours. It's more ornamental than anything else.

Felicity is having a marquee set up. She's covering the entire garden with a canopy of grey and cream Pierre Frey linen. Chelsea Garden Centre is bringing in truck-loads of gravel and bamboo. There will be several waterfalls. Her vision is Asian simplicity. Ecological sensitivity with Calvin Klein undertones.

Felicity has been to see her bank manager. He has offered her a sizable loan, and she has offered him investment opportunities in her new venture. She has called upon her richest friends. They are only too eager to buy a chunk of Felicity's guaranteed success. She thinks she may have found the perfect property, but the current owners are still haggling about the price. Arabs can be so difficult to deal with, especially when it comes to keeping appointments. She has achieved all of this in less than two weeks – not bad, even for Felicity.

She has been avoiding Sebastian since the embarrassing scene at the hospital when Sascha called him in. He really did appear quite concerned when he arrived, but once he realized that she wasn't dying he soon regained his composure, and his last words to her as he stormed out of the room were: 'I hope you rot in hell!' Not the kind of bedside manner one might expect in a private hospital room with Colefax & Fowler curtains and an en suite bathroom.

He re-employed a young under-porter during her two-day absence in hospital, and gave him a promotion, which struck her as rather odd because it was Sebastian who had dismissed the boy in the first place. Wayne Something-or-other. A shifty type, but good with the guests. She didn't bother to question Sebastian about the incident; surely he had his reasons.

Felicity isn't interested. She doesn't speak to anyone below management level if she can help it.

She saw Ross at his restaurant last night. She was dining out with Min Hogg from *The World of Interiors* and Piers von Westenholz. Ross watched them from his table in the corner. He sent someone else over with the wine list. It's all rather ridiculous for him to behave in such a childish manner, particularly as it was he who ended their relationship. It was all about money, obviously.

He sees Felicity as faded grandeur.

Mottled gilt and exposed gesso.

Like something that Piers might sell in his shop on the Pimlico Road.

Sod him! If he wants to be a restaurateur for the rest of his life, then let him. She has heard that he's seeing Bettina Carlton-Blye. They were spotted last week at some piss-elegant Soho restaurant that Felicity wouldn't be seen dead in. One of those places with flock wallpaper and hamburgers. Bettina has no style. A lot of money, but absolutely no style. She had her fortieth birthday party at Stringfellow's. She wears Zandra Rhodes and dyes her hair. She is seen around town with Joan Collins and that television chap who does the supermarket sweep game. Who cares? They're all a bunch of wankers anyway.

Felicity eats another praline and checks her watch to see if it's too early to call Tokyo.

'Miss Craven, I have a lady here to see you,' Marissa's voice interrupts over the intercom.

'I don't have any appointments. Who is it?'

'She won't say. She says she's an old friend.'

Felicity pauses. She doesn't have any old friends – none with whom she would wish to be reacquainted, anyway.

'Tell her to leave a card. I'm busy right now.'

'She . . . I'm sorry, you can't go—'

The door to Felicity's office bursts rudely open and in walks a striking woman wearing a Chanel suit and enough L'Air du Temps to fumigate a toxic dump. She has gold-heeled shoes and a diamond ring the size of a quail's egg. Marissa stands in the doorway looking helplessly unassertive.

'What is this?' questions Felicity sharply. 'You can't just barge in like this.'

'Why, I just knew you'd be thrilled to see me!' says the woman in a ghastly American drawl. 'I was in London for a few days, looking to buy a little piece of property, and I thought I'd call by and introduce myself. You have a simply charming place here, Miss Craven. May I?' And the woman indicates a small armchair opposite Felicity's desk. She sits without waiting for an invitation. Felicity shoots Marissa a look.

'I have to go to my dental appointment. I'm already late,' says Marissa apologetically.

'Oh, close the door and go!' says Felicity.

Charming as always.

Marissa closes the door of the office, leaving the two women in private.

'Angelica Schloss, I presume,' sneers Felicity.

'Right on the button!'

'What the hell are you doing in my hotel?'

'How gracious! You are no less generous in person than you are over the phone. I guess I wanted to see you in the flesh. After all, you were my worst nightmare for seven years. You could have ruined my life.'

'So you ruined mine instead? How thoughtful of you to come all this way to gloat. I hope it was worth it.' Felicity can barely contain her anger. She can feel her pulse pounding in her throat.

'I didn't come here to cause a scene, Miss Craven. I was hoping that maybe we could readdress the issue of reimbursement. I am still open to the possibility of giving you some cash, despite the fact that you were so rude to me over the phone. I have a conscience and I am a Christian. I cannot bear to think that I might be the cause of someone else's misery.' Angelica Schloss actually raises her clasped hands at this point, as though invoking some invisible power of goodness.

'You're wasting your time. Don't you have some shopping to do?' snaps Felicity.

'I cannot give you up. I will not be defeated by this. I must give you some recompense for the life you spent with David before he met me.'

'I told you before: I don't want your pity or your measly seven million. I can cope just fine by myself.'

'I have something for you.' Angelica reaches into her black suede handbag and removes a folded manila envelope. It is thick and heavy and it falls with a substantial thud on Felicity's desk. The pralines go skidding across the highly polished surface and land in Felicity's lap.

'What's this?'

'The deeds to the property you've been looking at in Green Park.'

'You bought the hotel on Clarges Street?' Felicity practically erupts with fury. It comes out as a dangerous whisper, choked and venomous.

'I sure did. That Mr Al Sabah is such a gentleman. I signed the papers just this morning.'

'You conniving, evil Yankee bitch!' screams Felicity, jumping up from her desk and jabbing her finger like a poison dart. 'Are you deliberately trying to make an enemy out of me or do you just get some kind of perverted thrill out of this?'

'Now, hold on there. Just stop right there, Miss Firecracker!' Angelica is crouching into her chair, clutching her handbag to her. 'I think you've got me all wrong. The deeds are in *your* name. I bought the property for *you*.'

Gobsmacked is a working-class word that comes to mind.

Felicity attempts to regain a modicum of composure. She returns to her desk and removes the papers from the manila envelope. There is her name, printed clearly at the top of the agreement.

'You just need to sign the places marked in yellow and return them to the lawyer's office before Monday.

It's a generous lease, and I've included two million toward renovations.'

'And what is your stake in this?' asks Felicity.

'Nothing. It is simply a gift. I have no legal rights to the property.'

'And can you keep quiet about this? I can only accept this if you promise not to blab your mouth off to everyone in town. I will not be perceived as a charity case under any circumstances.'

'You have my word, Miss Craven.' Angelica Schloss extends her hand across the desk. 'Is it a deal?'

'Not so fast. I still don't trust you. You come waltzing in here, expecting me to buy the fact that due to some innate social conscience you flew all the way to London to buy a hotel for me as salve for you guilt? You could have phoned. You could have wired the money without going to all this trouble. And how did you find out about the hotel on Clarges Street? It's supposed to be a secret.'

Angelica smiles. And when she smiles she closes her eyes, like a nun. Or a patient schoolteacher. Felicity would like to wipe that sanctimonious smile off her face with the back of her hand.

'I know several of the directors at Glendale Estates. Over the years I met them through business dinners and suchlike. I know that you approached Jerry Ackerman regarding an investment possibility in your new venture. Robin Bleesdale from Promotions has been particularly kind since David's death. We speak often. He was very close to David, you know.'

'Yes, I did know actually. I was David's wife, remember?'

'Excuse me, honey, I seem to have a knack for saying the wrong thing.'

'Excuse *me*, honey, you seem to have a knack for being an interfering cow.'

Angelica shrugs her black Chanel shoulders. Her hair is swept back to reveal expensively gaudy earrings the size and shape of golden croissants. Felicity recognizes them from one of her magazines.

'I did not come to London just to purchase your hotel, Miss Craven. I have reasons of my own to be here. I have been thinking of taking a second home in London and so . . . oh, to hell with it. You're going to find out sooner or later. I have bought Blythwood House from the partners at Glendale Estates. Robin told me it was going up for sale, and so it just seemed the perfect opportunity. I saw the photographs in *House & Garden* a couple of years ago – you have made it lovely. I just know I am going to enjoy living there.'

Felicity is stunned for a second time. This is almost worse than finding out that David had been cheating on her. Somehow this is more of a violation.

'You're like some kind of bloodsucking predator,' says Felicity in a controlled, unwavering monotone. 'Your sole purpose in life seems to be this pathetic, parasitic desire to steal my life from me and take it over. Are you so totally insecure that you have to aspire to be somebody so far out of your league they could be in another galaxy? You will never be me. You will always be just a poor imitation, like an old whore in an expensive but unsuitable dress. You can take my husband and you can take my money – hell, you can even take my house and everything in it – but you will never take my *class*. Now I suggest you get your arse off my upholstery and get out of this building before I do something unladylike. Do you get the picture, Mrs Schloss?' Felicity is standing now, grasping the edge of her desk with white-knuckled fingers.

'Snippy, snippy!' says Angelica Schloss, gathering her wits about her like a fallen cape. 'I should have known you'd be less than civil with your thanks, but I had to see this through. You're obviously still very bitter about the whole thing, but I can assure you that I came here only out of the goodness of my heart. The hotel is yours, Miss Craven. Do with it what you will. I've said my piece and I'll leave you alone.'

'Get out!'

Angelica stands. She must be wearing a Wonderbra to have a cleavage like that.

'He was going to marry me, you know.'

'You'd have been welcome to him.'

'I'm at the Ritz until Wednesday if you wish to call me.'

'Thanks for the information. I'll inform the IRA.'

Angelica smiles as she opens the office door.

Standing in the corridor outside Marissa's office is Wayne Briggs. He is holding a parcel, and he nods at Angelica Schloss as she departs.

'What are you doing loitering outside my office?' demands Felicity.

'There was nobody around, Miss Craven, and you need to sign for this parcel.'

'Why didn't you just knock?'

'I, er . . . You had someone in there with you.'

'Oh, give me that.' Felicity signs the clipboard and takes the parcel to Marissa's desk.

Wayne slouches off to the lobby.

There is a red light flashing on Marissa's intercom switchboard. A red light that indicates the connection through to Felicity's office is still operational. The entire conversation between Felicity and Angelica was broadcast to Marissa's office.

And the door was open.

And Wayne Briggs was standing in the corridor.

Felicity sighs.

So what? He's only a porter. Too dense even to knock on her door. Probably thinking about pop music and girls and going to the pub on a Friday night. She knows the type.

Thick as two short planks.

CHAPTER TWENTY-FIVE

'Mummy, this is Thierry. He lives in Brussels.'

Sabrina Craven appears confused. The poodles are snapping at her heels, barking and leaping in their coordinated housecoats. They think they're going out for a walk on the Heath.

'Terry who? I don't think we know any Terrys, do we?'

'*Thierry*, Mummy – it's French . . . or Belgian.' Sebastian looks at Thierry for confirmation.

'Hello, Mrs Craven, I am very pleased to make your acquaintance. Sebastian has told me a lot about you.' Thierry offers Sabrina his hand.

'There was Terry McMichael, of course, but he died in sixty-three. Fell off the end of the pier – completely sozzled, he was. I haven't been back to Brighton since.'

'I wanted to show Thierry the house, Mummy. Why don't you go and ask Mrs Leigh if she'll put out some tea in the drawing room?'

'She's been moving the furniture again. I keep bumping into things.' Sabrina puts her hand up to her head as though searching for something. 'My tiara – what happened to my tiara?'

'You don't have a tiara, Mummy. Now go and find Mrs Leigh. I'm taking Thierry upstairs. I need my tuxedo for the party tomorrow night.'

'There aren't any plums left. I ate them all,' she says as she leads the dancing dogs across the hall and into the kitchen.

'See what I mean?' says Sebastian. 'I don't know how we're going to cope with her tomorrow, but Felicity insists Mummy comes. We've hired an escort, but we've told Mummy that he's a bachelor without a partner for the night. Apparently he's very dashing.'

'This is a beautiful old house. How long has it been in the family?' asks Thierry, appraising the original mouldings along the top of the wallpapered dado.

'Three generations. My grandfather bought it in 1927. It was built in 1860 by a wealthy industrialist and his wife who was a painter. Mummy has an old visitors' book somewhere. William Morris stayed here several times, and a lot of the old Bloomsbury clan used to set up camp at weekends. Oscar Wilde came to dinner in 1895, a few weeks before he was jailed.'

'Sebastian?'

'Yes?' They pause mid-flight. Sebastian turns to look at Thierry on the step below.

'You really do not mind that Solange is staying at the apartment? You seemed a little upset when you came over this afternoon.'

'Of course I don't mind,' says Sebastian. 'I was just a little surprised to find her there, that's all. I'd been hoping we might have had an hour in bed or some-thing. I wanted it to be a surprise.'

'Solange would have understood, you know. We have been friends for many years and she would not have been offended if we had disappeared into the bedroom for a little nooky.'

'Sometimes, Thierry, there are some English expressions that you just shouldn't use. They don't sound right coming from you.'

Thierry reaches up and pinches a substantial patch of Sebastian's arse.

'Ouch!'

'Serves you right for being so rude. Now get up those stairs and show me where you used to fantasize about meeting a stunning Belgian man, when you were a little boy.'

Thierry chases Sebastian up the last flight of stairs and they grapple on the landing.

Little boys playing grown-up games.

Poppy chooses the restaurant this evening, a small, intimate place tucked away on a side street in Soho, and very popular with the camp theatrical crowd. The walls are dark green with huge pink flamingos. There are games on the tables and Steph, the hostess and namesake of the restaurant, leans provocatively across the small bar, exchanging wisecracks and pleasantries with her patrons. She kisses Poppy on both cheeks when they arrive.

'French-style, darling!' Steph screams, adding a

third kiss to the ritual of their loud and meretricious greeting.

Heads turn.

People smile.

Sebastian has never been here before, and he feels unsure of himself as he hesitates by the doorway, with Thierry and Solange close behind. Poppy's hippy friend Dee is with them. Sebastian has never met her before, but she seems like an interesting person.

Attractively boyish.

'Come on in, you lot!' shouts Steph, raking her fingers swiftly through the peroxide tangle of her hair. 'I'm not going to bite!'

Poppy finds them a corner table. They have Pick Up Sticks and a snowdome of the Empire State Building. A party of men at the next table are singing Happy Birthday to a caustic-looking old man with purple hair and silver rings. They applaud and shriek when he blows out the candle stuck in his bread pudding.

'I didn't think you still had it in you, Neville,' somebody shouts.

'I'm getting it in me a lot more often than you are, dear!'

More applause.

Thierry shoots a look at Sebastian, who in turn scowls and shakes his head as if to warn him not to offend Poppy. This is her favourite place in the whole wide world.

'Isn't this fabulous, darling?' she shouts above the din.

'It's very cosy,' says Sebastian, feeling Thierry kick him sharply under the table.

'Steph cooks most of the food herself, and it's all scrummy. Solange, have you ever tried steak-and-kidney pie?'

'I do not think so, but I do like kidneys very much.' Solange looks particularly beautiful in the half-light of the restaurant. Her eyes are like a husky's: steel-blue and ringed with dark violet.

'Sebastian tells me you come to London quite often.'

'Yes, every week or so. I sell art to galleries here. I like this city.'

'I've only been to Brussels once, but I remember that gorgeous old square with all the merchants' houses decorated with gold. We ate at a fish restaurant just off there – horrid displays of dead fish and octopus with lemons jammed in their gaping jaws. Very off-putting.'

'That is mainly where the tourists go,' smiles Solange condescendingly. 'We do not eat there.'

Sebastian sees Dee glancing at Solange as though she just spat on her shoe. He attempts to take the chill off the conversation by smiling brightly and leaning across to touch Dee's arm.

'I'm glad we meet at last. I've seen your picture on Poppy's kitchen mural.'

'What do you think of your own recent addition?'

asks Dee. 'It's considered quite a privilege to be included in that motley crew.'

'I feel very honoured,' says Sebastian, looking over at Poppy with affection. Poppy blows him a kiss and mouths, *Thank you, darling*.

They are given menus and they order drinks. The food is all good old-fashioned British stuff, the kind Sebastian has always enjoyed at The Forum. Yorkshire pudding with onion gravy, whiskied mackerel pâté – that kind of thing. He would be perfectly comfortable here if he didn't have to worry about Thierry and Solange. He's concerned that they might feel it's all just a bit too *pedestrian*.

Thierry in his Façonnable houndstooth check and Solange in her severe midnight blue.

'*Bon appetit*,' says Thierry when their starters arrive. Sebastian sees that both Solange and Thierry have ordered the same thing: a simple green salad with oil and vinegar.

'I'd like to raise a toast,' says Sebastian, lifting his gin and tonic. 'To new friends.'

'To new friends,' they cheer in unison.

Now they all fall silent and stare at their food. Sebastian is wondering what to say next when Poppy interrupts his thoughts.

'We had a very depressing weekend.' She looks at Dee. 'A friend of ours, a neighbour of Dee's, actually, has recently found out that she has leukaemia.'

A general murmur of detached concern.

'And she's pregnant.'

'How sad,' says Thierry. 'What happens about the baby? Will she have an abortion?'

'She doesn't want an abortion; she's against it,' says Dee.

'But won't the radiation treatment, or the chemotherapy, kill the baby anyway?' asks Thierry.

'She has decided not to have the treatment. She's having the baby at the cost of her own life. I'm not sure if she's very brave or completely misguided. Personally I would do anything I could to prolong my life. What happens to the baby when she dies?' Poppy allows her question to float between them.

'What about the father?' asks Sebastian. 'Surely he can look after it.'

'We don't know who the father is. Apparently she had a one-night stand with somebody from her office. She was a virgin. It's bloody typical: this fella just got her drunk, dragged her off to a hotel and practically raped her.' Dee voices her opinion in no uncertain terms.

'Has she approached him about the baby?' asks Thierry.

'He's dead,' says Dee. 'She hasn't told us what he died of. I get the impression it was some kind of industrial accident.'

'She has a lovely boyfriend,' says Poppy, mopping up gravy with a chunk of bread. 'They met through the classifieds and he's being amazingly supportive. Since he found out about her leukaemia he's been practically living at her house, trying to help her through the trauma of it all. It makes it all the more sad that she's met someone, when there's so little chance of them ever being happy together.'

'Do you think he will take the baby when she dies?' asks Solange.

'I don't know, they haven't really thought that far ahead. Claire's not wealthy, and she has no savings. Duncan's comfortably off but he's no Donald Trump.'

'What about relatives?'

'She doesn't have anyone. Her parents are dead. No brothers or sisters.'

'What a mess! It makes one realize just how vulnerable we all are, doesn't it? Somehow it brings things into perspective,' says Thierry.

'I think it's hard to even try to imagine how it must feel to be in that kind of situation. We all think we know what we'd do if we were given six months to live, but I honestly believe that none of us can really know what we'd do until we're faced with the ultimatum. Claire told me she'd always thought she would spend the entire six months in bed, crying, unable to carry on any kind of normal existence. And yet she's coping remarkably well. I haven't seen her shed a single tear, and she's been going to work as though nothing has changed. It's admirable,' says Poppy.

'I've always thought I would spend the entire credit limit on my Access card and travel to all the places I've ever wanted to visit,' says Dee.

'But how could you enjoy any of it, knowing that you were going to die at the end of it all?' asks Thierry.

'Now that's where the question gets more difficult. That's why we can't really tell how we would react until it actually happens. It's more likely that I'd try every kind of freaky cure that's available – move to California and let them pump me full of herbal infusions and squirt yogurt up my backside.'

Nervous laughter.

'Well, I'd have lunch at McDonald's every day for the entire six months and go back to smoking two daily packs of ciggies!' says Poppy.

'Sex without condoms!' joins in Sebastian.

'Sunbathing without sunblock,' says Thierry.

'Riding a Harley without a crash helmet, and bungee jumping,' says Dee.

'What about you, Solange?' asks Thierry. 'What would you do for your last six months on earth?'

'I'd probably kill myself,' she says, much to the disappointment of her companions, who were obviously expecting her to suggest something a bit less dramatic.

'How horrible,' says Poppy.

'I don't believe you,' says Thierry.

'It's true. I don't think I could just hang around waiting for it to happen. It would be like sitting in a jumbo jet that has just lost its engines and is plunging towards the ground. The tension would kill me.'

'But what if there was some kind of miracle? A cure, or something that suddenly allowed you to live for much longer than you had originally expected? Isn't there always that chance of survival?' asks Poppy.

'Maybe, I don't know.' Solange is obviously beginning to regret her rash statement.

'Well, I would never have the courage to kill myself. I'm too much of a coward,' says Poppy. 'I can't even shave for the terror of drawing blood.'

'I didn't know you shaved, Poppy,' laughs Thierry.

Dee nearly chokes on a gulp of white wine.

'My *legs*, darling. And sometimes, if I'm feeling particularly adventurous, my bikini line.'

'Since when did you last wear a bikini?' asks Dee, laughing.

'Never! But that doesn't mean I have to walk around looking as though there's a nest of mice in my knickers!'

'Now then, who's having the Lancashire hotpot?' It's Steph, helping their waiter to deliver the main courses.

Their morbid discussion is broken off, and with the main course comes a flutter of frivolous topics, giving way occasionally to a bite-sized chunk of culture introduced by either Solange or Thierry.

Twentieth-century postmodernism brushes shoulders with biorhythms.

Brad Pitt and Jackie Collins compete in the arena with Hieronymus Bosch and Aldous Huxley.

The conversation takes a swift nosedive into the pudding.

Treacle tart and jam roly-poly. And custard with everything.

'So, this girl with the leukaemia,' says Sebastian, for want of something better to say. 'Has she actually made any decision about what to do with the last months of her life?'

'Not really,' responds Poppy. 'She's going to keep on working until it gets too much for her. She's OK at the moment, but she gets tired easily.'

'Has she told anyone at work about this? Maybe they could help her out. Hang on, is this the girl you told me about? The girl who works for Glendale Estates?'

'Glendale Estates, that's it,' says Dee, innocently spooning her pudding to her mouth. Sebastian recognizes the expression of dawning realization on Poppy's face.

'That's your brother-in-law's company, isn't it?'

'Yes, it is. I wonder if I could have a quiet word with one of the directors – see if there's anything they can do,' suggests Sebastian.

'Oh, that would be great!' says Dee, momentarily forgetting her gingered rice pudding.

'Do you know what her position is?'

'She's just a typist, I think, but she's been there for years.'

'And the chap who got her pregnant – do you know anything more about him, apart from the fact that he's dead?'

'Well, surely there haven't been that many blokes in the company dropping dead over the last few months.'

'There's David, my brother-in-law, for one . . .'

'You don't think . . .?'

'No! It's not possible. David with a lowly typist? It doesn't make sense.' But Sebastian doesn't sound convinced.

'It was just one night, after a Christmas party. Lots of booze. A willing little virgin and an extremely powerful boss. Oh, my God, do you think that's how it happened?' Dee is mortified.

'There's only one way to find out,' says Thierry. 'You'll have to ask her.'

Poppy orders coffee and liqueurs.

Sebastian shakes the snowdome and a blizzard swirls chaotically around Manhattan. What would Felicity say if she knew about this sudden revelation? He can see his dear sister's sententious expression right now, as though he's peering into a crystal ball.

She's going to blow a gasket.

CHAPTER TWENTY-SIX

It's Hitler's birthday.

April 20th. They just said so on the radio.

Claire can't remember the last time she was hungry. She eats her Weetabix one spoonful at a time, pausing in between, watching the slurry in her bowl grow progressively more dense as the milk soaks into the bloated wad of wheat. She doesn't want it, but she has to have it.

For the sake of the baby.

'The time now is eight-forty-five, and here's another golden oldie from Neil Sedaka.'

Claire stares at the crack in the corner of the breakfast-bar melamine. It is an unhygienic crack filled with the crumbs of ages, packed down with layers of dishcloth grease and spilled drinks. The kind of crack they warn you about in domestic science classes, like bluebottles landing on the butter. It's a health hazard and should be avoided at all costs. Claire can see Mrs Leadbeater now, standing at the front of the school kitchens with her moulded white hair and her pinched, angular face. Rows of girls in aprons, hand-stitched in gingham and hessian. Rows of cookers like a gas showroom, back to back as though refusing to speak.

Claire still has her old school recipe book in the kitchen drawer, covered with cling film and Sellotape to save it from spills. It has rubber-stamp pictures on the front – a pie, a fish, a loaf of bread. Claire used to decorate all her school books appropriately, and she was commended for her originality. Inside the book, in Claire's schoolgirl hand, there are pages dusted with flour and splattered with milk. Recipes from a time before girls knew that they could be independently self-supportive, before microwaves and Marks & Spencer's prepared cuisine.

Queen of Puddings.

Mock Roast Pork.

Wartime recipes for women on a tight shoestring. Women who had nothing better to think about than a tasty meal for their hard-working husbands at the end of the day.

Cream of Tartare.

Crystallized Violets.

Batters that had to be beaten no more than forty times before they were in danger of curdling. Nothing curdles any more.

This is the first day that Claire has taken off work since she learned of her death sentence. It has been the long Easter weekend. Yesterday was a bank holiday, and Duncan took her to Kew Gardens.

When the alarm went off at six-thirty, she was already wide awake and staring at the Artexed ceiling.

She doesn't sleep very well these days, and yet she is constantly tired. Her bedroom has become a torture chamber filled with terrifying dreams, and she prefers to nap on the sofa with the electric fire on and the telly turned down low. That way, if she wakes up in the middle of the night, it isn't so frightening. She can look at the adverts and the strange programmes that they broadcast in the small hours of the morning, and she can pretend the world is carrying on as normal. People buying fabric conditioner. People planning holidays. People waking up in the morning and not having to face the sickening truth that they won't ever see snow again.

She watched a documentary about Pennsylvania in America. There are Amish settlements where the people still live on farms without modern conveniences. No electricity or machinery, and they ride around in horse-drawn buggies, like *Little House on the Prairie*, in bonnets and simple, home-made clothing. Something about the simplicity of Amish life offered Claire a brief spark of hope. Maybe in a self-contained world like that she could turn her back on modern-day life, and maybe leukaemia wouldn't exist beneath a patchwork quilt.

She can shed no tears. Her outward emotional responses are impotent, and she faces each day with the stoic expression of one about to swing from the gallows. The inevitability of death can sometimes seem to Claire as a relief. Let it come. Let it swallow her whole, and have done with all this supposition.

Everything is changed, spoiled and irretrievably altered, as though a black sock has been inadvertently dumped into her life along with the whites. The colours are insipid now, and what was once pleasurable is now painfully trivial.

Duncan has been remarkable. For someone who could so easily have walked away he has proved to be the light of Claire's life. He comes round every day after work, bringing with him food that he thinks she might want to eat. Food that sometimes she has to push down the sink with the tap running, so as not to hurt his feelings. He puts his arm around her on the sofa and they watch TV, not talking, just watching the normal lives on the screen. Sometimes Dee might pop over, and the three of them even manage to laugh. It's barren laughter for Claire, and light relief for the other two. An antidote for the tragedy which lurks in the corners, tainting the April atmosphere with its smell of November leaves.

Claire knows that they all think she's crazy to keep the baby. She knows that her decision smacks of martyrdom, but she's not doing this for herself. There are no thoughts of glory or heroism connected to this apparently selfless act; it is merely a question of morals. God will help her through. She honestly believes that, even though she stopped going to church years ago. It would be hypocritical to start going now, just because she wants something.

Dee says there is no such thing as God. Dee is an atheist, and she says that the human race is being presumptuous by believing in an afterlife. Do we believe in a heaven for insects and animals? Aren't we just tiny granules of nothing in a universe that could be destroyed as easily as a foot destroys an ant? What gives us the right to believe in heaven? It's just something thought up to keep us warm at night; a comforting story to be passed on in the nursery when children cry at the thunder. We've been burdened by our intelligence. We have too much time to think about things and too little courage to face the naked truth of the matter. We live, we die – end of story.

Duncan says he's an agnostic. He believes in something but he isn't quite sure what it is. It most certainly isn't the traditional image of God with a beard and a white robe, peering down through the clouds, and it has absolutely nothing to do with going to church and praying. But he believes in an afterlife; a kind of psychic energy that we create when we're alive and which lives on after we die. He thinks that it's something like soundwaves, a kind of uncoded frequency filled with the mutterings of ages past. It isn't a theory that offers much consolation, but it's better than nothing, and he hasn't ruled out the possibility of reincarnation.

Claire rinses out her breakfast bowl and swallows the pills the doctor has given her. It's a beautiful day – a mockery of everything she's feeling. The bulbs are up in the garden and there are fresh green leaves on the trees. What an unusually startling contrast against the clear blue of the sky. Two colours that Claire would never put together and which seem to make an almost perfect coupling: sky-blue and spring-green, like brush strokes on a china plate.

The post clatters through the letter box. She has another appointment at the hospital – an overnight stay this time. Debenhams are having an end-of-season sale. The water rates are going up. It's the kind of post she always gets, but today it seems particularly pathetic. Some people get letters written on pretty paper, and others get cards saying *Thank You* and *I'm Thinking of You*. Even at Christmas, Claire is lucky if she gets enough cards to fill her mantelpiece, and most of those are economy cards from Woolworths that come from the girls at work.

After the postman, just as Claire is standing in the hallway, Dee rings the bell. Claire knows that it's Dee because she can see her red jacket through the patterned glass.

'I noticed you were at home,' says Dee. 'Are you all right?'

'I've taken a sick day. There's nothing wrong, I just couldn't face going in after the weekend. Have you got time for a quick cuppa?' asks Claire, in her dusty pink candlewick dressing gown.

Dee glances at her oversized watch.

'Sure, just a quickie.' And she comes in, smelling of fags and bringing with her a stain of colour in a suddenly monochromatic setting.

'I was just feeling sorry for myself,' says Claire, filling the kettle. 'It's not a good idea to spend too much time dwelling on things. I'd have been better off going into work.'

'You deserve a day off. I'm surprised you haven't taken one sooner.' Dee seats herself at the breakfast bar. She doesn't smoke when she's with Claire now.

'How was your dinner last night?' asks Claire.

'It was rather nice, actually. We talked about you.'

'What?'

'Poppy was telling them about your predicament. Did you know that Poppy's friend Sebastian is David Glendale's brother-in-law?'

Claire has plugged the kettle in, and she doesn't turn to look at Dee.

'How does Poppy know Sebastian Craven?' Her voice is light.

'Oh, they've been friends for a couple of months. He rescued her when her car broke down. She doesn't live very far from Sebastian's sister.'

'Oh,' says Claire, messing around with the sugar container.

'Did you know David Glendale?'

'He was my boss.'

'It was a tragic accident, him getting blown up like that.'

'Mmm.'

'Can I ask you a really personal question? You don't have to answer it if it makes you uncomfortable.'

'What?' Claire hasn't moved from the corner of the kitchen. She's fiddling with the tie on her dressing gown.

'Is David Glendale the father of your child?'

'What on earth gives you that idea?' laughs Claire. 'He was my boss, a very powerful man. I only ever saw him once or twice a month. Anyway, he was married with two kids. Why would he look at me, of all people?'

'There's nothing wrong with you. Why shouldn't he look at you? And as for being married, I've never known a man who wouldn't jump at the opportunity to be unfaithful were the possibility thrown at him.'

'I didn't throw myself at him!' snaps Claire, before she has time to realize her slip-up.

'Oh, so it *was* David Glendale,' says Dee conclusively.

Claire practically runs over to the breakfast bar and grabs Dee's hand.

'You can't tell anyone about this, Dee. It's deadly secret. Promise me you won't breathe a word of it to anyone – not Poppy, not anyone.'

'Why are you so worried, love? He's dead – what possible harm can arise from telling people who the father of your child is? Sebastian reckons he can probably get you some kind of compensation from the company.'

'Oh, my God, you've *told* him?' Claire moans, raising her hand to her face.

'We kind of worked it out for ourselves.'

'I'll never be able to go into the office again! Everyone'll know and I'll be the laughing stock. Oh, God, this is awful, just awful.' She goes through to the living room and Dee follows her.

'Come on, Claire, this could be a really good thing. You could quit work, get a lump sum of cash and take things easy. They might even offer to help out when the baby's born. This could be the break you've been looking for. Sebastian is really nice; you'll like him.'

'I was such a fool, such a stupid idiot. I never thought this would get out. I never dreamed anyone would be able to find out that it was him of all people.'

'I don't really think it makes much of a difference *who* it was, love. The main thing is that now you've got the chance to profit from your mistake. God knows, you deserve a break.' Dee puts her arm around Claire, and Claire sniffles into the arm of the oversized sofa.

Pregnant with a billionaire's baby and now I'm crying in the arms of a lesbian!

'The kettle's boiling. I'll go and make that tea,' says Dee, disentangling herself.

Claire remains crushed among the cushions. This feels like a really bad thing. She feels like she's been dragged on to a fairground ride against her will, and the gypsy men are going to spin her round and round until the money falls out of her pockets and she's sick. She can't even begin to imagine Sebastian Craven hearing all about this over dinner in London. He must think she's some kind of common little tart in a short skirt with ladders in her tights. He probably laughed about her when he got home with his sophisticated friends; they would call her a whore and a slag and they would say it serves her right for sleeping with the boss. How degrading! How utterly horrible. She's cringing just thinking about it.

'Here's your tea, love.'

'Do you think he'll have told anyone at the office yet?'

'I shouldn't think so. It's only just after nine, and he's organizing a big party at his hotel today. Poppy's going with him, actually. Do you want me to give her a call?'

'Oh, would you, Dee? Tell her to call him and thank him very much for his concern, but not to tell anyone at my office. Tell him it's very important that no one knows.'

'Hang on, then. I'll give her a call now.' Dee goes to the phone.

Claire listens to the conversation, plaiting her fingers over and over again through a shredded Kleenex.

'She's going to phone him at the hotel, but it'll probably take them a while to track him down. I've given her your number so Poppy can call you back when she hears from him. Now I've got to be getting off. Give me a call at work when you hear from Poppy. And don't look so miserable, love. I'm sure he won't have told a soul. He's probably forgotten all about it by now.'

Dee kisses Claire's cheek and leaves her to fret in the little house with the blinds drawn and the tea going cold on the window sill.

*

Claire is still there at four-thirty. She hasn't moved; the phone hasn't rung. If she gets dressed quickly she could be in London by six-thirty. She has to look up the address of the hotel in the Yellow Pages. She has to find the nearest tube station in her A–Z. She has to get there before Sebastian tells a living soul about David Glendale and the consequences of his unfortunate indiscretion. It is of overwhelming importance, and Claire is the only one now who can save herself from this indecent exposure.

She goes upstairs and drags out the first thing that fits. Most of her clothes are now too tight, and she has to wear loose-fitting garments and elasticated waists. Her breasts have gone up one whole bra size, and they lie heavy at night beneath her reversible duvet cover. Is it her imagination or have her nipples become more sensitive too?

She's a mess.

Her hair hasn't been combed and she hasn't even cleaned her teeth.

In the bathroom mirror she looks like a wide-eyed witch: ragged and roughly sketched, as though waiting for someone to come along and colour her in.

No time for vanity. No time for anything more than a catlick with the flannel and a quick squirt of Yardley. She puts on clean knickers and a dab of Mum, just in case.

She has to find Sebastian before it's too late.

Chapter Twenty-seven

'What is it, Wayne?' asks Felicity sharply.

She is wearing Issey Miyake, a pleated sheath of bronze Fortuny silk that prevents her from walking with anything but miniature oriental steps. Her hair has been artfully ratted out, so that it looks as though she's just got out of bed and sprayed it with a can of lacquer. Charles Worthington came over this afternoon and had her hanging upside down over a stool while he raked through her wet hair with a diffuser.

'Can I have a word in private, Miss Craven?'

'I'm very busy. What is it?'

'It's sort of personal,' whispers Wayne, coming closer to Felicity – as a rat might approach a snarling dog.

'What could you possibly have to tell *me* that is personal?' Felicity recoils from Wayne's impertinent proximity.

'It's about your new hotel, Miss Craven.' Wayne practically has his head on her shoulder, and Felicity has to resist the urge to push him away.

'What are you talking about? What new hotel?'

'The one your husband's mistress bought for you.'

Felicity steps back and almost trips over the back of

her dress. She reaches out to steady herself against the wall of the conference room.

'Where did you get this information from?' She compresses the words between her tongue and the roof of her mouth as though they are made of gum.

'From the horse's mouth, so to speak,' grins Wayne.

The intercom. Felicity remembers now.

'Now, you listen to me, you sneaky little opportunist: if this is about money, then you can forget it. The hotel is no secret, and I certainly couldn't care less about who knows. As for the benefactor, the money belonged to me in the first place, so you're hardly going to start a scandal by going public with this information.'

'I think you're calling my bluff, Miss Craven. You want everyone to think that you've swung this new deal on your own. You'd be seen as some kind of charity case if word got out that the new hotel was given to you as compensation for your husband's screwing around. It'd certainly take the edge off your gala performance this evening, wouldn't it? I can see the headlines now.'

Felicity grabs Wayne by the elbow and pushes him into an adjoining office. She closes the door and glares at the porter with venom.

'How much do you want?'

'Now, who said anything about money?'

'Oh, quit the dramatic lead-up and tell me what you want.'

'I want a job in your new hotel. A managerial

position would be nice: something with a company car and a clothing allowance.'

'What the hell do you know about managing anything except suitcases? Why didn't you stay on at school and take your A levels, like decent boys of your age?' sneers Felicity.

'Who cares about frigging A levels? I didn't even take any GCSEs. I don't intend to do much work, anyway. Think of me as window dressing. I'm pretty good-looking, and the punters like me. I could be, say, part of the scenery.'

'You're asking too much,' says Felicity. 'It'd be less trouble just to let you blab to the newspapers. How about a couple of grand to keep your mouth shut?'

'I don't think so. You'll have to come up with something a bit better than that,' laughs Wayne, standing his ground.

'I need time to think about it. Today is not a good day to be talking about this.'

'It's now or never, Miss Craven. I intend to broadcast this news tonight, right in the middle of your poncey party.'

'You little shit!' Felicity slaps him with the expletive. 'You're going to regret ever having come to me with this. I am a very powerful woman, and I'm going to break you if it's the last thing I do.'

'Oh, such brave words from someone who has no choice but to back down. Do we have a deal, Miss Craven?'

'If you can call blackmail a legitimate deal.'

'Let's shake on it.' Wayne approaches Felicity with his hand outstretched.

'I wouldn't touch you with a bargepole,' snorts Felicity, swatting away his hand in disgust.

'Suit yourself, but a deal's a deal.' Wayne produces a folded document from the inside pocket of his uniform. 'Sign this. I had a lawyer friend draw it up for me. You're not the only one with friends in high places. Forty thousand a year and all the trimmings – non-negotiable.'

'You're not going to get away with this,' says Felicity, taking the papers.

'Somehow I think I will.'

And, for the first time ever, Felicity signs legal papers that she hasn't even read.

Not much point when you're dealing with a blackmailer.

When Claire arrives at the hotel she knows immediately that something is wrong. The place is deserted – not even a doorman in sight. The girl at the desk is eating potato salad out of a tub with a plastic fork, and watching a portable TV. The carpet is worn down to the underlay in places and there are greasy black patches on the wallpaper. This can't be the right place.

'Excuse me, is this Craven's Hotel?' asks Claire.

'Yeah,' replies the girl, without even looking away from the TV screen.

'Can I speak to Sebastian Craven?'

'Who?'

'The manager.'

'He's out.'

'Aren't you supposed to be having some kind of party tonight?'

'Not that I know of.' The girl looks at Claire with impatience.

'Are you sure this is Craven's Hotel?' Claire asks again.

'Here,' says the girl, tossing a folded pamphlet at Claire.

Craven Hill Hotel.

Claire looks at her watch. It's six-forty-five.

'Do you have a Yellow Pages?' she asks.

The girl points with her fork to a public phone in the lobby. The directories hang from a chain on the wall.

Bugger, bugger, bugger!

Sebastian is pissed off. Here he is in the lounge bar of Craven's in his tuxedo, with a Kir royale and Poppy trying to remain upright in a dress that quite frankly is too tight for her statuesque frame.

'I think it's jolly rude of him, actually,' he says, addressing the space that hangs moodily between them.

'I'm sure he's just trying to accommodate everyone. You know how thoughtful he is about this kind of thing,' placates Poppy, shifting to the left in an attempt to straighten the zip that is scratching the small of her back. The dress is dark purple, a colour that usually suits Poppy with her flame-red hair. Tonight she merely looks gaudy in a room filled with classic black and muted naturals.

'He knows how important this event is for us. I don't see why Solange couldn't just take a taxi to the airport; that's what most normal people would do.'

'I don't think Thierry realized that missing the first hour would upset you so much. I'm sure if you'd actually expressed these feelings to him, he would have changed his plans. You can't expect him to read your mind when you just shrug and say, "That's OK" every time he does something you don't like.'

'It's that bitch, Solange. I don't like her very much. She's a smarmy cow and she's always around. She's like a spy padding around his flat in her ridiculous nighties, loitering in the hallway smoking those filthy French cigarettes. Have you noticed how she never actually smiles? It's as though it would crack her face.' Sebastian finishes off his drink and grabs a glass of champagne from the tray of a passing waiter.

'I think you're just jealous of her because she's got a long history with Thierry. They've been friends for years, and they share something that you're not part of. Solange's OK; she's just a bit formal, that's all. Why don't you spend more time at *your* place when she's over in London?'

'Because Thierry doesn't like my place. He says it's *generic*. And it's not convenient for his work, whereas I, of course, am a gentleman of leisure and can get up at noon every day, irrespective of location.' Sebastian drowns his bitterness in another gulp of champagne.

'I think you're feeling sorry for yourself. You're trying very hard to find things to be upset about, when in reality things are going pretty well for you at the moment. Just look around you, Sebastian: this place runs itself while you reap the benefits, thanks to that much maligned sister of yours, and you've got a gorgeous, intelligent, aristocratic boyfriend who's great in bed and equally great out of it. I don't know what more you could want.'

'Oh, it always looks wonderful from the outside,' gripes Sebastian. 'You just don't understand the complexities of the situation.'

'I understand that you're going to ruin a perfectly good relationship if you don't lighten up. Now, wait here for me – I've got to go to the Ladies'. This damned dress is driving me up the wall. Next time I'll hire one, like everyone else.'

Poppy staggers off through the crowd, her hair a flaming beacon above the expensively coiffured heads around her. Sebastian sinks down into a nearby club chair. He's supposed to be circulating among the VIPs, but he prefers to leave all of that to Felicity and her entourage of sycophants. He knows he is not going to find the grace to forgive Thierry before the end of the evening. It's going to be miserable. He downs his drink and goes in search of another.

*

'So I said to her, if it's good enough for Lady Sarah Armstrong, it's good enough for me!'

Felicity reacts appropriately.

She's talking with a woman from Warner Brothers, who looks suspiciously like Daffy Duck.

'Please excuse me. I think I'm needed over in the marquee.'

She makes a nimble escape through the crowd, and leaves the hotel via the front entrance. They have closed off the roads around the square, and now there is a dark carpet stretching across the street to the main entrance of the marquee. The carpet has been lined on both sides with boxwood 'hedges'. It's going to be light for at least another couple of hours, and Felicity is anxious to create some atmosphere with candles and indirect lighting. At least it isn't raining, and there is only the gentlest of breezes to ripple the surface of her grey and cream linen canopy.

Cars arrive and cameras flash. Intrigued passers-by gather behind yellow police barricades to see if they recognize anyone. Some idiot is waving a Nuclear Disarmament banner for some unfathomable reason. Felicity offers a regal wave when she sees Terence Conran getting out of a surprisingly unpretentious little car. She wonders if Ross will come – she sent him an invitation. She would like him to see her performance this evening, when she steps up on to the stage to announce that this is her last night as manager of Craven's; that tomorrow she will be off to Crete with the children for eight days, before returning to

London to begin work on her new hotel. She can't wait to see the look on Sebastian's face. It will be priceless.

'Whose dress are you wearing, Felicity?' asks a cable TV reporter with an oversized microphone and an overweight cameraman.

'My own!' she jokes. 'It's Issey Miyake, actually. Isn't it gorgeous?' Felicity gives them an unsteady twirl.

'Is it true that you've invited Angelica Schloss to the party tonight?' asks the unsuspecting girl.

'Where did you get that ridiculous idea?' responds Felicity sharply.

'Well, didn't the two of you meet recently, here at Craven's?'

'I wasn't even aware that Mrs Schloss, or whatever her name is, was in the vicinity. Doesn't she live on a farm somewhere in Middle America?'

'So you didn't know that she's buying your house?' asks the reporter, gleeful with malicious intent.

'Of course I knew, but the house belongs to my late husband's company, and therefore they can sell it to whom they like – I had nothing to do with it. I was already considering a move, anyway; the house is old and needs constant maintenance. It's been decorated to within an inch of its life, and I'm ready for fresh pastures. Mrs Whatshername is welcome to it. I may even leave her the curtains!'

'So there's no animosity between the two of you?'

'Of course not. I don't even know the woman.' And

Felicity trots back up towards the hotel as fast as her Fortuny pleated silk will allow.

'Darling, how *are* you? You look marvellous!' she shrieks, throwing her arms around Tom Cruise for the cameras, and practically pushing poor Nicole into a potted bay tree.

When Claire sees the crowds outside the hotel, she realizes that there is no way in hell she is going to get inside with all that security and press to get through. She looks like one of the gawping bystanders pressed up against the yellow barrier, tired and battered by life but hoping to catch a glimpse of glamour as it passes by. Nobody gives Claire a second glance. She wonders how much more attention she would get if they all knew whose child she was carrying.

'Stay behind the barrier, love,' says a friendly bobby with a smile.

'I need to get inside the hotel,' says Claire. 'My brother's staying there and I said I would meet him in the lobby.'

'Is that right, love?' says the bobby, smiling at her as though she's in a straitjacket. 'And what's your brother's name?'

Claire has to think fast. She isn't very good at making up stories, and she can see that the bobby knows she's fibbing. 'Sebastian,' she says. It's the first name that comes into her head.

'Sebastian who?'

'Bentos,' says Claire, thinking of Poppy.

No lumps of fat or gristle guaranteed!

'I'll tell you what, miss, why don't I radio my colleague over there and ask him to check the guest list, eh?'

Claire nods. She wonders if she could run away when his back is turned, but he keeps his eyes on her as he speaks with his colleague over the walkie-talkie. He's checking out her tracksuit bottoms and padded jacket.

'That's right: Bentos.'

Claire pretends to watch the crowd with detached interest, hoping that she looks as though she isn't telling lies.

'There is a Bentos on the list, miss, but it's a lady, not a gentleman.'

'Oh, they're always making mistakes about his name,' says crafty Claire, wondering where her sudden inspiration is coming from. 'It's the S, you see: S for Sebastian. It often gets stuck on to the Mr part, and people think he's a Mrs.'

'A Ms *Poppy* Bentos?' questions the bobby, raising one quizzical eyebrow.

'That's his middle name,' says Claire.

'Poppy,' says the bobby.

'Yes.'

'Well, how about we send someone in to find him, and he can vouch for your identity?'

'All right,' says Claire, suddenly needing to wee rather urgently.

She hears a riotous cheer as somebody gets out of a car, but Claire can only see heads and anoraks.

After what seems like at least an hour, the bobby turns to Claire and pulls her forward through the jostling throng.

'Is this her, miss?' he asks Poppy, who's standing on the other side of the barrier in a shocking purple frock with her hair piled up in a kind of tumbledown beehive.

'Yes, that's her, officer, thank you.'

And Claire is admitted beyond the boundary of the hoi polloi, on to the crimson carpet in her Adidas trainers. Up behind Twiggy and that man from the ten o'clock news. Cameras blind her with their phosphorescent glare. Poppy holds on to her arm and leads her towards the entrance of the hotel, as if she's an undercover agent taking Claire off to a paddy wagon. How embarrassing. How terrible to be paraded up a crimson carpet between Twiggy and George Michael, with her hair unwashed and no make-up on. She has to look at her feet all the way up to the hotel doors.

Clump, clump they go on the crimson carpet.

Who the buggery is that? she hears them thinking. *That ordinary-looking woman in the Asda jacket with the frayed cuffs?*

When they get inside the lobby, it is crammed with bodies in all directions.

'What are you doing here, Claire? Are you mad?' Poppy has had to get close to Claire's ear in order to be heard. She overcompensates for the noise, and Claire nearly jumps out of her skin.

'I wanted to see Sebastian. He needs to know that he can't tell anyone else about the baby.'

'This is hardly the place, or the time. I was going to pass on your message, anyway. There was no need for you to come.'

'I really need to use the loo,' says Claire.

'Oh, right,' sighs Poppy, looking out over the sea of bobbing heads. 'Come with me.'

Poppy leads Claire over to the Ladies' Powder Room.

'I'll wait for you out here. You'll have to go as soon as you're done in there. You can't hang around for long.'

Claire pushes through the upholstered door.

There's a woman sitting on a golden throne beside a pile of towels and a collection box.

'Good evening, madam,' says the queen of the powder room in a voice that sounds pre-recorded.

Claire wonders if she's collecting for Cancer Research. She looks in her purse for some change.

The woman coughs and motions Claire over to the cubicles, shaking her head when she sees Claire's purse. She points to the marble-clad cubicles while avoiding Claire's eye. She knows Claire shouldn't be here at all, but she's too polite, or too uncaring, to be bothered. Claire locks herself in the first available loo, totally unaware that she is weeing right between Yasmin Le Bon and Delia Smith.

*

It's difficult finding a point of focus, with alcoholic fumes blurring the scene like the shimmer of sun on tarmac. Sebastian squints through his glass of champagne, to see distorted images effervescent with strings of tiny bubbles rising to its surface.

'You're drunk!' says Thierry.

'You're late!' replies Sebastian.

'It's only eight o'clock. I told you I'd be here once I'd dropped off Solange. It doesn't look as though I've missed much. Where's Poppy?'

'Gone off with a security guard. Haven't seen her for half an hour.' Sebastian feels comfortably upholstered, like the wadding inside a well-stuffed sofa. When he looks at Thierry he wants to reach out and touch him. He wants to kiss him and tell him that he loves him. Tears burn the edges of his bleary eyes.

'You look positively sozzled, old chap! Are you sure you're up to this thing?' Thierry's voice comes to him from the end of a very long tunnel.

'I'm fine. Jus' fine.'

'I just saw your mother with her escort. People are already walking over to the tent. She looks marvellous. Very regal.'

As Sebastian attempts to sit up in his chair, he spills what remains of his drink down the front of his starched white bib. 'Oh, shit!' he says, much more loudly than he imagines.

'What the hell's going on here?'

It's Felicity; she hisses into Sebastian's ear like a viper. She looks tall and skinny in her dress. Her scent acts like smelling salts for Sebastian, and he attempts to appear alert, but he just looks surprised.

'Is he blotto?' Felicity asks Thierry.

'It seems that way. I've only just arrived myself.'

'Christ! That's all I need, right when we're supposed to be giving our welcome address. I'll just have to go up on my own. Whatever you do, don't let him into the marquee. As usual, I'll have to shoulder all the responsibility. Take him home.' And Felicity hops off as fast as her dress will carry her.

'Come on, let's get you out of here.' Thierry takes the empty glass from Sebastian and helps him up from his seat. People are watching. People are taking note.

Thierry takes Sebastian out into the lobby, where the crowd has dissipated somewhat. Poppy is walking towards them with a rather plain woman at her side.

'Who's this, then?' asks Sebastian, pointing rudely at Claire and wondering if she's one of the cleaning ladies. Why is Poppy hanging around with a cleaning lady?

'Sebastian, this is Claire Brown, the lady I told you about,' says Poppy. She keeps her voice low and pulls Claire over into their circle of secrets.

'What lady? I don't know any ladies,' says Sebastian, laughing at his own joke.

'Shut up, Sebastian!' says Thierry. 'People are looking.'

'The lady with the baby. Remember?'

Sebastian remembers, and, as he remembers, his fuddled mind clears just a little. That's right! The woman who's having David's bastard child. The woman who is going to help Sebastian disgrace his sister. How utterly perfect! Here she is, standing right in front of him, when out there, in that marquee of grey and cream linen, Felicity awaits her audience. Couldn't be better!

'Pleased to meet you, Miss Brown,' he says, taking her tiny hand in his own. 'Glad you could make it. Aren't you a bit hot in that coat?'

'Hello,' says Claire. She is like a little mouse.

'You couldn't have come at a better time.'

One thing Felicity did not bargain for was the steepness of the five steps leading up to the podium. It isn't until she attempts to lift her foot on to the first of those steps that the dilemma becomes all too clear. Her blasted dress will not allow her to get up there.

She discovers that if she twists herself sideways she can take each step individually, as long as she's careful to maintain her balance on her unsuitably high heels. There is no handrail, no support of any kind, and she has already been announced by Bruce, the general manager. Applause spurs her on. She attempts a shaky smile and takes another crablike step towards the summit.

If Felicity were more of a good-time girl she might make a joke of the whole thing and tug the dress up around her waist, skipping smartly up on to the stage with self-effacing panache, but of course Felicity is not much of a good-time girl at all. She sidles up the steps, keeping her arms anchored stiffly at her sides. Cameras blind her with their intrusive flare.

Two steps. Three steps. The applause is growing thin as the audience holds its breath. Will she make it? Will she get up on to the stage to deliver her speech? She can see that Bruce is trying to decide if he should help her or not. He's right over at the other side of the podium.

On the fourth step Felicity catches the heel of her shoe on the corner of the carpet. For a moment she thinks she can regain her balance, but suddenly she finds her arms flying out to break her fall as she keels over and goes sprawling, writhing among the snaking wires of the sound system. She can't get up. Her legs kick inside the pleated sheath of silk and she feels Bruce's arms about her waist. The applause has stopped and people are staring at her with open-mouthed delight. The cameras flash gleefully and Felicity almost finds herself in tears of humiliation. Her hip is badly bruised. She has to limp over to the podium. She has somehow to regain her dignity. All eyes are upon her. All she can hear is the beat of her heart and the shallow gasping of her breath.

'Making an entrance again with my usual flair!' she says breathlessly into the microphone.

The laughter is satisfyingly supportive. Felicity settles her hair and smiles at Bruce.

This is not going as she had planned.

She decides to stick to her notes and just get on with it. She isn't very good at making jokes about herself. She has always found it easier to laugh at other people.

'I never knew it could be so difficult making it to the top! . . .'

More laughter.

' . . . but now that I'm here, I intend to stick around for a while.'

Felicity is finding her composure. She sees familiar faces all around her. She knows her speech without having to refer to her crumpled notes. Unfortunately, without Sebastian here on the stage, her announcement is going to lose some of its glory.

'Ten years ago today we opened the doors of Craven's to mixed reviews. Our critics heralded the hotel as overblown, over-decorated and over-indulgent. Who was going to pay upwards of nine hundred pounds a night to stay at a forty-bedroom boutique hotel, when they could be at the Ritz or the Dorchester? Well, as I look out tonight I can see at least two hundred of you who *were* ready to take such a step. In fact, by the time Craven's had been open six months, we had already met our target for the first year. And so it has been ever since, through a decade that economically has been disastrous for many of our competitors. A number of those early critics are now some of our most frequent guests.

'Although my father purchased this hotel as an investment, it soon became clear to me that it was to become my dream. For almost two years I organized the renovation and decoration of the hotel, making it what it is today. Of course, it wasn't all hard work. I got to travel the world seeking out materials and furnishings for each of our renowned bedroom suites. Glass from Murano, silk from Thailand, parquet floors from a demolished church in Poland. I wanted Craven's to be rich with history and culture, and no matter which of our rooms you sleep in, you can be sure that it will be an adventure in sensuous luxury.

'When my father passed away, the legacy of the hotel went to my brother Sebastian. He should be up here with me this evening, but unfortunately urgent business has called him away. I don't think Sebastian would take offence if I were to say that, although he is the owner of Craven's, he has always allowed me to think of it as my own, never standing in my way when I have been captured by yet another expensive flight of fancy. Well, tonight, exactly ten years since I unveiled my dream, I am here to say goodbye.'

Felicity pauses here. She wants them to wait.

'I have a *new* dream. Another hotel. But this time, one that belongs to me. Negotiations are already under way and I will be announcing the details within the next few weeks. Tomorrow I leave for a short holiday with my children. I think we deserve some time away together as a family, since this has been such a devastating year for us so far. When I return, I will begin massive renovations on my new property, which is scheduled to open in the next twelve months. It will be totally unlike anything that you have seen at Craven's. It will represent a new millennium: a simple design philosophy that combines abject luxury with the purity of twenty-first-century sensibilities. I am going to call my new hotel The Phoenix, and I am sure that for those of you who know me, the symbolism of that name will not be lost on you.'

It is at this precise moment that Felicity sees Sebastian standing at the entrance to the marquee. He is staring at her with something not unlike burning hatred. But that would be un-brotherly. He's with that outrageous woman in the purple dress. She's pulling at his arm for some reason, but Sebastian appears not to notice. His eyes are set on Felicity.

Then something very odd happens. Just as Felicity opens her mouth to conclude her speech, she sees a very common-looking woman running towards Sebastian from the hotel. She's wearing a tracksuit! Something of a scuffle alarms some members of the audience, and people begin to turn around. Felicity decides to forge ahead, anxious to avoid any kind of embarrassing conflict.

'The tenth anniversary of Craven's is a milestone, not just for me but for—'

Felicity is interrupted by her brother, who is now shouting from the back of the marquee. He is grasping on to the common-looking woman by her coat sleeve, and she appears to be very distressed. Thierry is trying to shut him up, but it isn't working.

'Ladies and gentlemen!' shouts Sebastian.

The audience turns its back on Felicity.

'As you have just heard, my sister will be leaving us

to start a new venture of her own, and of course we all wish her well.' He sways a little at this point, and it's obvious that he's drunk. 'Well, it's my hotel anyway, so who gives a fuck?'

There is an audible gasp of astonishment, and Felicity searches desperately for a security guard.

'For ten years Felicity Craven has taken the glory, while I stood quietly in the background. Well, now it's my turn. And tonight I want to introduce you to somebody you may not know. This is Claire Brown; she works for Glendale Estates, the company created by my late brother-in-law, David Glendale.' At this point Claire manages to break away from Sebastian's grip and she runs out of the marquee, only to be apprehended by two policemen who are guarding the entrance to the hotel.

Felicity is mortified. She can't get down from the stage without being carried, so she is forced to remain up here on the podium, watching her brother make an absolute ass of himself.

'I am sure that you are all aware that my brother-in-law was a bit of a bastard. As much as I dislike my sister, even I thought that he treated her with an unusual amount of disrespect. We all know about his mistress and illegitimate children in Texas, we all know about his corrupt and ruthless business history – it was part of his legend. Well, this poor woman . . .' and Sebastian points to Claire, standing between the two police officers, ' . . . is dying. She's dying of leukaemia and she only has a few months to live. She is also carrying David Glendale's child.'

There is a reaction from the crowd that sounds like approaching thunder. Chairs scrape, people mutter, photographers and reporters gather ranks and push towards the front to capture every word. Sebastian is loosening his bow tie. Claire Brown appears to be crying.

Felicity doesn't know how to react. She couldn't care less about that stupid woman and her claims that she is having David's baby – it is probably a hoax anyway. Felicity finds that her immediate emotional response is directed towards Sebastian. If she had a gun handy she would probably shoot him, but instead she leans towards her microphone.

'Will someone please see that my brother gets some attention. He is obviously in some distress and doesn't know what he's saying. This has been an intensive time for him, and it appears that he has been drinking. I am sure that you are all aware of his recent identity crisis, and I can assure you that he is receiving the very best of psychiatric treatment.'

The crowd don't know which way to look. It's like a game of tennis, with the ball being swatted from left to right, up and over the net, to be thwacked again and again.

'And you're a fucking bitch!' screams Sebastian, obviously unable to gather sufficient wits about him to make a less retaliatory statement. 'You're a bigot and a liar. You're a fascist, anal-retentive sociopath and you deserve everything you get!'

'OK, can somebody please get my brother out of here,' shouts Felicity, trembling with fury.

Security guards move in and virtually carry Sebastian out of the marquee as he continues to shout obscenities at Felicity.

Felicity indicates to the band to start playing. They break into a hurried rendition of 'Take Five'.

Dave Brubeck would never have imagined it being played at such a frenetic tempo.

PART TWO

CHAPTER TWENTY-EIGHT

Serendipity is the word that springs to mind.

But there is nothing random or accidental in the eclectic style of Thierry's apartment in Brussels. This is artfully arranged serendipity, a clever and educated juxtaposition of items seemingly unrelated and yet somehow perfectly balanced. It is nothing like the Bayswater flat above the toy museum.

It is nothing like Thierry.

May sunshine in all its midday clarity strikes the cobbled courtyard and spills over into the ground-floor apartment in dappled pools of white. It is very dusty, and the dust sparkles in the sunlight. Around the courtyard there is a portico of weathered terracotta columns, some of them eroded to the point of collapse. The canopy above is a rumpled blanket of sagging tiles and moss. Oversized urns and broken statues huddle in corners as though afraid of the light. There is a cast-iron bathtub with lion's feet, and it is filled with green, brackish rainwater. There are old iron gates and chimney pots, peeling paint and blistered stucco. The courtyard is perfectly decomposed, just waiting for a photographer to come along with soft lighting and grainy film.

Picture perfect.

Thierry is off in Liège. Sebastian sits alone in the apartment with a copy of *The Bulletin*, an English-language weekly filled with expats and classified adverts for moving sales and cleaning ladies. There's even an English-speaking gay group called EGG. Somewhere far away a clock strikes twelve. It is a melodic sound, unlike the solemn toll of the Westminster chime, and Sebastian wonders if there are mechanical figures moving in and out of doorways striking bells with golden hammers. It's that kind of sound.

He will be meeting Solange for lunch at one. He had hoped that just for one weekend he might spend some time without her being around, but it is beginning to appear that Thierry and Solange are practically inseparable. This is the first time Sebastian has been to visit Thierry in Brussels, and already he feels like an interloper. It was Thierry who arranged the lunch with her. He thought it would be nice for Sebastian to have some company on his first day. He doesn't seem to realize that Sebastian would be much happier wandering around the town alone, not having to make trite conversation, not having to be nice to someone he really doesn't care for.

It's eleven o'clock in England; it says so on the television. One can get the BBC in Belgium, and it's a better picture than Sebastian gets in London. There are other channels, of course, many of them subtitled in French or Flemish or Dutch, and the adverts are funny. Sebastian has been channel-hopping since eight this morning.

He arrived in Brussels the night before, and it was almost dark when Thierry brought him to the apartment. His flight had been delayed in London and there were road diversions outside the airport in Brussels. Thierry drives a BMW. It smells of leather and Solange's cigarettes. The ashtrays are overflowing with ash and folded filters. Along the way Sebastian saw a windmill, but Thierry explained that it was just a decorative structure, placed there to delight the tourists who stay at a nearby hotel. And then they passed beneath the Parc Cinquantenaire with its brightly illuminated triumphal arch, and Sebastian was filled with the delicious sense of being abroad.

The streets of downtown Brussels are narrow in places, opening out on to squares and avenues, with cafés and restaurants and tall slender merchants' houses leaning forward precariously from the weight of their age. Thierry lives right in the heart of the city, on a quiet street tucked behind a square called the Sablon. There is a shop on the street with dusty windows, where they sell wheelchairs and prosthetic devices. There is a bistro on the corner called Le Villance, which has striped awnings in sun-faded red and green. There are four apartments in the building where Thierry lives, one on each side of the courtyard. Thierry's family own all four, and rent out the other three.

'Home sweet home!' said Thierry as he struggled

with the key. The door refused to open. 'Can't see a thing in this light,' he said as he jingled through the bunch to find the right one. Sebastian could see light in the windows of one of the other apartments. The room inside was filled with books right up to the ceiling, and a man sat by the window with a magnifying glass and a newspaper.

'That's Monsieur Cavell. He's a retired professor of medicine,' said Thierry, looking up from his keys. 'Here we are . . .' He finally held up the key to his apartment.

On first impression, Sebastian imagined that he had entered a storage room. A huge metal clock face with roman numerals dominated one tall, whitewashed brick wall. It must have come from a church or a clock tower, it was so big. There was just the one room, so that all aspects of living had to be conducted within sight of the other occupants. Only the toilet was hidden away from sight within a tiny cupboard that looked suspiciously like an old confessional. Everything else was exposed.

'Goodness, this is rather unexpected,' said Sebastian as he dropped his bags to the floor. 'What happens if you have guests?' he asked, looking at the exposed bathtub raised on a platform of marble in one corner.

'One makes sure that one is well acquainted before one invites them to stay,' laughed Thierry, switching on several lamps, all of which cast little more than decorative lighting in the shadows of the room.

The bed was a four-poster with voluminously

threadbare draperies, but the sheets looked new. The living area was a jumble of oddly assorted furniture ranging from art deco club chairs in soft pink suede to regally gilded Louis XV salon pieces with brocade pillows and peeling veneer. The windows were large, and some of the panes were cracked or replaced with coloured glass, but there were no curtains.

'You're obviously not concerned about privacy,' said Sebastian.

'Who's going to look in?' replied Thierry. 'Only Monsieur Cavell, and he can't see newsprint six inches away from his face.'

'What about the other residents?'

'They do not overlook my apartment and they rarely use the courtyard entrance.'

'Felicity would love it,' said Sebastian, still unable to say his sister's name without a prick of remorse.

'And you?' asked Thierry.

'I shall have to get used to it,' was Sebastian's reply.

And he *is* getting used to it. He has been here for fourteen hours and it's growing on him. He has taken a bath, soaking up to his neck in bubbles with the thrill of being naked in such a wide open space. He has toasted pieces of baguette under the grill and drunk bitter coffee left over from the night before, heated up in a saucepan with a burned handle.

There is very little of Thierry evident in the apartment. Sebastian knows that most of his things are back in London. The wardrobe holds a couple of suits, the chest of drawers a few sweaters, socks and underpants.

There are no photographs, or letters, or dirty magazines pushed under the bedside cabinets. The kitchen cupboards are bare save for a few imperishable items, and the fridge is broken. The only thing that's new is the TV, and that is perched unceremoniously on top of a mound of yellowed newspapers.

Sebastian wears his new pink waistcoat. It's daring for him, a colour that normally he would not consider. Thierry picked it out for him at Simpson's, and it does look wonderful beneath his chestnut-brown jacket with the velvet collar. He doesn't wear a tie; he leaves the button-down collar of his shirt open and appraises this new casual approach in the cracked mirror above the washbasin. Sometimes he can see why people think him attractive.

It's a short walk to the Sablon. There's some kind of street market going on in the square, and a barrel organ churns out fairground melodies. The greasy, sweet smell of freshly cooked waffles infiltrates itself between the mangled mess of bric-a-brac and miscellanea. All around the perimeter of the square there are smart boutiques, restaurants and antique shops, and in the middle there is a church with beautiful stained-glass windows illuminated from the inside.

Sebastian finds Solange sitting outside a small café beneath an umbrella. She's reading a newspaper and the waiter has just brought her a beer. Seen from a distance, Sebastian thinks how impressive she appears, sitting there with her impeccably tousled hair. She is, of course, smoking one of those foul cigarettes, and she squints through the smoke as she turns the page of her paper.

'Hello, Solange,' says Sebastian, taking the seat opposite.

'Sebastian, you made it! Are you going to join me in a beer?'

'I'm not much of a beer drinker.'

'You cannot come to Belgium without drinking beer. It is one of the few things we do very well. Maybe you would try a Kriek or a Framboise? It is usually more for the ladies, but if you are not a beer drinker it might be better for you.'

Sebastian does not miss the slur, but he chooses to ignore it.

'I'll have whatever it is that you're drinking.'

Solange beckons the waiter and orders for Sebastian. She speaks in Flemish.

'I know that boy. He comes from Leuven,' explains Solange, stabbing out her cigarette.

'I find this whole language thing very confusing. Thierry tells me you can drive just ten miles outside Brussels and find that nobody speaks French at all.'

'Well, that's not completely true. Many of them *do* speak French; they just prefer not to. You will do better to speak in English when you are outside of Brussels. Most Belgians react kindly to your language. It is not, I think, very different from the situation you have with your Welsh and Scottish Nationalists.'

Sebastian's beer arrives. It is immediately refreshing but familiarly bitter – a taste he has never enjoyed. He knows that Solange is watching him with interest.

'You don't like me very much, do you?' asks Solange, her question sounding more like an affirmed statement.

'What on earth gives you that idea? I don't really know you,' replies Sebastian, taken aback by her confrontational tone.

'I am an obstruction between you and Thierry, this I can see, but you know, you are just as much an obstruction to me. I have known Thierry for many years, and he is my closest friend. I see that Thierry is very fond of you, and yet he is bound to his friendship with me at the same time. Who, I wonder, will be the victor in this battle?'

'Battle?' says Sebastian. 'I hardly think it's a battle, Solange. Yes, I admit that sometimes you are around just a little too often, but I have accepted that as part of being with Thierry. I can assure you that I have no desire to push you out of the way.'

'I can assure *you*, my dear Sebastian, that you could not push me out of the way even if you so desired.' This is Solange at her most pompous, and Sebastian has to resist the urge to retaliate.

'Well, then there will be no problem. I want Thierry's love and you want his friendship – surely they are two entirely different things?'

'You think so? Are you saying that you do not want his friendship and I do not want his love? That is a strange evaluation when surely the two things are closely related?'

'I think you know what I mean. We relate to Thierry in totally different ways.'

'It is true. You seek to gain his love, and I, of course, already have it. That perhaps is the difference you are speaking of?'

'Solange, I don't want to argue about this. We must beg to differ on the subject. Obviously it's something that troubles you much more than it does myself. Now, why don't we order some food? I'm ravenous.'

'As you wish. We can sweep this under the carpet. It will be interesting to watch as you discover more about our friend. Maybe you will not like the things you find.'

'You make that sound like a threat.'

'Think of it as more of a warning. I believe it is only fair to tell you that you have touched just the very tip of the iceberg.'

The waiter brings menus, and Sebastian refuses to allow Solange to order for him. He speaks to the waiter in French, and he doesn't have to worry about making any mistakes. Everything is ordered in the present tense and the waiter understands every word.

'Excellent!' says Solange.

'*Merveilleux!*' replies Sebastian, draining his glass and pushing the filthy ashtray over to her side of the table.

Chapter Twenty-nine

Here's something you don't see every day.

Wayne Briggs is stepping out of a taxi on to the gravel of Blythwood House in a rather smart-looking jacket and tie.

'Keep the change, mate. And I'll see you back here in twenty minutes. Just keep out of sight down by the gates,' he says to the taxi driver.

Blimey! This is like a fucking palace. He looks up at the white, white house with all its pillars and windows and chimneys, but barefaced Wayne refuses to be intimidated by its architectural superiority. He straightens his tie and marches right on up to the front door, bold as brass. The knocker is massive, and shaped like a lion's head.

Lovely pair of knockers you've got, Mrs Worthington.

Now where did that come from? A *Carry On* film, probably.

It takes ages for the door to open. Wayne is expecting a butler, or a servant of some kind, but instead he is faced with a teenage girl wearing a Walkman and ballet slippers.

'Hi!' she says.

'Hello, I'm here to see your mum,' says Wayne in his most polite voice.

'She's not here. She's in London,' says the girl.

As if I didn't know.

'You must be Sascha, Felicity's daughter.'

'That's right. Who are you?'

'My name's Wayne. I work with your mum at the hotel.'

'Oh, well, she won't be back until tonight. I'm only here because I've had the mumps. Where's your car?'

'I came by taxi.'

'Did you have an appointment or something? I could ring Mummy at the office if you like.'

'Well, we had a sort of appointment. Perhaps you should call her anyway, just to let her know I'm here. Can I wait inside?'

Sascha pauses for a moment, looks him up and down and then says, 'Yeah, you can sit in the hall.'

'What're you listening to?' asks Wayne, crossing the threshold.

'Spice Girls.'

'Which one's your favourite, then?'

'Baby Spice, but I used to like Ginger as well.'

The entrance hall is frigging wicked! A huge double staircase, all white marble and iron. The chandelier is like a big crystal spaceship. Wayne takes a seat on a little gold and red chair as Sascha goes to phone her mother.

This is all going according to plan. When Felicity hears that Wayne is actually in her house, alone with thirteen-year-old Sascha, she is really going to flip her lid. He wishes he could be in two places at once. He would love to see that bitch shitting herself.

He takes a peek into the room to the left of him. In it there's wicker furniture and potted orange trees. Very posh. Wayne wonders how long Sascha will be. Perhaps Felicity has told her to call the police, then hide in a safe place until they arrive.

Because he is sick and completely warped, Wayne has brought with him a Snappies bag filled with cock-roaches. Many of them are bloated with egg sacs. They crawl around inside the bag but Wayne doesn't shudder. Like him, they're just trying to stay alive. He opens the bag and scatters the insects around the orangery. They scuttle and hide beneath the furniture, away from the light, away from exposure.

And, just in case this house is so clean that the poor things can't find anything to eat, Wayne has brought another bag filled with cake crumbs which he sprinkles around the skirting boards, behind the sofa and the plants. A cockroach feast. A magnificent breeding ground for the slum-dwelling insects.

The taxi driver is back. Wayne slips out of the front door and pins a scrappy piece of Basildon Bond to the panelling, just below the lion's-head knocker.

Called but you were out.

'Can you take me back to the station, please?' Wayne asks the taxi driver.

He has to pinch the back of his hand really hard to stop himself breaking into hysterical laughter.

CHAPTER THIRTY

They are in B&Q buying laminated shelving. Duncan
is wheeling the trolley and Claire trails behind,
looking at grouting. It's Sunday afternoon and families
are out in abundance, filling the wide aisles with unin-
terested teenagers, and wives who would rather be at
home watching an old film with their feet up on the
pouffe. It wasn't so long ago that Sunday afternoons
were sacrosanct – no shopping allowed. High streets
were deserted, multi-storey car parks were empty, and
the only place you could get a loaf of bread or some
raspberry ripple ice cream was the corner shop.

Of course it's America that has spoiled everything.
Claire used to like her quiet Sunday afternoons, and
sometimes she would go window-shopping along the
lonely pavements, enjoying the bizarre silence that
existed in places where normally one expected noise.
Only the Wimpy Bar would be open, and that was
before they modernized them and got rid of the waitress service.

Plastic tomatoes filled with ketchup, and crusty
mustard bottles.

Beefburger, chips and peas for fifty-five pence.

These days there are queues a mile long in the food

hall at Marks & Spencer's, and you can have your lunch in a cardboard box from McDonald's for little less than a fiver if you go for a large milkshake and apple pie to follow. The old England that Claire remembers is disappearing beneath a mound of Happy Meals and DIY superstores, with vending-machine coffee and enough parking space to contain a small village. It makes her sad to think of things changing so quickly. She is young, she is only thirty-four, and if *she* notices these changes, what must it be like for OAPs, who were born when flapper dresses and the Charleston were the outrage of the decade? She thinks about her baby and wonders where it will all end.

Five months pregnant, and she is wearing a maternity smock from Mothercare. It isn't particularly attractive but it was in the sale, and Claire is watching her pennies. During the past month, since the papers got hold of her story and turned it into a human interest tragedy, Claire has returned over ten thousand pounds to generous strangers who have written to her, wishing her well. One newspaper offered her an indecent amount of money for the serialization of her story, but Claire refused the offer. She's a private person and she wants no pity. It has taken her a month to calm down after her ordeal at the anniversary party. She was on the front of every tabloid scandal sheet the following day, and even the *Guardian* had a little bit about her on the third page. She could have died of embarrassment!

They crowded outside her little house at The

Acorns, with their vans and their cameras. They threw questions at her like stones every time she walked down the path, and the pain brought tears to her eyes. Dee was interviewed by one TV reporter and they had to bleep out so much of her statement they couldn't use it. She told them all to fuck off. But they didn't fuck off for over five days. And then, suddenly, two women were concussed on the Old Kent Road by a chunk of fallen satellite, and the reporters left Claire's story exposed and bloodied on the front lawn, along with their empty film cartridges and their cigarette butts. It would appear that the expiry date on Claire was already up, and the women on the Old Kent Road were much more willing to talk about *their* ordeal.

Duncan walks on ahead. From the back he almost looks like any other man, but there are small, significant differences between Duncan and the others who wander the aisle in search of Sunday salvation. You might look at his khaki corduroys with the trailing hem and the threadbare pockets, and think he is hopelessly inept. You could assess his baggy fisherman's jumper with the patched elbows and class him as irredeemably ordinary. And his hair is unfashionably cut, like an overgrown schoolboy from the fifties. But Claire sees these things differently now. She sees those corduroy trousers and she knows their gentle, time-worn softness. She sees the rumpled jumper and she knows the man within. And his hair, so thick and abundantly tousled, reminds her that fashion is something that comes to those who have less important things to think about. Duncan has his priorities straight.

He wears Y-fronts and listens to Radio 4.

He doesn't know his Versace from his Liberace.

Claire worries about the sex. Still they have not made love, and she thinks that perhaps Duncan is frightened of hurting her, or maybe the baby. They have slept together on several occasions but Duncan always keeps his pants on, and Claire wears her powder-blue nightie like a chastity belt. He kisses her as though she might break beneath his hands. They sleep back to back with their bottoms barely touching, and Claire sometimes wishes that she was more liberated, like Dee; that she could just roll over and initiate something. But, despite these thoughts, Claire is a nice girl, and she knows that nice girls don't do that. Duncan will have to make the first move.

She really wants it to happen. She thinks about it to stop herself fretting about the baby and her fear of the future. She thinks she almost knows what it would be like. It wouldn't be like that first and only time with David Glendale and his precision-mounted penis. He had been a professional – a well-oiled piston with all the sensitivity of polished steel. Duncan, she knows, would be different.

'These brackets are the wrong size,' says Duncan, holding up a vacuum pack of metal shelf accessories. 'We'll have to go to Do It All. Do you mind?'

'No, I don't mind. Perhaps you could drop me off at home first. I'm feeling a bit tired.'

'Oh, I'm sorry, love. You should have said something. Do you want to go to the car while I pay for our stuff?'

'I think I'll just go and sit outside and wait for you.'

Claire doesn't like to admit to her illness. She has been practising Positive Thinking, but sometimes it just doesn't work. She makes her way through the browsers and edges between the checkout queues to reach the exit. There's a young man outside with a boy on his shoulders; they're waiting for a woman with a trolley full of wallpaper and paint.

'Look, Mummy, I'm taller than you are!' shouts the boy.

But the woman is too busy with her paint charts and her fabric swatches to listen to what he is saying.

Claire sits on a painted bench and squints into the afternoon sunshine. It's funny how quickly she has grown accustomed to the weight of her swelling stomach. She likes to rest her hands on it, contemplating the life within. It is a strange, bitter-sweet emotion. How can she explain the feeling of fear that sometimes threatens to overwhelm her completely? She looks at the sky, and it is as though she realizes for the first time in her life that the earth is suspended in space, spinning inexplicably in an endless universe of stars. Claire feels small. She feels less than small. When she looks at the stars at night, she knows that many of them are no longer there, that they burned out thousands of years ago, and that all she is seeing is the ghost of their memory. Claire is frightened that her child will one day see her as nothing more than an extinguished star – the faintest scent of a leaf pressed between the pages of a book. Her child will never know who she is. Her child will not know of this moment as she sits on a bench outside B&Q, with the breeze bending the weakling stalks of the newly planted trees.

The trees are surrounded by wire to keep them from falling over.

They will probably never see maturity.

'I got you a coffee,' says Duncan, appearing at Claire's side with his trolley and his laminated shelving. He presents her with a Styrofoam cup and a plastic spoon.

Claire smiles up at him.

She sees herself reflected in his glasses, and she wonders for how many millionths of a second her reflection would remain if she snuffed herself out like a candle. Is life really that short?

'Thanks,' she says, and she takes the coffee from Duncan.

A jet flies overhead, glinting in the sun, and they watch the vapour trail as it scratches the enamel of the sky with silent deliberation.

'You've been very quiet today – is everything all right?' asks Duncan, taking a seat beside Claire on the bench.

'Oh, I'm OK. I keep thinking about the baby and wondering what I'm going to do after it's born. If I don't think about the baby, then I have to think about myself, and I'd rather not dwell on that.'

'You know my offer still stands. If nothing else comes along, you can always count on me – I really mean it, Claire. I'm not just being polite.'

'Oh, Duncan, I know you mean it, but you've only known me for a few months, and I just wouldn't feel right dumping my baby on you for the next eighteen years or more of your life. The adoption agency said I could help interview prospective parents before the baby's born, so that I feel as though I have some kind of choice in its future. It would be kinder to let the baby go to parents who really want a child, people who will love it as their own and bring it up in the kind of way I would have liked myself.'

'And you're absolutely certain you don't want to try that treatment Dr Shaw told you about?'

Claire shakes her head and looks up into the sky. 'No, I just can't risk it. There's no guarantee that it won't hurt the child later in life. Those studies in America haven't been verified, and although the babies are born with no apparent defects, they don't know if the chemicals will affect them when they start to grow up.'

'I wish you weren't so obstinate. Can't you see that I'm being totally selfish here? I don't want to lose you, Claire.'

'Oh, Duncan, what use am I to you? I can't even offer you a normal relationship. I don't want you hanging around just because you feel you have to.'

'Is that what you think I'm doing?' asks Duncan, taking Claire's hand.

'I don't know. I just feel as though you're going beyond the call of duty. As much as I like having you around, I have got to sort this thing out on my own. Think of it as a kind of last request. My life has been pretty useless so far, and now I've got one final chance to do something right. I'm not going without a fight.'

'Sounds as though you've made up your mind.'

'I suppose I have. I just needed to hear it for myself.'

'So what's the first move?'

'If I knew that, Duncan, I wouldn't be sitting here wasting my time doing nothing. Every time I think I've come up with a good solution, I then come up with a good reason why it won't work. Dee says I should be more assertive, but that's never really been me.'

'You don't ever need to be something you're not. Some of us like you just the way you are.'

'Some of you are *stupid*!' laughs Claire, squeezing Duncan's hand.

'Well, tell me something I *didn't* know. Come on, it's time for some of that fruit cake and a cuppa.'

'Duncan?'

'Yes?'

'It is going to work out, isn't it?'

'Of course it is, love. You'll wake up one morning and you'll have it all sorted.'

But Claire isn't so sure. She follows Duncan across

the B&Q car park, and the weight in her chest hasn't shifted.

Every day is like looking at an old photograph and wishing that time hadn't moved on.

Chapter Thirty-one

Of course one would never find Felicity Craven in B&
Q. She would hate the long queues at the checkout,
and the polyester shell suits hovering around the bathroom displays. She drives past these places when she's
on the motorway, and she wonders why they have to
be so ugly.

Concrete and corrugated aluminium.

Bold primary colours intended to attract the masses.

Felicity prefers to deal with her little hardware shop
where Mr Gresham knows her by name and lets her
rummage through his stockroom. She dismisses the
idea of DIY, and instead she calls upon the services of
men in pristine white overalls, who charge her by the
hour to pay for their mobile phones and their letter-
heads designed by graphic artists.

Sunday afternoons for Felicity are a different kettle
of fish entirely.

Usually she spends the day at home, and,
depending on the season, she might set herself a
household task such as walking the grounds with her
gardener or showing her cleaning girl how to dust the
tops of the door frames without making the wallpaper
shiny. Sometimes she sits in the conservatory and

sticks press cuttings into a large scrapbook, and at other times she might involve the children in some kind of tranquil activity such as gilding flowerpots for winter narcissi, or making hand-marbled paper to line the bedroom drawers.

Today, though, she is sitting in the snug of an East End pub somewhere near Petticoat Lane market, with a man called Lou who has gold teeth and a missing finger. Felicity has never been to Aldgate before, and she is astounded by the noise and the filth. The market, despite its picturesque name, is situated alongside rows of ugly concrete council flats, wedged between the kind of buildings that she thought only existed in BBC soap operas. The pub is called the Four Bells and she is offered something in a bag called pork scratchings. She doesn't want to offend, so she accepts the snack but refrains from sampling the delicacy. Lou is drinking beer from a bottle, and Felicity has asked for mineral water. The barmaid gives her tonic water in a half-pint glass with a slice of lemon and two round ice cubes. The sound of the street market and the thump of the jukebox make discreet conversation impossible, although Felicity and Lou have the entire snug to themselves.

A month ago Felicity would never have dreamed that she could be having this conversation. It has been a difficult period, and she is having to adapt with the times. Since the outrage that turned her anniversary party into a disaster, Felicity has been in seclusion. The holiday with the children was a convenient getaway, but the newspaper speculation had swept through London like wildfire, and Felicity is still smarting from the assault. She is being painted as the insensitive rich lady who cares about nothing but her own empire. She is a bigot and a bitch. Her marriage was a sham and her lifestyle is extravagantly sinful.

OK, so it's true! But who wants it splashed across every cheap little rag on Fleet Street? And of course Felicity is terrified of any further scandal. Wayne Briggs has been taking advantage of this situation and his demands are growing increasingly unreasonable. His frightening visit to Blythwood House has really shaken her. That is why Felicity must resort to this – Petticoat Lane market on a lovely Sunday afternoon, with a man who looks as though he should be with a travelling circus.

'So you're a friend of old Ross?' asks Lou, eyeing Felicity up as though she has tassels swinging from the ends of her nipples.

'Yes, Ross and my late husband worked together for years. He said that you might be able to help me with a little problem I have with an employee.' Felicity sips her tonic water and attempts to ignore Lou's scarred hands as they dance nervously on the wooden table top. He wears three gold sovereign rings and a silver skull and crossbones with emerald eyes. His fingernails are cracked and dirty, his knuckles raw and scabbed. She's wishing that she had conducted this business over the telephone. But that would have been too risky. She wonders if people like Lou have access to fax machines or email. But, of course, clandestine meetings are always preferable in situations such as this. She's seen it at the cinema.

'So he said,' sneers Lou, picking his tooth with a cocktail stick and leaning back against the torn red leatherette of the bench. 'He also said that it'd be well worth my while. You see, lady, I don't do favours for anyone, you know. I was banged up for two years because of this kind of caper. I'm supposed to be going straight, as far as my probation officer is concerned. What's it worth?'

'Well . . .' says Felicity, looking around the empty snug and beginning to wonder if she shouldn't just bolt while the going is good. 'Ross said that you might consider two thousand?'

Lou allows this offer to roll around on the table between them like a dirty penny for a few moments. He sips his beer and plays with the diamond in his ear. He's like something dreamed up by Dickens, and Felicity imagines him enjoying the torture of young children and animals. She's scared of him. She's scared of this place. She feels overdressed and under-protected, and any minute now she thinks that she might be raped or murdered. It would be her own fault.

'Sounds OK,' says Lou. 'Did you bring the dosh?'

'Yes, I did,' says Felicity, opening her little black handbag and producing a satisfyingly fat roll of twenties. Ross told her that anything larger would be unacceptable in circumstances such as this. She puts the money on the table, by the tin ashtray with the stubbed-out beer logo. Lou looks at it but makes no move. Felicity sits with her knees pressed together, waiting for some kind of sign as to what she might do next.

'So who is this person?' asks Lou, finally reaching for the banknotes with nonchalant fingers.

'His name is Wayne Briggs,' whispers Felicity, afraid of the sound of her own voice. 'He is a porter at Craven's Hotel.'

'And you need me to give him a little warning, am I right?'

Felicity nods. Ross had made it all sound so easy, but now she is feeling particularly sordid. Dealing with gangland thugs isn't as glamorous as she'd imagined it might be.

'I brought a picture and some details about his home, and so on. There really doesn't seem to be any other way. I've tried to justify this over and over but—'

'Save it for the priest, lady – I don't need your excuses. Give me a week.' Lou finishes his beer in one final swig, pockets the money and leaves the snug by the back exit. Felicity is left alone with her tonic water and her fear. Any minute now the police are going to come in and say that they've been monitoring every word from an unmarked van out in the street – but nothing happens.

Oh my God, what have I done?

Felicity grabs her bag and rushes out into the crowded street. She is facing the backs of the market stalls. Cardboard boxes are piled high, and a dog watches her warily from between two dustbins. She looks up and down the street but Lou is nowhere to be seen. She has no contact number and no idea where to find him until this time next week. By then he will have carried out her request.

Felicity hurries out on to Commercial Road and hails a taxi. Nobody here will recognize her. She's wearing a black Afro wig and pink sunglasses.

Yes, it's tacky!

But, once an actress, always an actress . . . Isn't that how the saying goes?

CHAPTER THIRTY-TWO

'I would like to help you run the hotel,' says Thierry over a glass of barely sweet champagne.

They are eating *fruits de forêt*: tiny Alpine strawberries, blackberries and white-currants served in delicate silver bowls. De Ultieme Hallucinatie is pure art nouveau, as are many of the restaurants in Brussels, and the waiters in their traditional white aprons move around the salon with impeccable discretion. Sebastian feels exuberantly indulged and delightfully cosmopolitan. Beyond the fabric-covered screens they can hear the less decorous thrum of beery conversation in the wood-panelled tavern at the rear of the building.

'Don't you have enough on your plate without tackling Craven's as well?' asks Sebastian. He is wearing one of Thierry's more splendid jackets – bottle-green velvet with black frogging at the cuffs.

'I am thinking of easing up on my regular work, to commit myself to the hotel. I think you need some help, and I think I am probably the best person for the job.'

'Now that's what I call modesty,' laughs Sebastian, tipping his champagne glass in Thierry's direction.

'I don't mean to sound boastful, Sebastian, but you

have to admit that I am something of a good organizer, and I know how to make that place work. Felicity has allowed the hotel to remain stale for too long, and I think that together, you and I could restore some of its former cachet. What do you think, old chap?'

'I'm rather surprised, to be honest with you,' replies Sebastian, considering his friend's suggestion. 'Are you sure you want to invest your time in someone else's business? I thought of you as a dyed in the wool independent. There isn't much negotiable salary, I'm afraid, and you would have to answer to me on everything. Could you lower yourself to that kind of situation after being your own boss for so long?'

'I would consider it an adventure – and an investment. I am pretty sure I can turn that place around within six months, giving us ample time to beat that sister of yours before she opens her new place. I have connections and I have good taste, a winning combination that will put Craven's back on the map.'

It is well after midnight, and they have been seated since eight-thirty. Coffee has yet to be served, and Sebastian is feeling drowsy from the wine and the rich food. This is the first meal they have had alone since his arrival in Brussels, and it has been wonderful. Thierry is the most handsome man he has ever encountered. In this light, and bathed in the bleary-eyed tipsiness of late evening, he appears to Sebastian as his saviour. He feels that he would do anything for this person. He loves him. He really loves him, and that is a painful thorn of emotion that scratches his throat and pricks his eyes whenever he thinks about it. Every moment without Thierry is a waste of time. He watches the clock for his return. He stays awake at night to listen to his breathing. He smells the collars of his unwashed shirts. He collects the hairs in the bathtub. Nobody has ever affected Sebastian this way.

It is a sickness.

'I would *love* you to come and work with me at Craven's,' says Sebastian, placing his hand gently on Thierry's sleeve. Thierry leans over to kiss Sebastian on the cheek. They are on the Continent. They can do that kind of thing here.

'It will be wonderful, you'll see. We are going to have the best hotel in Europe.'

And with the coffee comes a small plate of heart-shaped chocolates, each one decorated with the tiniest piece of crystallized orange peel.

After dinner they go to a bizarre little place called Le Cercueil. It is tucked away on a narrow side street not far from the Grande Place. There is a black, dimly lit staircase which leads up to a small bar where ultra-violet light casts unearthly shadows across the black-painted walls. There are funereally draped velvets and black ostrich plumes, and full-sized empty coffins have been transformed into glass-topped coffee tables. Sebastian pauses on the threshold, but Thierry beckons him inside with an amused smile. A kind of moaning, chanting dirge swells and recedes like the waves of some demonic ocean, and Sebastian feels very uncomfortable.

They take a seat at one of the coffins, beneath a flickering electric candelabrum that emits no light. The barman ignores them and yet there is only a handful of people in the room – a youngish patronage who seem decidedly ordinary for such an extraordinary location. Sebastian might have expected the place to attract those punky, black-eyed weirdo types who call themselves goths, but the people here tonight are studenty Euro-travellers wearing Kickers and drinking beer from skull-shaped mugs.

Finally the barman offers them his attention, his dour expression glowering in the darkness. He brings them fluorescent gin and Sebastian is once again shocked at the price – Brussels is not for someone on a budget.

'How do you know this place?' he asks Thierry.

'Oh, it is not a regular hang-out, but it is always fun to bring people here just to see their reaction. Brussels is full of these crazy little establishments, which seems odd for a city with such a conservative reputation. There is never anyone here; I don't know how he keeps it open, quite honestly.'

'Well, at these prices he could probably retire after the tenth gin and tonic!'

'I wanted to talk to you about Solange,' says Thierry, with an unexpected change of temperature in his voice.

'What about her?' asks Sebastian, averting his eyes.

'I know that you don't like her, and she hinted at a little discussion the two of you had the other day over lunch. I'm afraid she can be rather possessive and jealous, but she means no harm.'

'I can understand her concern. She was your closest friend, and then suddenly I come on the scene and push her to one side. You've known her a lot longer than you've known me, and so I'm prepared to accept her animosity for the short term. Maybe she'll soften as time passes.'

'Solange and I have been friends for many years. Even when I was with Alfred, Solange was there by my side, especially when Alfred became ill and I had to look after him. Solange knows everything there is to know about me – good and bad.' Thierry smiles a sad smile and sips his gin.

'I just hope it's not going to get in the way of *our* relationship.'

Thierry's expression brightens, like a light coming on and blinding Sebastian to the hidden truth. 'That would never happen. Solange is just a friend, and you, my dear Sebastian, are my lover. An incomparable difference.'

'What does Solange think about you coming to work with me in London?' asks Sebastian.

'I haven't told her yet. I imagine it will not make much difference, as she is so often in London on business herself.'

'Yes, I suppose not,' replies Sebastian, attempting to take the sting of bitterness from his tone by swallowing the statement with a smile. He would like to keep Solange away from London. He wishes she would get a job in Brussels and stay here, but he knows that's not going to happen. 'You'd think Solange would get her own flat over there, since she spends more time in London than here in Belgium.'

'Why bother, when my place is perfectly large enough for three?'

Sebastian can't argue with common sense.

They finish their drinks and leave the bar. It is almost two o'clock, and the backstreets of Brussels are quiet. It is only a short walk up through the Sablon to Thierry's place.

'Did you leave the lights on?' asks Thierry as they turn into the darkened courtyard and see a dim glow coming from the murky windows of his apartment.

'I don't think so. It was still light when I left this afternoon.'

Thierry tries the door. It is not locked. He shoots a look at Sebastian that raises the hairs on the back of his neck. There is no sound from within. With a sudden lunge Thierry flings open the door and shouts: '*Qui est là?*'

Who's there?

Two people jump up from the tangled sheets of the four-poster bed. Sebastian registers an ample pair of breasts as Solange darts for cover behind one of the threadbare draperies. The other figure is a dark, hairy man with a beard.

'Solange! What the hell are you doing here?' asks Thierry in French.

'I could ask you the same damned thing!' she

replies, no longer bothering to hide her nakedness as she stands defiantly by the side of the bed. 'I thought you were in London. You told me you were leaving this morning, so naturally I thought this place would be empty.'

Thierry offers Sebastian a brief but enigmatic glance, as though attempting to weigh the situation before reacting further. Solange has snatched her dress from the back of an antique chair and is pulling it on over her frizzed-out hair. She looks remarkably young.

Thierry speaks to Sebastian in English. 'I'm sorry, Sebastian. They obviously thought I was out of town. It's all rather embarrassing.'

'Maybe we should just go out for half an hour?' suggests Sebastian, aware that something about Thierry's explanation does not ring true.

'No,' says Solange, 'that will not be necessary. We will leave.' And then, in French to the bearded man, 'Come on, let's get out of here.'

There are a few minutes of silent manoeuvre, with Solange seeming deliberately to take an age to find the rest of her clothes. She doesn't pull on her underwear until she has buttoned up her dress, and Sebastian gets the impression that this is a mark of disrespect, as though the display of her naked body is somehow a way of saying 'Fuck you!'

When they finally leave, Solange has the barefaced audacity to kiss Thierry full on the lips as she passes. '*Dors bien*!' she says, winking at Sebastian with all the friendliness of a Dobermann. The bearded man looks to Thierry and starts to make a mumbled apology, but Thierry just holds up his hand and closes his eyes.

'Please, Philippe, don't even bother . . .'

So Thierry knows this man?

They leave the apartment and Sebastian sits on the edge of a chair.

'Why were you so horrible to them?' he asks as Thierry closes and locks the door.

'What the hell does it matter to you?' snaps Thierry with an uncharacteristic snarl. His face is black with anger in the dim shadows of the room.

'You can't really blame them if they thought we were in London,' says Sebastian. 'After all, you did give Solange a key to this place.'

'I don't want to discuss it right now. I am tired and I just want to sleep.' Thierry throws his jacket over the back of the sofa and heads for the washbasin.

When Sebastian goes to tidy up the bed, pulling back the rumpled covers he finds the sheets are blotched with semen.

'I shall have to change the sheets,' he says.

Thierry turns to look.

'Bitch!' he screams, throwing down the towel he is holding and making for the door.

'Where are you going?' asks Sebastian, seeing the fury on Thierry's face.

'Leave me alone!' shouts back Thierry.

And he slams the door behind him.

Sebastian sinks down on the edge of the bed and runs his hand over his tired face. What has happened here tonight? He has the sickening feeling that none of this has anything to do with him at all. Sebastian feels superfluous, unwanted. And all around him there is the humming sound of the silence. Like the silence that follows immediately after an explosion.

CHAPTER THIRTY-THREE

Claire's calendar is from the Scope charity shop, and it has photographs of the English countryside in cheerful sunshine colours. She has taken to marking off the days with a green biro, and today is the last day of May. Time is moving quickly now that it is limited, and, whereas Claire used to rejoice in the turning of each month, these days she sees each thatched cottage, each poppy-strewn meadow as another milestone on her journey towards death. Baby Day has been marked with a pink felt pen, and Claire likes to flip the months over sometimes just to see how close she is to becoming a mother.

Will she make it?

How many days will she have after the baby is born?

Might she die in childbirth and never see her daughter's face? For she is sure now that she's going to have a girl.

Duncan has bought her a calendar for next year. It's a kind of wishful thought. Claire was surprised that they had even printed next year's calendars so early, but Duncan insisted on buying it for her because it had images of Pennsylvania and Amish folk on each picturesque page. There were proverbs and recipes, and the calendar came with a free sewing pattern to make an appliquéd apron. But Claire never wears aprons; these days most stains come out with a warm soak in Ariel.

'You're getting really big,' says Dee, sitting at the breakfast bar with a cup of instant cocoa and a packet of orange Club biscuits.

Claire pats her swollen belly and looks down at it appreciatively. 'I think it's just that I've got so scrawny since I started losing weight. I weigh two pounds less now than I did before I became pregnant.'

'What did the doctor say yesterday?'

'Oh, nothing new. They're still trying to persuade me to try that new drugs treatment, but it's still experimental and I'm just not willing to risk it. I think they've finally realized that they can't push me into it; they just suggest it regularly because they feel obliged to. The baby's doing fine, so there's not much more they can do until after it's born, and by then it might be too late for any kind of treatment to do me any good.'

'Poppy saw Sebastian last week. Apparently he still feels awful about that night at the hotel, and his offer still stands. I rather like him, actually, even though he was such a drunken wanker and got you into so much shit. It's that sister of his that deserves to rot. Did you see her talking to Lorraine Whatshername the other morning on breakfast TV? She thinks she's God's gift to mankind, with her hair and her teeth. She even made fun of Lorraine's jacket, and I thought that was a bit much when Lorraine is always so nicely turned out.'

'No, I didn't see it,' says Claire, busy with a herbal tea bag and the electric kettle. 'And as for Sebastian's offer, I might still take him up on it if all else fails. It's just that I don't really think it's his responsibility to set up a bank account for the baby.'

'So what are you going to do?' asks Dee. 'Time's slipping away, and the burden of this is left on your shoulders. Don't you even want to tell that stuck-up bitch what you think of her? She hasn't offered you a penny, despite all that stuff in the papers about her feeling so bad for you. It was just a load of propaganda manufactured by her press people when she thought public opinion might turn against her. People like her don't give a toss about people like us.'

'Now you're sounding militant again. You know I'm not much of a fighter, Dee, and I'm certainly not the type of person who goes begging for money from a complete stranger. I've got pride, and I won't reduce myself to the level of an emotional blackmailer just because I have the opportunity. There has to be a right way of doing this; I just haven't found it yet.'

'I'm gagging for a fag!' says Dee. 'I should go back home, I suppose, so I can inhale a packet of Silk Cut before I miss my daily quota.'

'You can have one here if you go out into the garden,' suggests Claire.

'Nah, I've got to go anyway. I'm rereading *She Devil*

and I've just got to the best part, where the police drag that dickhead Bobbo off for embezzling money from his clients. Ace!'

'Are you seeing Poppy later?'

'I'm going over to her place for dinner. She's got this new cookery book full of bean recipes, so I'm prepared for a fart-fest!'

'Dee, I've never said anything to you before because it's none of my business, but I do know about you and Poppy.'

'What do you mean?' asks Dee, looking uncomfortably compromised.

'Duncan saw you kissing her in your kitchen. I know that you're a—'

'I'm not anything, Claire!'

'Look, it honestly doesn't matter to me. You're my friend and that's all I care about. Poppy is a wonderful person.'

'Yes, Poppy and I have a bit of a thing going, but I *like* fellas! I really do! Poppy is just, well . . . she's different. She's not like a lesbian. I can't believe we're having this conversation – you of all people, Claire!' Dee is embarrassed.

'What do you mean by that? Do you think I'm so unworldly that I don't know about lesbians?'

'No, I just couldn't imagine you ever bringing it up like this. It's so . . . *cosy*. Here we are, having a nice cup of coffee and suddenly you start asking me if I'm a pervert.'

'I wouldn't use such a word.'

'Well, you know what I mean.'

'Look, Dee, you and Poppy can do whatever you like. I just wanted to clear the air between us, because we never talk about your personal life. You keep making lewd comments about blokes and I just thought you did it for my benefit.'

'But I *like* blokes!'

'Fine! So you're bisexual, then?'

'No! I'm one hundred per cent normal. It's just Poppy; she can be very persuasive when she wants to be. Claire, I'm not going to justify this – it's just *different*, that's all.'

'Look, you're always telling me to own up to who and what I am. Well, you should stick by your own convictions. There's nothing wrong with being gay in this day and age – look at Cher!'

'Cher isn't gay.'

'I thought I read somewhere that she was.'

'No, that's her daughter, Chastity.'

'Well, look at Pat Butcher in *EastEnders*.'

'Oh, God, this is getting too weird. I'm going home for a fag.'

Claire's phone rings.

'I'll let myself out,' says Dee. 'Oh, and Claire . . . you've got a smashing pair of tits!'

Claire rolls her eyes and goes though to the living room to see who's calling.

'Is this Claire Brown?' enquires an American voice.

'Yes.'

'Oh, hi! My name is Angelica Schloss, I'm a very

close friend of David Glendale. I hope you don't mind me calling out of the blue like this, Claire, but I've been meaning to get in touch ever since I heard about your terrible story on CNN. I've just come back from Hawaii, so this is the first opportunity I've had to call you.'

'Erm . . . I'm not sure if I know you . . .' starts Claire with uncertainty.

'Oh my Lord, aren't I just the *worst* person . . . I was David's *girlfriend*. You've probably heard about me – I live in Texas? The papers were full of it at the time.'

'Oh, yes,' says Claire, sitting on the back of the sofa.

'Well, you're probably wondering why the heck I'm calling you, I know *I* would be. Well, I wanted to offer you some help with the baby and all. I know you're sick and I know that you need money to support the baby when it's born. Well, I have a little proposition for you. I know this sounds real rude, and I honestly don't want to be, but would you consider allowing me to adopt the child so that I can bring it up in Texas with its little half-brother and half-sister? I wouldn't expect you to give up the child until you . . . well, until you can't look after it any more, and we could have an attorney draw up some kind of agreement between us saying that I will be legal guardian.'

Claire doesn't know what to say. This has hit her like a Frisbee in the back of the neck.

'Are you still there, Claire?'

'Yes.'

'I do hope I haven't upset you, honey – that really is

the last thing I would want to do. I honestly feel for you, and I just thought this might be a good solution. I love kids, and to know that your child was part of David would bring me as much joy as if it was my own. It would want for nothing, Claire – I'm a very wealthy woman. And you could come over here to see the house – all expenses paid, of course – and I promise I would not interfere with you and the baby until the time was right.'

'I don't know what to say. I was only just talking to my friend here about this, and wondering what I should do for the best. It's such a coincidence.'

'Probably some kind of mental telepathy, honey. I truly believe that we are all in the hands of Jesus when it comes to these major decisions. Are you a religious woman, Claire?'

'Well, I do try to pray at least once a week, if that's what you mean. I believe in God and all that.'

'Oh, I'm so glad. So many young people these days ignore the Bible and the Word of the Lord. I'm Presbyterian, and so are the little ones.'

'What are their names?' asks Claire, still reeling.

'Tori and Zane. Tori is five and Zane is just two. They are the sweetest things.'

'Well, I really do need to think about your offer, Mrs . . .'

'Schloss. Please just call me Angelica, honey.'

Angelica Honey? It sounds like something you'd smear on toast.

'I would like to meet you.'

289

'Of course! I'm coming to London in a couple of weeks. I'm buying a house, you know, and I need to start shopping if I'm to move in at the end of the year. Do you know that Harrods are giving me a personal shopper who will do absolutely anything for me? Isn't it peachy?'

'Lovely,' says Claire.

'And you are not to worry about money, honey, I would like to help you out over the interim period, you just need to tell me how much you need. If you give me your bank account I can have money wired over within twenty-four hours, and I can always send you a credit card in the mail for those little impulse buys. Sometimes it just isn't very convenient carrying wads of money around, is it? And it's not even very fashionable these days.'

'I don't need anything, thank you.'

'Of course you do! Everybody needs *something*, and I know you haven't been working. What about medical expenses; surely you're swamped with doctor's bills and medication charges?'

'Actually I get it all through the National Health.'

'What's that, honey? Some kind of insurance company?'

'It's socialized medicine actually – it's free over here, you see.'

'Oh, my goodness, you mean like in *Russia*?' Angelica cries.

'I don't know if the Russians—'

'I want you to go to the best doctors you can buy.

Don't worry about the money – let *me* deal with that. No wonder you're sounding so weak, if you've been relying on free doctors! You need *real* medical attention in your condition, not only you but that baby of yours. I'll call my friend at Glendale Estates and ask him to sort somebody out for you, but in the meantime I want you to give me your checking-account number so that I can wire you some emergency money.'

Claire hesitates.

'I won't take no for an answer, Claire. You're obviously a lady with principles, but principles don't get you anywhere in this life, and you'll just have to accept that David would have wanted me to do this for you. He was a very generous man.'

'I'll get my chequebook,' says Claire.

'OK, honey.'

And when Claire puts down the receiver to fetch her handbag, she doesn't hear Angelica Schloss covering her mouthpiece to whisper: 'I think she's going to do it.'

All Claire hears is the sound of approaching salvation.

CHAPTER THIRTY-FOUR

Felicity and Ross are back together. He has split up with Bettina Carlton-Blye and now he tells Felicity that it was all a big mistake. 'She was a bitch!' he says, nibbling on Felicity's ear and tweaking her nipple.

They've been back together now for a week, and Felicity is sore from all their making-up sex.

'It might be thrush, darling,' says Felicity, wincing as she hoists up her knickers for the second time that afternoon.

Ross is wearing one of David's old dressing gowns, and he throws himself back on to the bed with a triumphant moan. He's rather dishy in a grey-at-the-temples kind of way, and Felicity is glad to have him back. She no longer feels guilty about his long-suffering wife, Cybil, because rumour has it that Cybil is getting plenty of action these days from a young lifeguard at the municipal baths. Having Ross around makes everything feel that much more normal; even the kids seem pleased to see him.

'So how are things going with the new hotel? There's been a lot of speculation around the circuit. You'll have to take me over there when you get a chance.'

'Oh, it's abysmally slow, darling. There's so much tearing down to do, the place just looks like a bomb-site at the moment. I've got some dubious contractors – Scottish, cheap and cheeky. They completely buggered up the wiring on the ground floor last week, and it all had to be ripped out and done again. That's set me back a couple of weeks at least, and now they're trying to tell me that they're not going to start on the renovation of the ballroom until September. The entire basement is untouched!'

'Where are these temporary offices of yours? I went past them yesterday in a cab, but I couldn't see anything.'

'Oh, we're above Cullens. There isn't a sign or anything; it's pretty grim, actually, but it's cheap and I'm hoping to have my office ready in the hotel by August. Did I tell you that Marissa is still with me? She defected from Craven's and came begging for a job. Poor, misguided fool; I think she has some kind of persecution complex.'

'I thought it was her when I called the other day. And I notice you've kept hold of the old chauffeur.' Ross gives Felicity a roguish smile as he raises his arms above his head.

'Oh, come off it, darling! James might be built like a Chippendale but he's about as bright as a fifteen-watt bulb. Do you know, he's getting married? Yes! Some leggy bottle-blonde from Norbiton who demonstrates exercise equipment at Debenhams.'

'Have you heard anything about that young porter yet?'

Felicity sits on the edge of her dressing table stool and stares at her perfect reflection in the mirror. Even ravaged by sex, her appearance is that of a screen goddess.

'Oh, gosh, I still feel pretty crummy about that business. I can't believe I actually did it. Apparently he hasn't been into work since Tuesday, and nobody knows where he is. He hasn't called in sick, and nobody's seen him. I'm frightfully worried that Lou might have gone too far and put him in hospital or something.'

'When did you develop a conscience, darling? You're starting to sound like Mother Teresa. Where's that ruthless streak I always admired?'

'Oh, stop being so naughty! Wayne Briggs may well be a foul little guttersnipe, but I certainly don't want to do anything more than warn him off.'

'You still haven't told me why you loathe him so much. How on earth can a teenage boy find anything with which to threaten the invincible Felicity Craven?'

'Let's just say he knows more than he should about certain things. He snooped in on a business meeting and he's trying to blackmail me. Greasy little sod!'

'Is it that good-looking blond boy who used to work in the lobby?'

'Yes, that's him. You'd think butter wouldn't melt in his mouth. The ladies loved him; that's why we kept him on. Oh, God, just look at this cellulite! Two hundred quid at the spa, and it's still rippling across my arse like curdled butter,' cries Felicity, prodding her upper thigh with expensively manicured fingers.

'Fliss, you're incorrigible! There isn't a flaw on your body and yet you insist on finding fault with it whenever you can. Are you fishing for compliments, or are you just obsessed?'

'It's all right for you. Men get better-looking as they get older, but women just sag and wrinkle like deflating balloons. One has to be on one's guard twenty-four hours a day. I bumped into Twiggy the other day in Conran's and she looked bloody amazing. Of course she said the same thing about me, but then doesn't everyone when they're shocked by one's appearance?'

'I've had enough of this. I'm going to take a shower. Are you coming with me, or do I have to scrub my own back?'

'Darling, if you've got another hard-on I suggest you make that water *cold*, because my poor abused pussy is closed for the day!'

Ross climbs off the bed and makes for the bathroom.

Felicity lets out a hideous scream of terror and throws herself across the room.

'Good God, whatever's the matter?' shouts Ross, caught up in her hysteria.

'Cockroaches!' she screams. 'There, under the bed.'

It would seem that Wayne Briggs's little joke has just made it to the master bedroom.

Felicity's temporary office really isn't very glamorous. She has the attic rooms, and there is no lift. Just foot-worn stairs with painted banisters, and abused industrial vinyl on the walls. No concealed lighting. No arty prints or vases of flowers. Just dirty landing windows and fire extinguishers.

Marissa sits at a slab of glass that was virtually impossible to get through the door. It rests on glass pedestals. The room is startlingly white. There are white leather club chairs and a glass coffee table with carefully arranged magazines, and a bowl of white lilies which strangle the tepid atmosphere with their cloying perfume. The window is jammed shut with years of gloss paint. Outside, the window sill is spiked with metal to stop the pigeons landing there. Glossy pictures of Felicity and Craven's Hotel line one wall, in black maple frames.

Beyond the white-panelled door we find Felicity thumbing through some Pendaflex files. Her office has slanted ceilings and dormer windows, which she has draped so oppressively in grey silk that they look like eighteenth-century courtiers bowed under the weight of their finery. Felicity is humming a little tune, which is totally unlike her – as a rule she never hums. Her gorgeous hair is pulled back in a simple French braid, and she is wearing a new summer suit from Jasper Conran. She looks every inch the part.

There is a commotion outside in Reception, and Felicity can hear Marissa screaming hysterically. What's wrong with that stupid girl now? Probably a wasp – or full-fat mayonnaise on her tuna salad sandwiches again.

There's a clattering sound, and then the door to Felicity's office shoots open, and there stands Wayne Briggs with a huge plaster over the bridge of his nose and both eyes blackened with violently purple bruises. His lip is crusted with scabs and he has one arm in a sling. Felicity remains crouched by the filing cabinet, wondering if anyone might come to her rescue were she to scream out of the window into the street below.

'Sorry I didn't make an appointment,' says Wayne Briggs through painfully cracked lips. There's a whistling sound as though he has no teeth. 'My dialling finger is broken.'

'Marissa, go downstairs and call a policeman, or something!' shouts Felicity urgently.

'I wouldn't bother doing that, darlin',' says Wayne to the dishevelled secretary. 'They might be more interested in carting your boss away than making a move on me.'

'Marissa, I'll shout if I need anything. Just straighten up that desk and get yourself a glass of Perrier.'

Felicity stands up, smooths her skirt and moves around Wayne in order to close the door. Wayne grins at her like a ghoul, and Felicity sees that he has indeed lost his front teeth. The sight sickens her, and she feels ashamed.

'You'd better sit down,' she says softly, offering him a chair by her desk. 'Can I get you anything? Water, perhaps? Or a cup of coffee?'

'I didn't come up here because I was thirsty,' says Wayne, taking a seat.

'No,' says Felicity, unable to look him in the eye.

'I don't suppose I have to tell you why I look like this.'

'Have you been in an accident?' asks Felicity.

'Don't bother fucking me around, you bitch! You know damned well why I'm all bashed up. It was that fucking henchman you hired, and if you don't call him off I'm going straight down the papers to show them what you're capable of. I don't know how you thought you were going to get away with this, but if you think it'll scare me off you obviously don't know who you're dealing with. You and that wanker of a brother of yours – I sometimes wonder what public school did for you both. Common sense just doesn't run in the family, does it?'

'I don't know what you mean. Are you suggesting that I had something to do with your . . . accident?' Felicity is trying her hardest to remember how to appear shocked and disturbed, but she suspects that she is not doing a very good job.

'Save the crappy actress bit for somebody who cares! You can forget the job in your new hotel. I don't want to work for you; I just want cash.' Wayne shifts uncomfortably in his chair and stares at Felicity with undiluted hatred.

'It depends what kind of figure we're talking about. You know my money is all tied up in the new hotel. My husband left me a pittance, and I've got a family to support.'

'What about the money you got from that woman in America? You're hardly what I'd call poor.'

'Listen, what do you want from me? I will not be threatened by a teenager, especially when I don't know what I'm supposed to have done.'

'Five hundred thousand.'

'What!'

'And fifty thousand a year for the next ten years.'

'Are you mad?'

'Take it or leave it.'

'I don't have that kind of money.'

'Well, find it. I don't see you doing very well in Holloway prison with all those bull dykes and drug pushers.'

'I doubt very much if it would come to that. It's your word against mine, and I have friends in very influential places. You'd never win.'

'Well, it'd be worth the try just to see you squirm.'

'Oh, just get out of here. I haven't the time to sit and listen to your idle threats. If you want to make up silly stories for the papers, then go ahead. I will deny everything and you'll end up looking like a pathetic like trickster. Now clear off before I really do call the police and have you arrested for being a public nuisance.'

'On your own head be it. But I'm telling you right now – you're going to regret turning me away like this. One day soon I'm going to be holding the barrel of a gun to your head and you're going to beg me for mercy. And I can tell you now, no amount of begging is going to stop me pulling that trigger and blowing your fucking brains out all over your expensive upholstery.'

'Get out!' shouts Felicity.

'And you'd better keep an eye on those precious little kids of yours an' all. I know which schools they go to, and I know where they are every fucking minute of the day. Remember that when you're making the arrangements to get my cash.'

'Get out!' Felicity screams again.

'Toodle-pip!' mocks Wayne.

And he leaves the office with a sardonic smile.

As soon as the door has swung closed on its safety hinge, Felicity punches Ross's number into her phone. Her heart is beating wildly and she can barely breathe.

'Ross?'

'Fliss?'

'I need to meet that man again, Lou.'

'What's happened?'

'I've just had a rather unpleasant visit from that porter chap – Wayne Briggs. Can you set up a meeting with him for this evening? Same place, at eight o'clock?'

'Do you want me to go with you?'

'No, I don't want you involved, darling. It's all getting a bit out of hand and I need to put a stop to it before it goes any further.'

'Give me a few minutes and I'll call you back. Are you sure you're OK?'

'I'm fine, darling. Just hurry up and call me.'

Felicity goes through to see how Marissa is. The reception area is empty, and magazines and lilies still scattered across the carpet. Marissa can't have gone far because her handbag is still slung over the back of her chair.

There really is no alternative now. Felicity has to put a contract out on Wayne Briggs before he ruins everything. It sounds extreme, but Felicity feels strangely detached from her decision. It's easy to think of killing someone when they are as manipulative and evil as Wayne Briggs. It's not as though anyone would miss him.

The phone rings. It's Ross.

'Fliss? Bad news, darling. Lou Baker was found dead last night on the edge of Hyde Park. It was murder, Fliss. Somebody clubbed him to death with a length of iron railing.'

Chapter Thirty-five

'Is it me, or do these scones taste like washing-up liquid?' asks Poppy, screwing up her nose.

'Well, I wasn't going to say anything, but they're not the best I've ever eaten,' agrees Tony, Sabrina's hired escort.

'It's our new pastry chef,' says Sebastian. 'Thierry brought him over from Belgium this week after he sacked Michel. I think I'm going to have to have a quiet word in his ear. The éclairs are a bit soggy, as well. How's yours, Mummy?'

Sabrina is spitting her scone into a napkin, dumping it unceremoniously on to the restaurant carpet with a resounding 'Blah!' which seems to amuse some of the other diners, who pretend not to look.

'Mummy! That's not very polite, is it?'

'Where are the Hob Nobs?' Sabrina asks in a loud and demanding tone.

'Mummy, there aren't any Hob Nobs – this isn't Littlewoods' café, you know.'

Sabrina picks up a smoked-salmon sandwich from the tiered platter on their table and dunks it straight into her cup of Earl Grey. Tea goes flooding in all directions across the white tablecloth.

'Oh, for God's sake, Mummy!' Sebastian is exasperated.

Tony reaches across the table and takes Sabrina's delicate wrist.

'Sabrina, that's enough. You're behaving very badly, and I'm not going to take you out again unless you start to buck your ideas up. Now, do you want that sandwich, or are you just being obstreperous?'

Sabrina looks at Tony as though she is about to leap from a tall building. She smiles brightly, squeezes his hand and starts to mop up the spilled tea with a fresh napkin.

'Oops!' she says. 'I've made a bit of a mess. I'm so sorry.'

'It was an accident,' says Poppy, looking at Sebastian as if to say, *Wow, this chap is marvellous!*

'Thanks, Tony,' says Sebastian. 'You really are a great help.'

'All part of the job,' says Tony, causing Sabrina to flutter her navy-blue false eyelashes at him in unabashed flirtation. Sebastian suspects that Tony is a bit of a gigolo on the side, but the money's worth it because Mummy has been remarkably calm since he came on the scene.

'How's everything working out with Thierry?' asks Poppy.

'Well, it's only been a week but he seems to be rampaging through the place like a bull in a china shop. He's already sacked two chefs, the housekeeper and several office staff, and replaced them all with people he says he knows from other hotels. The new housekeeper is a particularly odd individual – a Russian lady who I swear is completely sozzled all the time. She reeks of vodka fumes and eats raw onions, which she stores in the back of the linen cupboard. When I tried to tell her that this wasn't a good idea, she started crying and ranting in Russian, and it took several shots of vodka to get her back on her feet. Thierry says she's incredibly cheap and surprisingly efficient, but I am yet to be convinced.'

'Are you sure he really knows what he's doing?' Poppy jangles her bangles as she flips her hair deftly over one shoulder.

'He's very confident. At least we're still at eighty-five per cent occupancy and he's brought in an awful lot of new business. Two wedding parties and a coach-load of Japanese businessmen who are going to take over the hotel for five days next month.'

'I thought you didn't do that kind of thing – block bookings and weddings.'

'Well, that was one of Felicity's rules about keeping the place exclusive, but Thierry reckons we can make a packet on these corporate deals and budget week-ends for out-of-towners. We're going to be included in the American Airlines London Mini-Break catalogue this autumn.'

'Sounds a bit iffy to me. Surely that's more for your Trust House Forte clientele? For Yanks who want to stay at the Café Royal or the Waldorf and pretend that they're seeing the real England.'

'Well, I'm leaving it up to him. As long as we keep making a profit, I don't mind what he does.'

'Felicity's going to have personal assistants for every guest in *her* new hotel,' says Sabrina, crumbling a pastry on her plate and dabbing at it with her fork. 'She told me there'll be free chocolates and a flip-top bin in every room.'

'A flip-top bin?'

'She means a laptop computer,' says Tony.

'Well I just hope she's not overextending herself. This isn't the eighties, you know, and she doesn't have the budget she had when Father bought this place.'

'She's got loads of money. She told me,' says Sabrina.

'But where did it come from?' asks Sebastian. 'I know it wasn't from David's will.'

'Felicity strikes me as the kind of woman who has friends in very high places,' says Poppy.

'Yes, well, I hear she's back with Ross Peters. Bettina Carlton-Blye soon dumped him when she realized that he hasn't got two pennies to rub together. His restaurant isn't doing very well according to Cybil, and he owes a ton of money, apparently. I don't know what Felicity sees in him, quite honestly.'

'He's good in bed,' says Sabrina. 'Felicity told me he's got at least eight inches.'

'Mummy! What *are* you talking about?' says Sebastian, looking nervously around to see if anyone is listening.

'His dick, darling! Apparently it's enormous.'

'I can't believe Felicity told you that, Mummy. Are you making it up?'

'No, I heard her on the phone to her friend Courgette.'

'It's *Georgette*, Mummy.'

'Well, anyway, I heard her.'

Poppy is trying really hard not to laugh and Sebastian has to kick her under the table.

'I think it's time we got you home,' says Tony, pushing back his chair.

'I'm not going into a home,' says Sabrina firmly, holding on to the edge of the table with her lips set in a determined line.

'Come on, the car's waiting for us outside.'

'What? I'm sorry, but I don't think we've met,' she says, staring at Tony with a bemused smile.

'Off we go, then.' And Tony takes Sabrina's elbow and leads her out of the restaurant. Sebastian and Poppy follow and wave them off at the door.

'It's a shame. She's still a very beautiful woman,' says Poppy.

'At least she's not in pain,' says Sebastian. 'And Tony is incredibly good with her.'

'Do you still think it's a good idea for her to have such an elaborate birthday party?'

'That's Felicity's grand idea – let *her* deal with it. If it's a disaster, then it'll fall on her shoulders, not mine. I think Mummy will be oblivious to the entire thing, quite honestly.'

'Have you spoken to Felicity yet?'

'No, she sends me faxes.'

'I wonder if she's heard about Claire's little wind-fall?'

'If she has, she's been keeping quiet about it. I don't imagine that Angelica Schloss is one of her most favourite people.'

'Well, she's certainly more charitable than Felicity.'

'Poppy, *anyone* is more charitable than Felicity!'

'I am thinking that perhaps we should redecorate some of the bedrooms. One or two of them are looking particularly dated,' says Thierry, sitting in what used to be Felicity's office.

Sebastian is not really interested in talking about the hotel. It seems that Thierry is still ignoring the scene they had in Brussels when they discovered Solange and her boyfriend in Thierry's apartment. He refuses to talk about it, and they haven't seen her or mentioned Solange's name since.

'Whatever,' says Sebastian. 'But put a budget together before you go ahead with anything.'

'I've got this incredible decorator who has just finished doing up a nightclub in Berlin. Very innovative, but not famous enough yet to cost a fortune. I am most eager to get rid of Felicity's influence in this place. She still haunts us like a kind of ghost.'

'That new pastry chef you hired, are you sure his credentials are accurate? I wasn't very impressed with the afternoon tea today.'

Thierry looks at Sebastian as though he is completely crazy.

'He is the best! Everybody wanted him when he left his last place, and it took quite a bit of wheeling and dealing to persuade him to come here.'

'You seem to be enjoying this, Thierry.'

'Of course I am enjoying it. I get a chance to prove myself to you – show you what I'm made of.'

'I already know what you're made of. I also know that there's another side to you that I know absolutely nothing about.'

'What on earth do you mean?' Thierry looks startled: caught out?

'Well, that business with Solange for a start.'

'Oh, *that*.' Thierry seems relieved. 'I told you – I was just angry with her for taking advantage so, and for spoiling our lovely evening. I would think that you would be pleased to have her out of the way. You told me yourself that you didn't like her.'

'Well, yes, it *is* nice to have you to myself, but I'm just concerned that there was something more to your reaction than you're telling me. You came back that night as though you'd just murdered somebody.'

'I've told you everything, Sebastian. I can do no more.'

'OK, OK. I suppose I'm just being paranoid. Things are all a bit topsy-turvy for me at the moment, with one thing and another.' Sebastian squeezes Thierry's shoulder and kisses the top of his head. 'You know I love you very much.'

'Ditto,' says Thierry.

'What's this?' asks Sebastian, holding up a brochure.

'Oh, karaoke machines. I thought it would be fun to have one in the upstairs bar. The Japs will love it, and we can have special nights to attract non-residents.'

'I don't think that's a very good idea, Thierry. This isn't a pub, you know; we don't serve scampi in a basket and lager shandy. Upstairs is supposed to be a piano bar where residents can relax with a martini or a glass of champagne. You'll be suggesting a jukebox and a dartboard next!' Sebastian laughs.

Thierry just looks at him, straight-faced.

'Do you want this place to make money, or not? The bloody piano bar hasn't made a penny of profit since this place opened.'

'It's not supposed to make a profit. It doesn't stand on its own as an independent business, you know; it's supposed to be part and parcel of the money we make on the rooms. I doubt that Tom Cruise and Nicole Kidman are going to pay eight hundred quid a night to eat cheese and onion crisps while a load of Japs sing "Wake Me Up Before You Go-Go".'

'I think the rooms are overpriced. We need to make them more accessible to the general public, instead of catering just to the rich and famous.'

'But that's what Craven's *is*, Thierry – a boutique hotel, not a four-hundred-bedroom West End giant. It was never intended to compete with the conglomerates; that's why we attract the people we do.'

'Do you want me to run this place or not? You

didn't seem to have any opinions when Felicity was in charge; are you suddenly assuming some kind of authoritative position now that *I'm* doing the job? Because if you are, then I don't think I can do this. I need to have the authority to make changes without being shot down every time I make a suggestion. I'm doing this for you, Sebastian, for your company and for our future. You want to remain wealthy, don't you?'

'Of course I do, but I'm just a bit wary of making so many sudden changes. Our clients expect certain things of us, and I don't want to lose them because of a drop in standards. I rather like hobnobbing with these celebrities.'

'There is more to running a successful hotel than sharing a bowl of macadamia nuts with Mariah Carey, you know! We could have this place bursting at the seams every night if we go about it the right way. Believe me, Sebastian, I know what I'm doing.'

'OK, OK, but no karaoke machine – not yet, anyway. Let's take one thing at a time.'

'Fine, have it your own way, but I'm telling you it would be a great investment.'

Right at that moment a man in overalls glides past the office window on an electric crane.

'Who's that?' asks Sebastian, going over to the window to look out.

'Oh, it's the men from Woodbridge and Carter. They're installing our new neon sign.'

'*Neon?*'

'Yes, I had them jazz up the logo a bit. It's going to

310

be very jolly, so that people can actually tell that we are a hotel and not some sort of private health club. I've always thought it looked awfully intimidating from the outside.'

'Good God, Felicity's going to have a hissy fit when she sees that monstrosity.'

'Well, Felicity doesn't have anything to do with it any more, does she? Anybody would think you were scared of her or something.'

'Of course I'm not scared of her,' says Sebastian uneasily. 'It's just that I'm nervous of all these changes, Thierry. You could have at least consulted me about the sign. And why are they unscrewing the chrome plaques on either side of the doors?'

'Oh, I've had some better ones made with the new improved logo. They light up as well.'

Sebastian refrains from comment.

He has a sinking feeling that everything is about to go horribly wrong.

CHAPTER THIRTY-SIX

Angelica Schloss looks like a rhinestone cowboy.

Claire is propped up with pillows on her living-room sofa. She doesn't feel too good today, and Duncan has been feeding her tinned chicken broth with wholemeal toast. She feels like an invalid, and she knows that her hair is greasy and flecked with dandruff.

The visit is unexpected, inconvenient. And most of all, it's embarrassing.

'I am truly sorry to burst in on you like this, Claire, but I'm only making a flying visit to the UK on my way to Paris. I just couldn't pass by without calling on you. I do hope you'll forgive me for this intrusion.' Angelica removes her cowboy hat with the turquoise stones, and places it on the armchair.

'You look pale as a ghost. Have you been to see that Harley Street doctor, like I said?'

'She has an appointment on Friday,' says Duncan, still standing by the door looking slightly apprehensive. 'Today hasn't been a good day. She hasn't slept all night.'

'Please don't talk about me as if I wasn't here,' says Claire, clearing her throat and trying to sound assertive. 'I'm just a bit tired, that's all. I wish you could have warned me that you were coming, Angelica. I would have tidied up a bit and washed my hair. I feel terrible.'

'Oh, nonsense, child. I didn't come here expecting tea and crumpets. I'd been hoping that maybe we could go shopping together, get to know each other a little better, but it looks as though I chose the wrong day for that.'

Angelica is wearing jeans with creases ironed into them. Her pointy boots look like snakeskin and her wide leather belt has a silver buckle that could double as a drinks coaster.

'Oh, I'm all right really. I've been sitting here all morning like a scarecrow. I could do with a bit of excitement.'

'Claire, love, I wouldn't recommend—'

'Oh, Duncan, stop being so overprotective. I feel like some fresh air, and a trip around the shops might do me good. I'm not dead yet, you know!'

'Oh, honey, what a thing to say! Of course you're not dead. Why don't you wash up and I'll get my driver to take us into town for an hour. Do you have any shops here, or do we have to go back into London?'

Claire manages a little laugh.

'Yes, we have a shopping centre, and a Debenhams.'

'What's that, honey?'

'It's a department store.'

'Oh, like Harrods?'

'Not quite.' Claire laughs again. Duncan helps her off the sofa and she goes upstairs, one step at a time, to make herself look presentable. She can hear Duncan and Angelica exchanging concerned whispers downstairs in the living room. Sometimes it's like being present at her own funeral, and she hates the way people talk about her when she leaves the room these days.

The baby struggles in her stomach and she pauses to place her hand against the thin wall that separates them. At least the baby's full of life. Claire catches her reflection in the bathroom mirror and is horrified by what she sees. Her cheeks are sunken into dark hollows and her hair is plastered to her head as though it is wet. Even her eyes are dull and lifeless, as if she has already died on the inside. There isn't much she can do to improve her appearance, but she rakes a comb through her hair, sprays some perfume and adds a dab of lipstick that instantly transforms her into a kind of horror monster, like the living dead in a Michael Jackson video. She has a spot right at the corner of her nose, but she hasn't the energy to squeeze it.

'All ready!' she announces, standing on the stairs in her white cardigan.

'Great!' says Angelica enthusiastically.

Why do Americans always sound as though they're about to recruit you to join a cult, or something?

'Are you going to come with us, Duncan?' asks Angelica, putting on her cowboy hat with a flick of her suede-fringed shirt.

'I think I'll stay here and clean this place up a bit,' he answers, winking at Claire and kissing her on the forehead.

'You've found yourself an absolute sweetie-pie,' whispers Angelica as she leads Claire down the path, avoiding the cat poo with a diplomatic swerve to the left.

It is a lovely afternoon.

June flowers and butterflies. Gardens overflowing with colour and fragrance. The Acorns has never looked more lovely, and Claire is proud for Angelica to see it this way. Claire hasn't been out for several days, and now – in the back of the huge leather-upholstered limo, with the windows down and the breeze smelling of warm asphalt and roses – she can feel her spirit rising to the surface.

'This *is* a tonic,' she says, smiling at Angelica.

'You look better already, honey. It can't be good for you sitting in that house all day.'

'I just haven't felt like going out. I get really tired. Some days I don't even get out of bed because I feel as though all the strength has been sucked out of me.'

'Well, I just know that Jesus is watching over you, Claire. You made this very brave decision to keep your baby and to bring a new life into the world. Sacrifice never goes unnoticed – I firmly believe that.' Angelica takes Claire's hand in her own, and Claire does not feel embarrassed. Which is odd, because this kind of thing usually makes her squirm.

'You must miss David,' Claire says.

'Oh, honey, David is always with me. I don't suppose you saw the best side of him – he was never very good when he had drink inside him, but that was the stress making him be that way. His life was a terrible burden for him, and I think I was the only person who saw his better side. Felicity was not good for him; she just added to his troubles. I suppose I was like a kind of confessional – somebody he could turn to when it seemed as though the whole world was fighting a lawsuit against him. I was truly blessed the day David Glendale came into my life.'

'It must have been awful for you not being able to go to the funeral.'

'It was hard, yes. I watched it on a TV news channel. But, you know, I never truly felt that I needed to be there. I have my own rewards, Claire, and I don't just mean the house and the money.'

'That's where I met Duncan,' says Claire, pointing out the Jolly Roger. 'We met through a personal ad in the local newspaper.'

'You did? How *special*. He's a bit of a hunk, isn't he? I was expecting somebody a bit less *epic* in proportions, if I'm to be truthful.'

'He plays rugby,' says Claire proudly.

'That's kind of like our football, right?'

'I'm not sure, actually. He's big but he's really kind and nice underneath.'

'A sort of gentle giant,' says Angelica. 'I used to know a guy like that at high school: Brian Fielding. He took me to the prom one year and he was my first ever real-live boyfriend. He's married now, with three kids. Funny how things work out.'

'What's it like in America?' asks Claire. 'Is it all skyscrapers and big cars like on the telly?'

Angelica laughs. 'Well, it can be if you live in Dallas, but for most of us it's just home, and we live a very simple life not that different from your own. You should come over some day and see what it's all about.'

'I've seen a documentary about Pennsylvania. That looked really nice.'

'I've never been: it's a long way from Texas. Is this the mall?'

'The shopping centre, yes. We can get out here.'

'Give us a couple of hours, John,' says Angelica to the driver.

'People are wondering who we are,' says Claire, noticing the inquisitive stares from the lunchers eating their pre-packed shrimp and mayonnaise sandwiches on the public benches.

'Well, let them wonder,' says Angelica. 'Now then, let's go and get you one heck of a makeover. I'm going to take you back to Duncan looking like a million dollars.'

'What's that in pounds?' laughs Claire, suddenly finding a bit of a spring in her step as the pigeons scatter to let them through.

*

The afternoon is an unmitigated success. Claire gets her hair done at Lobby Toffs. Thirty-five pounds for a shampoo, cut and blow-dry. She doesn't know she has so much hair until Trina, the stylist, fills it with volume and makes her look like an air hostess. She has her nails done at the same time, and Angelica chooses a very pale natural pink, because she says that Claire is a mother-to-be and anything else would be vulgar.

In Debenhams they get the woman on the Estée Lauder counter to do her face. Claire is perched on a high bar stool with cotton wool wrapped under her collar and her new hair bound back by an elastic strap. The Estée Lauder woman looks like an air hostess too, but she has a really strong Cockney accent and she keeps calling Claire's cheekbones 'stunning'. When she has finished, Claire is allowed to look at herself in the oval mirror. She still has an unnaturally pale complexion, but now it looks more interesting, as though it is supposed to be that way. Angelica buys all the necessary ingredients, plus toners and moisturizers, and the Estée Lauder woman acts as though it's Christmas, throwing in free samples and sucking up to Angelica as though she's royalty or something.

'I've never seen one of these,' says the assistant, fiddling with Angelica's platinum American Express card. 'They cost a bomb, don't they?'

'Excuse me?' says Angelica, not understanding.

'She means the membership fees — they're expensive,' explains Claire, aware of her Feline Frost lipstick.

'Oh, honey, I have no idea what I pay for that darned thing.'

The Estée Lauder woman looks very impressed, and throws in another sample of White Linen.

'Do you have a Pea in the Pod?' asks Angelica, straight-faced.

'Erm . . .' says Claire, not sure if this is a joke or something.

'The *store*, honey. Pea in the Pod – maternity clothes.'

'Oh, I've never heard of it. It must be an American shop. We've got a Mothercare.'

But Angelica is not very impressed with Mothercare, so they end up in a little shop called Bonne Maman, where a thin woman with a bun and red shoes helps them choose a very expensive dress made from a light, floaty fabric printed with pale, shadowy roses. It hangs from just under Claire's bust and drops in lovely folds to her ankles.

'I look like an air hostess at a garden party,' she says.

'You need some better shoes,' says Angelica. So they go to Freeman Hardy & Willis and get her some ivory-coloured court shoes. Angelica can't believe how inexpensive they are, so she buys Claire two pairs. 'Just in case they fall to pieces,' she says.

And then it's time for coffee and buns at the Doughboy Café, before they return to the car, which is waiting for them outside Ryman's.

'Doesn't she look great, John?' Angelica asks the driver as they climb into the back of the limo.

'You look pretty as a picture, madam,' says the driver, with a tip of his hat.

The two women drive back to The Acorns with their shopping bags and their big hair, as if Angelica isn't a millionaire and Claire isn't dying of leukaemia.

'Good God!' exclaims Duncan when he opens the door.

Claire gives him a twirl on the doorstep.

'How did you do that?' he asks.

'With about five hundred quid,' says Claire, looking at Angelica.

'Now, don't start obsessing about the money again, Claire. I've told you, David would have wanted me to do this, and it really is nothing.'

'I've just put the kettle on,' says Duncan.

'Oh, I can't stay. I've got to be at Heathrow by six-thirty. I'll call you when I get back into London next week – maybe we can all get together for dinner or something. And let me know what the doctor says. Here's my number in Paris – call collect.'

Claire assumes that Angelica is going to kiss her on the cheek and so is unprepared for the hug that squeezes the breath out of her.

'I feel as though I've made a new friend today,' says Angelica.

She returns to her car, where John is waiting to open the door for her.

'It's another world,' says Duncan, watching the limo

as it glides out of sight behind the ice-cream van parked on the corner.

But Claire has already gone inside.

And that's where he finds her: crumpled in a heap of pale shadowy roses at the bottom of the stairs.

CHAPTER THIRTY-SEVEN

Sometimes one can almost feel sorry for Felicity Craven. She doesn't seem to have much fun, despite all the trappings of success. She kids herself that spending money makes her happy, that the contents of an expensively produced carrier bag with fabric handles will offer her something to be thankful for. But how long does that kind of happiness last? Not very long. Sometimes it doesn't even last as long as it takes to get the bag home and unloaded.

The last time Felicity was really happy was probably, oh, about fifteen years ago, when she first met David. Before their children came along and cluttered up the equation. In those days it was still thrilling to buy jewels at Asprey, to have flowers delivered from Moyses Stevens. Materialism has left her jaded after so many years of excessive indulgence. She knows people who still hum and ha over the cost of a diamond solitaire the size of a bread crumb – she has seen them standing outside the windows of H. Samuel with their Tesco bags and their hooded coats. It isn't really a question of how happy is Felicity Craven; it's more a question of how sad are those people who can't even afford a poxy little diamond?

But things are not going her way at the moment, and she's feeling the strain. Her aromatherapist has administered lavender and clary sage, but they aren't doing much to brighten her spirits. Apart from Ross and a couple of fair-weather girlfriends, she has no one to talk to. The children are away at school, and, even before the bust-up, she and Sebastian had never been particularly close. Mummy used to be a good listener before she cracked up, but these days it's like talking to a child. Felicity lives with her own thoughts, her own fears. And every day it's as though she's being tested.

Lou Baker is dead. Somebody thrust a spiked metal railing through his chest, and killed him like a modern-day vampire. Felicity is frightened but she doesn't know what to do. She *should* go straight to the police and tell them everything she knows about Wayne Briggs. She should, but she knows she won't. She doesn't know why exactly, but it has something to do with a fear of being caught out, for Felicity herself is not beyond reproach in this matter. In a way, if it hadn't been for Felicity, Lou Baker would still be alive, living his life of petty crime, earning his money with a knuckleduster and a sawn-off shotgun. What if Felicity is the next victim on the list? She has been keeping herself locked in. Wayne Briggs is nowhere to be seen.

In the summer months, London really isn't very pleasant, and usually Felicity goes somewhere nice with palm trees and four-star service. This year, however, she has to stick around because of the new hotel. Every day is another dilemma. The city is full of tourists. Even sacrosanct places like Fulham Road and Chelsea Harbour are peppered with foreign accents and ethnic minorities. Today, in Piers's antique shop, an American couple in trainers and baseball caps shelled out thirty thousand on a pair of threadbare Aubusson *entre-fenêtres*. Felicity can't even imagine what they will do with the things – probably hang them up on either side of some ghastly pseudo-French fireplace with gas-burning logs and a glass screen.

It's stifling in the temporary office. There's no air-conditioning and the windows will not open. Marissa has brought in a couple of fans but they don't do very much apart from stir the already stale air around in circles. The only bright spot of the day is the recent magazine article about Craven's. Felicity keeps it on her desk, along with the family photographs.

Hotel du Lack: celebrity haunt loses cachet after management reshuffle.

There is a photograph of the new neon sign.

The article is scathing. Guests are complaining about the sudden changes. Emma Thompson has moved out and Gazza has moved in. The sushi bar has been rented out to Johnny Rockets. There are plans for murder-mystery weekends, and a German *bierfest* in the marquee. Felicity hadn't imagined it could all happen so quickly. She only wishes now that her own hotel was up and running, so that she could offer a suitable alternative. At least the article includes a marvellous profile of Felicity, and practically begs her to open The Phoenix as soon as possible. She has already received phone calls from perplexed celebrities who no longer have a safe and stylish refuge in London.

Everything is going according to plan.

'I'll be out for most of the afternoon,' she tells Marissa, as she passes through the outer office wearing a straw sunhat that resembles a wilting king-size pizza.

'Fine,' says Marissa sullenly, and she fans herself deliberately with a piece of folded foolscap to demonstrate her annoyance at being left with the heat and the boredom.

Outside, it's not much better. The midday sun slices cruel segments of pavement, causing people to squint and cower against the buildings. Beneath her hat, and with her expensively understated sunglasses, Felicity is well protected. She is actually glad there is no breeze today. Her hat cannot contend with anything more than a whisper of wind before it lifts up like a Dutch nun's headdress and has to be held firmly in place. Today is perfect. Her sandals make a cool sound against the pavements of Green Park, and all around her there are buses and taxis and work-day people in unsuitable clothes, trussed and decorated like sweating turkeys.

Felicity walks up the road to L'Odeon. It isn't one of her favourite restaurants, but it's close by and at least it's stylish. She has booked a window table so that she can look down into Regent Street, far enough away from the piano player for his music to become pleasant background noise. She knows she's taking a bit of a gamble meeting like this in a public place, but she's tired of sneaking around like a fugitive. For once she isn't particularly concerned about being spotted by Wayne Briggs, because she knows he would never be in a place like L'Odeon. No, today she's more worried about seeing her brother, Sebastian. Even though she checked with his secretary to ensure he was out of town.

One can never be too careful in matters of such delicate subterfuge.

She is the first to arrive. The hostess seats her and brings a bottle of mineral water, along with the menus. Felicity nods and smiles at an acquaintance across the way. The restaurant manager comes over to say hello and to ask how the new hotel is coming along. She knows he's worried about the competition, but he feigns friendship and offers her a complimentary bottle of wine with her lunch.

How kind.

'Right on time, darling!' says Felicity, standing to kiss her lunch guest on both cheeks. 'You look fabulous, as always. Is that a new jacket?'

'Olivier Strelli. He made it for my last birthday,' says Solange as she accepts a seat pulled out for her by the waiter.

'I keep thinking Sebastian is going to be hiding somewhere,' says Felicity with an amused, conspiratorial smile. 'Imagine his face if he saw the two of us together like this.'

'I can see you are really enjoying this, Felicity,' says Solange in her MTV Euro-accent. 'It couldn't be going much better, could it?'

'Did you see the article yesterday? How is Thierry moving so quickly? I think we all underestimated your husband's influence over Sebastian. I think my brother must have truly fallen head over heels for him. Isn't it fabulous?'

Solange doesn't look too convinced.

'It is not doing very much for my marriage, Felicity. When Thierry caught me in bed with Philippe we nearly gave the game away. Now he's not speaking to me, and the tension is running dangerously high.'

'Well, now, darling, you only have yourself to blame. I think it *was* rather reckless of you to jump into bed like that when there was every chance of being discovered. I didn't even know you were seeing anyone on the side.'

'I wasn't, but with Thierry concentrating on Sebastian, I was feeling a bit left out. Two months without sex and I was ready to drag anyone into bed – and Philippe has been looking for an opportunity to sleep with me for years.'

'It's a good job Sebastian is smitten, otherwise he would have suspected something was wrong by now.'

'Well, I think he suspects nothing. Your brother is in love with Thierry, and even the sex is getting better between them, so why should our plan not work?'

'So Thierry really *is* bisexual?' asks Felicity, politely removing an olive stone with her napkin and placing it in the saucer provided.

'Oh, God, Thierry would sleep with anyone and anything! I think he prefers women, but I have known several men who have been besotted by him. My close friend Henri was in love with him for months after a short-lived little *affaire vigoureuse*. Thierry is a very potent personality.'

'Well, at the rate he's moving with the destruction of Craven's, it won't be long before you can have him back and we can leave my dear brother with the spoils of your husband's genius. I nearly died when I heard about the sushi bar – what an absolute hoot!'

'You know, I think Thierry is actually enjoying it. His conscience bites him because of Sebastian, but he finds much fun in thinking up new ways of making the hotel *médiocre*.'

'So Thierry *likes* Sebastian, then?' asks Felicity, imbuing the word with scorn.

'We all do, Felicity. Your brother is, I think, a very kind and gentle man. None of us can see why you hate him so much. Surely it cannot be because he is homosexual? You have many such friends in the business.'

'Oh, the *queer* thing isn't really the reason why I want to see him ruined. It's more to do with the hotel and the fact that he was never generous enough to offer me any help or give me a share in the place. Daddy really didn't know what he was doing to me when he left it all to Sebastian – I was in shock for months, and nearly jacked it all in right then and there. I would have walked away if there had been an alternative, but David was a miserly bastard and I just couldn't stomach the idea of being beholden to my husband twenty-four hours a day. And then, of course, there was that bloody awful fiasco at the anniversary party. I can never forgive Sebastian for showing me up like that.'

'He told Thierry that he still loves you, despite all the harsh words between you.'

Felicity doesn't want to consider that, so she waves her menu at the waiter and they order their lunch.

Baked Icelandic cod in a pecan and garlic crust with puréed peas and potato galette.

No dessert.

Black coffee.

'What kind of person shops at the Scotch House?' asks Felicity, staring out of the steeply arched restaurant window.

'I think maybe Americans,' replies Solange, 'or middle-aged schoolteachers from Yorkshire.'

'Do you know, it'll be ten years since you and I met, next week,' says Felicity.

'What anniversary is that? Is it wood or iron or something boring like that? We should find out and buy gifts,' laughs Solange. She has been drinking most of the complimentary wine.

'I thought you were a fool to marry Thierry,

you know. You seemed so much more intelligent than he.'

'Well, we proved you wrong, didn't we, *ma chérie*. Our marriage has been a good one.'

'Until now.'

'Well, thanks to you and your grand schemes. If it wasn't for the money, none of us would be doing this.'

'And our friendship, of course.'

'That goes without saying: sisters under the skin.'

Felicity looks at Solange and wonders how some people can be so stupid.

Intelligent people with university degrees.

People like Solange and Thierry.

Neither of them has bothered to question Felicity's motives, or to enquire about their eventual financial guarantees. Blinded by greed and power, they have fallen in with the plan without question. Felicity hasn't even resorted to her bogus legal contract, the one she had written up should it be requested. She's dealing with amateurs. She has offered them temporary pleasure in their pursuit of fortune, and both of them are so caught up in their illusions of grandeur that they are unaware of the pitfalls ahead of them.

The rented flat in Bayswater. The rented apartment in Brussels. The expense accounts. The bank accounts. The cars, the meals and the borrowed family ancestry. The trappings of the rich and famous have been theirs because of Felicity's apparent generosity.

But they are heading for a fall – a gaping pit of their own ignorance and making.

Felicity congratulates herself.

She is good at this game.

She is very good.

CHAPTER THIRTY-EIGHT

It's sickening the way these people lead their lives. One would think they might have the common decency to cover up their legs when walking around Bond Street, of all places.

Sebastian looks at the shorts and the sandals, and he is certain that the young men with rucksacks must be German. It just goes to show, doesn't it? Nobody has any values these days.

Sebastian is thoroughly cheesed off. He is really, really bored, and doesn't know what he wants to do. He has just had a solitary lunch at The Forum, and the Eve's pudding sits stodgily in his stomach. He had seconds, too.

The heat doesn't help. He's wearing his linen suit, but his collar feels too tight. It says 15½ on the label but he suspects that, because it didn't come from Jermyn Street, it's probably wrong. One can't trust off-the-peg clothing, and normally he wouldn't even consider a shirt from Next, but it had been a present from Nanny Freemont, and he had called in to see her this morning for elevenses.

He isn't needed back at the hotel. Thierry is so busy these days that there's no time for fun, and Sebastian is tired of hanging around in the hope that somebody might give him something to do. Not that he really wants anything to do, but it would be nice to be asked. He hardly recognizes half the staff these days, and all the good people seem to have resigned in disgust at Thierry's new regime. Sebastian wonders where it will all end, and he's sure Felicity must be laughing about him behind his back. Just like she always has.

If the truth be known, he's scared to say anything to Thierry. He's scared to say how much he disapproves of the slot machines in the bar, the paper towels in the toilets, the artificial flower arrangements in the lobby. He knows that Thierry is trying to reduce the day-to-day costs of the hotel, but Sebastian loathes anything second-rate. Sebastian is also worried that Thierry is now more interested in the hotel than he is in their relationship. Since he moved to London they have barely spent more than a few hours together, and they haven't had sex in weeks. Sebastian has taken to buying magazines in Soho and playing with himself when the bathroom door is locked.

Like an adolescent once again.

He hasn't been to his flat for weeks, and he's afraid to go there now because he knows it will smell of a life passed by. The curtains will be drawn, painting the living room in shades of drab and olive, and in the kitchen there will be the remains of a treacle sponge cake left to go stale on the table. The dishwasher's crammed with filthy pots and pans. Forty or fifty copies of *The Times* piled up on the hall marble. He stopped paying the cleaning people when he practically moved into Thierry's Bayswater flat above the toy museum. All his clothes are there now. His CDs, his toiletries, his toaster oven for breakfast croissants.

At least that heinous Solange isn't around any more. She hasn't spoken to Thierry since the fateful night in Brussels when they caught her in bed with that chap. She's probably too embarrassed to show her face. Still, Thierry had overreacted, causing Sebastian to wonder if perhaps there was something else going on. Were Solange and Thierry more than just friends? He had caught Solange gazing at Thierry sometimes, and more than once she had made thinly veiled comments about their past. Sebastian hopes he is wrong.

And now he's got to contend with this ridiculous party that Felicity is giving for their mother's birthday. He refuses to have anything to do with it, and he's leaving everything up to Felicity – just the way she likes it. His mother wants to have a fancy-dress party, with a theme. Felicity came up with the awful suggestion of a sixties retrospective, because Sabrina loved the era so much. Unfortunately Sabrina adores the idea, and now they're all going to be forced to wear polyester lounge suits and miniskirts, like a load of idiots. If it wasn't for the sake of his mother, Sebastian would certainly not be going. He's taking Poppy and Dee – and Thierry if he can drag him away from the blasted hotel.

Someone else he hasn't seen recently is Wayne

Briggs. He hasn't been in to work, and he hasn't called in sick. Sebastian hopes that perhaps he has been caught by the law for doing something illegal. Drug pushing or soliciting, maybe. Perhaps he's twenty feet down in the Thames, with bricks tied to his ankles. That would be marvellous! One less thing to worry about. Thierry had wanted to stop Wayne's wages being paid into the bank, but Sebastian had felt too afraid of the consequences, so he persuaded Thierry to leave things as they stood. He made up a lie about Wayne being from an underprivileged family, with an invalid mother and a father in prison – they relied on the money, and Wayne was a good worker. Hah!

When Sebastian surveys his life like this, he wonders what the bloody hell he is doing. Nothing seems to be going right and he's miserable. Every day gets a bit worse, a bit less fun, and he doesn't see any of his old friends now because Thierry doesn't like any of them. What happened to the carefree playboy he used to be?

He isn't at all interested in the hotel, even less so since it turned into an amusement arcade. He has absolutely no ties, nothing to keep him here. He could sell up and move on. There would be enough money from the sale of the hotel to keep him for years with clever investments, and he could move to another country – France perhaps? Or maybe Portugal. It seems like such an attractive idea that he calls Thierry on his car phone.

'I don't understand you, Sebastian. You called me

out of a meeting to tell me your pipe dreams? Are you quite crazy, old chap?' says Thierry, obviously unamused by Sebastian's wild suggestion.

'It would be so great! No worries, no stress: we could live a life of leisure. There's nothing in London any more, and I'm really fed up with the bloody hotel. I never see you these days, and I'm tired of everything. Let's just pack it all in now and do something impetuous.'

'Have you been drinking?' asks Thierry.

'Of course not! I'm just bloody sick and tired of my life – Felicity, the hotel, all of it. I want some fun.'

'Well, excuse me if I sound just a little sceptical, Sebastian, but do you know how old you are? You're talking like you're back at university, like some crazy kind of kid. Grow up, will you? And don't call me out of a meeting again just because you're bored.'

Thierry is gone.

Sebastian is left staring up through his open sunroof at the sky, where an unexpected air balloon drifts uneasily across the London skyline.

The tithe cottages on Broadbent Lane paint a perfect picture of bucolic peacefulness, as the late-evening sun casts improbable golden shadows across thatch and brick. The cottage gardens are worthy of a Hallmark calendar, and Poppy sits on the front step hulling strawberries into a pottery bowl. Dee is down by the fence, smoking a cigarette from which a single strand of lazy smoke rises. Sebastian pulls up in the car. He has the sunroof open and Mahler on the CD.

'You look like a bloody nursery rhyme,' he jokes as he gets out of the car. 'All you need is an apron and a poke bonnet and it could be a scene from *The Mill on the Floss.*'

'Not so romantic when that flood comes and drowns us both!' laughs Poppy.

'Did they smoke Silk Cut in the mid-nineteenth century?' asks Dee, stubbing out her cigarette on the fence.

'Clay pipes, I think.'

'And opium.'

Sebastian kisses Poppy's cheek and steals a strawberry.

'What are you doing here?' asks Poppy.

'Oh, I was bored with London. Nothing to do, and Thierry is working as usual. I thought I'd take a leisurely drive up the M1 to see what you two were up to.'

'As you can see, we're up to nothing much. We've just pigged out on barbecue beans and cauliflower cheese, and we're about to embark on an orgy of strawberry shortcake and ice cream. If you're very nice, you can join us.'

'I thought you might be at the hospital with Claire Brown. I was going to go up there, too. I've got some flowers in the car.'

'Not much point, really. She's stable but they're keeping her pretty sedated. The contractions have stopped, temporarily at least, but they're afraid the baby's still going to be premature. Duncan is beside himself. Hasn't left the hospital for three days.'

'Has anyone told the Texan fairy godmother yet?' asks Sebastian, leaning against the porch where cabbage roses droop with fragrant fatigue after a hot, sultry day.

'Duncan phoned her in Paris. She sent flowers, and wanted to get Claire out of the local hospital and into a private ward somewhere. The doctors think she's still too weak to be moved. I think Duncan said that Angelica's coming back to England at the end of the week.'

'I still can't believe that woman. Do you really think she's doing all this out of the goodness of her heart?' asks Dee, swatting at a cloud of gnats with a broken twig of tarragon.

'She's religious, Duncan says.'

'Guilty conscience maybe, because of David?'

'Or maybe she has a saint complex and wants to be the all-encompassing benefactor?'

'Whatever she is, she's definitely the right thing for Claire at the moment. I was beginning to think she would die penniless, and that baby would end up being adopted by strangers.' Poppy puts aside her bowl of strawberries and wipes her hands on a tea towel.

'It's a shame you two couldn't adopt the baby,' says Sebastian, testing the suggestion as one might test the bathwater to see if it will scald.

'What would we want with a baby?' asks Dee defensively.

'I just thought . . . Well, wouldn't you make good parents?'

'Hardly, darling!' says Poppy. 'Whatever gave you such a strange idea?'

'Look, how come you two want to keep your relationship such a bloody secret? I tell you all about my own sordid sex life, and yet the two of you seem to hide yourselves away as though you're actually ashamed of being gay. Surely I'm the one person you can confide in? I feel as though you're treating me as an utter fool sometimes.'

Poppy and Dee exchange glances. They look uncomfortable.

'Neither of us is comfortable with the term "gay", Sebastian. We hate the term "lesbian" even more. Actually, neither of us thinks of ourselves as lesbians, neither of us has done this kind of thing before, and I suppose we're just still a bit shy of owning up to certain things.' Poppy looks to Dee for affirmation.

'We're very good friends who just happen to sleep together, OK?' says Dee.

'Fair enough,' says Sebastian, 'but I still don't know why you never explained any of this to me earlier. It's very awkward at times.'

'For that reason exactly. It's very awkward for us too, and we don't want to be judged because of it.'

'Fine, fine. I'll keep my trap shut in future,' sighs Sebastian.

'What has got into you, darling? You look as though you've just lost sixpence and found a penny.'

'Oh, I'm bloody fed up. I feel like I need a holiday or something. Thierry and the hotel just aren't working, and I really think I might like to get rid of the place and move on somewhere more interesting.'

'Now this *is* new! Where did all this come from?' asks Poppy, returning to her seat on the step while Dee goes in to make the coffee.

'It's been coming for a while, I think. Thierry, of course, thinks I'm a loony and refuses to listen.'

'Darling, let's not forget whose hotel it actually is. If you want to sell it, then you don't have to get permission from anyone – least of all Thierry.'

'I know, but he's working so hard on my behalf.'

'A bit too fervently if you ask me, darling. Did you ever stop to wonder what he's getting out of this?'

'He's doing it for me, I suppose.'

'Oh yeah, and I'm selling earrings at Camden Lock every weekend because I like the fresh air, I suppose! Sebastian, darling, how much are you paying Thierry, if you don't mind me asking?'

'He's on a normal managerial wage, plus expenses. About thirty thousand, I think.'

'And he gave up his own business to earn thirty thousand plus expenses? I don't think so, darling. Something doesn't compute.'

'But he looks at us as a marriage, Poppy. It's what we earn collectively that matters – that's what he told me right from the beginning. What's his is mine, and so on . . .'

'Very cosy, but not particularly clever for someone who is supposed to be such an astute businessman. Just be careful, darling. You haven't known him very long, and I'd hate to see him take advantage of you. Why don't you spend a little more time at the hotel with him? Sit in on the meetings. Offer your suggestions, and don't let him bully you into anything you don't like. He's very persuasive, isn't he?'

'But I love him. Surely that counts for something, doesn't it?'

'Darling, some of the most horrible, ruthless people I have ever encountered in my life have been those I've loved. They get you into bed and suddenly they imagine they can do what they like with you. It's as though they lose all respect for you as a human being once they've seen you without your underwear.'

'That's a bit cynical, isn't it? Surely not everyone thinks that way?'

'Let's hope not, for the sake of humanity. I'm just trying to tell you that you're being too soft with Thierry. You've got to assert yourself a bit more; he seems to have drained all the life out of you. It isn't attractive, darling. You've become a bit of a drip, actually.'

'Thanks! That's all I need. A lecture from my friend on top of everything else.'

'Oh, come on, darling, let's go in and get some coffee and shortcake and stop all this serious stuff. It's up to you how you handle Thierry, but you should seriously think about what it is that *you* want.'

'So does that mean I can leave him to it and run away with the under-gardener?'

'If that's what blows your whistle, darling go for it!'

Sebastian kisses Poppy's hair.

'What would I do without you?' he asks.

'Probably find yourself another Titian-haired beauty to spill all your troubles to.'

'Red hair, no knickers, my mother used to say.'

'Shows how much your mother knows then,' says Poppy. 'I can assure you that my bits and pieces are under cover at all times.'

CHAPTER THIRTY-NINE

Claire lies very still. She has been lying still for two days and two nights, afraid that one sudden movement might bring back the contractions. It's like waiting for the dentist's drill to hit a nerve. Or seeing a hurtling truck in the rear-view mirror and anticipating the impact.

She cannot be moved to a private hospital, despite Angelica Schloss and her money. She must remain calm and still, staring up at the prefabricated ceiling tiles, making acquaintance with the yellowed leak stains that seep along the cracks between them. The fluorescent light has a plastic cover that is filled with dead flies and moths, and the bulb has an irritating, undulating light that makes Claire cross-eyed if she stares at it for too long.

She shares this room with three other women. Josie with the ruptured spleen, Tracy with the acute haemorrhoids and Gill who had a breeze-block dropped on her head. Tracy is very funny and makes them all laugh, but Claire has to hold in her laughter just in case it jiggles her baby back into action. There isn't much to laugh about, but strangely enough Claire still finds it possible to react to the outside world as though she is still part of it.

The doctors are very concerned about her health. The leukaemia is raging through her blood cells, making her so weak she can barely feed herself. She doesn't eat very much because everything makes her feel sick, so she sips water and pushes her food around on the plate with listless fingers. Sometimes there is pain and she has to ring the bell for the nurse, who brings her pills in a little plastic cup. It looks as though it's going to be a race between the cancer and the baby. Which will finish first?

Duncan has gone home for a couple of hours to shower and change. They don't allow him to stay in the room outside of visiting hours because of the other women, but he has been keeping vigil outside in the waiting room. Claire feels very guilty about Duncan. It seems that she has given him nothing and he is giving her everything. He would have been better off never meeting her in the first place. Tracy in the next bed reckons she's going to steal him away when Claire isn't looking. 'He's got a smashing bum!' she laughs.

Hospitals are dreary places. They give you too much time to think and too little time to adjust. Death and disease lurk in every corner, with a stink like disinfectant and school dinners. It's like sleeping in a DSS office; even the orange plastic chairs are the same and the walls are painted institutional green and cream, half and half, in glossy, bumpy paint that's easy to swab down. The only attempt at cheerfulness is a cheap framed print of a waterfall. The window looks out across institutional rooftops. Flat expanses of rippling tarmac and raised skylights.

Claire has signed the papers. She's giving Angelica the right to become the legal guardian of her baby when she dies. Angelica can adopt the child and bring her up with Zane and Tori, her American half-brother and half-sister. Angelica hasn't asked for proof that Claire's baby is David Glendale's; she accepts Claire's word on the matter. How different Angelica is to Felicity Craven, who has been screaming about blood tests and written testimonies. No wonder David spent so much time in Texas. It must have been very difficult for him not being able to divorce Felicity without immediately losing half his fortune. Angelica says that she begged and begged him to walk away and forget about the money; surely he was rich enough to survive on half his amassed billions? But David was a miserly man, and he hated his wife so much that he couldn't bring himself to let her get away with it. You see, he knew that Felicity would like nothing better than to get her hands on all that money, so that she could live the life of a queen without the limitations of the palace purse strings.

Poppy called in last night. She brought some beautiful flowers from Sebastian Craven, all wrapped up in cellophane with pink and blue ribbon and a card that said, *Please call if there is anything I can do*. He had underlined *anything* and written his home phone number. Poppy said that he genuinely wants to help.

Claire doesn't blame him any more. It's a total waste of energy, and it really doesn't change anything.

Tracy joked about Poppy when she left. 'She's like a bleeding centre forward! I bet she doesn't have to worry about keeping mace in *her* handbag!'

At a quarter past five Claire's waters break. She thinks she has peed herself, but when she lifts up the sheets there is a rank stench, and she knows it is a bad sign. She calls the nurse, sobbing because there are still seven weeks before the baby is supposed to be born, and the nurse pulls a curtain around Claire's bed and brings a doctor, who announces that the head is engaged. She is going to have the baby.

The contractions return later that night: subdued at first, and then gradually stronger until they become uncomfortable. They wheel her into the labour ward and Duncan sits by her side. This was supposed to be an exciting, joyful experience, but all Claire can do is cry. She wonders if she can hold the baby inside just another day. Will one more day give it more of a chance to survive? How much can a baby develop in twenty-four hours? A fingernail, perhaps? A millimetre of lung tissue? Claire defies her contractions, refusing to work with them, refusing to bear down. The nurse tells her to go with the pain, but Claire breathes in and clamps her muscles as tight as she can, even when the pain is like a burning fist inside her. There is an unbearable urge to open up, to push with all her might, but Claire fights and clings to the edges of the bed until her fingers go numb.

'You've got to let it go, Claire,' says the nurse. 'Stop tensing up like that.'

'Sod off!' pants Claire. 'Who asked you for your pissing opinion?'

The nurse has heard it all before, and she winks at Duncan.

'Come on, love, there's no point in going against it now. It's going to happen and you might as well accept the fact. You're just making it harder on yourself,' says Duncan, wiping Claire's forehead with a damp cloth.

'I don't have to accept anything. Keep your trap shut and – aghhh!' Claire raises herself up from the damp sheets and holds her breath as a wave of pain ripples from her breasts down to her toes. She finds herself bearing down involuntarily. Panting, moaning, she swears like a trooper, and then something gives. She is disembowelled. It feels as though her insides have just slipped out on to the bed, leaving her with a muscular throbbing that ebbs and twitches.

'Is it the baby?' she gasps, squeezing her eyes tight shut against the truth.

'It's a little girl, Claire,' says the nurse.

But Claire can't see her daughter. She can't touch her daughter.

'Is she alive? Is she OK?' asks Claire, trying to sit up but unable to focus her vision.

'She's breathing, but we'll have to put her in an incubator. She's very tiny.'

Something strange happens next.

Claire opens her eyes, and it is as if she's looking

into a mirror. Very close. Right up until her nose is almost touching the reflection.

There she is.

Sweaty. Pale and sad.

Looking right back at Claire with an expressionless, glassy-eyed stare.

The nurse is barking orders to her assistant, and Duncan is still holding Claire's hand. Claire steps back until she is somehow suspended above the scene, looking down over the entire room as though through the lens of a camera. She sees the top of Duncan's head, and the label sticking out of the back of his shirt collar. She sees her own broken body lying twisted on the bed in a pool of blood, as though she's been wounded in the groin. She's just lying there, looking blankly up at the ceiling.

Duncan has been watching the nurses, but now he returns his attention to Claire.

'I think it's going to be OK, love,' he says.

But the body on the bed does not respond. Claire can see from her high position in the room that she is dead. She doesn't know *how* she knows exactly, but it's just like looking at a wide-eyed fish in the market. An empty shell of a person, discarded, an overcoat that no longer fits.

'Claire?' says Duncan, more urgency in his voice. He shakes the body slightly and the head lolls to one side.

'Oh, Christ! Claire! Nurse! Nurse! I think she's dead. Oh, God, oh, God . . .' Duncan is standing now, shaking the body, screaming to the nurses. Frantic. Frightened.

Then there is chaos: nurses, doctors and people shouting and administering needles. They are banging on her chest and blowing air into her mouth.

Claire watches with interest. She feels a pair of strong hands on her shoulders but she cannot turn around to see who it is. She feels certain that the hands are going to pull her away, and she prepares herself for this eventuality. And then, with a breathtaking shove, Claire is propelled downward at great speed. She lands with a gigantic thud and sits straight up with her eyes stretched wide.

'Oh!' she says, sucking in air with a desperate gasp.

She stares at the doctor with the electric paddles just as he lifts them from either side of her chest.

CHAPTER FORTY

Wayne Briggs stares at the front of the *Evening Standard* with disbelief. Why would she do this? Why would Felicity Craven suddenly announce to the world that Angelica Schloss put up the money for the new hotel? Here she is, shaking hands with the Texan slag outside the Ritz. What is the silly cow playing at? This is everything she didn't want to happen. This is why she's paying Wayne to keep his mouth shut. Well, actually, she still hasn't agreed to pay him anything, but he does have the signed contract regarding a secure position at the new hotel. That means he can forget about the hundred thousand and the ten-year retainer; he's going to have to settle for the job at The Phoenix instead.

What a crappy fucking day it's been. He had to go to the magistrates' court this afternoon because of that little matter back in April with the 'pretty policeman' in Leicester Square. The judge was a fat old prat who gave Wayne a warning and a fine of five hundred quid. Patronizing git! On the way out of the courtroom Wayne had looked at the cop who testified against him and had blown him a kiss.

His arm is still broken and in a sling, so everything

is twice as much hard work as it should be. The simplest things are now a chore; even having a slash is a balancing act and his pants get splattered with piss. At least he's got two new front teeth. Wayne hadn't been to the dentist for years, so he had to go private to get the bridge made. The dentist was pretty cool, actually, considering he was a bit of an old codger. Gave Wayne some laughing gas and it didn't hurt at all. Until he had to get his chequebook out.

There hasn't been a peep about Lou Baker's murder: nothing in the papers, nothing on the telly. Wayne reckons he's got away with that one. For a spur-of-the-moment attack, it had been remarkably successful.

Wayne is not pleased with this news about Felicity, not pleased at all. And he cracks the front of the rented sofa where he kicks it with his Timberland boot. There's nothing on the bleeding telly except snooker and gardening, and he's read the *Auto Trader* from front to back, even the adverts, so he hasn't got anything to look at in bed tonight. He hates the summer. Still light at ten o'clock, and the local pubs all crammed with Sloaney wankers who sit outside drinking white wine fucking spritzers and laughing about how much money they've made on the stock market.

She has obviously done this as a way of telling Wayne that she isn't going to be blackmailed any more. She must have looked at her choices and decided to cut her losses. He feels offended, as though Felicity is breaking some kind of honourable contract, and he can feel anger bubbling up like fermenting yeast in his throat.

This is war!

That's how people like Wayne Briggs think. They think in terms of violence and retribution because they have no comprehension of peaceful negotiation and compromise. A length of lead piping speaks louder than words. A well-aimed revolver achieves more than idle threats, and it's much more sexy.

Felicity slag-arse Craven is going to realize that she can never gain the upper hand with Wayne Briggs. He knows he will not sleep now unless he has his revenge. He's racking his brain to think of a gratifying way to send his message, but he doesn't even know where he could find her at this time of day. Probably not at Blythwood on a weeknight. Certainly not at the new hotel site. Wayne knows she's renting a flat somewhere in Holland Park, but he doesn't know the address. So that leaves the office in Green Park.

He looks at his watch. It's barely ten-fifteen.

He needs to wait until at least two o'clock before he attempts anything, but that's good because it gives him a few hours to prepare.

He's blinded now by a sense of injustice, and nothing will appease him until the deed is done. Now he's excited. Like he's going to have sex with some-body really brilliant.

Under his breath he repeats his litany of hate.

'*Ladybird, ladybird . . .*'

He loves that rhyme.

'Your house is on fire and your children are gone . . .'

The first thing he has to do is get to the phone box on the corner to call in a couple of favours. Then he has to go to the Late-Nite general store on the Brompton Road for the second part of his plan.

The store is busy, even at this time of night. Girls in office blouses and blokes in loose ties and pinstriped suits buy convenience foods for their flat-share suppers. They're playing Enya to make the place seem posh, and the shelves are all made of real wood with brass lights. That's Knightsbridge for you. Two quid for a bottle of Welsh rainwater.

Wayne catches the eye of the cashier: a big bloke with a beard and earrings. Wayne reaches up to take a bottle of champagne from the top shelf, the one with the astronomical price tag, and carries it over to the glass door of the shop, pretending to hold it up to the window so that he can read the label. The big bloke is watching him intently, even though he's ringing up someone else's purchases at the cash register. Wayne lifts the bottle of champagne in one hand and hurls it violently at the mirrored panel behind the display of tropical fruits, at the same time screaming 'Bastards!' at the top of his voice.

The bottle shatters the mirror and champagne sprays everywhere. Shoppers scatter. A woman with a bun screams and falls to the floor, in a very expensive-looking suede skirt. The bearded cashier grabs Wayne and hoists his arm up behind his back.

'OK, wise guy, what the hell do you think you're playing at? Meena, call the police.'

In Knightsbridge the cops come in less than three minutes. Flashing lights, handcuffs – the lot.

'All right, son, it's down to the station with you.'

Wayne goes without a struggle.

He sits in the back of the cop car and smiles to himself.

Cuvée spéciale, 1984.

He reeks of it.

CHAPTER FORTY-ONE

Here is the silver-backed brush and the antique scent bottle. Here is the perfumed candlelight and the feather bed.

Felicity is alone tonight.

The flat in Holland Park is far from perfect, but it's better than sleeping at Mummy's place in Hampstead, and it's much closer than Blythwood during the week, when the children are at school. Felicity has shipped them off to summer school in Lyons for three weeks, before they come home for the rest of the holidays.

She savours a Fauchon truffle from the tissue-lined box by her bed, and allows herself the luxury of triumph. She is finally getting everything she wants. With Thierry doing such a terrific job with Craven's, Felicity can see that The Phoenix is going to be much in demand by the time it opens. She can already picture the opening night in her mind, and she is impatient for it. Impatient for the celebration of her power, her style, her creativity and business acumen. She's going to be back at the top of every A-list in Europe, and she craves all that sycophantic attention. Her announcement today has caused a surprisingly small ripple of gossip. People don't seem to care very much how she got the finance for the new hotel; in fact some of them actually applaud Felicity for being so enterprising and 'forgiving'. After all, Angelica's the one who stole everything from Felicity in the first place.

Now that sleazebag Wayne Briggs can sing for his supper. No more blackmail; no more threats. Felicity can turn him over to the police if he bothers her any more. The ridiculous work contract she signed will never hold up in court, and it's his word against hers.

A cat can look at a queen.

But not much else!

Felicity is renting this flat from her friend Georgette. Georgette has gone to Japan for six months to get revenge on an old boyfriend, so the flat is conveniently free. It isn't exactly what Felicity is used to – the unlined curtains, the vinyl flooring in the kitchen, the *entertainment centre* – but it's a quiet refuge and nobody knows where she is. Not even Ross. She has given out the phone number but not the address. Originally this had been a necessary precaution because of Wayne Briggs, but she has grown to enjoy the anonymity, and now she intends to keep things this way.

She has tried talking to Sebastian about their mother's birthday party, but it isn't easy. If things are difficult between them now, what are they going to be like once he realizes what she has done to him? That she's in cahoots with Thierry and Solange? That they have plotted and schemed to ruin his business and to punish him for . . . for what? Felicity is finding it more and more difficult to remember exactly what it is her brother did to her that was so bad. So, he humiliated her in a drunken public scene at her anniversary party. Is that so awful? He called her a bigot and a bitch in front of her friends and her most influential clients – not to mention the press. He never once offered to make her a partner in the business, and yet he allowed her to do all the work. He made her the snigger of conversation at every cocktail party in South Kensington and Chelsea when he announced his homosexuality in such a flagrant manner. Oh, yes; to a woman like Felicity these things should be punishable by hanging. She can organize the birthday party without him.

And it's going to be one hell of a bash, for Felicity has had the most brilliant brainwave. She's going to throw the party in the original ballroom of her new hotel before the workmen begin renovations. It's the perfect space for a sixties retrospective, and an ideal opportunity for Felicity to introduce everyone to The Phoenix. The ballroom is immense. It was designed in 1959 by some American designer called Rex Williams, and it's a homage to bad taste – perfect for her mother, perfect for a sixties party. It will be the antithesis of everything Felicity Craven stands for.

It's warm, muggy. Felicity has the bedroom window open but there is no breeze. Just dogs barking and the sound of traffic two streets away. She feels restless, and she knows there's no point trying to sleep. She's thinking about Angelica now, that strange Texan woman who seems impervious to Felicity's hostility. How can she be like that? Does the woman have no natural animosity, or is she just dense? Those religious types are sometimes a bit odd.

'Good luck, honey,' she had said when they parted this afternoon.

Felicity hadn't bothered to reply. That woman gives her the creeps. And now she's made friends with that loser, Claire Brown – the one who has just given birth to David's bastard child. Why would Angelica Schloss want to fly all the way here to get involved with somebody like that? It just doesn't make sense to Felicity. Felicity doesn't even give money to charity unless her name is going to appear in the programme. What is Angelica Schloss getting out of this deal? And who's looking after those circus children of hers while she gallivants all over Europe buying houses and giving money to perfect strangers?

She's thinking of changing her hairdresser. Charles Worthington is becoming too much of a celebrity these days, and she doesn't like the fact that he's been appearing regularly on breakfast TV. She dumped Nicky Clarke for the very same reason three years ago.

Is this new alpha-hydroxy lotion really working around her eyes?

How much longer can lavender and apple-green last, and is it worth using them in one of the rooms at The Phoenix if she tempers them with cobalt?

The phone rings just as she has dropped off to sleep. It's three-fifteen.

'Fliss? It's Ross, darling. I've just had Marissa on the phone. The landlord of your office building got hold of her – there's been a fire.'

'Oh, my God,' says Felicity, sitting up in bed with her nightdress all twisted.

'The whole top floor went up in smoke. Very bad, apparently. They reckon it was arson but they won't know until they've investigated. You don't think it could have been that under-porter of yours, could it?'

'Who else could it have been?' asks Felicity without hesitation. 'Well, this time I'm going to get him put away. He's not holding anything over me now. I can do what I should have done months ago.'

'Are you sure it was him?'

'Ross, don't be so naive. I made my announcement today in the newspaper, and then tonight my office burns down and they suspect it's arson. Coincidence? Hardly, darling! I'm calling the police right now.'

Got him!

And Felicity pops a truffle in her mouth before dialling 999.

Felicity knows that there are some people who, because she is rich and beautiful, think she deserves everything she gets. She knows how people gloat over the downfall of those more fortunate than themselves, reading their lurid newspapers over bowls of

Weetabix, rushing to get to the horoscopes and the sports page.

People with melamine 'Tudor' and leaded glass from Magnet & Southern. Spice jars filled with coins and paper clips. The working classes and their envy.

There's nothing left of Felicity's office. The whole top section of the building is blackened and hollow, like the carcase of a Christmas turkey that has been picked clean and thrown into the fire. Smoke still rises from smouldering timbers and the acrid smell of it lingers in the air.

Somebody broke into the building. Somebody went straight up to the top floor and set fire to the hall carpet with a liberal dousing of petrol. Could Felicity think of anyone who might have done this kind of thing? Does she have any enemies? The investigators are young but they wear their authority like an expensive suit.

'I think I know who did it,' says Felicity. She passes on the relevant information.

It comes as some disappointment to Felicity several hours later when the police inform her that Wayne Briggs was in their custody at the time of the arson incident, and therefore could not be held accountable for the crime.

'He could have paid somebody to do it for him,' argues Felicity.

'Yes, madam, he could, but at this point in time that is mere speculation on your part, and therefore we have no grounds on which to arrest him.'

Bollocks!

Felicity slams the phone down and stares miserably at the insurance claim forms.

Will they believe her if she claims five thousand for a pair of hand-made silk curtains?

CHAPTER FORTY-TWO

'But what will you do with the money if you sell Craven's?' asks Thierry, uncharacteristically clad in nothing but Liberty-print boxer shorts. (A gift from Sebastian before he really understood Thierry's taste in expensive clothes.)

'I don't know yet, but I honestly can't stand back while you single-handedly turn the hotel into a Las Vegas-style mediocrity.' Sebastian registers the look on Thierry's face. 'I'm sorry, Thierry, this is not a dig at you and your efforts on my behalf. It's just that I feel as though you're taking my grandmother, or somebody I've loved and respected all my life, and you are parading her around town in fishnet stockings and crotchless knickers. It's sad and humiliating. Craven's bears my name, Thierry; it represents my family, and I don't want my name to be associated with bargain-break weekends and HP Sauce. I like to think that I'm above that kind of thing.'

Sebastian is sitting in bed with a thin white sheet pulled up to his waist. Once again Thierry has performed astoundingly well, without showing the slightest indication that he was getting anything out of the experience himself. When Sebastian touches

Thierry's penis he can almost feel the skin recoiling, his balls retracting. They've tried talking about this before, but Thierry becomes defensive and difficult, and so Sebastian has learned to keep his mouth shut. The subject of the hotel and Sebastian's decision to sell it is a substitute discussion, but Sebastian feels that somehow the two subjects are related. How long can one person love a man who shows absolutely no desire for him?

'I think you should wait another six months,' suggests Thierry, looking out at the first signs of morning through the open bedroom window. 'You can't really judge my improvements at this point. I am thinking that you need to wait a little longer before you make any rash decisions.'

'Craven's could be worth twenty-five per cent less if I leave you in charge for another six months. Don't you see, the hotel was only worth so much because of its reputation. Every neon sign, every karaoke machine is chipping away at the property value, and if I am going to sell the place I want to get maximum returns. Felicity was right. The hotel is nothing without her.'

'Oh, you sound like a defeatist. I thought you were more of a fighter, Sebastian. You disappoint me.'

'Well, I'm sorry about that, old chap, but I've made up my mind. You've still got your own business to go back to, so you haven't lost anything at all, and I will, of course, reimburse you for the time you've spent working for me. Thierry, you have a family and a life in Brussels that you gave up to help me, and for that

I'll be eternally grateful. Can't we just go back to how it was before? Before Felicity dumped the hotel and left us floundering in her wake? I want to concentrate on our relationship instead of arguing day and night about work issues.'

Sebastian climbs out of bed and pulls on his pyjama bottoms.

'Look, just give me a few more weeks to turn things around,' says Thierry, almost wringing his hands with despair.

'I don't know why this is suddenly so important for you. I know this was your chance to prove yourself to me, but you'd already proved yourself the minute I met you. Why not go back to the success you've already made for yourself and stop this destructive, macho 'I can do anything' routine? It isn't impressing me.'

Sebastian attempts to put his arms around Thierry, but he finds himself shrugged off. Thierry moves over to the empty fireplace. In the pale, pale light he looks almost luminescent.

'Well, excuse me, Sebastian, for trying to help you out. I do not impress you? I think you have said enough. You really seem to have no idea what I have done to help you. I gave up a lot of things to be with you on this: more things than you will know. You are being ungrateful and you are making me very angry. You might just as well have thumped me in the stomach.' Thierry's English is sounding stilted, as it usually does when he becomes agitated.

'Look, I'm not trying to insult you – far from it. I appreciate everything you've done, but I just don't think that it's the direction in which I wish to go. I could sell Craven's and we could start some new kind of venture together. Maybe move to another country, or develop your own business and I could help you instead.'

'Don't you see, Sebastian? There *is* no business! I have nothing to fall back on without the hotel!'

'What on earth do you mean? You didn't get rid of your business? I thought it merely went back into the hands of your family. Surely they'll return it to you if you explain the circumstances?'

'What family?' shouts Thierry. 'My family does not exist. It was a fabrication to make you like me.'

'What? You made up your family, thinking it would impress me? I don't believe it,' says Sebastian. He feels strangely flattered.

'I do not wish to talk about this now. It is five o'clock in the morning and I am tired. You simply need to know that without the hotel I have nothing. No aristocratic family, no business, no nothing!'

'Thierry, darling, you have *me*. I'm not going to dump you just because you don't have some fusty old family relics in your lineage. I've got enough family heirlooms for the both of us, and the money from selling the hotel will give us the chance to go away together, to start a new life somewhere. I love you; doesn't *that* mean anything to you?'

Thierry doesn't answer. He grabs his shirt from the back of the chair and pulls on his trousers.

This is just like the evening in Brussels all over again. Why does Thierry run out every time he's faced with some kind of emotional dilemma?

'Where are you going now?' demands Sebastian.

'I need some air.'

'We need to talk about this, Thierry. You can't keep running away every time I bring up the subject of our relationship. Answer me this one simple question: do you love me?'

The question thuds to the ground like a dead weight.

Thierry doesn't have to answer. Sebastian can see it in his face.

The reality wraps itself around Sebastian's throat and strangles him with an indescribable pain. He sits on the edge of the bed – the bed whose sheets are still rumpled from their lovemaking just minutes before.

'Why did you do it?' Sebastian asks. He feels defeated.

'I really like you, Sebastian. I really do. I just can't love you.'

'So what is it, then? Is it about money? Were you just hanging around because of my connections? What?'

'Something like that. I don't really know. I've got to go.'

Thierry is tying his shoelaces, and Sebastian can't bear to see him leave. At this time in the morning, with the sun threatening to come up over the trees at any moment, it feels just too tragic. Too bloody awful to contemplate.

'I don't know what to do,' says Sebastian; his voice is small and squashed with emotion.

'I am not worth it,' says Thierry. He touches Sebastian's shoulder, and Sebastian clings on to him with a sudden fierceness. It's all hopeless now, he can feel it. It's like an empty bag. A table strewn with last night's crumbs.

'Please don't go.'

'It's all too late, Sebastian. We have to stop this ridiculous game; it has gone on too long.'

'Was it just a game, then? It felt like much more than that to me.'

'Perhaps I do not choose the right words. You have been deceived, Sebastian, and I am very unhappy about the way things are turning out. There are many things that you do not know about me, and I am too ashamed to tell you about them. Let me just say that I am not proud of what I have done, and, even though I know you will finally hate me, I want you to know that I did not do any of this to hurt you. It was purely a business deal. Having spent these last months with you, I have grown to hate myself for what I am doing and I cannot allow it to continue.'

'What are you talking about? A business deal? How can you call our relationship a business deal? Are you that cold-blooded?' Sebastian feels sick.

'I am married, Sebastian. Solange is my wife. It was all a fabrication to fool you.'

'And you expect me to swallow that?' asks Sebastian, pushing Thierry away.

'It is the truth. We did it for money. The plan was for me to bomb your business, leave you with the ruins and go back to my wife with our pockets full of cash. You have been swindled, Sebastian, by the person you most trusted.'

'You mean this was planned right from the beginning? From that very first day at The Forum, when you brought me here that afternoon? I can't believe it. Craven's was still under Felicity's management, and she hadn't made any announcement about quitting. How could you possibly have known that she was going to leave me in the lurch like that?'

Thierry turns away and reaches for his watch on the bedside table.

'Did you know before the rest of us that . . .? Oh, God, no . . . was it Felicity who put you up to this? Did you know Felicity before you ever met me?'

'I have to go out,' says Thierry, avoiding Sebastian's glare.

'Oh, my God. Oh, Jesus Christ! That cold-hearted, scheming cow!' Sebastian is on his feet now. He has his head in his hands and he's pacing the floor. Thierry stands frozen by the bedroom door, like a child at the bars of the lion's cage.

What can he do? Sebastian is trapped inside his own boiling anger. He understands now why people in films slam their fists through windows and smash their heads against walls. It is all he can do to stop himself from flying at Thierry. But Thierry has gone. Sebastian hears the click of the lock on the hall doorway.

The first glint of sunrise shows itself through the lowest branches of the chestnut trees, and Sebastian falls to his knees by the open bedroom window and starts to sob. With his forehead resting on the painted window sill, he clasps his hands to his face and feels the poison in his veins.

The birds sing a joyful song.

It is going to be a beautiful day.

CHAPTER FORTY-THREE

'He knows everything, Felicity – I had to tell him. I just couldn't let this go on any longer.'

If Felicity could spit blood, she would splatter the carpet with her fury.

'*You* couldn't let this go on any longer? What the fuck does it have to do with you? Since when did you start making the decisions around here?'

Thierry is pacing the carpet. They are meeting in the lounge bar of a small hotel on Brook Street.

'Look, he is going to sell Craven's, and there is nothing I could have done or said that would have changed his mind.'

'But, Thierry, pardon my apparent ignorance, but I don't see what that has to do with you telling Sebastian everything else. You *do* realize that you've ruined everything, not only for me, but for you and that dumb bitch of a wife of yours as well? I should have known you weren't up to it when I met you. Well, you've really done it now.'

Felicity can barely keep her voice from breaking. She is shaking with rage, and her head feels as though it might explode at any moment. She's finished: there can be absolutely no way out of this one. Sebastian is going to grind her into the ground like a cigarette filter.

'Look, Sebastian isn't a bad sort, you know. He has compassion, he can forgive you. Maybe he'll leave you alone when he's got over the initial shock.' Thierry doesn't sound too convinced, but he's obviously trying to wheedle his way out of this compromising situation.

Felicity looks at him, and all she sees is his failure.

'You realize that you get nothing? You and Solange can clear off back to Belgium, back to your crummy little flat in Antwerp, back to the pathetic little life you had before I came along. I don't owe you a penny.'

'But . . . what about all the time we have invested, our jobs . . .?'

'I could ask you the same thing. Do you really care what happens to me now? If you'd just kept your mouth shut a little longer, we could have rescued the situation. I don't want to see or hear from you or Solange ever again, do you understand? And if either of you contemplates any kind of counter-attack, I shall contact my friends at the embassy in Brussels and make your lives misery.'

Inside her handbag, Felicity's mobile phone begins to chirp.

'Just get out, Thierry,' she snaps, flipping open her phone and glaring at him with something close to murder in her eyes.

'Felicity? This is Sebastian. I think we have to talk.'

'You'd better tell me where and when,' she says.

And Felicity Craven slumps back into the pillows

of the sofa, totally unaware that she has a ladder in her tights and chewing gum stuck to one sole of her Italian crocodile shoes.

Felicity meets Sebastian at Craven's.

Even in her abject state, she notices the silk flower arrangements in the lobby as she passes through to her old office.

Hideous!

There is an ethnic-looking receptionist who has customized her uniform with cheap lapel pins. She's having a laugh with one of the new porters: a greasy-haired boy with trousers too tight and gravy stains on his jacket.

Thierry really knew how to ruin a good thing.

Felicity hardly recognizes her old office. Without the drapes and the furniture it looks bereft. The light is different now that the window is bare, and there are sad, flat patches in the carpet where her things once stood. It even smells different.

Sebastian is sitting at an oversized mahogany partner's desk. He does not appear angry or agitated, as Felicity might have expected. He merely looks defeated.

Crushed.

'You'd better sit down,' he says, indicating a tweedy armchair that Felicity recognizes as a relic from the pre-refurbishment days. Thierry must have gone rooting around in the basement for that old thing.

She places her handbag on the carpet and sits

quietly, unable to say anything to her brother. There is nothing she can say now, and she knows it.

'Well, it appears that you have won, Felicity.' Sebastian's voice is small in this big, empty room. 'You have surpassed yourself this time. You have proved to me that there really are no lengths to which you will not go in order to get your own way. I still can't believe it. If Thierry hadn't told me to my face, I would still think that this was just some twisted little lie you'd manufactured in order to make me feel inadequate. Just like the old days when we were kids.'

'Sebastian—' Felicity begins, leaning forward as though painfully encumbered.

'Don't bother, Felicity,' interrupts Sebastian, halting her words with the palm of his hand. 'You really shouldn't say anything at this moment. I don't want to hear your voice or your excuses – though, God knows, they would make entertaining fodder for some second-rate novelist with a penchant for bitchy villains.'

Sebastian turns away to gaze out of the window. He affords Felicity a few moments to wallow in her despondency before he turns back to face her. His eyes are deadened with sadness and confusion. To Felicity this is much worse than the anger and retribution she had expected.

'What can I do?' she asks. Not because she actually wants to do anything, but because she doesn't know what else to say. Even under such damning circumstances, Felicity finds contrition practically impossible.

'You can start by explaining to me exactly why you did the things you did. Do you really hate me so much that you had to ruin me, both financially and emotionally? I find it hard to believe that we are actually related. Are you sure we come from the same parents?'

'You know, Sebastian, you may feel justified in being supercilious at this moment, but may I remind you that just a few months ago you were calling me a fucking bitch in front of a celebrity audience at our tenth anniversary party. That is hardly the action one might expect from a doting and loyal brother, now is it?'

'And let me remind you, sister dear, that the reason I was calling you a fucking bitch in front of a celebrity audience was because you had just announced that you were leaving me high and dry to start your own business, without even discussing it with me beforehand. Not only that, but you had denounced me to the tabloids as disgusting and depraved, and turned my friends and family against me.'

'You were caught with an under-age rent boy, for God's sake! Don't try to twist this whole thing around as though you're blameless, Sebastian. If you hadn't been fiddling with young boys in the first place, if you hadn't hogged the entire Craven's empire to yourself when Daddy died, if you weren't such a fucking exhibitionist, then maybe none of this would have happened.'

'I can see that you don't regret one thing, do you? You don't give a toss about other people's feelings. You're a selfish, egotistical, cold-hearted manipulator, and I think it's about time somebody brought you down a peg or two.'

Sebastian is no longer looking defeated. He's standing behind his mahogany desk. His eyes are no longer glazed with sadness. His hands grip the arms of his chair.

'You can't touch me,' says Felicity, practically smiling with self-satisfaction. 'I've never needed you, Sebastian, and I don't need you now. My hotel will be up and running by the new year, and you couldn't manage this place on your own if your life depended on it. Why don't you just sell up and bugger off? Nobody wants you around here any more.' She's laughing now. 'And to think of how you loved Thierry – what a joke! According to him, he couldn't even get it up for you!'

'You're despicable. Yes, you are a monster. No wonder David hated your guts. No wonder he left his fortune to Angelica. Well, I've got news for you, Felicity. According to my solicitors I can slap you with an industrial sabotage charge. I can sue you for purposely attempting to ruin my business. I have no doubt that both Solange and Thierry will back me up if the fee is right, and I could take you for every penny you've got. So forget your precious new hotel, because I can pull it from under you feet and wipe that smile off your face before you can say bankruptcy.'

'You're bluffing,' says Felicity, although her smile is not quite so broad.

'Try me,' says Sebastian.

Game, set and match.

CHAPTER FORTY-FOUR

'We have no way of explaining why these things happen, Claire,' says kindly Dr West, with his hairy ears and his stethoscope, 'but it is one of the unpredictabilities of cancer.'

As remarkable as it may seem, it looks as though Claire Brown has gone into total remission. The doctors are astounded. They seem to think it's a miracle.

'Of course, there's no way of saying how long this condition will last. It may be just a few months; it may be a few years. I have patients who have been in remission for over ten years and still look fine.'

But Claire knows better than to spill the beans to Dr West about her near-death experience in the hospital delivery room. She doesn't want to come off as one of those spiritual loonies who appear on late-night TV wearing sandals, and rattling on about the healing power of crystals and astral projection.

Claire *was* clinically dead for ninety seconds after she gave birth to baby Claire. Duncan recounts the experience to anyone who'll listen, but Claire doesn't have to be told because she was there, watching. The doctors shocked her back into life like Frankenstein's monster. But it wasn't the jolt of electricity that returned Claire to that hospital room. It was the hands of God. She has no doubt about that.

'So what happens now, Doctor?' Claire doesn't seem able to take it all in.

'You go on as you would if you were perfectly healthy. Of course, we will need to monitor your progress with regular check-ups, and when the cancer returns, we will be able to deal with it this time using the appropriate treatments.'

Now that it is September, Claire can look back over the past few weeks and see it all in its entirety, like a spool of film unwound and projected by light on to the wall of her very soul. Does that sound too sickeningly romantic? It is difficult to describe her feelings without coming across like a doorstep apostle. She feels different since it all happened. There's a crack inside her that has opened up and spilled a soothing liquid, like treacle, through her body and her mind. Like breaking through the crisp menthol shell of a Locket before the honey drips down your parched, sore throat.

Like balm to a burn.

Like sugar to a grapefruit.

There are people who have this jolt of surprise in their lives. People who survive plane crashes, coming out unscathed when all the other passengers are killed. People who watch helplessly as a load of bricks drops from a crane to crash down on the exact spot where they were standing only a minute ago. People who are shown just how close they are to death. They are the chosen ones. And life is treated thereafter as a reward, and not a birthright.

Everyone is crying. It's a miracle.

But Claire doesn't feel overwhelmed any more. The truth is, she almost expected it to turn out this way.

Claire goes to church whenever she can, but not beyond reason. Of course, they all think she's just offering up her thanks to the Almighty for saving her life and that of her child. That seems natural. She likes to go on weekday afternoons, when she is the only person there. When the little votive candle burns brightly in its red glass jar, and the sunshine makes jewels of the stained-glass windows. She takes a bus to Oakdowne and walks up the lane to the tiny stone church with the crooked gravestones and its smell of ancient ceremony. The oak beams are black and mouldering, and the edges of the pews are polished where generations of hands have clutched and prayed. It is here that she feels the bond between earth and heaven. It is here that she feels those hands, the hands that rested so lovingly on her shoulders before she was pushed back to life.

Duncan made love to her for the first time last night.

It happened after they had heard from the hospital

that baby Claire was going to make it. She's going to live. She is going to breathe on her own, without the machines, without the drips and the needles. Claire was very calm when she heard the news. She didn't cry, or throw herself into Duncan's waiting arms. You see, she had known all along that baby Claire was going to survive. Why else would God have sent Claire herself back to earth if not to care for her child?

Duncan took her gently. It wasn't the thrusting, bloody mess that Claire had shared with David Glendale. Duncan kissed her with such tenderness it made her shiver. She discovered that the most unexpected parts of her body were erogenous zones. Claire wonders how many women actually wait until they love a man before they allow him to touch them in this way. It *has* to be better. It is a spiritual experience all on its own, and it can bring tears to the eyes of a non-believer. It is the way it was meant to be.

Angelica has been an angel. She has paid for the very best of medical care, and she has been with Claire for almost the entire time since baby Claire was born, even though she misses her own two children dreadfully.

'You should go home, Angelica. You've done more than enough for us,' says Claire, squeezing her friend's hand.

Sometimes it seems as though Angelica has something that she wants to say – like now – but she shakes her head and smiles. 'Maybe I will, now that the baby is doing fine.'

She has given Claire a pair of David's gold Tiffany cufflinks. They are engraved with his initials. 'For the baby, when she grows up and wants to know about her father,' says Angelica.

Duncan takes Claire to Heathrow to wave Angelica off at Terminal Three. Her luggage is matching: Louis Vuitton. The real thing.

Poppy and Dee take them out for dinner. There is an Indian restaurant in the high street that has half-price specials on a Thursday night, and the drinks are potent.

'Sebastian is insisting that you both come to his mother's birthday party,' says Poppy, resplendent as always in lavender fake-fur-trimmed velour.

'We don't even know the woman,' says Duncan.

'We won't know anyone there. We'll be out of place,' says Claire.

'You'll know us, darling, and we need somebody to share a table with, otherwise we'll get stuck with some snobby old farts from Kensington.'

'But you said it's fancy dress. I've never liked that sort of thing. I'm too much of an introvert.'

'Claire, darling, you are not an introvert. Anyway, it's not so much a fancy-dress party, it's more of a *theme*. You could go to a charity shop and buy a costume for a few quid.'

'I hardly even remember the sixties,' says Claire, blowing on her masala.

'Well, I do,' states Duncan. 'And I wish to forget them, quite honestly.'

'Anyway, does Felicity know that Sebastian has invited us? I can't imagine that I'm one of her most favourite people.'

'Darling, since Sebastian had that gigantic show-down with her about Thierry, she's willing to do just about anything her dear brother tells her to. I never believed Sebastian could be quite so ruthless.'

'Surely he's not going to forgive her for that awful business?' asks Claire.

'Not on your life. He's going to make her life an absolute misery for as long as he can. He's threatened to sue her for industrial sabotage; his lawyers say he has a really good case against her, and she could lose every penny she's got. Meanwhile he's holding it over her like a hand grenade, and she's being all sweetness and light.'

'What happened to Thierry?' asks Duncan.

'Disappeared off the face of the earth, darling. Probably hopped back to jolly old Belgium with that ghastly wife of his, never to be seen or heard of again.'

'Poor Sebastian,' says Dee. 'I don't think he deserved any of this. He looked bloody done in when we saw him last week.'

'He really loved Thierry, didn't he?' asks Claire.

Poppy nods. 'What a bastard, eh?'

Then Dee breathes in a chilli pepper, and has to be whacked on the back while waiters rush around with natural yogurt and iced water.

It is an ordinary evening.
Half-price curries and plastic tablecloths.
But to Claire Brown, it is an evening to remember.
She is alive.

CHAPTER FORTY-FIVE

The security at Felicity's new hotel is shockingly inefficient. There is none, actually – the wide-open entrance is covered only by plastic sheets and scaffolding. During the day it is filled with workmen who eat sandwiches wrapped in cling film, and smoke cigarettes which they stub out in the rubble.

Funny how workmen feel that vulgarity is part of the job.

Is it in their job description?

They talk about Felicity when she isn't there. They call her a whore and a bitch, and they wonder what it would be like to shag her. Frigid, probably.

Wayne Briggs joins in with the conversation.

He has been hanging around the builders for the last few days. He has told them that he's with the catering company that will be organizing the food for tonight's party. The builders like him because he brings them fags and cans of lager, and tells them lurid stories about Felicity Craven and her little perversions.

She doesn't look like the kind of woman who would like that kind of thing. Does she wash it off immediately, or does she roll around in it for a bit? Phew! That must stink!

It doesn't take much for Wayne to get caught up in the bustle of preparations. Caterers, florists, display artists and lighting technicians fill the basement ballroom with their equipment and their staff. The main entrance to the hotel is being tarted up to look like the old shop frontage of Biba. Wayne has absolutely no idea who Biba was, and to him it all looks like a load of shit. They're putting up massive black and white photographs of old film stars around the ballroom, with lights around them.

'Who are these people?' Wayne asks a girl with a staple gun and a pincushion strapped to her wrist.

'Well, that's Julie Christie, and that's Alan Bates. This one here is Lawrence Harvey, and that one's Dirk Bogarde.'

'What's the point?' asks Wayne.

'It's the sixties. Black and white is the theme. It's the old glamour of London in the sixties.' The girl obviously doesn't know what she's talking about, because she's probably only twenty-odd herself. What the fuck does she know about the sixties?

Someone is blowing up white balloons with a big can of gas. They float up to the ceiling and start to create an effect. The lighting people all seem to have ponytails and ripped jeans, and they shout things like, 'Chuck us that bit of rigging, Tone!' and, 'Where the hell are those coloured gels I asked for, Kev?'

Wayne prefers it upstairs with the builders. He likes the dust and the destruction they cause. They call him Squirt, and punch his shoulder when he tells them a joke. A couple of the blokes aren't half bad to look at, and Wayne wouldn't mind getting off with them. They would smash his face in if they knew what he was thinking, so he makes up some more lurid stories about Felicity, and they let him join in with their pissing competition behind the skips.

Felicity's heart just isn't in it. She stands in front of the bedroom mirror in a white satin cocktail dress of her mother's, and she feels about as festive as a coffin-bearer. The hairdresser did a terrific job with her hair, teasing it up into a huge mound of pin-curls, with corkscrew tendrils down both sides of her face. The make-up is authentic. They had someone come to the house to do it for them. Baby-pink lipstick and silver-white eyeshadow, and huge black eyelashes that are stuck on with glue.

Sabrina is wearing another original sixties garment, something she hasn't worn since the photo shoot she did for Get Set! setting lotion in 1969. It's a triangular A-line number that barely touches her knees, in black and white chequerboard with a matching cap and knee-length white leatherette boots. The hair and make-up are just a slight variation on her usual look.

'Isn't this exciting, darling?' says Sabrina, having been allowed a weak gin and tonic before the car arrives.

Felicity smiles bravely at her mother in the mirror, and messes with her fringe. She really wishes this night could be over. There's no joy in it now that

Sebastian has ruined everything for her. She really hates him. He's lording it over her with this stupid threat of a lawsuit, and her solicitor has warned her to keep quiet until it all blows over. Tonight was supposed to be *her* night, an opportunity to show everyone her new venture, but it has been spoiled by the fact that Sebastian will not allow her to make any kind of speech or to take the limelight away from their mother.

'It's her party, for God's sake, Felicity, not yours. Some day you'll have to realize that the entire world does not revolve around Felicity Craven.'

Damn and bugger!

Her arse sticks out like a pair of watermelons in this sodding dress.

Sebastian has offered to drive everyone to the party himself. He has hired a super white Rolls, and supplied them all with champagne as they glide down the M1. Duncan is sitting up front with him, and he looks rather amazing in a second-hand white satin Nehru jacket with gold naval epaulettes *à la* Sergeant Pepper. In the back, the three women are laughing hysterically because one of Claire's nipples is poking through her white crocheted top.

'You'll have to tell everyone that it's bubble gum!' screams Poppy, holding her sides and making her mascara run.

Dee has spilled champagne on her black leather miniskirt.

'I'm going to bloody well wet myself,' laughs Claire.

'I already have!' says Dee, mopping her skirt down with a tissue.

Despite recent events, Sebastian is actually looking forward to tonight. He has invited a lot of old friends, and it should be a good way of reacquainting himself with some of them. He has been out of circulation for too long, and since Thierry went back to Brussels there has been a sad and empty period of late-night films and microwave meals served in plastic containers.

Sebastian has put his flat on the market. He can't face the sterility of his former life now that he has experienced something less ordinary. He's buying the Bayswater flat above the toy museum which was, of course, rented by Felicity for her nefarious schemes. Even the wonderful antique bed that was supposed to be Thierry's heirloom was in fact rented from Felicity's friend Piers, along with most of the other antiques in the place. Although to others it might seem that Sebastian is attempting to wallow in sentimentality by moving into the flat, he feels that he's doing exactly the opposite. He is changing his life.

Since he met Poppy and Thierry, Sebastian has been introduced to a less predictable existence, and he finds it too depressing to go back to the Hooray Henry, Champagne Charlie life he was leading before. The flat above the toy museum is perfect in every way, and Bayswater, although not as fashionable as neighbouring Notting Hill, is far enough away from

Kensington to be considered wildly bohemian by most of his friends.

'I'm surprised you can sit down in those trousers, Duncan,' shouts Dee from the back seat of the car.

'We've fastened the fly with safety pins, under the jacket,' says Claire. 'There was no way we were ever going to tuck all of his tackle into that small space!'

'Didn't realize you were so well endowed, Dunc,' cackles Dee, dribbling champagne down her chin and on to her *Love & Peace* T-shirt.

'I keep my assets well hidden,' laughs Duncan, giving Claire a loving wink over his shoulder.

'It must be hard!'

'Most of the time it is, yes!'

And they leave the M1 and head for the West End, soliciting envious glances from fellow travellers along the Hendon Road.

The guests will soon be arriving. Felicity and Sabrina won't be here until after everyone else, because they want to make a grand entrance. Wayne knows the entire schedule for the evening, and he too has got everything planned to the last detail.

He has changed into his disguise.

He hired it from a theatrical suppliers on Cambridge Circus, and it cost him an arm and a leg. He has a blond page-boy wig made from real hair: the assistant in the costume shop called it the Herman's Hermit, whatever that means. He also wears small, round John Lennon sunglasses, a droopy blond moustache and a kind of hippy sleeveless sheepskin coat that goes down to his ankles and has flowers embroidered around the pockets.

He checks the service lift to see if anyone has moved his parcel, but nobody has been round to visit the old catering kitchens, because they are roped off with yellow tape and declared dangerous owing to reconstruction. Strings of naked lightbulbs illuminate this area with a harsh, cruel light, but there's nobody around as Wayne picks his way carefully over bags of cement and metal girders.

The service lift is enormous: big enough for trolleys and deliveries from the ground floor above. There in the corner of the lift is the beautifully wrapped present, about the size of an electric toaster. It doesn't tick. That would be too predictable. These days such things are timed by sophisticated electronics, and Wayne's contact has told him that this is made to IRA specifications. How's that for a recommendation?

Wayne looks at his watch. It's almost seven o'clock. He has two hours exactly to get the present up to the ballroom and be out of the building before all hell breaks loose. This he cannot do until everyone is assembled, because he doesn't want anyone moving his package once it has been set down on the gift table at the back of the ballroom. Felicity is due to arrive at eight; that will give him plenty of time.

Alongside the present, Wayne has his Adidas bag with a change of clothes, money and a train ticket for Glasgow. He's going to spend a few days with his old friend Johnny up there, until all the fuss has died down.

The letter has already been posted.

South Kensington postmark.

Meticulously typed on Craven's notepaper by the hotel computer and printer.

By the time the police receive the letter, there will be no way of knowing if Sebastian wrote it or not. Sebastian and that slag-bag of a sister will be splattered across the ballroom ceiling, along with most of the other guests. And Sebastian's letter, accepting responsibility for the tragedy, will prove to everyone that Sebastian never really forgave Felicity for every foul deed she had done to him.

Wayne Briggs returns to his hiding place behind the temporary stage in the ballroom, and waits for it all to begin.

CHAPTER FORTY-SIX

'You look positively ridiculous!' says Sascha to her brother, in the back of the limousine.

'You stink like a cat fart!' is Josh's doltish reply.

'Will you two just stop it now!' snaps Felicity, who is facing them from the middle seat with Sabrina and Ross on either side. 'I've had enough of this constant bickering, and if you don't stop it now I'm sending you both back home with James.'

'She started it,' says Josh.

'She started it,' mimics Sascha.

'I don't care who started it. I'm sick of hearing you both.'

Felicity has such a short fuse these days. She should think of going on Prozac.

'We're here,' announces Ross, peering out of the tinted window and shaking Sabrina's arm.

'Where's Tony? Will he bring the Beverley Sisters?' she asks, looking anxiously for her escort.

'Don't worry, Mummy. He's inside.'

'Wow, it looks like a nightclub,' says Sascha.

'What does Biba mean?' asks Josh.

'It's a fashion shop that they used to have in the sixties, darling. Please spit out that gum. It doesn't look very smart, you know, to go into a party with a mouthful of that horrible stuff.'

'It's Bubblicious!' says Josh, spitting it into the ashtray in the car door.

'It's vile,' says Sascha.

'You should know,' he replies, sticking out his tongue, which has turned a dark shade of purple.

They step out in front of the fake entrance of the hotel, and several cameras flash. There are red cordons to keep back the riff-raff, and Felicity is disgusted to notice a couple in vest tops eating chips out of newspaper. *Honestly*!

Tony is there to take Sabrina's arm, and they walk through the makeshift passageway to the top of the grand staircase leading down to the ballroom. White satin drapes and strings of white lights lead the way, along with poster-size photographs of Sabrina in her modelling days.

Here she is, astride a Honda Melody with the front basket filled with daisies.

Here she is, lounging on a fox-fur rug with a silver halter-neck and a glass of Cherry B.

'Oh, darling, this is thrilling!' says Sabrina to Felicity. 'Where on earth did you dig all these up from?'

'Archives, Mummy. You'd be amazed what they keep on record, you know.'

'Golly, Tony, look at me here with Glenda Jackson. Shame she became so political, she used to be such a lovely girl. Poor Kenny Russell hasn't made a decent film since Glenda stopped flashing her boobies for him.'

Felicity is smiling, but she feels less than cheerful. Ross is grating on her nerves and she has a nagging headache that threatens to become another sinus infection. She is wearing a g-string because of the sheer satin dress, and the thong part is cutting into her buttocks like a piece of dental floss.

Down in the ballroom Sebastian stands with his little entourage. They are drinking champagne cocktails beneath pictures of Leslie Caron and Pat Phoenix. The room is crammed with famous people, and Claire has been stunned into silence by the sheer glamour of it all. Everywhere she looks there is another immediately recognizable face, and she is quite overwhelmed with excitement. Who would have thought it? She looks at Duncan to see if he's watching her, but he's too busy ogling Marianne Faithfull, who has just walked by with a cigarette holder the length of a broom handle.

'She makes a marvellous Holly Golightly,' says Sebastian.

'*Breakfast at Tiffany's*, darling,' says Poppy, seeing Claire's puzzled expression.

The ballroom is enormous, and the ceiling is a single mass of white balloons with black and silver streamers. White searchlights sweep the balloons, and every table has an arrangement of white flowers and candles. It's like a wedding reception – they even have a table for the presents. Claire feels bad because they didn't bring anything, but Sebastian has said his mother would never notice. It's not as though she actually *needs* anything.

Duncan has asked Claire to marry him.

It happened a couple of days ago when they were watching a repeat episode of *Murder She Wrote*. He just dumped the suggestion on Claire's lap as though it was a tray of baked beans on toast, and then left the room to make a pot of tea. When he came back with the teapot and a packet of garibaldi biscuits, Claire couldn't say anything other than yes.

They are planning a Christmas wedding.

A small informal do at the registry office and a little party afterwards at Duncan's house. Sausage rolls, vol-au-vents, that kind of thing. Angelica offered to do something much more elaborate for them, but Claire has had enough drama in her life this year, and she doesn't think she could cope with the whole church-and-bridesmaids thing.

'Here they are at last,' says Sebastian as the ballroom lights dim and a single spotlight looms in on Sabrina and Tony at the top of the grand staircase.

There is a round of applause and the band plays 'These Boots Were Made For Walking' as Tony leads Sabrina down the steps. Felicity, Ross and the children follow close behind, and the applause swells again as the spotlight lands on Felicity. She attempts a modest

smile and raises her hand, but Sebastian is pleased to
see that she doesn't make a grab for the microphone.

It is almost eight-thirty. Sabrina and Felicity were
late arriving, and Sebastian knows that the caterers
will be ready to start serving dinner almost immediately. Nobody is sitting down yet; they're all too busy
circulating. It's the kind of event where the drink, the
clothes and the networking are far more important
than the food or the *raison d'être*.

'Do you know where the loos are, darling?' asks
Poppy, towering magnificently, her red beehive
stabbed with rhinestones.

'I think they're back there,' says Sebastian, pointing
to some swing doors through which he has just seen
some hippy type with a sheepskin coat disappear.

'If you see Mick Jagger, I want his autograph,' she
says as she teeters off in search of the ladies' room
with Dee on her arm.

Wayne has thirty minutes to get his parcel on to that
gift table and get out of the building. He's left it all a
bit late because he wanted to make sure Felicity was
going to turn up. There had been rumours going round
that she might not, because of her falling-out with
Sebastian. Thank Christ she did, otherwise what
would he have done with the sodding parcel?

He jumps over the cement bags and opens the
doors to the lift. The music from the party echoes
around the catering kitchen, but it is distant and
ghostly, as though it belongs to a different time zone.

This could be another planet, and Wayne could have just stepped through the portal. He imagines the kind of space creatures that might live in this barren terrain. They would have scales and blubbery lips, and they would probably leave a trail of slime behind them.

As he reaches for the parcel he hears voices, and when he looks up there are two women wandering towards the kitchen. One of them has massive red hair, and the other is tarted up in a black leather miniskirt. They are giggling and clutching on to each other.

Wayne presses the button to close the lift doors and stands there in the metallic silence, waiting for the women to go away.

Sabrina is finally at her table. She wants to know where the Beverley Sisters are. The lighting operator flicks a switch to illuminate the entire ballroom with flashing strobes and white lasers, which fan through the air on a cloud of dry ice, spelling out Sabrina's name on the sea of balloons above. There is a drum roll. Strobe lights flash and searchlights sweep through the expectant crowd. Felicity stands next to her mother and indicates to the lighting technician that he should lower the six suspended go-go cages, each one containing members of a dance troupe who gyrate and swing to the sound of Burt Bacharach and his orchestra.

As the cages begin to descend from the ceiling, there is an unscheduled blackout. Every light in the ballroom is extinguished and the music from the speakers is suddenly silent.

'Those bloody cowboy electricians!' hisses Felicity. 'The fuses have blown again.'

Applause and light-hearted jeering rises from the crowd, who are now bathed in the flicker of candle-light. The percussion section in the band starts to play 'Boom Bang A Bang', and Felicity pushes her way over to the lighting chaps to see if they can fix the problem. None of them wants to touch it because of union rules, and they don't want to get blamed if something else goes wrong. It's the responsibility of the building contractors.

'Cash in hand,' begs Felicity. 'Name your price.'

One of the ponytailed technicians offers to take a look at the fuse boxes.

Poppy and Dee are stuck in the sudden all-encompassing blackness of the catering kitchen. They stand there with their arms around each other.

'It's OK,' says Poppy, feeling Dee tense in the dark-ness. 'The lights'll come back on in a minute and we'll be fine.'

'I'm claustrophobic,' says Dee, sounding unusually frail. Her voice is swallowed by the absorbency of the impenetrable gloom.

Wayne Briggs can hear them through the doors of the service lift. He too is stranded in the dark, and the buttons on the control panel are no longer operational. He pounds on the metal doors and shouts.

'Oi, you out there! I'm trapped in the lift!'

'We don't know where you are,' shouts Poppy. 'We can't see a bloody thing in here.'

'You've got to get help,' shouts Wayne. 'I'm stuck in this frigging thing.'

Stuck in this frigging thing with a birthday present that is due to explode in about fifteen minutes.

The caterers are serving up the smoked salmon, and the band plays on. It's all rather romantic by candlelight, and Claire holds Duncan's hand under the tablecloth. She really, really loves him. Now that they are actually having sex, she feels she can say that without one smidgen of doubt. She had her first orgasm and thought she was fainting. Duncan has surprised her with his knowledgeable technique.

'Where are Poppy and Dee?' she asks Sebastian.

'Went to the loo. I'd better go and see if they're all right. They might be lost in the dark somewhere.' He puts down his napkin and wanders off with a candle and a glass of champagne.

Upstairs on the ground floor of the hotel, Felicity stands holding a torch while the ponytailed technician fiddles with the fuse box by the service lift. They're in the back corridor that leads to reception, and it's piled high with building supplies and lengths of scaffolding. Felicity is totally pissed off. Just what she needed tonight! She wishes she had never come. Wait until she gets her hands on those bloody building contractors: she's going to wring their scrawny Scottish necks.

The technician, who is called Dave and reeks of garlic, pulls out fuse after fuse and announces each of them intact.

'Here's your problem,' he says, pointing to several red trip switches that have flipped themselves off. 'Looks like somebody jerry-rigged the system. We probably overloaded this ancient wiring when we started with the lasers. This isn't legal, I can tell you that much.'

He flicks the row of switches and immediately the dark corridor is thrown into shadow and light by a string of naked lightbulbs.

'Thank God for that!' says Felicity, brushing dust from the hem of her mother's white cocktail dress. 'I was ready to call the whole thing off.'

There is a whirring sound, a mechanical cranking of metal and electricity.

'There's somebody in the service lift,' says Dave the technician, and they both turn to see who it might be.

The doors of the lift open, throwing a soft, golden light across the rubble and debris that is scattered across the bare floorboards of the corridor. A hippy-type person with blond hair and a moustache runs towards them, waving his hands frantically in the air and screaming blue murder.

It must be nine o'clock.

'What the hell . . .' says the technician.

But his words don't make it much further than his open mouth, as the service elevator suddenly erupts in all directions, hurtling a fierce ball of flame and metal straight at them.

Poppy and Dee hear the explosion above them just fractions of a second before they are bombarded by an avalanche of falling bricks and girders. The entire far end of the catering kitchen collapses under a wall of flame and twisted metal, and Poppy is thrown backwards against a pile of cement bags.

Sebastian, who had only just walked into the area when the lights came back on, flattens himself against a wall as water spurts from broken pipes and flames rush across the ceiling, setting alight exposed timbers and filling the air with a thick, rolling black smoke.

There is momentary blackness, and Sebastian's lungs burn with such ferocity that he drops to his knees with the violence of his choking coughs. He is kneeling in water, but he can't see anything. Then there is a second explosion, which appears to bring down part of the ceiling, revealing flames and light from the floor above. Suddenly he is encompassed by a hellish scene of destruction.

Poppy appears to be trapped beneath a fallen beam. Dee is already scrambling over bricks and rubble to try to free her, but a constant stream of water gushes over them both, making it virtually impossible to manoeuvre. Sebastian crawls on his hands and knees through the water and attempts to help Dee with the heavy length of wood that is crushing Poppy's legs. Poppy appears to be unconscious and there is blood on her forehead.

'I've got to get help,' shouts Sebastian.

'There's no time. That ceiling's going to cave in any minute,' screams back Dee, pointing to a large section of plaster that is suspended above Poppy's head by nothing more than a tangle of metal strips.

'OK, let's both pull at this thing on the count of three. One, two, three . . .'

They hoist with all of their combined strength and the beam moves several inches, but not enough to free Poppy's legs.

Sections of metal air-duct plummet downward just a few feet away from where they are crouching, and where the service lift had once stood there is now a blazing inferno of spiralling smoke.

'Try again!' Sebastian shouts. 'One, two, three . . .'

This time they get the beam down to Poppy's ankles.

'I can't breathe,' gasps Dee, coughing violently.

Sebastian's vision is blurred by the stinging, acrid smoke. 'We've got to try one more time,' he splutters, barely able to contain his desire to head back towards the ballroom, away from the imminent danger and the asphyxiating smoke.

On the third try they actually get Poppy's legs clear, and Sebastian is able to drag her body away from the cement bags and into the passageway behind the ballroom.

'I think she's coming round,' he says, cradling her head in his lap. 'Go and get some help, Dee. The ballroom is just through there.'

Poppy is groaning. Her legs are in pretty bad shape and Sebastian is concerned by the amount of blood she's losing. He moves her head gently and attempts to take a closer look, wondering if he might fashion a tourniquet from a ripped piece of her skirt. The fabric is sodden and stuck to her skin. When he tries to pull the skirt away she begins to moan, and it seems that more blood pulses out.

'I've got to try and stop the flow of blood, Poppy,' he says. 'I need to tie a bit of your skirt around the top of your leg. This is probably going to hurt, but I can't think of any other way.'

Sebastian pulls at the fabric as quickly as he can – as though removing a Band Aid – and Poppy practically doubles up with pain.

What Sebastian sees when he looks down at Poppy's mangled thighs is far more shocking than he had bargained for, and his hands falter in mid-air.

Poppy has a penis.

Dee returns with two other people.

'She's a man,' Sebastian says, looking up at Dee with his bloodied hands outstretched.

'There's no time for that now,' says Dee. 'We've got to get her to a hospital. The ambulances are already on their way. It's pandemonium out there.'

'You knew all the time?'

'Yes, I knew. Now let's get her out of here before the whole blasted place falls in on us.'

Sebastian helps them lift Poppy on to a tablecloth that they have brought with them from the ballroom, and they hoist her up on this makeshift stretcher and carry her out through the double swing doors.

The only thing Sebastian sees as they struggle through the riotous crowd is a young go-go dancer in tasselled bra and cowboy boots, dangling perilously from the ceiling as she prepares to leap from her swinging gilded cage.

CHAPTER FORTY-SEVEN

We wonder, would Felicity have approved?

There is gypsophila among the funeral flowers.

There are Twiglets at the wake.

Sebastian has attempted to make it as tasteful as possible for his sister, but he has never had her innate artistic flair, and this has not been an easy week.

Racked with guilt and silently grieving for all he has said to his sister over the last few months, Sebastian is an emotional wreck. Tranquillized and stupefied, he attempts to justify his recent actions, but Felicity's tragic death seems to override all rationalization.

She was killed instantly, they say.

Wouldn't even have known what was happening.

Cold comfort for those who remain behind. Fodder for the journalists who peck and squawk like crows over a burst bin-bag.

Sabrina doesn't seem to understand what has happened, and she keeps asking for Felicity as though she has only just left the room.

'When is she coming back with those Hob Nobs?' she says, watching *Blue Peter* with the dogs leaping around her feet in specially fashioned baseball caps. Tony feels that it's time to think about a day-care centre, or even full-time nursing, but Sebastian doesn't want to consider that just yet.

It doesn't seem possible that someone as young and callow as Wayne Briggs could have caused such terrible chaos. Sebastian once again feels guilty about this, because he doesn't know why Wayne would have targeted Felicity unless it had something to do with his own involvement with the boy. Obviously he was unbalanced – why else would anyone take revenge to such epic heights? Ross has explained all about the blackmail, and the murder of that gangster chap they hired to rough Wayne up, but Sebastian cannot help but feel responsible. After all, if he hadn't picked Wayne up in Piccadilly that night, none of this would have happened. The newspapers are having a field day with each new revelation.

At least Poppy seems to be doing OK. She might be able to leave the hospital next week, and it looks as though she will regain the use of both legs after physiotherapy. Sebastian has not been to see her – things have been too hectic – but Dee gives him a constant up-date and he has talked to Poppy on the phone.

'Do you think I'm a freak, darling?' she asked him. 'Half man, half woman, like one of those Victorian circus acts?'

'Of course I don't. I have to admit that I really haven't given much time to the thought, but I doubt it'll make much difference to me. So, you're a man who lives as a woman – I've heard of worse! The strangest part for me to swallow is that you're a *straight* man who lives as a woman. That's a bit of a mind-twister.'

'Most transvestites *are*, darling. Poor Dee has to cope with being called a lesbian when really she's getting poked nightly by a former truck driver with hairy thighs, and, I'm proud to reveal, a larger than average appendage.'

'I've already seen it,' says Sebastian.

'Not at it's best, darling!' jokes Poppy.

'I always thought there was something a bit butch about you. A kind of Danny La Rue aura, always larger than life, and that voice . . .'

'So we're still friends?'

'We will always be friends, Poppy. Nothing's going to change that, dick or no dick!'

So what is he going to do with himself now?

Sebastian Craven stands on top of a mound of rubble and surveys the devastation around him. It's hard to see clearly through the smoke, but he knows that there must be a glimmer of hope somewhere just beyond the burned-out shell on the horizon.

He is going to keep Craven's and restore it to its former glory, with the help of a designer woman who was a close friend of Felicity's and knows her style well enough to emulate it. It's the least he can do, and it will give him something to concentrate on until he gets his life back in order.

He might have dinner at The Forum this evening.

It's a place of constancy, where he can sit in the

familiar dining room and read the gold Latin mottoes while he tucks in to a plateful of suet pudding.

'Will that be all, sir?' asks the young under-porter as he hands the car keys to Sebastian.

He wears the Craven's uniform well. Fills it out nicely.

'How old are you, Steve?' Sebastian asks.

'Twenty-two, sir.'

'How are you finding the job? Everyone treating you well, I hope?'

'Oh, yes, sir, everything's pukka. Thanks for asking.'

'Jolly good. Keep up the good work.'

Sebastian pushes his way through the revolving glass door with a barely perceptible backward glance.

CHAPTER FORTY-EIGHT

Water, like silent lakes of frozen skimmed milk, appears periodically through winter branches in the early evening light. The sky is layered in transparent shades: faded purple, growing gold towards the horizon. They are still on the main highway north, but the road is very quiet and the views are becoming more interesting since they are away from the larger towns.

Duncan is driving. Claire has abandoned the road map now that they are nearing their destination. She has a sheet of notepaper and handwritten directions on her lap, but it is almost too dark inside the car to read them. Duncan turns on the headlights and switches off the radio, which has been fading for about ten minutes as they climb higher into the Pocono mountains. They have given up trying to find another station – everything is clouded with static, and the only thing they can hold on to for any length of time is a local country and western station. The peace inside the car matches the tranquillity of the passing countryside, and Claire holds her breath for a few seconds, trying to penetrate the black shadows inside a dense thicket of stripped, upright trees.

'The turning should be about two miles up ahead,' says Duncan, breaking the silence.

Claire holds up the written directions and peers carefully to read what they say. 'Angelica's writing is terrible.' Claire can't tear her eyes away from the passing scenery. 'Isn't this beautiful, Duncan? It's just like it was on that television documentary.'

'It's hard to believe we're actually here, isn't it? There was a time when I really thought this couldn't be possible. Six months ago I would have considered it a miracle to have just six more *days* with you.'

'And here we are, a new year about to begin and so much to look forward to. I honestly believe that we've been blessed, Duncan. I know you don't like me going on about God and everything, but Angelica believes so too.'

'We've certainly been lucky, but you really have deserved it, love.'

'What time did we leave Washington?' asks Claire.

'About twelve-thirty.'

'We've been driving for almost five hours. It was six o'clock last night when we left Houston, and there's a two-hour time difference between Texas and Pennsylvania. That means it is . . .' Claire counts off the hours on her watch, 'half past two in Texas and half past nine in England.'

'We'll soon be there,' says Duncan, placing his hand on Claire's left knee and turning to smile at her in the twilight. 'You're excited, aren't you? I can tell. You've been twitching in your seat for the last hour or so.'

'I'm nervous, actually. I hope it's not going to be awkward when we get there. Thank goodness for Angelica.'

It's the time of year between Christmas and New Year when everything seems to be suspended in mid-air, waiting for the final exhalation. They are headed for a secluded country inn that Angelica picked out, where they have huge breakfasts, log fires and four-poster beds. Baby Claire is silent in her bundle of blankets, strapped into the back seat of the car. She has been sleeping for most of the journey.

They turn off the main highway and start down a smaller road which winds through dark woodland. They follow a narrow strip of evening sky which is sprinkled with early stars and occasionally, through a clearing of trees, they catch the cupped sliver of a crescent moon. Suddenly, to their left, the trees part, and they are driving along the side of a very wide frozen lake. The sun has left a scrap of orange in the sky like egg yolk on the indigo blue of the horizon. Duncan pulls over into a small gravel lay-by and kills the ignition, plunging them both into a new, intense silence. They get out of the car and walk over to the edge of the lake.

'Somebody's been ice-fishing,' comments Duncan, pointing out several circular holes cut into the solid surface of the lake. He steps out on to the ice and looks back at Claire with a reassuring smile. 'It's OK. This ice would hold an elephant.'

'What about Claire?' she says, looking back at the car. 'We can't just leave her.'

'She's fast asleep, love. We'll hear her if she starts crying.'

Claire is nervous about going out on the ice.

'Come on,' says Duncan, holding out his hand as though coaxing a recalcitrant child through the doors of a dental surgery.

Claire steps gingerly on to the ice. It isn't sleek or slippery; it's dusted with a fine layer of snow, and the bare patches that show through are scratched and opaque like pieces of beach glass. In the dim evening light the lake is the colour of battleship steel. Claire follows Duncan out as far as the first fishing hole, and they peer down into the ominous depths, trying to see water. The ice is over six inches thick and the hole is black. It seems to Claire that the two of them are like a pair of tiny black dots being watched by a satellite. She looks around and there is nothing but the expanse of the lake and the vast dome of the sky. The silence is complete.

'We should have brought some skates,' says Duncan, breaking the spell.

'I can't skate,' says Claire.

'Of course you can. You've just never had the right teacher,' says Duncan, taking hold of Claire's arm and leading her out towards the second fishing hole.

'Shouldn't we go back to the car?' asks Claire, holding back.

'Just a few more minutes. I want to see what's around that bend in the lake.'

They step further out, testing the ice with careful tread, holding on to each other in an effort to gain the courage of their convictions. They reach the second hole, and the ice here is not quite so thick – probably about four inches. 'I dare you to put your hand into the hole and touch the water,' says Duncan.

'Why?' asks Claire.

'I dare you,' he repeats obstinately, releasing Claire's arm.

'It's just water,' says Claire, looking down into the black hole without the slightest scrap of curiosity.

'So touch it,' goads Duncan.

Claire looks across the lake, as though someone might be watching, and then kneels at the side of the fishing hole. There is a very slight breaking sound far below the surface, like a fractured bone wrapped in velvet, and Claire crouches by the hole for a moment, straining her ears for something else.

'Come on, then!' says Duncan, rubbing his hands together and looking back at the car.

'Just wait a minute,' answers Claire.

'It's getting cold,' complains Duncan.

'This was your suggestion,' says Claire, pushing up the sleeve of her coat and leaning over the hole.

She can't admit that there's something menacing about putting her hand into the unknown depths of the frozen fishing hole. She has irrational thoughts of sea creatures with snapping jaws, or the grasping hands of the undead, like in the final heart-jerking scenes at the end of a bad horror movie. She lowers her hand into the hole and it descends slowly, anticipating the first sting of icy water against her fingertips. Suddenly, without any warning, Claire is jerked towards the hole so that her shoulder is lodged against the ice and her feet fly out from under her.

Duncan lets out a frightened shout which rips through the silence and startles a flock of birds out in some distant shrubbery.

Claire pulls up a fistful of water and swats it at Duncan, rolling on to the frozen lake, convulsed with laughter.

Duncan looks both shocked and humiliated, but struggles to appear a good sport, so he laughs weakly and says: 'Bloody hell! You had me worried for a minute there!'

Claire stands up and wipes her arm down the side of her jeans. It is almost dark, and she can't see much of Duncan's face. The sky is almost the same colour as the lake, and she can only just make out the silhouette of the car.

'Time to go,' says Claire, still catching her breath.

'You devil!' says Duncan, making as if to punch Claire on the arm.

They cross the lake, past the first fishing hole, and reach the safety of solid land. A vehicle approaches, headlights cutting a swathe through the darkness, before it crunches into the lay-by and stops beside their own car.

'It's Angelica!' announces Claire, peering through the half-light to see inside the vehicle. 'They must have come to find us.'

Angelica steps out of the passenger seat. She is wearing a huge fur coat and matching hat. She looks like a Hollywood version of a Russian émigrée.

'Hey, you guys, we thought you'd gotten lost.' She peeks in to look at the baby, and rubs her hands together. Then she looks back at her car.

'Come on out, honey. They're not going to bite!' she shouts to the driver of the car. Claire can see him dimly through the tinted window.

David Glendale steps out of the car.

But it is not the David Glendale that Claire remembers from her days at Glendale Estates.

'Hello,' he says, standing there in his three-quarter-length camel coat, with a shy expression on his face.

'I've heard a lot about you,' says Duncan, being the first to approach David and shake his hand. Claire is surprised; she thought that Duncan might be jealous or spiteful because of her past association with him.

Because of baby Claire.

Because of that scene in the Dorchester hotel room just twelve months ago.

Blood on the sheets and snow on Park Lane.

Angelica insists that he has changed, but Claire is uncertain about this meeting.

'Pleased to meet you, Duncan,' says David in his clipped, upper-crust accent that makes Claire shiver.

'Hello, Claire,' he says. 'Is this frightfully awkward for you?'

'A bit,' says Claire, smiling.

Angelica intervenes. 'Come on, honey, there's been a lot of muddy water under the bridge. Why don't you two kiss and make up?'

A rather unfortunate expression, Claire thinks, as she shakes David's warm hand.

'Your face . . .?' she whispers.

David touches his cheek with a finger. 'Ah, yes, the plastic surgery. Just in case Felicity ever got wind that I was still alive. Better to be safe than sorry, and I'd always wanted a straighter nose.'

'They did a beautiful job, didn't they, Claire? He was handsome before, but now he's perfect.' Angelica links her arm possessively through David's.

'So, you've finally got the chance to move back to England, then?' says Duncan. 'The coast is clear now that Felicity's dead. You must be anxious to reclaim your children and the house.'

'Oh, the kids are fine with their grandmother for a couple more months, until I get all the legalities sorted out. I think it's best that I don't make my reappearance until early next year, by which time I'll be ready to face the uproar. It's all going to be frightfully traumatic for the family, and for my partners at Glendale Estates. Maybe, in the long run, a simple divorce would have been easier, but Felicity would have screwed my arse to the ground and wiped me out financially. I couldn't do that to Angelica and our children, so we came up with our bizarre little plan. It worked better than either of us ever imagined. If Felicity hadn't died, I would have lived out the rest of my life in Texas, pretending to be someone else, and no one would have been any the wiser.'

'I still don't really understand why you contacted *us*,' says Claire. 'I know you wanted to help when you heard about my baby and everything, but why did you risk exposing your secret for the sake of somebody you didn't really know?'

'He's got a conscience, honey,' says Angelica. 'That is a rare commodity these days. And I have to admit that I had more than a little to do with the suggestion. The hardest part was giving the money to Felicity for her new hotel. I had to grit my teeth to stop myself punching her in the face. So ungrateful – and David still feeling guilty for hiding away all his money in Switzerland so she couldn't get at it. It was his little consolation prize, wasn't it, honey?'

'I suppose I just felt rather uneasy about leaving Felicity in the lurch like that, despite the animosity between us. We were married for a long time, and I just couldn't cut her off completely after all. I've put everyone through an awful lot of pain and suffering. Have you both forgiven me?' asks David.

'How could we not?' says Duncan. 'Look what you've done for us: you've turned our life around.'

'You must learn to rely on us from now on – after all, we *are* family,' smiles David, with a breath of white vapour.

'Let's go, guys. I'm ready for a cocktail, and I know Duncan is always in the mood for a nice cold beer.' Angelica takes control. 'You follow us. It's only a couple of miles up this road.'

They get into the car and Duncan starts the engine. The headlights illuminate a clump of reeds, bleached white and eerie against the blackness of the lake.

Before they move off, Claire looks across at Duncan, his face ghostly in the faint green glow of the dashboard.

Duncan senses her scrutiny and looks back at Claire. 'What?' he asks, smiling.

'David – he seems like a totally different person now. More relaxed, I suppose. I think it's going to be all right, don't you?'

Duncan reaches over and squeezes Claire's hand. 'It's going to be *marvellous*, love.' And he leans across the creaking leather seats to kiss Claire lightly on the lips.

As they pull away from the side of the road, Claire winds down her window and takes one last look across the lake, trying to imagine that they have just been out there on its crusted surface. She imagines, for one fanciful moment, that she can see the two of them crouching over one of the fishing holes like a pair of shadows in the gloaming.

'What's up? Did you see something?' asks Duncan, slowing down to peer into the darkness.

'No. I thought for a minute that we'd left something behind, but I'm just being silly. We've got everything here.' And she looks at baby Claire, still sound asleep in the back seat.

Duncan puts his foot on the accelerator and the car crunches out into the road, heading for the inn. Their lights disappear through the tangled branches of the trees and all that remains are two sets of glittering tyre tracks ready to be covered by the next fall of snow.

The End

TOM SHARPE

Grantchester Grind

Pan Books £5.99

A Porterhouse Chronicle

Crisis time again at Porterhouse – where crises never come singly.

The formidable Skullion – previously Head Porter, now elevated to Master – is showing signs of physical frailty after his stroke, though as cunning as ever. So the tricky business of appointing a new Master must start all over again.

Meanwhile the College's monstrous debts refuse to go away, and a sinister American media mogul seems determined to make a television documentary on the premises, destroying part of the chapel in the process. Moreover, the widow of the previous Master is convinced that her husband was murdered, so she plants an agent in the Senior Common Room to dig up an unpleasant truth that everyone else would prefer kept under the carpet.

Faced with such continuing crisis, the instinct of the true Porterhouse man is to reach for the bottle . . . or to fall back on the subtle and traditional Cambridge skills of blackmail and kidnap. But will these be enough?

'Has all the ingredients of a classic Sharpe novel –
grotesque characters, outlandish plot, scabrous dialogue'
The Times

TOM SHARPE

The Midden

Pan Books   £5.99

Timothy Bright doesn't exactly live up to his name. Brought up to regard copious flows of money as his birthright, he can't understand why the funds have been cut off, nor why friends he recruited as Lloyds Names no longer want to talk to him. When gambling fails, Timothy turns to embezzlement, but it's the lesser offence of helping himself to some strangely aromatic tobacco that propels him up the motorway and into bed with the Chief Constable's wife.

The Chief Constable has just survived charges of bribery and perjury, and is not too concerned that his efforts to dispose of Timothy involve false imprisonment, breaking and entering and a spot of GBH. It is when the Chief tries to frame his old adversary, the upright Miss Midden, that things begin to go seriously wrong as his underhand ploy opens up the way to spectacular mayhem